DEMON FALLOUT

BY
MARK TUFO

DevilDog Press

Edited by Sheila Shedd

Cover art Dean Samed

Dedications -
Writing a book seems like it would be a solitary endeavor, such is not the case.

I would first off like to thank my wife who had the patience to listen to me ramble about a completely different realm within the Talbot universe.

Next we move on to my editor Sheila Shedd, who was able to take some mis-formed sentences and ill-advised story twists and help shape it into the novel you hold in your hands.

Then there is the small army of beta-readers I enlisted for help to make this as error free a novel as it possibly could be, Patti Reilly, Kimberly Sansone, Jeff Shoemaker, Vanessa McCutcheon, Giles Batchelor and a special thank you to Christy Thornbrugh taken from us far too soon, may you rest in peace.

Last but not least my dear reader is you, without you, none of this happens, and I cannot thank you enough.

Just a quick shout out to Sean Runnette, the voice talent for the audio versions, I hope you know how much I appreciate all you do my friend.

To the men and women of the armed forces and that thin blue line we are thankful for all your sacrifices.

DEMON FALLOUT - THE RETURN

Author Notes

Hello dear reader if this is the first book of mine that you have stumbled upon, first off I want to thank you for taking a chance on it and it is my sincerest hope that you enjoy it. Now with that being said, I truly meant this story as a standalone, meaning you would not need any other references to understand some of what is happening here. For the most part this is a true statement, but I have created what some call the Talbot-verse, the main character Michael Talbot fluidly flows through a great many of my books and series, mostly due to circumstances beyond his control. Demon Fallout immediately follows the Lycan Fallout Universe which itself follows the Zombie Fallout World. I am going to include after the prologue, the ending to Lycan Fallout 4 which at the very least will set you up for this book. As always if you have any specific questions please feel free to reach out to me.

PROLOGUE - REFLECTIONS

WHO DEFINES WHAT IS GOOD and what is evil? Us? God? Satan? Are we the best—are we even qualified—to judge right and wrong? Can an act be inherently good or evil, defying judgment? Do we decide it's so? Male lions, when taking over a pride, often times murder the male offspring of the outgoing king—cubs, sometimes. Is that evil? Western morals say that it is wrong to kill innocents. But their behavior is instinctive; nature requires the elimination of competition. Weasels steal the eggs of nesting birds; orca swallow whole adorable seals, sometimes in sport. These acts are not evil; they are necessary for the continuation of their respective species, and all that depend on them in turn. Only man thrusts his beliefs upon the natural world, labeling these actions "good" or "evil". Laws are set in place to define and enforce man's conception of morality. I'm not sitting here arguing that we should be able to do whatever we want, when we want. I'm merely wondering why we can't.

Helping a little old lady to cross the street is a classic example of a "good" act; such helpful civic behaviors make us feel "good" inside. But a serial killer will tell you there is no more exquisite feeling than the slight pull as his blade slides across the pulsing, heated skin of a human neck, the brief tug while cutting through arteries, the splash of crimson life expelling onto the cold, indifferent ground. We deem this act "evil" because a book of doctrine, written over two thousand years ago, says it is so, because society and its laws say so. Circular argument? Maybe. But I had a little time and thought perhaps writing these thoughts into words might produce clarity. It did not.

ENDING OF LYCAN FALLOUT 4
IMMORTALITY'S TOUCHSTONE

I DRANK MORE THAN ANYONE has a right to, so it stood to reason that sometime during the night I was going to have to get up. I reached over to Azile; she was on her side facing me, clearly asleep. The babies' crib was next to the bed on her side, both of the munchkins were fast asleep as well. I was going to do my absolute best to make sure that they all stayed in their current condition. Wasn't going to be easy, considering I was still roughly five sheets to the wind, it was dark as pitch in the room, and I was unfamiliar with my surroundings. I sat up, hoping that my eyes would adjust to the gloom, which made absolutely no sense, though. My eyes had been shut; wasn't going to get much darker than that. My night vision was as good as it was going to get.

I started weighing options, like maybe I could hold it for a few hours more, or what would be worse? Me waking everyone up when I fell over a table, or me wetting the bed when my bladder had had enough?

"I'll just go slow." I glacier-like slid off the bed and had a moment of panic when my foot came up against something furry. Took me a second to realize it was Oggie, that meant Sebastian was close by, and if I so much as looked at her crossly, she would start mewling incessantly. I did not pick up my feet so much as shuffle them, figured the odds of stubbing a toe were much decreased that way. Something was niggling in the back of my mind as I navigated around the animals and headed to the bathroom. It was quiet; so quiet as to be called silent. Oggie usually snored loud enough he would wake himself up. If he was already up, he would have most certainly greeted me as I got off the bed.

And then there was Azile; I don't know if I've ever encountered a lighter sleeper in my life. There were times I'd gotten out of bed without waking her, but never without slightly disturbing her to the point she would roll over. "I'm like a ninja," I said, right as I plowed my toe into a table leg. "Cocksucking whore of a biscuit eater." I waited until the initial burst of pain subsided to the dull ache of a broken toe, then I completely forgot about my newest injury and the pressing need of my bladder. Something was amiss. I'd now certainly made enough noise that everyone in this room should be looking at me with accusing eyes for disturbing their slumber. Right this very second it was so quiet I could have heard a cricket fart in the far corner of the room. Speaking of which, is that actually a thing? Can that happen? I would have dwelled on it longer, but something had me on the verge of being terrified.

I was even now wondering if an assassin had found his or her way into the room and was stalking me as its final kill because everyone else had already been taken care of. No matter how hard I strained to see, it was as if a curtain had been placed over my vision. There was no doubt in my mind it was darker than it was supposed to be. There are degrees of dark. Being outside in the pitch black of Maine during the dead of winter is dark; being a hundred feet underground in a cave is another type. What I was experiencing now was that closed in, total lack of light. It had a weight and a claustrophobic feel to it. It wasn't natural; this was the point I started to think that quite possibly I was in the midst of a world-class nightmare.

"That's it," I said, realizing how flat the words felt as they hit the deadened air. "Your bladder is so full it's affecting your second brain and you're having a doozy of a dream right now." I knew the cure to wake up was to just take my junk out and start pissing. My mind would start to wonder how I could go for so long without feeling relief. Worked like a charm every time, because invariably my body would say screw it and would be on the verge of releasing everything for real. That's when I would awake. But as much as I wanted this to be a dream, I knew it wasn't.

I turned back and got low, blindly reaching out with my hands. I touched fur, but it was the cat. I nearly recoiled because her first reaction should have been to jump up, hiss like a snake, and take a razor sharp claw swipe at me. Nothing. She did not move. There was heat coming from her body, but I could detect no sign of her breathing, no rise and fall of her chest. I ran my hands over the length of her trying to see if I could feel some blood or a wound. Again nothing. She could have been a statue out in a park on a warm spring day. I moved to Oggie; my heart missed a beat or two as I got the same result. I knew there was no possible way I could go over to Azile and the babies. If the same thing happened, I was pretty certain I would spin into depths I would not recover from.

"Dream, Talbot. This is all a dream," I said as I stood up. The word "enchantment" drifted into my head, uninvited. "Who, though? Ganlin is gone. His brother, maybe? His ex-wife pissed off that she was no longer going to get alimony payments?" I was heading back to the bed, not that I wanted to, but I needed to know. And if anyone could break through a spell, she was lying on our bed. Maybe I could shake her awake, maybe kiss, maybe I could just randomly wave her arms about and mumble incoherently; I was bound to strike on something that would work. I was absolutely terrified that this was my new reality. I would be surrounded by those I loved but would never again be able to interact with them. That seemed exactly like what a lesser god would do to someone like me.

There was some laughter out in the hallway beyond our door. It trailed away in a dying echo. I was on the move, about to chase whatever or whoever that was to the ends of the world if need be, for some answers. That was right up until a tapping came on the window. When you're twenty feet from the ground and there's a knocking on your window, that gives you pause for concern. Now I was frozen. It's one thing to chase, it is quite another for something to be bold enough to come a-calling. As distasteful as it was to head toward something deep, dark and dangerous which had absolutely no fear of me, it was where I needed to go. I ripped the right window off its hinges; the left was going to need some work as well.

A figure, blacker than the surrounding darkness, was somehow visible, if only because the dark around me swirled into it. I knew what it was long before it spun its head at me and exposed its white eye. It was the raven, my raven. Light brighter than the surface of the sun poured out from the eye, over and through me; illuminating the room so brilliantly it washed out all the other colors. I had to turn away from the intensity of the vision before me. Azile was still on the bed; she appeared to be resting as comfortably as Snow White—and had the pallor to match. Then came a voice I thought would snap off a thick blood clot from somewhere in my leg and lodge itself into a deeply folded part of my mind, choking off all flow and hopefully killing me instantly.

"I need help, Mr. T!" Tommy begged.

DEMON FALLOUT: CHAPTER ONE
MIKE TALBOT JOURNAL ENTRY 1

"NO, MIKE. JUST DAMN NO! Please?" Azile pleaded.

Maybe it was a split second after I heard Tommy begging for help or maybe it had been twelve and a half hours as I sat on the floor in a catatonic stupor, but Azile, the babies, Oggie, and even the fucking cat all woke at the same time. When the raven left, there was a loud popping as if it had created a vacuum between the worlds it inhabited, and by leaving, the bubble burst.

"You didn't hear him, Azile." I'd told her everything that had happened. That I'd awoken to something strange, that she and everyone else in the room were under an enchantment, about the raven, and the message. Like pretty much normally, she looked at me like I was nuts. I think she was looking for signs of the blood clot that was even now cutting off vital blood flow to some part of my brain. But, meh. This was my brain, so how vital could it be?

"Are you sure you heard him? If I'm to believe everything you told me, then Tommy is in the underworld."

"Wait…" I stopped her. "If you're to believe me? What the hell does that mean? I was *dead* Azile, and soulless; yet here I am, mostly intact." Sure, I was of sound body and soul, but it would be a stretch to say I was of sound mind. When's the last time I could really say that? When I was fourteen, maybe? And even that was questionable. If I remember correctly, that was the year I raced a train across a trestle in the hopes that I would get to see Meghan Grendler's bra. It was only partially successful. I mean, I didn't get hit by the train so that was a plus, but as for the bra, she pulled up her sweater and dropped it back into place so fast I hardly got a glimpse of some frilly pink material covering her budding breasts. Well, it was fodder enough for many a night, so I guess it worked out better than being scattered across a train track. What the hell was I thinking?

"I'm not doubting what you believe you heard," Azile started, shaking me out of thoughts revolving around a rosebud decorated training bra. "But those you encountered could have made you believe just about anything…couldn't they? How could you know you weren't being manipulated?"

I wanted to argue. I mean who wants to think that they were led along like a puppy? But she was right; how could I not? I'd taken on a five-hundred-ton machine for the chance to see a cloth covered mammary or two. I was not the toughest person to force into a bad situation, plus I'd been in their world, whoever *they* were. They could have done just about anything. "It was Tommy."

"Even if it was, Mike, what are you going to do about it? You can't just run into the underworld and rescue him and his sister. You do realize she's part of the equation?"

"I can, with your help," I fired back, and as much as I was in a rush to save Tommy I wanted nothing to do with Eliza. I had no basis for the hope that she could indeed help. The way she clammed up was all the answer I needed though, to realize the truth in my statement. Then to further reinforce my words, she redirected.

"You have a family now—a family that needs you."

I think she would have been better saying "a family that loves you." Of that I'm sure. That needs me? Well, that's pushing it. Me and trouble are like wet is to water, hot to fire, gross tasting to cherry filling, you know, that kind of thing.

"Tommy is family, too," I told her. I'd adopted him before I'd even met the scared girl I'd rescued from a semi all those years ago. She couldn't argue that.

Her head sagged. I was gaining ground in a fight I wasn't so sure I even wanted to win. Did I want to help Tommy? Of course, I did. But I'd really like to help him in that traditional way, like he was out at two a.m. and he had got a flat and like most irresponsible kids he had already used his spare four months ago and never replaced it or repaired the other tire so now he was stranded in some town an hour away and I had to go and *help him* and I'd be super-tired for work the next morning. But it would all be worth it when I saw the relief on his face as I pulled up. Yeah, that kind of help I was willing to give. But this? This was different. This wasn't even about just giving up a life, which I was willing to do. This was about giving up the *afterlife* as well. Lot more at stake in that outcome. Mortality is fleeting. Even immortality, surprisingly, has its limits. It's once we start traveling the realms of the gods that we begin to understand what eternity really is. To normal people, it's a word that doesn't carry much weight, like "infinity" or a "quadrillion." Sure, we know what they mean on a basic level, but we're not built with the capacity to truly comprehend the vastness of some things. And maybe because it was something I could not wrap my mind around, I felt that this was still something I needed to do, and might be capable of doing.

"I can help," she finally said.

It's weird for me just about any time that I actually win a fight with a member of the opposite sex, I don't feel certain of the victory until I see results. That I did so now should have been cause for celebration, so why did I feel the need to go and hurl up everything I'd eaten that day?

"But we do this my way or not at all, Mike," she added, though I barely heard it for the torrent of bile worming its way back up my throat.

"What does 'your way' entail? And what are the drawbacks?" I asked, probably not the best phrasing, but it was out there.

"I don't know just yet. It's not like I send many people into the underworld to retrieve wayward souls."

"Fair enough," I told her.

CHAPTER TWO
MIKE JOURNAL ENTRY 2

I SPENT THE FOLLOWING MORNING with the twins, mostly just looking at the tiny creatures who were spending a disconcerting amount of time staring back at me. I was under the impression infants only had an attention span of a few seconds. Sure, that was a second or two longer than me, so theoretically they should have gone back to cooing and gurgling and looking for their fingers a good long while ago. I fed them and changed them. Funny. After all the things I'd been through in this extended life, all the horrible and disgusting things I'd seen and done, if I'm being honest, dirty diapers trump it all. I don't know what ungodly thing happens in the digestive system of a baby that can turn their mother's milk into a black, tarry substance that smells far worse than ordinary shit and sticks to everything like it has superglue for a base. I had my shirt pulled up over my nose and a plastic shopping bag on each hand as I worked through half a tub of wipes and a bath towel getting them cleaned up. On a side note, all the crinkling had the babies fascinated, kept them from pumping their legs too much, which was a good thing because that only tended to spread the goop.

"You have got to be kidding me," Azile said from the doorway. She had a slightly bemused expression on her face. "The savior of the free world taken down by some baby poo."

"Baby poo my ass. Whatever this was, it was belched from the bowels of some large primordial monster. I'm surprised it didn't eat right through the diapers."

"Not an enemy in the world would fear you right now if they could see you."

"There's not an enemy in the world that would dare come in here to see me."

"Let me finish up." She sidled me out of the way before I could protest, not that I was going to.

I wanted to leave the crib side, the room, possibly even the house to clear my nose out, but I stayed. I stayed because these moments are fleeting. When you're lifting a baby's ass into the air so you can wipe it, time seems to stand still, but before you know it, they're asking for the reins to the horse-drawn carriage and then heading off to the barn dance. Plus, well I think if I looked hard enough in a mirror I'd be able to see the large hourglass shimmering above my head, and if there were any sand remaining, it would be draining fast through an abnormally large opening.

"What the fuck?" I asked when I realized I was the only one in the room. While I was distracted by deep thoughts, Azile had taken the babies into the kitchen and had made herself some coffee. I guess preparing for the afterlife is a tiring job. I picked up the babies' blankets and inhaled deeply, enjoying the unique scent that only a new human being can make before they are tainted by the evils of the world. I had fought hard and I'd fought long for what I had now. Why shouldn't I get to enjoy it? Sit back and just revel? I was ready to live the life of faded glory, to look back on the good old days, gloss over the bad and magnify the good. If there were a scale for that I rated it. Didn't I? Had I really done so much evil that I would never be free? Would Poena forever torment me? Or was this her final cruel act: to allow me to have everything back only to yield it once again? Fucking spiteful demi-gods. What gives them the right? Doesn't she have a supervisor or something she needs to answer to? And could I get a call into him or her? I would not survive another set of calamities, another loss. I threaded the needle every day of my existence. If something were to happen to Azile or the babies I would spiral out of control; there would be no telling what I would be capable of in my never-ending grief. I was now gaining some small understanding of the things that drove Eliza to the acts she'd committed. Revenge is a mighty powerful motivator, and it doesn't give two shits who pays its price.

"The babies are ready for a nap...and I'm just about ready, too."

"Huh?" I was on the floor in the nursery. "They just woke up."

"Been three hours, Mike. You've only moved to sit."

I wanted to ask her if she was kidding but there was no merriment on her face. At some point, Oggie had come in and was lying down in front of me. Pretty hard to miss a hundred-plus pound dog making an entrance. It seems I was already partially traveling into alternate realms.

"What am I doing, Azile? I'm terrified and I'm not sure if I'm doing the right thing. I love you all so much; I don't want to leave." Fat tears rolled down my face as I hitched a sob.

"You're right, Michael; Tommy is family. That's always been the most important thing to you. Would you be able to live with yourself if you didn't do this?"

I looked at her through the watery haze I had created. "If I drank enough I could probably push through."

I WALKED AROUND THE ENTIRE day on self-imposed egg shells. Azile gave not one hint that she was upset with me. The contrary, if anything. I just figured that at any minute she was going to tell me it was go-time. So by the time night started closing in on the home, I had to ask. We had finished dinner and Azile had just put the babies down. I met her in the hallway.

She did something wholly unexpected. She lifted the hem of her dress, letting it ride ever so slowly up her right thigh. With her left finger pressing her bottom lip, she had a pin-up expression on her face like, "Oops…what have I done?" All thought of the underworld was pushed from my mind as all that existed was the softness hidden just up that skirt.

After a beautiful marathon stallion session of thirty or forty hours, I emerged from the bed, the sex god that I am. Victorious and full of swagger! Not even close to actual events– but, hey, it's my journal. It started off tenderly enough and we were perhaps fifteen minutes in when one or both of the babies decided that we were having too much fun and needed to put the kibosh on it. We went from tender arousal to needing to fulfill an intense itch right now, if you get my meaning. If not, well, I don't think this is the place to explain it. Anyway, by the time it was all said and done I'd rolled or been pushed out of the bed hard, landing squarely on my ass.

"Take care of that," Azile said breathlessly pointing toward our bedroom door and the squall beyond.

"I feel so used," I said as I got up and rubbed my ass.

"Like you care," she replied.

I tilted my head sideways. "Yeah, you're right—not so much."

I was back in a minute or two. Alianna had stolen MJ's bottle, thus giving her two to his none. "Better get used to it little buddy, that's pretty much how it's going to be for the rest of your days." I smiled as I bent over and kissed them both.

I came back to Azile sitting on the edge of the bed.

"Sit." She looked over at me.

"I didn't do it," was the first thing I could think to say.

She ignored my well-practiced expression of innocence. "We need to discuss what's going to happen."

I sat down heavily. I could have almost forgotten, lost within her warm embrace. "You're not going to like it," she said.

Wisely, I said nothing. I already didn't like it; how much more unpleasant could it get? I'd no sooner let that thought run around inside my head when I wished I'd been able to pull it back.

"Sebastian will be going with you."

I thought so little of the cat, I'd forgotten the vermin actually had a name and it took me a few seconds to reconcile the two. I stood up quickly. "No." Pretty sure I shook with rage.

Azile smiled then started laughing.

"What the hell is so funny, woman?" I demanded.

"It's pretty difficult to take you seriously with that…appendage flopping about from side to side," she said as she pointed to my wilted manhood.

I suddenly got self-conscious of my nakedness, which is rare for me, but I didn't want it to detract from my adamance. I muttered as I pulled on some bed clothes. "Unfair tactics," I think I may have said. She was still on active smile suppression duty. "I am not taking the cat!" I made sure to exclaim, as I once again stood. "And stop looking at my damn crotch!"

Things took a hard-left turn when she reached out and rubbed where she'd been looking. I jumped into the bed faster than I'd exited and we did get that long, sweet session we'd been striving for as Alianna kept her bottle-stealing mitts to herself.

I was so spent by the time she brought the Sebastian thing back up I couldn't even think to protest its presence. "He's going to be important to you down there," Azile said bolstering her argument.

"You sure he isn't just going to turn me in at the very first opportunity?"

"Well, I can't make any guarantees, but I strongly doubt it."

"Wait, I was sort of just kidding. That could actually happen?"

I could hear the sheets rustle as Azile shrugged.

"Oh yeah, that makes me feel way better. My traveling companion may or may not double cross me."

"The benefits he brings will far outweigh whatever negatives you fear."

"So you say."

"There's more."

"You sure we shouldn't just dive into round three so you can explain all of it while I'm sleeping?"

"While that would be preferable, it is more effective to keep you in this awake and semi-compliant state."

"Let's get this over with."

"Lana, Mathieu, and Gabriel will be here soon."

"Why?" came out of my mouth though I already knew the answer. Gabriel was the opener of doors, the bridger of worlds, so to speak. "Is he in any danger?"

"Constantly," she replied quickly.

"Okay, is he in more danger by doing this for me?"

"I do not believe so."

"Azile? Make me feel warm and fuzzy about this or I'm going to turn them away on our doorstep."

"His mere existence puts him in danger; having him be part of this quest puts you at somewhat less risk."

That wasn't enough, not nearly enough. I would never put a child's safety behind my own and the look I'd given her completely conveyed that message.

"Look, Michael. He is safer here than anywhere else. I swear that. You have to listen to me before you make a rash decision. I can send you alone, but without him I cannot so easily pull you back. In fact, I'm not sure that I can at all."

Not gonna lie—that was cause for concern. I mean no one really wants to take a one-way ride to hell. I mean that would have been like going to Miami in July. Or Alaska in February, or Detroit in, well, any time of the year. "Keep going," I said.

"I can shove you through that opening, but it seals once you are in. Gabriel has the ability to keep the gate open. I can't even begin to understand how, but that is the way of it. And as long as it is open, I can bring you back, Michael, all of you. And if I don't have a way to bring you back, I won't send you through. I don't care that it's Tommy. I love the boy, maybe as much as you do, maybe more. We spent many a long year together while you rotted away in your brother's basement. But I will not lose you in a doomed attempt to save even him."

I paused. In my own selfishness, I'd never really stopped to think about their relationship. They'd been friends for decades upon decades, relics from the previous world, while I languished in my own personal prison. They'd had countless more time together than I'd had with either of them. I was struggling so desperately with my own grief I couldn't even conceive that someone else was hurting as badly; the fact that she was so very near and dear made me feel even worse. I had been so self-absorbed that I couldn't even see it.

"Can you forgive me for how pig-headed I've been?" I asked as I pulled her into a hug.

She seemed confused. "Wait…for which time?" she asked.

"Can I maybe go with a blanket coverage on that?"

"Pretty big blanket. More like a tarp—a stadium tarp, even."

"You done? I meant in terms of Tommy. I guess I always thought you two were like acquaintances that met occasionally for tea and to talk about me or something."

"We were friends, Michael. For a while, he even lived here. We had so many shared experiences, and he was someone from somewhat of my own era; it made him easy to talk to. This may come as a bit of a shock to you, but I had few friends when I was growing up, and have even fewer now."

"What?" I asked incredulously. "Someone nicknamed the Red Witch doesn't have a throng of followers and friends tripping over themselves to be with her? How shocking. And this, ummm, Tommy thing…it wasn't a 'friend with benefits' type of arrangement, was it?"

The pillow that launched itself from the bed nearly crushed

my nose.

"It amazes me that you have somehow not fallen into that large disconnect between your brain and your mouth."

"I'll take that as a no," I said as I vigorously rubbed my face.

CHAPTER THREE
MIKE JOURNAL ENTRY 3

THAT MORNING AS AZILE FED the babies, I made a grand breakfast of eggs, pancakes, bacon, and hash browns. I noticed many a sidelong glance from MJ as he watched me eating bacon.

"Trade you," I told him, holding the bacon out to his tiny nose. Azile laughed and pushed my hand away, the baby firmly attached to her nipple. When we were finished eating and cleaning up, Azile bundled the kids up and escorted me to the porch where we sat, each holding a little one. They were so wrapped up from the cold I wasn't even sure which one I held. I also wasn't so sure why we were sitting out there. It was a beautiful day, and the scenery was breathtaking as we looked out over a small lake and some rolling hills and all that, but I'd done enough sitting and staring for an eternity. I was okay with not revisiting that time of waiting. I should have known there was a real reason we sat there in relative silence. Not more than ten minutes later we heard the echoing of horses neighing, then the lively chatter of a toddler. As if I needed more clues, I was given the singsong laugh of Lana the Ninja. I stood. While I was happy to see Gabriel and even Lana, the thought of Mathieu being here lifted my spirits immeasurably.

"Hello, you blood sucking sprite!" he yelled from his mount.

"It is good to see you as well you miserable cur!" I told him. "Lana!" I smiled, helping her and her growing belly dismount. "Have you got his flea problem under control yet?" I whispered loudly as I kissed her cheek.

"I may perhaps harbor a few pests, oh ancient one, but you, sir, are an infestation," he said as he grunted to get off his horse. I would have helped him, but he would have seen this as a show of weakness, and I don't care what age it is, that isn't allowed. He put all his weight down on his prosthetic leg. He must have been getting a lot of practice because he looked pretty stable in the maneuver. Lana had helped Gabriel from his pony. The boy was a bundle of smiles. Hard to believe what he was capable of; such devastating potential hidden in such a small, vulnerable package.

We laughed and enjoyed our meeting, as friends should do. It was only after the sun went down and the kids went to bed that the conversation turned serious.

"No, Michael," was all Mathieu said as Lana sat down next to him.

"Yet, you came with Gabriel. Your actions speak much louder than your words," I said.

He looked over to Lana and nodded his head. "My beloved feels differently than I do."

I reached over and put my hand on his shoulder. "If it were me trapped in another realm would you come to help?"

"Neither Heaven nor Hell could hold me back."

I nodded as he said those words.

"And this man means as much to you as you do to me?" he asked.

"He doesn't brew beer, but he does mean a lot to me, Mathieu. I would do the same for anyone in this room. Except Sebastian."

The cat hissed as it jumped up into Azile's lap. "You should be more kind to the one that will guide you on the path." Azile stroked the large cat's back.

Oggie came and pressed his body up against my legs. He seemed to know something was up as he stayed close for as long as he could, even whining at the door when Azile and I wanted some alone time. Maybe not so much with Oggie, but that damned cat knows what's going on and I for one am not into an audience. That's just some freaky shit that people with peculiar discernment go for. Used to think I had some exotic tastes, once upon a time, then I discovered the internet and it turns out I was about as straight-laced as they come. People are a strange animal. I mean, I once saw this thing with two male midgets, an Amazonian woman, a twelve-foot rubber snake, six or seven…oh, forget it. No sense in me giving that imagery away; I've been trying to forget it for over a hundred and fifty years and it's still stuck there like a malignant tumor.

"How are you even going to know what to do?" Lana asked.

Azile couldn't help herself as a small laugh-slash-snort erupted from her mouth. "You mean like a plan?" she asked.

"Sorry." She was looking at me.

I sighed. She was right to laugh. Last time I had a plan, I think I was four and I was figuring out how to get at my sister's brand-new box of crayons. It's worth noting that she caught me and tickled me to the point I almost wet myself. Funny thing about being tickled; sure, you're laughing your ass off, but it's more of a panicked, manic thing. Someone literally has to hold you down as they tickle you, otherwise you'd run as far away as possible. Hardly seems like something benign. I got my revenge a week later. I showed our dog where they were and he tore the box to pieces and ate the crayons. My mother was not a happy camper with all the brightly colored shits he took for the next couple of days; obviously these had to be collected from the yard because they looked like melted chocolate Easter eggs. My sister couldn't prove anything, but she had her suspicions.

"I don't know what I'm going to do," I said in all honesty. "I don't even know how I'll find Tommy or what I'll be able to do if and when we do meet. I'm going under the assumption he'll somehow find me. Is that reasonable?" I asked Azile.

"He found you here; he should be able to find you there." She said the words but I didn't hear any assurance behind them. "There's more, Mike. I know this won't dissuade you, but you should know. Your destination will be so foreign to your base of reality that your mind is going to attempt to fill in what it perceives as gaps. It may even overlay what is actually there in front of you with things and situations you can more readily understand."

"What does that even mean?" Mathieu seemed more distressed than I; maybe because I had the attention span of a horsefly at a stable: "Woo Hoo! Just look at all those asses to bite!"

"Michael, are you listening?"

"Yeah. Something about horses." I stood up. "The raven is back." I had goosebumps up and down my arms and all along my spine.

Azile spread her hands, they were roughly as high as her head as she spoke an incantation. Lana looked to her sword which sat across the room, though I didn't think that steel would do much good right now. Everybody's head turned to the stairs as we heard a tapping on the window.

"What is this evil?" Mathieu stood, he was on the verge of changing over.

We went up the stairs as a very tight-knit, cohesive unit. I was terrified that at any moment they were all going to freeze in time like had happened a few nights previously and I'd have to do my best to keep them from tumbling down. When we all made it to the landing I was finally able to let out a small sigh. I should have felt better for it, but the tapping grew louder and more incessant and then there was the tinkle of glass; I pictured that black beak poking a bb sized hole straight through the pane.

"He must not be allowed to gain entry." Azile moved quickly to the door. She hesitated slightly as she caught sight of the large bird. I'm pretty sure a normal raven stands around two feet high and has roughly a four-foot wingspan. By any standards that's a big bird. The monster standing on the sill was close to double those figures. I felt like with a proper harness I could maybe cruise the skies with that thing as my ride.

Azile gasped as the bird swiveled its head, his white eye

casting an impossibly dark, white light throughout the room. It illuminated nothing yet cast our shadows against the far wall, creepy as fuck, that was.

"Need help now…" fluttered on the softest of air currents. If not for the hole in the window we may not have even heard it. "…by the burning bridge," was all we heard before the bird squawked loudly and lifted off. Lana had somehow got her sword and it was at the ready. Mathieu had changed over, Azile was saying a spell to dispel the evil that clearly lingered, and me? Well, I was standing there with my mouth wide open waiting for something to fly into it I suppose.

"Was that Tommy?" Mathieu asked in that gravelly voice he had when he was in mid-morph back to his human form.

My first inclination was to say, "yes." Azile beat me to a response.

"It may have been; it may not have, as well."

If she was trying to sow seeds of doubt in my mind, she was successful. It had taken root and was actively sprouting at this point. "What's that mean?" I asked.

"You said it yourself, Michael. You were only allowed to regain your soul in the hopes that you would one day yield it to the great deceiver. Perhaps he grows impatient."

"This…all of this is a lie?" I knew the answer before the words even made it to the ears of my audience. The great deceiver would be able to pull off something like this, so, why wouldn't he? Shit pretty much seemed right up his alley. He knew about Tommy and me; most likely knew all about my impetuous behavior. He could pull just about any string he so desired and watch me come running down the hill full-tilt, trip, skid and tumble straight into whatever trap he had erected. He didn't even need to do anything; I was about to come willingly. Probably be a bigger thrill for him to capture that which had not earned its way to him; big joke on the hairless ape. "I guess I just…just figured I had more time."

"You cannot go; you must see that now," Mathieu said in desperation.

"Hold on. We don't know that it *wasn't* Tommy," I said in defense, though I wasn't so certain I wanted any. Defense I mean. "The bird is a messenger, right?" I asked Azile.

"But from whom?" Lana asked astutely.

"The bird is more than that…I…I don't quite know all it is." Azile seemed to be racking her brain.

"But is it good or bad?" Mathieu needed an answer.

"It is both; or rather, it is neither," she replied cryptically. "It walks on the edge of a razor; minor fluctuations temporarily give more weight to one side or another but never for long. Its reason for being is balance; it makes no judgement, holds no allegiance." Azile seemed to be speaking from far off as she pulled knowledge, a long-ago legend from a distant past.

"It's time." We spun to see a sleepy-eyed Gabriel wiping his eyes.

I swallowed the lump in my throat that was my heart trying to lurch its way out, so I guess in the end even with all that was going on I managed a status quo, seemed about right for me. Much ado about nothing. Thank you, Shakespeare, for stating every human dilemma so very eloquently.

In the dark of night, after that horrifying experience and now the questions of doubt being raised by my most trusted allies, I was far less inclined to go than I had been just ten minutes before while in the warmth of the living room, surrounded by friends and the comfort of a roaring fire.

"I'm not ready," Azile said.

"Does not matter. *They* are ready," Gabriel replied. Oh yeah, that made me feel better.

"Who exactly are 'they,' honey?" Lana asked.

He shrugged his shoulders and kept vigorously working at his tired eyes.

"Are you sure about this Michael? I have not yet been able to weave all of my protection spells."

"I don't think there's time now," I said. "You all heard the urgency in Tommy's voice.

"Or the deceiver is fearful that Azile could somehow prevent him from obtaining that which he wants," Mathieu chimed in.

"Thanks for that," I said sarcastically. "You wield that kind of power?" I looked to her.

She shrugged, much like Gabriel had.

"Huh. Lot of shrugs going on around here. The last time I saw that many, my kids were much younger and I was trying to figure out who ate a hunk of birthday cake a day early. Yup. Bunch of shrugs then, too."

"We need to get you into a comfortable position, for once you are in place, it becomes crucial you are not moved; not so much as an inch, or there could be...problems when you realign with your body."

"Realign with my body? Wait. What?"

"You are not traveling in the physical sense, at least not as you perceive it. Surely you knew that?" she asked.

Somewhere inside of me, I guess I knew that. Just hadn't really paused to put all the puzzle pieces together, I guess. Plus, some things my brain deliberately hides from me to keep me from freezing up. "Like astral projection then?" I tried to make it sound like a clarifying statement; don't think it worked.

"Something like that, though I won't be able to slap your foolish self awake," she snapped.

"Slap? Why would you want to slap me awake?"

"Even you cannot be this thick," Mathieu said as an aside.

I wisely said nothing more as Azile led us all to the master bedroom. "Lie down," she commanded.

I was going to ask her where she would be sleeping but I got the distinct impression she would be doing precious little of that while I was gone, and I didn't want to be slapped prematurely. I did as she asked, lying on my back. I clasped my hands over my chest. Azile gently undid my hands and placed them down by my side. "You may cut off the circulation if you keep them that way," she said gently.

"Just now you looked like how we laid you the first time," Mathieu replied with a shudder.

"Michael, you need to listen to me. You can be injured; you can die where I send you. This physical body will remain here, but you will have a physicality there, as well. I know it sounds strange, but do you understand?"

"Yeah. It's like I'm getting cloned."

"You can think of it like that, but this isn't a body double. Your spirit can only inhabit one shell. Your clone dies, you go with it."

"I should look into a better stunt double."

Azile was muttering something, and for the first time in the last few minutes, Gabriel looked like he was awake.

"Are you ready?" he asked as he reached for my hand, never waiting for my response as he clasped it tightly. I'd like to say it was like being in a Star Wars movie, more specifically in the Millennium Falcon when it went (successfully) into hyperspace; at least I would have experienced a transition. In one moment, I was on my bed in my home next to my wife; the next, I was on a bed of thorns in the middle of a vast field full of them.

"Listen to Sebastian…" drifted out from a distant somewhere. I was afraid to move; it felt like my body was being used like a pin cushion, because indeed, it was.

"What are you doing there?" I gently turned my head to the sound and clenched; I think I would have been better off shoving my head into the thorn pile and hoping for the best. It, this…creature, was somewhat like Sebastian, though it was probably ten times the cat's normal size. Its ears were much larger, elongated. The razor-sharp fangs in its mouth were at least six inches long and stuck out of its mouth, much like I figured a saber tooth looked like. The only thing that made me think it was Azile's familiar was that the colors and striations were the same–oh, and the blatant contempt it had for me. That seemed about right. Other than that, this was a completely foreign animal. Plus, the thing was talking to me.

In typical Talbot fashion, the smartest question I could manage to ask was, "You talk?"

"Not as such. It is *you* who understands *me;* you are thinking in felinese."

"Huh?" I shifted, slightly fearful I was going to put a thorn through my ass.

"What does one with such greatness see in someone like you? No, I'm honestly curious. She has had many suitors, all were much more deserving of her gifts and beauty, yet she has settled for…I mean chose, of course, someone so…pedestrian."

"Take the cat, Michael. Listen to the cat. Follow the cat's lead, she says. I wonder if she knew the cat was such an asshole."

Sebastian let go something between a lion's roar and a red fox scream. It was unsettling, frankly it was terrifying. I got a good long look at multiple rows of pointy teeth. I'd not known the cat had a little bit of shark in it.

"I could kill you right here at this very moment and no one, not even Azile, would be the wiser. This is where my spirit dwells; this is my kingdom."

"I wouldn't get so high and mighty, cat. It's an arid shithole covered in barbs. I guess just the kind of place something like you enjoys." He approached. I noticed he was not walking atop the thorns but rather floating an inch or two out of their reach.

"I am not going out like my friend." I rolled over, my hands taking the brunt of the maneuver. "Death by cat makes sense in an ironic twisty sort of way, but I've got work to do."

"I respect Azile. She will be one that lives long in the annals of time. I will honor her request that I protect you. But know this, Michael Talbot, I will not place myself in harm's way to save you, not at any time."

I couldn't help it and I was pissed that it happened, but I shied away a bit when the cat reached out a large paw and touched me on the shoulder. I was surprised that I did not feel the pain of his claws dig into me or a torrent of hot blood flowing down my chest. What I got instead was a light and airy sensation as I began to rise. I was still on all fours, but up in the air. I was trying to get my balance as I magically hovered.

"What the hell is happening, cat?"

"I have given you a rise above the grip of the thorns. I could allow you to walk among them, if that is what you would prefer."

"Let's not get hasty." I felt like I was on a sheet of ice; my hand or knee would sometimes shoot out at a strange angle as it sought to gain traction on seemingly nothing.

"It is easier if you do not dwell on it. I would assume not thinking on something would come naturally to someone of your intellect."

"A cat with jokes. Just what everyone needs in their life." My right hand shot out and my head dipped down. The point of a thorn came within millimeters of my left eye. Would have popped it out like an olive on a toothpick.

"My name is Sebastian. If you call me 'cat' again in this realm, or in any realm, it will be a mistake you will regret."

"Where are we?" I asked, instead of letting spill a bunch of words that would surely get me in a bucket of hot shit. And believe it or not, I was smart enough to realize when I was completely outclassed and out of my element.

A Cheshire grin appeared on Sebastian's face as he once again reached over, this time he was not so gentle as he batted me in the side. I spun in place like a suspended ball of yarn.

"Where are we?" He repeated my words as I flipped over again. "We are at the gateways to the underworld."

"And you're the...err...gatekeeper?" I asked, holding back a little bile.

"I and others like me, yes," he said as he reached out and, thankfully, stopped me. Without any friction, there was a good chance I would still be spinning around a hundred years from now. Some poor traveler would come across my shriveled remains still going strong like a grotesque pinwheel.

"That's true? I always said that because of my dislike for your species."

"It appears in your ignorance you were right, for once. What is that aphorism? Even a clueless moron can fall down on the correct spot occasionally."

"I don't think that's how it goes," I mumbled. "Your job is to keep people out?"

Sebastian laughed. "If only our task were so simple. That is but a part, a very small part. There are all manner of creatures that we must keep behind the gates. For those fools that willingly enter, well, we simply don't have the resources available, or the desire, really, to stop them."

"How far are we from the gate?"

"An eternity, or the mere blink of an eye. Though this is accurate, because of your limited brain power, I do not mean to be metaphorical. This world is not how you would expect it to be."

"Gee. Thanks, I think."

"As a human, most of your kind live in only one dimension, and are very reluctant to consider the possibility that more exists beyond what you can see, feel, or touch. You limit yourselves to the few senses you are most familiar with to keep you in tune with your existence. Even those that are open to the idea that there may be other worlds beyond theirs, still believe that their world is far more vast and more significant that any other. In terms of realms, yours is middling at best, perhaps even somewhat below the median."

"This ain't my first rodeo, Sebastian. I have been to a realm or two. I know mine is not the only one that exists. As far as ranking goes, I'll leave that to others, but of course I am going to give more weight of importance to the one I inhabit."

The cat regarded me for a moment. "This is true; I had nearly forgotten that you escaped the clutches of the passing. I'll admit I was surprised that someone of your stature made it back. Those journeys are usually reserved for gods, or at least legends—neither of which you are."

"I hope whatever we have to do here is quick because being around you for too long is its own type of hell."

It smiled again. Pretty disturbing sight. "I can understand that from my point of view. We will travel to the burning gates; that may be the best place for you to go through."

"Me? What about you? And why are so many things down here burning? Nobody paid taxes for the fire department?"

"I cannot go through!" The cat seemed alarmed that I would even suggest such a thing. "It is forbidden."

"Oh, that's just great. Typical feline response. When someone is in need, just turn away so we can all see your swishing tail."

"I will allow you this slip in judgment because you are ignorant in the ways of this world. I have no choice in this matter. I do not choose to stay behind simply because I loathe nearly everything about you. I am bound by laws down here that are not as easily breakable as the laws of Man seem to be. I can no more travel across the gateway than you can harbor an intelligent thought."

"Fuck. If that wasn't coming from you, it would almost hurt. What do I do once I'm past the gate?"

Sebastian paused and licked his front paws, very reminiscent of a normal house cat as opposed to whatever this gargoyle-like thing in front of me was. "I do not know," he finally said when he was satisfied.

"Having a hard time figuring out why I need you here."

"Should you somehow survive, which I am hoping, and predicting, will not be the case, you will need to cross back over. That is why you will need me."

"Yeah, about as much as I need my own nipples," I muttered.

"Come, we venture." He started walking, well, floating, away.

I moved my legs hoping to keep pace. I was basically just spinning my gears, like a truck with a burned-out clutch or possibly Wile E. Coyote as he flies off the edge of the cliff and has a delay before he drops.

Sebastian looked back; disdain was clear amongst his features. "If walking is going to be this much of a problem perhaps you should just go back now and Azile will somehow let Tomas know that you have failed. Pity. For a soulless one he is a rather exemplary being."

"I'm not throwing in the towel just yet."

"I would not wait much longer; this place will not be safe for long."

"Not safe? Not safe from who?"

"Whom. It is from whom."

"Oh come on. A grammar nazi in hell? Well, wait. Actually that makes sense."

"*What* comes, I can neither prevent, battle, nor hide from. We must leave here. It may be better if we ask Azile to call you back now and we can attempt a new insertion point."

"How do I do that? How do I go back?" I wasn't in a panic just yet, but a feeling was starting to bubble to the surface as if my instincts were becoming vaguely aware of a threat coming our way. Maybe the cat had me spooked, or maybe some deep, primordial part of me was wired to know when something super fucked up was heading my way. Like Spidey.

I expected Sebastian to put his paw to his forehead and shake his head back and forth. Pretty sure he sighed. "You must fix her image in your mind; concentrate on the love you feel in your heart. You must smell the scent of her in your nose, the warmth of her touch..."

The sight of Azile's image began to brighten in my mind. "I'm doing it, I see her!" I said excitedly. "It's like she's on T.V.."

"I have no doubt it is more her keeping the lines of communication open than your superlative cognitive abilities."

"I am about sick of your fucking tongue. How about if I come over there and wrap it around your neck..." Unbeknownst to me at the time, Azile could see me, too. I was making my way to him in good fashion before she spoke.

"Michael?" she asked. There was genuine concern in her voice. "Are you in trouble already? You have been gone less than five minutes."

I heard Mathieu in the background like we were talking over a phone. "Well, if anyone could get into trouble that fast it would be him."

Sebastian seemed bemused as I nearly glided right past him. "Can we go now?" he asked.

"Just checking in," I told Azile. "Is this how I get a hold of you when I need you?"

"It is, Michael, and Gabriel and I can bring you back easily enough when you are on this side of the gate. Once you cross over it cannot be done."

"Like, at all?"

"At all." This from Gabriel.

"Is Sebastian helping?" Azile asked.

I wasn't sure how to answer that. "Did you know what he looks like down here?" I asked quietly.

"Of course. Are you two getting along?"

"Along? I wouldn't go that far."

"Pay attention Michael; listen to him. Do not let your old biases hinder your ability to let him help."

"You realize that he hates me, right? That he would rather see me dead than succeed, and that he could easily eat me."

"That's just him warming up to you."

"You two certainly have a way of sticking together."

"We must leave now, Azile. Bledgrum comes," Sebastian said.

"Go, Michael. Leave now!" There was a panicked dread in Azile's voice that easily and quickly transferred over to me.

"How bad can this Bed-gum be? And I thought this was your territory?" Yeah, I had asked the questions with a sort of bravado but we were already on the move and I was doing all I could to stay up with the cat-monster.

"Most of my power, our power, is concentrated at the gate.

Out in the open, even I would be no match for what comes."

We started hearing noise behind us, sounded like a live, six-point caribou being force fed through a meat grinder. Now in honesty, I have no idea what this would sound like, but it would be horrifyingly disgusting and terrible and loud. Sebastian's face wasn't overly expressive, but I could easily detect the mask of good old-fashioned fear covering his mug. His eyes were open wide and his teeth were exposed in a grimace.

"We're going to have to hide," he said as he lowered himself down into a thicket of thorns. I don't think he so much as parted his fur with the barbs. I, however, could have supplied the Red Cross with a couple of pints of blood and had some slopping off the table as well when he reached up, grabbed my ankle, and yanked me through.

I was about to rail on him for purposefully trying to eviscerate me by brier. I would have, too, if he hadn't stuck a paw with fully extended claws straight into my maw. Look at that! Damn near a Dr. Seuss verse, albeit with a darker slant. He had effectively sewed my mouth shut with four razor-sharp talons. If I dared to speak he would rip deep gouging wounds through my lips and gums. I could not pull back for fear of shoving a spike through my spine. Involuntary tears rolled from the corners of my eyes. He pulled his grapnels back, leaving his paw there. By now I was well aware that speaking wasn't a great idea. The ground I was kneeling on was thrumming as if it had been electrified. At first, it was a low-level current, and then the intensity built up, along with the thrumming hum. The ground shook so hard we were now bucking like a heart attack patient getting defibrillated. Whatever it was had to be huge, so naturally I had to see it. I find it funny that they say "curiosity killed the cat" because Sebastian, if anything, was sinking lower to the ground while I was slowly rising up.

I went far enough to just peek my eyes over the curtain of brambles we were enshrouded by. I had a fascination with

Godzilla in my youth, and by youth, I mean all the way until the z-poc started, when suddenly we had more immediate threats to deal with. But there was something about that two hundred or so foot-high monster that intrigued and terrified me to no end. Kind of funny; I had watched Godzilla before we started learning about dinosaurs in school. I remember being wholly unimpressed with a forty-foot tall tyrannosaurus-rex once we finally got to the natural history museum. The "terrible lizards" were nothing compared to the king of all reptiles; it didn't matter that they had actually terrorized the earth. Then I got my first glimpse of Bledgrum, four hundred feet...five hundred, maybe? It, (I'm sticking to It, otherwise I have to assume there are two of these beasts and they somehow copulate and there's only so far I can carry this bad dream) looked like one of the pyramids of Giza had fallen through some quicksand, been deposited in this hellish landscape, come to life, and was now bent on harassing the locals. A lot like Godzilla, when you think about it.

I wouldn't doubt if the ancient Egyptians had somehow witnessed this monstrosity and constructed their monuments with it in mind. Size and shape notwithstanding, that was about it for the similarities. Instead of a sandstone shade, it was more the drab gray of a subway tunnel. Its skin, if that's what it was, had a coating of thick slime that reminded me of a garden slug. I thought it might have had some sort of facial features but its...head, I guess...was so high up and the light was suspect; it was impossible to tell. Tentacles by the dozens protruded from every side in random order and lengths. They flailed about as if independent from each other, a handful of blind snakes escaping through giant, gray, slimy fingers. Sometimes they seemed to be randomly flogging the creature for merely having the audacity to exist, often times they would whip down, grip great swaths of thorny vines, rip them free of their mooring, then toss the heavy vegetation high and far so that it came down much like a missile would. Explosions of plant life, dirt, and dust plumed from every strike point like a full-scale nuclear war was being waged upon the battlefield.

Hundreds of legs supported the base of the beast, each as thick as an elephant's. Again, much like the tentacles, they all seemed to be operated by their own driver who had not a clue what the rest of the others were up to. A chill swept down my spine as I watched dozens of legs snap in half as they tried to go against the majority, they would flop around and be dragged on the ground; following this hideous slapstick routine would be this awful grinding sound as bones reset and the legs were once again able to be used, though they never seemed to learn the dance and would once again be broken, dragged, reset; as It would stumble on.

"What the…?" I asked aloud and too loudly apparently before Sebastian knocked me flat on my ass.

"Quietly or he will hear you," the cat hissed.

The thing was maybe a mile away and over five hundred feet tall; I was having a hard time believing it would be able to do that, unless it had ears the size of ship sails, and I saw no such organs. But I believed the cat, completely.

"He knows we are here," Sebastian said.

Again, I trusted him; nothing can fake that kind of terror. I could have started with the "Hows and Whys" but what was the point? It wouldn't change the facts.

"It's your soul, it's as out of place here as you are in Azile's home."

"Fuck, Sebastian, even when we're about to die you dig in an extra one."

"The truth may be spoken in all places and times."

"Wait, what about your soul? It could just as easily be tracking you."

"Impossible; I do not possess one. I volunteered its release so I could guard the gate."

"Do all cats do this?"

"Do all humans join the military? Only the bravest and fiercest are allowed to become Gate Keepers."

"But why the cost of your soul?"

"So that we cannot be tempted over the threshold. We lost many great warriors in the first few millennia of our war. Either they would follow an enemy too far in the hopes of finishing the demon off, or else they would be seduced to pass over, believing in so doing they would obtain powers beyond imagining."

I had so many questions regarding where these souls went. Was there, like, a Souls Storage Warehouse? And did this mean that demons also possessed souls? Probably, but I didn't know for sure. Not sure if that helped or not, but the thought was there now and I could chew on it later. The great beast was still lumbering along, sort of, but not mostly, in our direction. As it searched, the monster made a fearful racket— a great cracking sound as if giant sequoias were being uprooted and snapped in half by a raging tsunami. At first, I assumed that this was just a normal sound caused by the movement of one so big and unwieldy, but Sebastian said otherwise.

"It grows angry. Azile is giving him false leads." This time the cat's smile was more smirk. "Its roar is meant to drive us from our hiding hole."

"It's working on me; how about you?"

"I, too, would very much like to leave this place."

"Look at that! Only takes the threat of being smashed into atomic particles to make us bond."

"We are not bonding. I merely do not wish to die."

"Fair enough, I didn't think we were bonding either, but we are definitely seeing eye to eye."

Sebastian shook his head. "I believe Tomas and his sister are doomed, and now we are not far behind them."

"It's turning." I had poked my head up. That it was turning meant absolutely nothing; its four sides were indistinguishable from each other. "It's coming this way." My heart was beating faster and working harder to push blood that was beginning to thicken from the cold. Even if it never saw us we would surely be trampled to death as if we were Mufasa and Bledgrum was the wildebeest. I thought back to a moment ago; I hadn't caught it then. "Sebastian, if he is looking for me, couldn't you escape?"

He regarded me, without saying anything.

"There is no sense in the both of us dying. I could die knowing I had at least attempted to save Tommy. I would feel better if I did not add you to the scales."

"It is not an easy death Bledgrum offers you. Those tentacles have needle-like barbs on them; he will suck your soul from you, leaving the dead husk of your body behind."

"I mean, yeah, sure, that sounds pretty bad but…"

"You do not understand; you cannot. Your soul will reside inside of that beast for thousands of years as he slowly digests it. You would remain completely aware and in unbearable pain the entire time, conscious, unable to pass."

I was feeling slightly faint; okay, more than slightly.

"What remains of you, your id, will be sent back to purgatory where the thousands of years of torment that your soul endured within the beast will be nothing but a footnote in the novel of the eons you will sustain there."

"Yeah, but we can outrun that thing, Sebastian. Can't we?"

"No, that time has passed. He is in search mode. If we were to run, we would simply become prey; we would stand no chance."

"I'm listening."

"We wait for Azile to come up with something."

"That's it? That's your plan? I could have come up with that and I'm the master of disastrous plans. What if we pull the plug? Can't we just pop out and pop back in somewhere he isn't?"

"Yes, but if we leave it may be months, or even years, before you are capable of returning."

"You didn't say anything about that before."

Sebastian shrugged.

Whatever was going on with Tommy, I was sure he did not have that kind of time. I concentrated on Azile. I could make her out on the couch; she had heavy beads of perspiration on her forehead.

"Hey, Azile," I said, through gritted teeth.

"I am busy my love," she forced out.

"We may need an extraction."

"How close?" The effort to say anything was clearly visible.

"Quarter mile and closing."

"I must do what I can to keep you there; I will give you the ability to talk directly to Gabriel."

"This is fucking great. My life is literally in the hands of a gigantic cat and a six-year-old."

"He can hear you," Gabriel replied.

"Sorry kid. Wasn't expecting this."

"I have not told Azile because she has too much going on right now, but someone has tampered with our connection."

Dread, which was free-flowing through me, was beginning to lessen as panic began to rise. "What's that mean, Gabriel?"

"I can't get you back."

"This isn't a really good time for games, Gabe." I was looking at the squirming, limb-snapping, slow-digesting, gray beast coming our way. The ground was now hopping up to meet us from Its footfalls.

"This has never happened," he explained, apologetically. "Something or somebody has cut the link, and I do not know how."

"We're in trouble Sebastian." I looked over to him.

"You don't say? Perhaps Azile believes she can somehow improve you through her influence," he said after a moment of reflection.

"If you weren't the size of a mountain lion right now, I'd shove your head in some kitty litter. My connection to the upper world has been terminated. Gabriel does not know how. But you should be able to get back, right?"

"That is without a doubt. This is my domain; I have spent far more lifetimes here than I have in your world. I can't help but respect your decision to die alone. Most would be much more selfish in their desire to be in the company of others in their greatest time of need; in their final moments, in your case. I will not soon forget this."

"Don't get too choked up, it's not like we're life-long friends. Maybe a moment of peace and quiet before I am no more would be more comforting. Well, I mean until my parts are separated and forced to suffer forever." I was watching Sebastian; he was not moving, his eyelids furrowed down as his iris expanded from a small slit to completely open. Didn't take a lot of figuring to realize he was stuck as well, he just didn't want to let on.

"I felt it would be nobler of me if I were to, that is, *witness* your devastation. To give Azile that final measure of closure so that she could move on and find someone better."

"Mighty magnanimous of you."

A clod of earth the size of a dump truck was ripped up no more than a hundred feet from where we hid. It landed another hundred feet past us. The thing had thrown tons of material nearly the length of a football field and that was with only one of its tentacles; it was chewing up the landscape faster than a herd of goats with tapeworms. Soon we would be in a barren, pockmarked field. There was little chance for escape and no place to hide.

"I have an idea," I said to Sebastian.

He was looking to the opposite side from where our pursuer was coming. His body was tense and his tail moved slowly back and forth; suddenly I thought he was gearing up to make a run for it and see how that worked out. Now I had to ponder whether he had known that this thing would hone in on me all along and had me hide here in the briar patch on purpose so it wouldn't take as long and he could go back to Azile, all sad and sympathetic. If he knew he could "pop out" whenever he chose, what was the risk to him? He did not turn when I spoke.

"You told me running would not work."

"Not likely when he is this close," he answered. "Perhaps if I had gone sooner…" he seemed to lament.

"What if I had gone sooner?" I asked. He did not answer; I think maybe he realized his mishap.

"What is your idea?" He turned to face me.

"The legs."

"You wish to be trampled by his legs before he can skewer you with his barbs? That is a pretty good thought for one like you. The chance that he can get a hold of your soul is greatly diminished that way."

"Only greatly diminished? Not completely out of the question?"

"The quicker you die the better. Your soul will be confused for a moment as you make the transition; the quicker you regain your wits, the better off you will be. As you try to grasp the concept that you do not still physically exist you will be the most vulnerable."

"Got this all figured out, don't ya?"

"I believe it bears repeating. There are not many aspects of you I admire, maybe none at all, actually." He tilted his head to think on this.

"Should have known a cat would be my undoing. Some sort of cosmic karmic fuck up the old ass."

"I told you not to call me that again."

"Screw you, cat. I'm out of here." I made the best version of a beeline that I could to get to Bledgrum. In some spots, the thorns were too thick; in some, I had to go down one side of a huge divot and back up the other. In a couple of areas, I actually had clear sailing, and not more than a whisker away was Sebastian, who I think was attempting to gut me, or at least fantasizing about it. The monster spun our way faster than should have been possible for something so mammoth and uncoordinated. When you think huge, you think lumbering, slow, and maybe deliberate in its steps. An economy of movement because of the energy required to ambulate something so vast. Well, if I needed any convincing that this world was vastly different from my own, here it was. A tentacle lashed out; I dodged to the right.

Not more than an inch of that slimy appendage touched me, I mean just the tip, but it had enough force to send me sprawling and it stung like hell. I was rocked sideways, my left shoulder made contact with the packed ground first. Some of the impact was absorbed as a lot of the momentum was expended as I slid. I immediately felt the piercing of my skin. I was wondering what it would feel like to have your soul sucked through the world's largest silly straw. Took me a second to realize I was on the move again, this time in the mouth of Sebastian. It wasn't tentacle barbs but rather large feline teeth that were making me bleed my own blood.

"Can you stand?" he asked with his mouth full as we got closer to the beast.

"Yes," I managed to answer as tentacles rained down all around us. The ground was being beaten into submission by the strikes. Sebastian shifted his body and swung his massive head, giving me some momentum as I tumbled from his mouth. I hit the ground, spun once, and was up and running before I could get hit again.

There was sort of an "eye of the storm" type of feeling about five feet from Bledgrum. He could not see, nor could his tentacles reach me, though he tried valiantly. As of yet, I was not a direct obstacle to the hundreds of feet and legs thrusting about in their broken puppet type of way. I think it was me staying in that sweet spot that ultimately saved Sebastian and I'd let him know when I got the chance. Bledgrum knew his deficiencies and was prepared to take steps to correct them, and by steps, I mean he started running toward me in an effort to crush my ass. This was when I helped Sebastian up before he could become ground chum. Now we were both making a run for it, and Bledgrum was having none of it. He changed direction faster than an NFL running back. A tentacle swept dangerously close; my hair moved from the wind it pushed.

We turned to follow suit. Slick, but it would only be a

matter of time until we tired or made an errant turn and those tentacles would be the end of us. I moved in past the sweet spot, to the swirling, stomping mass of legs. The dust storm his feet were kicking up was a choking clog of fine debris turning to mud in my throat and lungs. It took every sense available to me to avoid being trampled and still I would occasionally be nicked from the side or pushed from behind.

"Think, Talbot. What would I do in this situation?" I took my belt off. And yes, while I was scared enough to shit myself, I wasn't in any imminent danger of doing that just yet. Maybe later, if I lived. I'm sure there were still plenty of nightmares ahead to witness. Anyway, this wasn't your traditional leather belt with drilled holes and a buckle; this was more of your garden variety rope I just used to hold my pants up. Amazing how you can keep a physique when there're no more fast food or snack cakes available. I scanned quickly, looking for one of the legs that didn't quite have its shit together as well as the others. Like, at some point it had just quit working properly and Mr. Bledgrum had not yet gone to the orthopedist to get it checked out. I found a perfect one that was mostly just getting dragged along.

Bledgrum again changed direction rapidly. It seemed he was actually helping me out as his busted limb now rushed up to meet me. In hindsight, it may have appeared that Bledgrum knew exactly what he was doing. My next set of maneuvers, while not technically flawless, were still adequate enough to get me perched up on the knee joint of the bum leg with the rope completely looped around it. I had an end of the rope in each hand, and while not the most comfortable mode of transportation, I was moderately safe. Then I had the crushing thought that all he really needed to do right now was sit down and my hitchhiking ride was over.

I was feeling somewhat pleased with myself at this very moment, you know, having averted death and all that with nothing but my brains and my belt. My heart was starting to come down a couple of hundred beats per second. Sweat was still dripping in my eyes but that was to be wholly expected at this point. Yeah, that's when it got interesting; there seemed to be a reason this leg had problems. It was littered with soccer ball sized pustules. They were dark gray, almost black—hard, knotty bumps that seemed to have a lot in common with warts. Only these were festering and oozing a greenish, slimy puss. So, what I thought was sweat upon my brow was actually some sort of stinking demon virus.

"Oh man, this can't be good," I said as I twisted my head from a rivulet of the substance nearly a hand span across. It didn't help that as this leg was dragged along it continually opened up scabbed-over sores. Soon I was covered in a thick viscera of hot, sticky fucking goop. I'm not even the slightest bit ashamed that I puked, at least twice. And still, that smelled better than the ulcerating holes. What I am a bit ashamed about admitting was I'd not even taken a moment to try and locate the cat. He had saved me, that was for sure, though I don't know why. I doubt there could be a worse fate than what Bledgrum proposed should he catch me. But, I guess there is always worse; maybe Sebastian wanted to make sure I got the uglier fate. Had the cat been upfront from the beginning I think perhaps we could have outrun the brute and possibly found a safe haven. Then again, maybe I was giving Sebastian too much credit. He was still just a cat, after all.

I spun my head around as I caught sight of something streak past; it was Sebastian. Not going to lie, there was a huge stab of jealousy as he jumped and grabbed hold of a leg with his claws fully extended. In two seconds, he'd settled in on that leg. I wasn't jealous because of the claws, but rather that the leg he'd chosen seemed to be free of any and all wart-like protrusions. I would have paid him handsomely to share his ride.

I read somewhere that dinosaur nervous systems were so slow it could take minutes until they registered pain caused by an injury; that was not the case with this guy. The moment Sebastian sunk his claws into that leg, Bledgrum had let loose with that woeful clacking racket. He started staggering back and forth in obvious pain.

"Big motherfucker like this is crying for his momma from cat claws?" I yelled out.

"There is a venom in them," Sebastian answered, smugly, I thought.

"You put them in my mouth! Will it kill him?" I hoped and didn't.

Sebastian shook his head.

"Silver have any special effect?" I asked as I looked to my axe.

"Does he appear to you to have any werewolf traits?"

"I hate you," I spat out as a particularly thick globule of something slid past my lips. I could ride the phlegm express into eternity or I could do something. I chose to do something because when one is as bright as I am it is not wise to sit around and think too much; can get into *way* more trouble if given enough time to come up with something sound.

"I would not do that if I were you," Sebastian warned as I climbed higher up the leg.

"There's a reason we are who we are," I told him back. It was an easy enough climb as I used the burgeoning crusty sores as handholds. I just hadn't realized how high I would have to go. From a distance, the legs had seemed pretty short, and in comparison to the rest of the beast they were. But I was still somewhere in the neighborhood of the top of a traditional telephone pole by the time I got to where the leg joined the base. In the grand scheme of things, forty feet doesn't sound so high, but I can guarantee if you were sitting on the top of one of those poles with nothing but a dinner plate-sized scab to hold on to, you'd be as terrified as I was right now.

Sebastian had much more easily climbed up his appendage. "What are you doing?" he asked.

"Payback."

"Payback for what? He has done nothing to us yet."

"Proactive revenge."

"There is no such thing."

"There is now!" I yelled as I dragged the blade of my axe against the soft, gray underbelly of the hideous thing. The flesh parted easy enough as my blade was sharper than it had a right to be. What I had not accounted for was the seven or eight feet of blubber that needed to be carved through to get to anything vital. As if in reward for my courageous action, large, yellow gelatinous chunks of congealed matter poured down over my head to the point where I had to stop what I was doing and hold on for dear life lest I be forced from my perch by the deluge. This probably doesn't need further embellishment. Once most of the disgusting innards had fallen out I crawled back up. I was three feet inside the monster, and the smell will probably take years of hard drinking to purge from my memory, but I'll give it a shot. It smelled as if I'd crawled up the rectum of an E-coli victim who had eaten a particularly bad batch of pulled pork soaked in blue cheese. Yeah. Hot, liquefied shit with the taint of rotting bacterial infection. That basically sums it up.

I was gagging something fierce; long ribbons of drool hung from my mouth but I just kept cutting away. And still, I wasn't clear for what purpose. I hacked and slashed, cutting great swaths of fibrous material. At this point, I was so lost in the savage act I never once pondered the ultimate outcome. I dared not go any higher up, afraid that I would forever become entombed within the beast, which is where I didn't want to end up in the first place. I reached up and gave one final hack. A small pink ribbon of intestine pushed through like a hernia and then the weight of it forced the opening wider as if Bledgrum were giving birth to his guts. I was almost rendered unconscious as that first piece bounced off my head and unwound its way to the ground.

"What have you done?!" Sebastian shouted.

I climbed down about ten feet and went to the far side of the leg as the small gap I'd created had begun to widen on its own. It was like watching the San Andreas fault widen right before my eyes and it got wider and longer with every step Bledgrum took. Intestines free-flowed like a plate of spaghetti tilting into the sink, though this was pasta I never wanted to have. Huge sections plopped out, some never making it to the ground as they became entangled in his legs; those that did were summarily mashed into the ground. The clicking intensified as Bledgrum was in some serious distress. Mile after mile the beast plodded on, tripping on its own innards, leaving a slime trail that I'm sure was visible from space. He was doing irreparable damage to himself as he tore through and crushed everything that fell from him.

"We're going to need to leave," I said to Sebastian as a giant rippling tremble shook Bledgrum's entire body, I knew a death rattle when I felt one. Bledgrum was moving much more slowly when my feet touched the ground, making the escape from the many legs less dangerous, as any freight hopper will tell you. Five minutes later Sebastian and I were off to the side and behind the behemoth. If he could still detect me I was no longer of importance as he stumbled forward.

"This isn't good." Sebastian seemed exceedingly nervous.

He plodded on. More and more material gushed out; looked like a garbage truck that had sprung a bad leak and some of the foulest refuse known to man was pouring into the street. There weren't ever going to be enough hazardous material teams to deal with this cleanup.

"Souls must be a pretty hearty meal." I managed to say. For the life of me, I could not look away from the spectacle ahead of us.

Sebastian said nothing. Bledgrum began to wobble in earnest as more and more of his legs stopped working or got knotted to the point where they could no longer move. He listed heavily to the left, sort of corrected himself, and then just toppled over. The thunderous sound and impact must have been heard multi-dimensionally because within a moment we had Azile on the spirit hotline. "Killed Bledgrum? What?" She seemed perplexed and was firing off questions faster than

Sebastian or I could register.

"There are consequences, Michael!" she exclaimed.

"You know, dear, I was a little under the gun. I had to do something," I explained. "And I'm not understanding why this is such a bad thing. He was a huge monster that did horrible things. If anything, I think I should be getting some sort of medal, maybe a key to the underworld or something."

"I'm sure the citizens will be lining up," she said sarcastically. "I want you to think about spiders, Michael."

"Why? I hate those fucking things."

"Do it!"

"Great! Okay…I'm thinking of those eight legged freaks of nature. Now what?"

"Let's pretend Bledgrum represented every spider on the planet and you just eradicated them."

"Holy fuck—I *am* a hero!"

"Just because you can't stand them doesn't mean they don't play a vital role in the balance of the universe."

"Meh. There were people that would have argued clowns had a purpose at one time. If you ask me the world is much better off since they stopped existing."

"We're not talking about clowns, Michael! Spiders consume more insects than any other species on the planet. Without them, we would be overrun by pests; disease and plague would run roughshod over the world. It would only be a few years before not much existed on the planet, save them. It would be worse than the zombies and the Lycan combined."

I was beginning to get an inkling that I had screwed up on an epic scale, but it had been him or me and it still didn't stop me from trying to justify or at least minimize my actions. "Yeah but, um, Bledgrum isn't a spider. Plus, he wanted to kill me first."

"I realize he wasn't a spider. You of all people should recognize an analogy!"

Holy shit. She was pretty hot under the collar. Probably a good thing we had a dimension separating us.

CHAPTER FOUR
MIKE JOURNAL ENTRY 4

SEBASTIAN AND I DIDN'T HANG around long; what was happening now did not need to be witnessed. Things, lower on the food chain, were coming up out of the ground and eating Bledgrum's parts. I say "things" because to describe them turns my stomach. They were roughly human-shaped, albeit much smaller, a third of the size I guess, somewhere in the fifty-pound range, so, human-child size. At first, I thought it was some sort of rainstorm as the ground began to swirl in dozens, then hundreds, of places. Then the earth began to swell in those spots like a rapidly expanding pimple on a teenager's face. Then it would burst and instead of the welcome white glob of grease, out came these carnivorous parasites. They were bipedal; that's all we had in common. They were a deep, coal black; their feet had large hooks, much like the vestigial dewclaw dogs have, though this one they used to dig at their food. They did not possess hands; rather their arms ended in a flat, pointed appendage, like a broad scythe, useful for fast digging. I could see no eyes; I guess they would have no reason for them at the depths they lived.

Tiny slits on the sides of their heads were, I imagined, for hearing; occasionally they would swivel those slits our way and listen intently. It was unnerving, being detected by these things, though I doubted they ate much live meat. Their mouths were a black hole, somehow impossibly darker than the rest of them, and in stark contrast to the white razor-sharp, interlocking teeth. Was sort of happy those things were more on the scavenger side than predatory.

"What are those?"

"You can call them sand sharks."

"Good enough. We should maybe get out of here," I told him.

"Gabriel says your connection has been restored. Azile wonders if perhaps you have done enough and should go back," Sebastian relayed. I was doing my best to hide from the incoming calls; I didn't need caller-id to know who was trying to get a hold of me.

"I'll decide that at the gates. As of yet, I have done nothing."

"Oh," Sebastian looked back, "I think you have done plenty."

We walked for hours; the light never wavered from an odd, twilight hue— a sort of un-light. Seemed like something important I should ask in regard to, but I was still completely covered in a thick layer of Bledgrum's bodily fluids and now that it was solidifying, movement was becoming hindered, and well, just plain disgusting, and it was all I could think about.

"Anything like a river run through this place?"

"No," came quickly and succinctly.

"No body of water I can use to clean up?"

"None."

"I feel like you're lying; either one: because you don't want to take the time to let me clean up, or two: you enjoy seeing me in such distress."

"There is what appears to be watering holes here, but they are made of lies. You would be better served diving into a pool of lava than dipping into these illusions. There are many things here that will appear very much as they do in your world; this is a deliberate attempt to ensnare the unsuspecting. Ironically, the things that appear to offer the most comfort or salvation are the ones you must be the most cautious of. There is no easy succor here; do not look for it."

"I guess we should stay close, then," I told him.

"Dangerous things in your world are still dangerous here." He turned what I'd hope was levity on its ear. "It would be wise to stay away from those things as well."

The landscape seemed to be devoid of life, though there were times I could see something flit past from the corner of my eye or scurry along a hillside, creating a small amount of scree. The terrain itself held no plants, harbored no trees. It was rocky and barren like the photos of the surface of Mars that I had seen. Though instead of the heavy, iron-rich reds, we were stuck with the more spirit-crushing drab grays that seemed to be prominent in the underworld. If this place wasn't in need of a paint job I don't know where was.

I really didn't know what I expected the gates of the underworld to look like—perhaps some formidable, burning mountainous wall with large, grated steel doors nearly a hundred feet tall covering a gaping wound in the cliffside, keeping in all that would seek to bust out. It should have been something epic; hell, I would have even taken that huge wooden gate that led visitors into Jurassic Park. What I got instead was something that looked like it had been built by a couple of kids with stuff they'd salvaged from an old barn.

"You were expecting something like St. Peter's gates I assume?" Sebastian asked as he looked over at me.

"I'll be honest; I don't think much about that barrier, but I figured something that was designed to keep in the worst this place has to offer would look more formidable than an old horse gate, maybe something like the black gates of Mordor."

"There is a lot of power down there."

"Magic?" I asked.

"Perhaps in your eyes it would appear as magic, but magic implies something can come from nothing. There is a great energy source used to thwart nearly every attack."

"If you say so." I started hiking down the small ridge we found ourselves on and was heading straight for it.

Sebastian bounded in front of me. "I understand my words matter little to you, but I will say them nevertheless so that I may keep peace with Azile. Not for me, mind you, but for her."

"I'm listening."

"Once you cross over, you are dead."

"That simple?"

"Your body, the one which lies upon Azile's couch, may resist for a moment or two, then it will convulse, gasp for a last breath, and be done."

"I don't believe you. I don't think Azile would have let me come if it was that easy to drop dead."

Sebastian said nothing for a moment. "Perhaps she had planned just this course."

"Naw. There's easier ways to get rid of me. She could just let me cook breakfast or something, probably spill hot bacon grease on myself and fall into the oven. I don't need elaborate, otherworldly scenarios to do me in."

"If you say so."

"What else? I feel like there's more."

"Is that not enough? I just told you that you will terminate your physical presence and your soul will be trapped. This is a doomed attempt at salvation; surely even you must realize that? Not to mention it is conceivable that this entire thing is a set-up. I heard you talking to Azile about the deal you made. Does this not seem like something He would do to retrieve something for which He feels entitled to?"

It was hard to argue that, but I did anyway. "You were in a trance or something when I got the message; there is no doubt in my mind it was Tommy that sent it. As for the other, he's in it for the long game. How much sweeter would it be for him if he were to gather my soul after I'd tipped the scales in his favor? If I'd done such irreparable harm along the way that salvation could never be won?"

"You are nearly too stupid to live. You were and are a vampire, a soulless one that has regained the unattainable. If ever He wanted a feather in that large cap of His, you would be it. You have been touched by the one God; you have been a valiant warrior in the grand-scale game of good versus evil. Perhaps He does not want to give you the chance to ascend."

I'd never done overly well with thinking out all aspects of

any particular scenario. For some fucked up reason, I'd always believed over-thinking a problem was worse than diving in. Right now, though, this wasn't about doing a bong hit followed by a shot of Jeff Daniels…or is it Jack? and a shotgunned beer. Which, by the way, put me on my ass, where I stayed for about ten minutes while I tried to regain my bearings. This was about my life. I was okay with putting that on the line for a family member—wasn't the first time and I guarantee if I made it through it wouldn't be the last. But that damned pesky soul…that was a whole other thing entirely. Death was finite and unavoidable; one second you were there, the next you weren't. Just the way it has been since mortality reared its ugly head.

That soul, though. Eternity would be making me its bitch, pretty much slapping me back and forth across the face with a wet salmon, bitch, for fucking ever. As much as I hated to admit it, Sebastian's words had a clear peel of truth to them.

I thought I knew what he would say if I asked, but again, I did anyway. For the most part, the answer was what I thought it would be, but for different reasons. "What would you do?" I asked.

His cat-chuckle was disturbing. "I would not go. There is no chance of a successful mission here. There are no odds that could be swung in your favor that might help your endeavor; no amount of dumb luck can better those odds. You will be beyond your God's help and beyond Azile's, and once you cross that line, you and I become enemies."

"What?" That I was not expecting. "Aren't we already?" I asked, looking for some humor; pretty much pancaked. Meaning it fell flat, if I wasn't clear enough.

"Even if you somehow miraculously found Tomas and his sister and managed to get them back to the gate, we could not and would not allow you back over."

"This isn't some twisted cat humor, is it?"

"As surprising as this may be, felines are not big on humor."

"Yeah, right shocker that is."

"Michael, this is not something to take lightly. When we fight back the demons that attempt to exit we do not know their intent, neither do we care. Each and every one that comes to that gate seeking a way out is met with unbridled and unrelenting fury. We have heard every deceitful plea spanning millennia untold. The gatekeepers are an integral part of the grand design. We have been tirelessly keeping vigilance; when we falter the world above pays greatly for our missteps."

"Ah ha! So, some *have* got past!" I saw a lifeline and was reaching for it.

Sebastian sighed. "Five times since the dawn of this age we have failed. Three of those errors set free what your kind called an 'anti-Christ,' though what happens here far outdates that."

"Five times? So, it can be done."

"Yes, five times. Five times out of billions upon billions. You would have an easier time getting hit by a bus."

"How hard is that?"

"There are no buses anymore."

"I didn't know you were being literal. So…five, though. It can be done."

"NO! It cannot!" he yelled. "If you crossover, you will be gone forever. Those few that made it through had enormous resources at their disposal. An amassing of power so great we could not contain it. Even then they were barely able to succeed. You will have no allies there. It will be you against everyone and every*thing*. The Lycan wars which nearly ended your existence numerous times? You had help. You were saved by others—others who risked their lives for you, for your cause. You will not be afforded that once you cross over."

"If I didn't know better it would almost sound like you care about what happens to me."

"You are thicker than a slab of bacon. Something is happening here; I sense there is a reason you were called to this realm now of all times, and I'm afraid you may be some sort of trigger event that ripples outward."

"Like a disturbance in the force?"

Sebastian didn't understand the reference, I let it go. I was torn damn near in two. Tommy, my son, needed help—that much was beyond question. But he chose this path knowing the dangers, and he was much better equipped to handle them. He called upon me in full knowledge of my limitations; what the hell did he think I could do if even he couldn't extract himself from this shitty situation?

"Turn around, go home, find a way to cope with your grief. He is lost…forever."

I did start to turn, his words so convincing. "I can't. He would do it for me."

"Then you are both fools that the world will not miss." He stepped aside.

I paused a handful of steps from the gate; a patrol of super-sized cats were milling about. A few glanced over and immediately dismissed me. They gave not one shit that I was sneaking into hell. I got the impression they figured I should already be in there.

"Azile," I said thinking desperately about my wife.

"I am here."

"You knew?"

"I did. Left to follow the voice of your own heart, I had thought perhaps you would find more reasons to stay amongst the living rather than venture among the dead." She was choking up.

"It's family; I don't have a choice in this matter."

"That I know as well," she replied through a sob.

"Is what Sebastian said true?"

"I cannot help you once you cross over the dark veil; in that, yes."

"I love you, Azile, you know this. I love the kids. Please tell them every day for me."

"You just come back. Some way, somehow, Michael Talbot, you come back to me."

"I promise," I told her as I took a step. With one foot I had crossed the imaginary line in the sand. The cats, which had seemed completely unconcerned with my presence, were now inching closer and watching intently. Some had even gotten down low in the classic ready to pounce stance.

"Well, that's pretty fucking unnerving. Is this what the end looked like for you buddy?" I was referring to my friend Paul, who had died a vicious death in a house full of starving cats.

I was having a hard time convincing myself to put my right foot over.

"I am here my love."

I almost pitched forward and fell back; I was rocked so hard by the words. And I know I did not imagine it; the cats were also looking around, some of them mewling—whether in anguish or ecstasy, I do not know.

"Tracy?" I asked hesitantly.

"Though you may not think so, there are always reasons for the things you do; we can never see all ends. Trust in who you are and what you do, and I will be there for you."

"Where were those words when we were together?"

I felt mirth, though I did not hear a laugh. "I was always there, though I did not always agree with you."

"I'm afraid, Tracy. I'm afraid we'll never be together again and that is something I just cannot reconcile."

"Whatever you have been told, you are not alone, neither on this side nor beyond this gate. Be strong. Not all that wish you harm are mortal enemies." And with that, I felt her leave as quickly as if she had been wrapped up in a soap bubble that had landed on a razor's edge.

"What the fuck does that mean?" I asked as I absently stepped over, and for the second time in about a year, I was dead. I thought there'd be more fanfare; must be one of those things where it happens so often I'm getting desensitized.

CHAPTER FIVE
MIKE JOURNAL ENTRY 5

IN TERMS OF LANDSCAPE, NOT much was different; it was like crossing over from Maine to New Hampshire. The big difference was where I was at and why I was there. And, oh yeah, the toll was much, much higher. Used to cost three bucks to cross that border; now it's a life.

"Not so bad," I said as an assurance to myself. Those words took a major hit when I turned around. There was what looked like a hundred huge, feral cats on the other side, all looking directly at me like I had just opened a giant can of tuna. As if that weren't a big enough issue, it was like I was looking at them through a glass shower door—one of those ones with the ripples in the glass that frustrated the hell out of me when I was a young teenager and the beautiful heroine in the movie stepped out of her towel as she stepped into the stall…when she closed that door you could barely make out she was human much less see any of those feminine attributes my hormones were starved for.

"Once a jarhead always a jarhead," I said as I steeled myself for something I was pretty sure was going to hurt. I reached out and pressed a finger against the strange rippled barrier. It may have yielded but I wasn't sure, I'd been forced back pretty quickly. Not like I'd stuck a fork in a 240-volt outlet forced back, but there was certainly a repelling. That, and when I'd done it, the cats had gotten so close together, from my vantage point it looked like they were congealing. They were extremely agitated. I hovered around the barrier for a few minutes, now completely baffled as to what I should do. It had all seemed so clear in my head; cross the border that can't be crossed, save Tommy, assuming he was in danger, cross back—a feat no one accomplishes, become alive again, and go home. I'm not sure why things don't ever translate smoothly over into the real world, or whatever world I find myself trapped in.

Movement on the other side of the curtain caught my attention. From the coloring, I was fairly certain it was Sebastian, and that was confirmed when he spoke, though, it sounded like one or both of us were underwater.

"Do not linger at the gate, Michael. Just because something is trying to get out doesn't mean it won't take the time to stop and kill you," he said.

"I fucking hate this place." I thought about waving to the big cat; didn't figure he'd return the gesture. That was alright, confirming I had company in this world was still a thread to cling to; I didn't want to walk in this place bearing solace. For what felt like a mile or so of walking I had my head down staring at my boots. I wanted to punch myself in the noggin for being so stupid. But fear and doubt had to be left behind; I needed to be irked or maybe even mad, to burn out the feelings of dread. I walked for a while, maybe even an entire day, possibly two. Saw nothing or nobody and as lonely as I was feeling it was better than the alternative.

"You're in enemy held territory, Talbot. You have no friends but you have a mission. Lift that dense head of yours and stop staring at the..." I was going to say "dirt" but it wasn't. I reached down and grabbed a little; felt like rubber with maybe some cork mixed in. Not a bad surface to be treading on; kind of nice on the joints if I had to admit it. I was just picturing a long-ago playground that had something like this under the swings. Then something strange happened, stranger, I mean. Not much of a shocker, given my location. I didn't think anything of it when some of the particles rolled out of my hand, but when some of them continued to roll when they hit the ground, that was when I figured another Bledgrum or something equally as large and terrifying was coming, causing the ground to quake. But that wasn't it—not at all. It was the ground itself, like, the whole surface of the world. It was dropping away around me like we were negatively charged. I was sinking, but my feet were still standing atop a platform of the spongy material. It wasn't like I was being swallowed up, exactly, more like a hole was being dug around me.

I couldn't see a scenario where this worked out in my favor. I was roughly knee deep in comparison to the rapidly rising rim around me when I started to move. The faster I ran the quicker the material moved away from me. I was losing ground faster than I could make it up, like climbing stairs in a nightmare. The rim had traveled halfway up my thigh and still, I pressed on. I was running in a blind panic now, as the world's surface rose past my navel. In my ever-optimistic mind, I had two leading theories. The first was that once I was deep enough, all the material would come rushing back in and completely cover me in my own permanent plastic wrap. The second was that the hole would just continue to deepen and I would be forever stuck in a massive pit constructed solely for me. Both meant being buried alive, and having once experienced that, these outcomes held no allure for me. I knew it had to have an end, I mean, right? Otherwise, this would be all this shithole had to offer and I think I knew enough to realize that couldn't be the case.

"Think, Talbot. You've just hit some sort of quicksand field; it can't be infinite." What I didn't tell myself was that it didn't have to be endless at the pace I was losing height, it only needed to expand another mile or so wide to trap me here, and for all I knew there could be a continent's worth of this useless ground or whatever that shit was. I stopped, hoping to survey the area and gain some bearing. When I did, I noticed that the material slowed its pace as well almost so as not to disturb me; sneak up around me while I stood there thinking. I wonder how many poor, weary travelers awoke from a slumber to find themselves possibly a hundred feet down a well, drowning in some insidious substrate they'd assumed was stable.

"What are the chances if I walk backward it will start filling in?" I walked a few steps in this manner, did not get the results I had been hoping for. The rim was up to my chest; it wasn't going to be long until I lost the line of sight past the wall building up in front of me. Physics-wise this was an impossibility; I should have been able to climb up the wall, the hole should not move with me. Dammit, I knew I should have paid more attention in school. Maybe there was a chapter on weird anomalies. While I was looking around, dumbfounded, I noticed these black spots on the ground. In fact, the area was littered with them, like someone with huge golf cleats had just marched past. They were holes much like my own, and for good or bad, I was going to check them out.

I was inclined to run, but I walked for a couple of reasons. First, the material moved away slower, sort of like that running in the rain thing. The faster you run, the wetter you get. I never really understood that, I mean, sure, you catch raindrops you may have missed if you were going slower, but what about the ones you avoided? I dismissed that fact as myth until I started driving. I'd been in rain showers where I had to stop the wipers at a red light, but once I got the car rolling along, I'd need the wipers going at speed. I forced myself to move slower but my heart kept picking the pace up—being buried alive, I think, is at the top of just about everyone's biggest fears, and I certainly wasn't the exception to that rule. By the time I got to the closest hole, I was about neck deep. In hindsight, I should have felt at ease; that's about where I'd been the majority of my life, neck deep in trouble, I mean. I know…I know—fairly obvious punchline, not sure why I felt the need to elaborate. I ramble when I'm terrified out of my wits.

I paused, forcing my heart to slow down before it forced me to stop altogether. Whatever trick or spell was going on, it would not allow the two holes to merge. Close, like maybe the thickness of a finger, but that was it. I dug into the wall and my hand was met with something that no longer felt like rubber but was harder, significantly more unyielding. I took out my axe and tapped, lightly, at first and was rewarded with a firm knocking sound, as if I were tapping on wood. This was all good, but I had a feeling force wasn't the answer and that if I tried to hack my way through, all I would succeed in doing would be to dull or possibly break my only weapon. Not sure it would matter at this point. I peered over the lip of my hole and down into the next. Whatever or whoever had been down *that* pit of despair was no longer in view. I got at least one question answered and you know what? Sometimes it's better to stay ignorant.

It didn't appear that the holes had any limit to the depths they could go; of course, I had no way of knowing what depth that might be. The bottom seemed lost in the inky depths of hell; it could have gone for miles. Knowing what I do about sinister phenomena, the hole most likely stops digging itself once its host dies. Not sure what I'd hoped for when I got to this neighboring hole, maybe an ally? Someone to commiserate? Got neither. I shouted down into the abyss then tilted my head listening, naively, for anything in return. However, in addition to the material being all around douche-like, it had a sound absorbing quality that had me thinking my yell hadn't traveled more than ten feet or so. This place would make an ideal practice spot for a heavy metal garage band. I shrugged and did the only thing I could think to; I slogged on to the next hole, which wasn't more than a couple of hundred yards away.

What sucked was that by the time I got there I could no longer see out of my own hole unless I looked straight up, and all that view gave me was of a darkness I guessed was some sort of sky, though I could not see anything celestial there. I jumped up to grip the lip of my hole. I found that if I pressed-off rather than pushed-off I could gain a slight spring. I hung at the top and could see into a shallow basin, well, more of a dent in the surface…I mean this thing wasn't much deeper, or as wide across, as an office trashcan.

"What the fuck?" At first, I didn't see the creature because it was so small, hardly bigger than a standard beetle, but relative to its size, the hole it was in was cavernous.

"What are you looking at?" the thing shouted at me. I was so surprised at hearing a voice, any voice, even a hostile one, that I fell back into my hole and looked around, ready for anything. When nothing immediately happened, I once again hopped up and looked at who, or what, I figured had made the rude inquiry. I was straining to see what was down there. It wasn't a beetle, that was for sure. I had no point of reference for what I was seeing, so it's impossible to describe accurately; it would be like describing television to a blind fish. I'm just trying to get you in the ballpark and putting these labels on it was an aid for my brain to make sense of it as well. I'm going to go with the face of a dog…but not of any dog you've ever seen before and not like one of those dogs that is so fucking ugly it's cute, either. Like a two-year-old with limited skills in wood carving had created his interpretation of a dog's face. The snout was elongated; at the end was the dark nub of what I assumed was its nose, could have been its anus, for all I knew. Its eyes were the black pearly pellets of a rodent.

Now I got the joy of trying to make out its body, like understanding the shape of a constellation. It was standing on two legs; they were jointed backward like a kangaroo's, though these were covered in shiny silver scales, not fur. It did have two arms which ended in two fingers and a thumb. Its chest was barrel shaped, and I guess for whatever this thing was, it would be considered buff in its world.

I said the only thing I could think of that made sense. "My name is Mike."

"You're the ugliest thing I've ever seen in my life," it replied.

"Really? In a world that has a Bledgrum, I'm the ugliest thing?"

"That beast is here?" the thing asked, turning its head to peer around.

"Naw, I killed it."

The thing leveled this piercing gaze at me. I'm telling you, I felt thoughts and memories shuffle around inside my head as it did so.

"Interesting," it said after a minute. "I wouldn't have thought the beast capable of dying, especially at the hands of something as ugly as you."

"You believe me then?"

"I'm a Breatine. It is impossible to deceive us. My people have been used for countless centuries as mediators during difficult negotiations to ascertain and ensure everyone stays honest and aboveboard."

"Is that weird? Never being able to tell a lie? I can't even begin to imagine how much jail time I would have ended up doing if that were the case."

"Please tell me that you are not as stupid as you are ugly; that would be a terrible combination to possess. I did not say *I* could not deceive; I said I could not *be* deceived. Vast difference. My people have shaped the destiny of our world with what we allow revealed or kept."

"Sneaky bastards. I know your type on my world. Gain the trust of those around you and then make sure everything that happens is in the best interests of your kind. Now I know why you're down here. How many wars are you personally responsible for starting?" I asked.

"Yeah? And what are you here for, not distributing enough doughnuts to the old-folks home on Sundays?"

"You know about baked goods and old-age homes? And I wasn't sent here; I came voluntarily to help someone."

The weird little creature gazed at me again; I felt memories shift aside as he dug through and found what he was looking for. It was a disconcerting feeling.

"You *are* as dumb as you are ugly! You voluntarily gave up your life and soul to be here?" It was shaking its head back and forth. "Concerning baked goods and old age homes, yes we are from differing realities, realms, dimensions, whatever you want to call it—but for all these differences there are also a great many similarities. That you came here of your own volition tells me that you are familiar with the theory of a great many worlds existing within your own. Is that not true?"

I begrudgingly told it "Yes." We looked at each other for a moment longer. I was at a loss, really, of what to do and this thing didn't seem like it was going to help me very much, but since my options were extremely limited, I persevered. "What's your name?"

"Go stare in a mirror."

At first, I thought this was some sort of deeply philosophical, thought-provoking inquiry, then I realized it was its version of an insult. It thought I was so ugly that to stare in a mirror was a bad thing, an otherworldly "Go fuck yourself." I was not offended. "Don't you have people where you're from?"

"We do; they are usually in cages at a zoo or used in sideshows at oddity carnivals. Do you have those? The ones with the *freaks*?"

"You know what, I think I'll leave you to your hole." I slipped back into my own prison. It wasn't long before its voice shouted out.

"Linnick."

"What? Did you say Limp dick?"

"Linnick," it said again.

"Little dick?" I asked.

"Linnn Nnnick!" it shouted with more force than I anticipated; I did not laugh.

"Pin prick?"

"Do not fool yourself. You are worthy of this place."

"I'm sorry, err…Linnick. It's in my nature." I wasn't sure how to broach this subject and probably it was something that didn't need broaching, but that is not my way. "You male or female, Linnick?"

There was a long pause, filled with that one kind of silence. Yeah, I'd definitely made a social faux pas. "I will blame your ignorance upon your incredible stupidity and gut-churning, grotesque, grisly, horrid, and repugnant physiognomy and forgive it in my endless benevolence."

"Female. I get it, you're female."

"I am considered of great beauty amongst my people."

If I'd eaten anything in the last twelve hours and it had not been completely digested, it would have shoved its way up through my esophagus and into my mouth where I would be forced to re-swallow it. For some reason, I was imagining two Breatines copulating, and well, it wasn't pleasant. I figured they were much like Praying Mantises; she'd have to rip the head off her partner—that way they wouldn't have to look at each other during the deed.

"Linnick, if I told you I have an idea, would you trust me?"

"Trust that you think so, perhaps, but believe it true? I doubt it. That you have an idea at all seems beyond your scope."

That stung. "We don't even know each other."

"I know enough. That you came here without duress speaks volumes."

"Fair enough. I still have a way we might possibly help each other, but I don't know if it'll work."

Silence, possibly a sigh, then, "I have been here for nearly seven days. I am hungry, thirsty, and exhausted. I would be willing to grasp at anything."

I grabbed the lip of my hole and pulled myself up and was hanging one foot over into her hole while I straddled the opening between us and my other foot hovered above my ever expanding hole. Not a maneuver I recommend for those that are not too flexible like myself.

"Is this your idea to help? Extinguishing my life?"

"What? No! Move to the side—I'm going to put my foot down and then pick you up."

"That…that might work. This dendrun hole is meant specifically for me; it may not be able to adjust itself to you." It didn't matter that she was a completely foreign species to me; I could still register the hope in her voice.

I had to get over the skeevies as I picked her up. By the way she braced I could tell she was no fan of this contact either. "I'm going to put you in my chest pocket. Are you alright with that?"

"It is preferred over the hot, clamminess of your hand."

With Linnick in my pocket, I was once again able to survey the landscape. In the distance, I thought I may have seen a mountain range. I was about to take my first step when she screamed.

"Do not take your foot out of this hole!"

My boot was hovering less than an inch from the ground. I pulled it back quickly.

"What the hell are you talking about?"

"This specific hole is my trap. If you step outside of it, you will trigger another trap."

I thought on her words and our predicament. "Linnick, you've got to be kidding me. I can barely fit my feet in here, much less be able to walk. I'd have to shuffle. You know how long that would take to get anywhere?"

"Shuffle or die. It appears our lives are in your mucid hands."

"I don't know what 'mucid' means, but I'm going to assume it's unpleasant."

"Look at you! Growing smarter by the moment."

"That way?" I pointed to the prospective mountains.

"Slide one foot in front of the other. I'm going to get some sleep."

"Must be fucking nice," I mumbled.

The hole did get deeper as we moved but since it was indeed custom designed for Linnick, it dropped at such a slow rate I don't know that we lost more than an inch over the mile I had shambled. Though, even at that rate, if I went enough miles we would be in trouble again, but I didn't give a shit. I was not finding another Breatine hole. A disgustingly ugly bug capable of revealing all your lies and truly insulting your species was not something I wished to make friends with or have many around. I don't know how much farther I'd gone, but my thighs and calves were on fire. My crotch as well. I'd been scraping my legs together for so long I'm surprised a blaze hadn't started. I made sure to keep my feet in the hole, but I had to sit.

"We're not there yet?" Linnick asked as she looked above the lip of my pocket. "Perhaps if you were not sitting we would have made more progress."

"Not all of us have the luxury of napping during their travels."

"I highly recommend it. Your pocket is slightly claustrophobic but otherwise warm and dry. Now if I could only have food served in here, it would have been perfect."

"What do you eat?" I asked absently.

"Internal organs. We burrow into the navels of live animals and then eat everything we get our mouths on from the inside out."

I looked down to her and was wondering whether I should smash her where she was or pull her out and fling her far away by one leg.

"I am joking, giant ape-creature. Grains. I mostly enjoy grains. My kind are vegetarians though in times of necessity we are quite capable of eating meat. I was not sure your ugliness could get worse, I was wrong; you should have seen your face. It seems that we will be spending some time together; I know you said your name but I have already forgotten it."

I was reaching down and rubbing my calf. This put Linnick nervously close to my face.

"Michael Talbot."

"Tallboat?"

"Talbot."

"Tallboat. That's what I said."

"Are you getting me back for my mispronunciations?"

"I am saying what you said: Tallboat."

She seemed genuine, and honestly, I didn't give a shit what she called me. As soon as we were out of the dendrun hole area, she and I were going our separate ways. "There is an end to this place, right?" I had to ask because, in reality, I didn't know.

"I did not have a chance to read the travel brochure before I came down."

"Funny."

"I believe we can deduce that this is a finite place, otherwise we would never hear stories about it. All who experience it would be lost."

"Not sure if that would be a bad thing, Linnick."

"Truly you believe this? Do you not think before you speak?"

"Not all the time."

"If everyone were to get stuck in their holes forever, we would not be talking and you would not have your opportunity to escape and help your friend."

"I meant everyone except me…and—and you, of course." I stammered.

"I do not need special skills to recognize your pathetic attempts at deception."

"Yeah. I would never have made it as a lawyer or a politician." Don't know if she knew what that implied, but she didn't question me on it either.

"We should not linger too long. I have seen Gargoyles in the sky."

"What?"

"Gargoyles. Does this word not exist in your world?"

"In my world, Gargoyles are stone decorations that adorn buildings, mostly used for water spouts and bird perches. I think they are supposed to provide symbolic protection from other mythical monsters, or something to that effect. They don't fly; they're not real…unless you live in Hollywood."

"They are quite real in my world, though they are rarely seen. Here, they are more numerous and much like they are there, scavengers looking for an easy meal."

"Scavengers? Then why should we care?"

"They are easily three times your size and you can barely move. I would consider that an easy scavenge."

"Are you kidding me with this?" I stood up, did a quick scan of the sky and started in again with my impersonation of Tim Conway's The Oldest Man. We'd been going a good long while, enough that Linnick once again got sleepy from my rhythmic swaying and went to lie down. At first, I had not noticed anything out of the ordinary; I should have realized something was up when I felt a cool breeze against my face. It would have been the first indicator of any type of atmospheric change down here. It turned out to be the flap of a great wing that got my attention next.

"Shit," I said as I turned to see something flying past. It went until it was almost out of sight and then made a broad, swooping turn coming back our way. I started shuffling like mad, even pumping my hands, as if that were going to make a difference. When I realized the futility of this I stopped to reach down and grab my axe.

"What are you doing?" Linnick said groggily. When she saw me looking up, she turned to the sky. She was able to pick up real quick on what was going on. That and my wildly thumping heart was nearly bouncing her out of my shirt. "How many?"

"*What!?* There could be more than one?"

"They're scavengers, Tallboat. They usually work in pairs or trios, especially when they're targeting something still alive."

"Oh, this is utter bullshit. I think there's only one; we may be alright."

Linnick and I watched as the beast dipped down low to get a look at us before flying off.

"Must have scared it off," I said.

"Or that was a scout and it's going back to get its mates," Linnick replied.

"I think I'm starting to hate hell. If I wanted everything I encountered to try and kill me I would have just stayed home."

"Have you ever stopped to ponder that perhaps there is a reason everything wants to kill you?"

"I choose to believe that it is dark forces that seek my demise in order to extinguish the beacon of hope and light I represent to the world."

"You say this in a mocking manner, yet there is a kernel of belief behind your words."

"I have to rationalize some reason as to why I have been on the top of so many 'to murder' lists."

"You need to shuffle faster before they return. I do not wish to be with you when you finally meet your heroic end at the hands of evil."

"Gee, thanks."

"I did not mean that to sound quite so harsh. It is my hope that this will not be the time that you ultimately meet your fate; I would just rather be on the safe side."

"I guess that's better." I started pumping my arms again, hoping I could create some more speed, though that seemed unlikely.

A turtle on some performance-enhancing drugs could have made better time than me. Shuffling is shuffling; how in the fuck anyone ever got caught by old-school zombies is beyond me.

"Morticia Addams!" I shouted out. "Sorry," I told Linnick when she looked up at me. "Television character…gorgeous…used to wear these tight dresses that ended like an octopus at the floor. She used to wiggle across the room with her knees together, though she always appeared to glide, now that I'm thinking about it."

"Does this help us in any way?"

"None at all. Pure distraction for an over-taxed mind and quickly tiring body." I looked up in time to see two Gargoyles lazily circling overhead.

"Still too few; they will wait for more before they attack."

"I can't even begin to tell you how much better that makes me feel. Are they made from stone?" I asked looking to my blade wondering if it could cut through rock.

"Have you been knocked into the dumbs?"

"Really? That's the expression that transcends dimensions? How about this one?" I flipped her the finger.

I think it was "aghast" that displayed across Linnick's features but she quickly passed that on to me when she spoke. "I'm going to assume, Tallboat, that gesture means something completely different in your world. Here, you have just asked if we could mate."

I had to think on that for a second. "Huh. Still a pretty close translation, though in my world it is more of a negative statement rather than a hopeful question."

"You are like a Drellting that has received a new plaything."

"Huh?"

"Easily distracted. There are now three Gargoyles. And to answer your question, in this world rocks do not have the ability to fly."

"That's good to know." Three seemed to be the magic number as they began to spiral leisurely toward us. They looked huge from up high, as they swooped in closer, I realized just how huge. Lycan wearing strapped-on wings; that was roughly what I was looking at. Unlike the giant wolf-beasts, these creatures were furless; their skin, I guess, was the gray of the stone I imagined them to be. They had the pushed in faces of gorillas that regularly smashed themselves straight into parked buses. Four-inch saber tusks jutted up from their bottom jaw to frame out their flattened noses. My balance was compromised as I twisted backwards to watch one approach from behind; add in the downward force produced by its fifteen-foot wingspan and I nearly fell over.

"Linnick, how the fuck am I going to kill three of them when I can't even maneuver?"

"You don't need to kill all three. What's with you and the

killing? Sufficiently wound one and the others will retreat…for now."

"I can probably manage that." I crouched down to make a smaller target of myself and bring one of the Gargoyles in close; I could hear the heavy beating of wings coming from behind me. Crouched down in a narrow hole made it impossible to turn so I did my best impression of a penny on a train track. It wasn't good enough, as something incredibly sharp ripped into my left shoulder, forcing my face into the ground. I spat out a mouthful of the black rubbery crystals that made up this terrain. At least it kept me from screaming.

"Are you bleeding?" Linnick asked.

"I think that's safe to say," I said through gritted teeth. My back was on fire, the Gargoyle had shredded through the latticework of scar tissue I had back there. I gingerly rotated my arm, it still moved, though it sounded a bit like I was making popcorn inside the socket.

"They will become more aggressive now that they smell blood."

"Too bad. I was hoping they had a fear of it, like, maybe a healthy dose of hemophobia."

Even though she whispered it, I clearly heard Linnick say, "Struck with the dumbs. Might have been better off in the hole."

The Gargoyles clearly saw their advantage. Coming at me from the back, left me completely exposed and them completely safe from retaliation.

"I'm going to need your help, Linnick. You in?"

"My choices are either help you or be eaten?"

"Are you really thinking about this?"

"Okay, I will do it."

"Didn't think I was going to have to strong arm you for that. I need you to be my rear-facing eyes."

She crawled out of my pocket and up onto the collar of my jacket. She was peering to my back. I suppressed a shiver from having her that close to my ear. There was a fear she might seek refuge in my ear canal and then burrow her way into my brain. Yeah, yeah, I get it—she wouldn't get much of a meal if she went that way, but it was still my brain. I needed to keep as much of it intact as I could.

"Two are coming…lined up behind each other."

"How far?"

"Three hundred flegs."

"Flegs? What the hell is a fleg?" If it was yards I had a moment if it was inches I was about to be skewered.

"It is a unit of measurement," Linnick replied.

"Yeah I get that! Just tell me when to…"

"NOW!" she screamed. I would not be surprised when later I would wipe the side of my face to find dried blood. The volume in her tiny body had torn through my eardrum. A lot of simultaneous movements followed automatically that I wasn't sure I could pull off; it wasn't like I'd practiced anything like this before. I hopped up and out of the hole as I twisted my upper torso. I was still spinning around as I forced myself backward while bringing my axe up. My left leg missed the hole completely, pushing me back harder and faster than I'd meant to.

That supposed misstep might have actually been the only thing that saved me. A claw with talons to match its teeth just missed latching onto that already damaged shoulder of mine. Still ended up getting close enough to pierce me with one or two of them. My back thudded off the ground and I bit down on my tongue; by this point, my axe was nearly forgotten, but I swung and missed wildly. I had much more luck as the second Gargoyle, upon seeing my stunt, was attempting to move away. The problem with trying to change the direction of something that big with that much momentum is that it is going to take a while; gargoyles do not turn on a dime. He was the Titanic and I was the iceberg, or at least my blade was. I hoped this was the same one that had torn me apart earlier because there was a cosmic justice and a very satisfying plunge as my axe bit deeply into his left shoulder. A hawkish screech, albeit much louder, erupted from his mouth as I dragged the axe down until it lodged into his clavicle, shattering the bone but also dislodging my weapon completely from my hands.

He was swooping away and taking my weapon with him. I could only watch helplessly. Blood began to pour from his wound and he was listing heavily, favoring that side and not able to flap that wing with the speed he needed to keep his flight controlled. The change in the other two was immediate; I became an afterthought as Gargoyles two and three began to make swooping dive attacks on their stricken compadre.

"No honor among scavengers, I guess," I said as I sat up and tried to get a reading on how badly I'd been injured.

"We've got problems," Linnick said.

"Yeah. I don't have a weapon and once those two are done with their cannibalism we'll be back on the menu. Well, I mean, I will. I can't even imagine they'd bother with you."

"I'll have you note that I've been told Breatines are delicious!" She seemed genuinely upset that I'd excluded her from the Gargoyle diet.

"I'll keep that in mind if I get hungry."

"You wouldn't dare!"

"Yeah, probably not. I'd eat a cherry glazed ham Pop-Tart first."

"You stepped outside of my hole."

I looked at the ground, scanning it rapidly. Nothing was happening. "Yeah, so? I think we're alright."

"We're not." Linnick pointed off into the distance. I could not tell what I was looking at. Then it struck me; there was a campy movie back in the early 90s, called *Tremors*, had Kevin Bacon in it. Oh man, what I wouldn't do for some bacon. Anyway, it was about these giant worms that traveled, pretty fast, underground, and then would pop up and eat some poor unsuspecting person, in the most violent, low-budget way possible. The relevant point I'm trying to make here is that as they traveled, puffs and plumes of dirt would occasionally shoot into the air and that was what I was seeing here. Though instead of some space worm racing to eat me, it was the damned hole I'd escaped, and with the way material was flying out from it, I'd imagine it was getting deeper at an alarming rate to make sure I could not once again escape its clutches.

Not a thought crossed my mind as I took off running. Being a vampire had certainly enhanced all of my abilities; I was much faster now than I had ever been, but even that wasn't going to be enough. Whatever force was propelling that hole was quicker by far. Linnick had kept her place by my shoulder, keeping an eye on things behind me.

"A thousand flegs," she said evenly.

I thought about doing the math. With a calculator, a slide rule, a computer, and a teacher that actually knew math, I could have probably figured it out eventually. I mean, I had some of the variables. At three hundred flegs I had a Gargoyle flying at a very high rate of speed, roughly forty miles per hour and he hit me in under three seconds so…carry the five…divide by a factor of pi, add in the theory of relativity…yeah, I had no fucking idea. I kept running. Arms were pumping, legs were thrumming. Not entirely sure if it was by fate, but the two Gargoyles that were dining in were directly in my path. As of yet, they had not taken notice.

"Suicide by mythical scavenger creature. I wonder if that's what they'll write on my tombstone." In an ideal world, I would startle the creatures and they would take off for flight but before one could get high enough I would grab hold of its mighty legs and it would lift us to freedom. I had a better chance of getting a happy ending at the butcher shop. No fucking idea why I put those two together. I mean, I love a good steak as much as the next guy, but, umm, not in that way. I did indeed startle the giant swine-looking things, but for all their size, they were agile enough to get up and gone long before I could even make an attempt for them. Not the one I'd clipped, though, he had more holes ripped into him than I could count. Somehow, it was still breathing. I could see the rise and fall of my axe head glinting some light. I grabbed the handle, hoping it wouldn't slow my momentum as I sped past.

It released with an audible plop and I was off and running, barely losing half a step. Not sure what I was going to do in an axe versus a hole bout, but I felt better for having it.

"Five hundred flegs. Should have stayed in my own hole."

"There's an idea. How about I put you down and we summon your hole."

"DON'T DO THAT! Yours will be here first and even if you drop me and go your way I will still be stuck in my hole. Your repugnancy is without limits, yet I do not wish to die alone."

I mumbled something about her wanting to be in her own hole and then not. I am truly convinced it does not matter the species, females are a special kind of nuts. Listen I'm not saying males are completely sane either—we're just different types of crazy. For instance, once I realize I am wrong I will concede to reason whereas a woman will sometimes fly into the face of said reason and battle her opponent into exhaustion, thus forcing compliance, heedless or even contemptuous of all facts and figures to the contrary. (Note to self: hide journal from Azile.)

"I don't want to die at all—at least not down here," I pushed past my teeth. I was running at full sprint; there was only so long I was going to be able to keep this pace up. I was worried that I would have an eternity to think about how short I had come up; by how many flegs I had failed. There was a small break in the terrain, maybe a half mile from our location. It was a ribbon of white in an otherwise black-gray sea. For all I knew, it was just more of the same, a trick of the light, but since it was the only thing that was remotely different in this place, I veered towards it, and to my left. With a destination in sight, I felt spurred on, I was squeezing my adrenal gland like it was a dry lemon and I wanted one more fucking sip of lemonade.

"Four hundred flegs."

"Linnick, I don't have a fucking clue what a fleg is. Look to our front and tell me how far that white line is." It took all I could do to get that sentence out. It was forced and broken up as I whispered each word during exhalations, but luckily, she was close enough to hear what I had to say.

"Too far," was all she said.

"How...many...fucking...flegs?" That one extra word took a serious amount of effort, but I felt I needed it to get my point across. Sometimes you just need to swear. Nobody ever hits their thumb with a hammer and shouts: "dandelion, bunny rabbit, sphincter!" Hey, it's my finger. I can shout whatever I want to.

"Seven hundred flegs," she sighed with obvious resignation.

The desire to give up, to just stop running, was at the highest level I could ever remember. In war, your enemies tire; sometimes you can outwit them, you can turn and give battle, you can surrender—fight another day. But when the very ground beneath your feet is out to get you, no malice, no agenda, no quarter...well, I was having a difficult time seeing the point to continue. I was one against all.

"Will you eat me when you begin to starve?" Linnick asked.

I wanted to tell her I was more likely to strip my own flesh before I would eat something that looked like her, but I have heard these trick questions from females before and there is no right answer. Instead, I used that image as a reason to keep going, to fight against odds that had never been in my favor. Almost my entire life, I had been staring uphill. Why would it be any different down here? I was a soldier in a war much bigger than myself. Soldiers do what they must to survive, but above it all, they do what they must to make sure the person next to them survives. And maybe we weren't allies in any true sense, but we faced a common enemy and I was going to use Linnick as my reason to keep going. If I had been alone, maybe I would have stopped and lay down, catching my breath, resigning myself as the hole swallowed me up; maybe not. It's easy to find an ocean of excuses to support the easy side of an argument; it's much more difficult to wade through the muck and pull the truth free.

"Tell me when the hole is ten flegs away," I said to Linnick. I'd slowed my pace considerably, to hardly more than a jog. I needed to catch my breath and do what needed to be done. I hoped physics played its part down here. You know, the part where a body in motion tends to stay in motion type of thing.

"One hundred."

My heart jumped a beat; it was so close and I totally had no clue if what I was thinking would happen would even happen. I was mere flegs away from knowing, though.

"I wish you were still running," Linnick said, then added. "Fifty."

"Forty…. thirty….twenty…ten!" she shouted

"Hold on," I told Linnick. At twenty I had sped back up to full sprint, though it was severely lessened; at ten I pushed off and dove as far as I could to the right; I struck the ground with my right shoulder and rolled two complete somersaults. I was more than expecting to feel that horrible falling sensation as I tumbled down something I figured was close to a hundred feet deep by now. What I got instead was a heavy spray of material that was being ejected from the charging hole and a large blast of air as the trap screamed past.

"Fuck yeah! Physics," I said as I got up on a knee.

"What just happened?" Linnick asked, orientating herself.

"Reprieve." I knew it was only a matter of time until the hole figured out I wasn't in it and I wasn't going to waste my hard-fought victory. I was back to moving at a decent clip, better than a jog, but much slower than a sprint. Conservation of energy was going to be the key here; the first rule of out distancing. What was strange now was the role reversal. I was the one doing the chasing, well not really; it was just that the hole was going in the direction I needed to be. Had to have taken the intelligent dirt another two hundred yards to stop its momentum. Now I didn't really know if this stuff was alive enough and cognizant of being played, but I had definitely anthropomorphized that hole; made it somehow easier to fight, thinking I might affect its strategy, put it off its game. When it finally did stop, there was a huge plume of dirt as it seemed to puff its cheeks in fury before once again charging at me like a great bull.

I've been accused before on many occasions of actually running headlong into my death; usually it's not quite such a literal translation, though.

"Tallboat! What are you doing?" Linnick sounded extremely nervous.

I wasn't even sure I could answer that question. Step by step we were on a collision course. I didn't know if it had been better to have the thing chasing me so I couldn't see it or to be fully aware of exactly where it was. In truth, both vantage points sucked.

"Tallboat?" I could just see Linnick's head swiveling from me back to the hole, repeatedly.

I could not spare the air to tell her anything. I didn't think she'd like what I had to say anyway. At fifty yards, I almost failed entirely. I'd hit some imperfection in the ground—a crippling pain shot up my calf, rocketed past my thigh, and plumed in my skull as my ankle turned; I ran through it like a thoroughbred at the final turn. "Five more steps, Talbot." I urged myself on. Right, left, blinding pain, right, left, red flash across my vision, right—I pushed off and launched straight ahead like an Olympic long jumper. My field of vision was impaired by the water that ran from my eyes; I wasn't even sure if I'd taken off too soon. I hoped not; in all my years I'd never been known as a premature ejaculator. I think I wore a grisly smile as I looked down at the fathomless pit that was rushing past beneath me.

Linnick screamed as she somehow lost her grip; I swung quickly and wildly with my free left hand, somehow catching her in my palm. I felt a savage pain in my thumb which I would learn was her biting down to anchor her position. I can't say I blame her, but holy fuck it was like a piranha had taken hold. There was another fifteen feet of hole to glide past and I was already on the dropping part of my flight. I swung my axe hand, sticking it deep into the level ground as my body fell into the pit. I was hit hard in the chest as the back wall of the hole slammed into me and hurtled me up and out. I flipped four or five times in the air before landing roughly on my back. The wind had been pushed out of me so violently it was all I could do to breathe.

"Tallboat, you should get up." Linnick had thankfully let go of my thumb and crawled up my chest and into my much safer pocket.

I was sitting up; seeing stars would have been welcome. I was seeing a pinprick of light off in the distance which I hoped wasn't just my vision tunneling as I forced my body to do things it was by no means ready to do at the moment. "Mind over matter, if you don't mind it don't matter." A faraway voice started off as a small spark inside my mind as I urged myself on, attempting to incite a conflagration by using an old Marine Corps chant. "Talbot? Sounds a lot like malcontent! I'm going to keep my eye on you!" That was my introduction to my drill instructor in boot camp; funny how close to the truth he actually was. I continued my trip down boot camp lane, using every bit of forced motivation I could muster to get my body up and moving.

I more lurched forward than walked, stumbling to one knee when my injured left ankle reminded me of itself. It did allow me a few beats of my over-taxed heart to regain and reassess. Linnick had climbed from my pocket and was looking over my shoulder again.

"It has stopped."

I knew what that meant. It would huff and puff like the big bad wolf and start coming my way again. And speaking of big bad wolves, at least of the werewolf variety, save one, they can all go fuck themselves. Seemed like a lot of quantifiers, but oh well, there are exceptions to every rule. I stood and did my own version of a huff, though mine was much more anemic and made me cough. I walked, increased to a testing jog, pressed on to a run, then abandoned all pain and thought and made a full-on sprint. I said, "fuck you" every time I brought my left foot down. My foot didn't care. The leading edge of the new terrain had taken shape and definition; it was a wall of sorts, a miniature cliff of Dover. Couldn't have been much more than seven feet tall, but that was seven feet that I was charging toward.

I was hyper-focused on that boundary. I don't know how I knew, but I was positive that hole couldn't pass. I once again saw Linnick peering behind us, then to my face, then forward. She wasn't saying a word, which was unnerving in its own respect; it's when they get completely silent—past comment that you know you're in trouble. I couldn't tell if she was hopeful we would make it or grieved that we would fail so close to our goal. I was more than expecting at any moment to start falling backward as my foot slid out from under me and we tumbled to our painfully long deaths. We had to make it; if they got me again I was certain the fates that ran this place would make sure I could see the cliffs from where I lay—a true torturer's device. To be caged and dying of thirst is one thing; to see a clear river running just out of your reach is quite another.

"Run, Tallboat! Please!" Linnick begged, though I'm not sure what she thought I was doing. I was flat out running as fast as I could; I wasn't holding anything back for another day—there was no 'other gear'. I know this is going to seem movie-cliché, but this is the way it happened, there is no need for embellishment. This will be something I add to my ever-growing list of nightmare inducing events. The timing had to be right. If all had been well with my body I would have pushed off when my left foot hit, but it was damaged and I didn't think I could get the necessary thrust. If I waited another cycle—micro-second that it was—for my right to come down, it would be too late. I was already being sprayed with the up-swelling ground from the pursuing hole. Nope. I was going to have to take off just slightly further from where I wanted to be. I somehow found the ways and means to wrestle an ounce of strength from a leg that felt like a wet noodle.

Linnick was speaking rhythmically, not in English. Had to be some sort of prayer. The ground was solid as I launched, it gave way just as my toes lifted off. I turned to look down at the gaping wound rushing beneath me; the bottom was as black as the heart of Eliza. This time we were keeping pace with each other; if I came down early, I would never come back up. Linnick knew we were going to come up short long before I did; she left the relative safety of my pocket and headed for my shoulder. I cried out as she bit down on my earlobe. As much as that hurt, it had nothing on the crushing impact as my chest crashed into the cliff side. My arms were on the ledge, only because that was where momentum dictated they go. My legs were independently seeking purchase on the slick side, and the hole? Well, it waited below like a patient shark or crocodile that can see its prey is in trouble and knows it doesn't have to do much more than wait with its mouth open for the meal to fall.

My feet were sliding like I was skidding on ice. The only thing keeping my upper half from tumbling over backwards into the pit was I think I had embedded myself into a crag. I popped two fingernails completely off as I fought to dig my hands into the tough soil. I wouldn't be surprised at all if I was tearing all of the skin, tendons, and muscles off my fingers and hands as I scrabbled to hold onto something, anything. When I did finally find something that did not give way immediately, it felt suspiciously like a bone, possibly a femur. At that exact moment, though, I was going to thank whose ever leg it was for giving their life for mine and Linnick's. I pulled up past my chest; I had my entire upper half over the lip when my left foot found an outcropping. I pushed myself about five feet away from the cliff edge. I crawled another ten feet before I rolled onto my back and passed out from exhaustion.

"I didn't think you'd be able to do it; I said my prayers of finality." Linnick whispered as I flowed from the world of the dead to that of dreamland—or so I thought. Dreams of a sort began, and good ones, thankfully.

"Michael, is that you?" It was Azile. She sounded like she was speaking through a rusted out and dented tin can; she looked like she was being broadcast over the air and I was attempting to receive her picture through some bent bunny-ear antennas extended with tin foil, but every part of it was welcome.

"It's me," I said, reaching out with my hand. She came in clearer, like I'd found the sweet spot with the antenna.

"You look awful," she said tenderly.

I wanted to tell her that I was having some serious doubts about coming here, but there was nothing she could do about it, not now. All I would succeed in doing was making her even more nervous.

"Stumbled over a hole…twisted an ankle. I'll be alright. Made a new friend." Of course, I glossed over everything. One look at me and she knew I was lying through my teeth.

"This the type of friend that is trying to kill you, or a bona fide one?"

"I think mostly bona fide."

"Allies in the underworld? I did not think such a thing possible. You must be careful."

"Yeah me neither. And sure—I always am."

Very loud silence came from her end in response. Then she finally spoke. "What is his name?"

"Linnick, her name is Linnick."

"Her?" I heard a stab of jealousy.

"You afraid I'm getting some hellish side action, woman? Let me put your mind at ease. She's about the size of a Matchbox car and looks like something you would find under a disposed of mattress that a hobo has been using at his underpass hovel."

She didn't seem completely convinced; I can't blame her. If Linnick was an Amazonian supermodel I doubt I would describe her as such to Azile.

"Oh woman—I love you. And even if we weren't a couple and Linnick was gorgeous, this place isn't really all that conducive to romance."

"I love you, Michael." Before I could say goodbye, she faded out. The connection had been broken.

"Tallboat…Tallboat…" This, whispered in my ear. Literally. Linnick was resting on the outer edge of my ear and was speaking softly. "Do not speak, do not move; breathe as shallowly as you can." The words were spiked with fear. Not sure how long I'd been asleep, but I felt better for it. I was trying to blink away the fog of my mind and was having a difficult time deciding whether I was awake or asleep or in that in-between strange zone where weird and unnatural things happen. I could feel my eyelids flutter, but there was no difference in the pitch of the darkness. I was as blind with them open as I was with them closed. I was convinced I was in that fugue state that I entered when I would astral project. I was aware enough to know my consciousness was separated from my body; I had partial control of my physical form, but not enough to make it operate adequately. It was a strange line to straddle. It had been highly enjoyable in my youth, but right now it pretty much sucked some of Trip's oily mud hens through a bent straw. I focused hard and moved my right hand to wipe away the veil I felt was across my face. Linnick nearly lost her mind.

"If you even think about moving again I will tear a chunk of your meat free and make you eat it," she hissed. I believed she could do that; it was cause for concern.

As I let the all-encompassing panic of potentially being blind wash around me, I heard something; this time it was not Linnick. It was on the far side of the cliff, away from the hole. It was soft, subtle even, the scraping of a fleshy scale against an imperfection in the ground. *Snake* was all I could think. Either one extremely large one or dozens of smaller ones were wriggling around not more than ten feet from my present location. It was impossible to tell if they were just passing by on a snake super highway or they were actively hunting for something, for me, maybe. When I heard the sniffing, I knew this couldn't be snakes, at least not like any I had ever seen. I started running through a visual list of all the grotesqueries and carnival side-show freak images that I could. Snakes with pig faces. Humans with snake bodies. Scaly cats. Each image worse than the previous. Maybe this was something from Linnick's world.

I tightened my grip on the axe handle I still comfortingly held in my right hand. Linnick must have sensed something on my part.

"It will kill and devour you before your mind can process the information." She delivered this without a hint of aggrandizement and I had no reason to doubt her words. I had a dozen questions, none of which I could ask. Lying helpless in wait is not one of my strongest positions. Something was making its way to me; not sure if it was an entire beast or maybe just an exploratory tentacle. The sniffing increased, stopped, then started again. I was holding my breath at this point. What was circling in was enormous—not Bledgrum enormous, but perhaps more powerful...certainly at least as deadly. This thing was intelligent, too. From one predator to another, I could sense its skill as it hunted in the dark. It was quiet, cautious; it used what was a detriment to most everything, not being able to see, to its benefit.

Something rustled not more than a foot from my head. I thought this was going to be it. I was desperately firing signals off from my brain to make my muscles move when I heard a shriek that sounded like a man getting his genitals caught in a wood chipper, minus the sound of the wood chipper. The tentacle or arm or whatever this thing was feeling around with reeled itself in rapidly, something terrified caught in its grasp.

There was a heavy crunching as if the monster was biting through an animal covered in body armor, a turtle, perhaps some large insect with a thick exoskeleton. The slurping wet noises were disturbing, but substantially worse were what sounded like sighs of satisfaction from the monster as it ate. I did my best to pretend it was just some large man sitting at KFC going to town on some extra crispy chicken wings as he occasionally brought their slogan to fruition and did some serious finger lickin'.

At some points in your life, like when your favorite girl dumps you, or you end up in a hot zone during a war, or a loved one dies, you just figure that this is "it." There is nothing that can ever be worse in your life. But for whatever inscrutable reason—the fates, the destinies, the malfeasant demi-gods—they prove you wrong, over and over again to the point where you would almost be better off embracing the current shit storm for what it is and thank it for not beating you any bloodier. Certainly, that's not the usual human way of thinking; we generally don't live long enough to learn that lesson. But when you start to carve into your two-hundreds…let's just say I like to think I am beginning to catch on.

But the smell. If anything about my situation was going to make me move my ass, it was the smell of this thing. Now, I'm going to work on this for a minute and see if I can get it right. We'll start with a port in New Orleans that has been besieged by industrial tidal waste and low tide. But that's just the opening salvo. Picture a blue chem toilet next to this port; this particular honey pot is devoid of all blue chemicals, but full of everything else. The day is ninety-seven degrees, with ninety-two percent humidity. The air so wet that when you speak, the words drip to the ground. Nothing can escape the grasp of the moisture, especially not scent, which takes on a liquid quality. I see the bulb gaining brightness over your head.

For some reason, the National Fiber Board has decided to do a Summer rally here, kale freaks and steel-cut oat hippies are everywhere. There are brown rice brownies, bran flake bars, and Brussel sprout bites everywhere. Beano vendors are selling out of stock at a record pace; scientists are wondering if they could somehow harness the flatulence to power the city for the month before the ozone layer above the city is gone forever. Alan Harkman of Idaho Falls, Idaho has found himself in desperate need of relief; his split pea almond soup has started to work its magic on the two quarter pounders with cheese he devoured on the sly, while his girlfriend Kaitlyn, a self-described vegan of over ten years, sleeps.

Alan hated pretending to be vegan, but it was worth every bean burger to look at Kaitlyn's lithe and toned body when they made love; besides, she usually lacked energy from not eating enough protein and fell asleep early, at which point Alan could eat anything he liked. Although he thought she might be getting suspicious. He'd gotten sloppy once and left an Arby's wrapper at the top of the trash. He'd lied and told her they had veggie wraps now. Big mistake; because now she made him get her one at least once a week. He had to go halfway across town to Pete's sandwich shop, get what she liked, then go back to Arby's to get a wrapper for it. The charade would be over soon but he was going to ride the bumper cars until the carnival barker told him to get off.

Anyway, back to Alan's expanding colon. The dearth of so many overstretched anuses has taxed the limits of the un-chem toilet. Bricks of feces, having forced all the liquid out of the bowl and onto the floor and surrounding ground, gave the area around the toilets a greenish, alien landscape feel. Fat sweat droplets fell from Alan's forehead as he waited in line; pain racked his gut, causing him to double over more than once clutching at his stomach and sometimes at his rear, he was flexing his butt cheeks tight, in the hopes of keeping what sought the light securely in the dark. By the time big Betty Bartholomew birthed her own brown baby, Alan was hunched over as he duck-walked into the now empty potty.

The heat inside was unbearable, as if the contents of the

bowl were on the verge of spontaneous combustion. He panicked for a moment when he did not feel that he could get enough air. He closed the door and simultaneously fumbled with the turn lock and the button on the top of his pants. The button would not yield and he was forced to push his pants down without undoing them. A lot of very unfortunate events rapidly transpired next. First, Alan did not spare a glance behind him as he sat. Had he done so he would have realized that big Betty had filled in the remaining crevasses within the toilet and she'd actually made a "grunt sculpture" that came up and over the rim and was parked halfway onto the seat. He sat on it, rather in it, causing the artwork to flatten out and coat his left leg from knee to ass. If this is making you gag, stop reading now, for if this was not bad enough, as he leaned over to puke, his balls and penis sank down into the mounds of muck and bile, the warm feeling not completely unwelcome to his junk until his brain realized exactly what he was linking with. He lost all ability for rational thought, yet his colon still had its own pressing needs.

Another strike against Alan was that Kaitlyn was very much into hipsters and their skinny jeans. Alan had previously made fun of those males preening around in their restrictive pants, but when Kaitlyn had bought him a pair and thought he looked wonderful in them he'd had no choice but to wear them, especially when it seemed that she wanted to take them off of him almost as fast as he put them on. Because he had not been able to get the fly or zipper undone, his legs were therefore locked together tight from ankle to knee, leaving very little separation for his butt cheeks. This caused the voluminous sewage that erupted from his ass to plume behind him as if it were a column of water shot from the back of a Sea-Doo. The shit aerated past the cinched-up anus as if it were coming from an aerosol can, coating the wall behind and Alan's entire back. For seven minutes, Alan alternated between vomiting, dipping his balls into warm rectal feedback pudding, and sending showers of shit up and behind him.

Many people in line vacated their spots to avoid being anywhere near what they figured was to be a crime scene. Alan's retching and shrieks of misery brought others to witness what was happening. When he finally emerged from the environmentally friendly, paper-less hut of hell's candy, he was covered nearly head to toe and even had dollops rolling off the top of his head. He walked straight across the broad, littered beach and straight into the foamy bay. It has been rumored the stink that came off of him was tangible and likely responsible for three deaths that day. Kaitlyn broke up with him that weekend, telling him that no vegetarian could possibly smell like that.

That…THAT, my friends, is what the beast next to me smelled like. I could hardly breathe; it was so thick I was filling up on the crap molecules I was taking in. I could tell Linnick was trying to take in the smallest breaths possible as well. The stench waxed and waned and eventually dissipated, yet the monster did not move off. In fact, it seemed as if it were about to take a nap after its particularly big and tasty meal. I was tensing up, hoping I could move slowly away.

"Do. Not. It is awake. It knows something is still out here and is attempting to lay a trap."

I wanted to ask her how in the hell she knew but that was not possible; I had to take her word for it. I was in a slightly awkward position and the more I dwelled on it the more I wanted to adjust and of course, in addition, I had four active itches on my body that fully demanded I take care of them NOW. I did my best to still my mind, using techniques Tommy had taught me, it worked about as well as you could expect. "Easily distracted" doesn't even begin to describe my pathetic attention span. ADD would be an improved diagnosis in my particular case. I have something more like Insufficient Interest Turmoil. My head moved of its own volition when, to my monster side, I heard what sounded like hundreds of poisonous darts being shot from long blow tubes. Fortunately, I'd not known then how close to the truth I was.

"Flutchers," Linnick said, though it sounded like a swear. She attempted to move farther into my ear, which was adding a whole new dimension to my jimmy legs. Try keeping still while a talking beetle crawls into your ear canal.

Whatever flutchers were, they were landing around the entire area in, I guessed, a three sixty pattern. I couldn't help but flinch when the first of them made contact with me. There was a sharp hiss from Linnick as I did so.

"This is going to be bad, Tallboat. You must stay quiet and still, though you will yearn to do anything but."

Honestly, I thought she was full of shit and that I was some sort of superhero as the flutchers bounced harmlessly off my exposed skin and certainly off the parts of me that were covered by clothing. "Ha! Gonna have to do better than that, assholes. I'm too strong for your bullshit pointy things," was what I said just as I felt the first pinch. Then another, then dozens, perhaps hundreds. The fire-ant torture from Lunos and Ganlin was excruciating; I'd thought that was "it" for me. But I'd yet to fully realize the depths of pain someone can experience. My blood felt as if it were boiling tomato sauce, erupting in huge blisters everywhere a dart had pricked my skin, my skin felt like it was spewing a caustic cocktail of lava and pus from the…pustules. My heart rate had to be closing in on two hundred beats a minute—if I could have had a thought, it would be that I was revving the engine to an unsustainable rate, about to crack the block.

"Deep, heavy breaths…quietly. You will get through this. They are not causing harm, only pain." Linnick was talking in as soothing a voice as possible. I wanted to shear her head off with my molars. The pain was unlike anything I had ever experienced in my life, I wanted to writhe in agony but did my damnedest to hold still. The pain; so immense I didn't know how I could possibly hold on to my self. There was not one goddamned fucking fiber of my being that was not aflame with horrendous hurt. Linnick continued whispering psuedo-comfort babble into my ear; it was like she was inside my head; well, she was. It was only a short matter of time before my mind snapped and reeled itself in, pulling as far away from the shock of my body as it could. My back was arching and my jaw was clenched shut with teeth shattering force.

I was way beyond my ability to stay in control. The fiend was on the move; something somewhere had made a run for it—for all I knew it could have been me. Each second was dragged out in exquisite, eternal pain. I didn't even notice when it started to get lighter around me; my eyes were clamped as tight as my mouth. My back was so highly arched, the only points of contact I had with the ground were the flats of my feet and the crown of my skull. You could add in breaking my spine to the list of injuries I was likely to endure from "holding still."

Linnick had crawled out from my ear and was still talking as she scoured my body, pulling flutchers out. The relief was instantaneous from each extraction. The dopamine that had been flooding my body to counteract the pain was now making me loopy. So much of it had poured into my system and was no longer in combat that it caused me to hiss-giggle uncontrollably; tears ran past my temples. My back slowly straightened itself out and slid to the ground. My breathing was labored and I choked on acid reflux as Linnick raced to get every one of the poisonous spines out of me.

"You still with me?" she asked.

It took many seconds before I had the faculties to clear my throat and produce a response. "Where else would I be?"

"Most lose their minds in the first minute."

"What…was that thing?" I asked.

"A Polion. I thought it was a myth. I read they were once pets to the demons down here but turned on their masters and were banished to the wastelands. Supposedly they've been cursed with perpetual darkness."

"What?" I wasn't following.

"The demons thought that they were so evil, that they made sure no light could exist around them."

"The flutchers?"

"They have adapted to their surroundings."

"How do you know about all of this?"

"How do you not? Underworld history and mythology is of a great interest to my world; your education is incomplete without absolute knowledge of the demonic realm."

"Out of necessity or academic curiosity?" I sat up, expecting to see rivers of blood from the dozens of flutcher wounds. What I got were raised bumps that a mosquito may have left.

I gasped as she threatened to shove a discarded flutcher back in. "Thank you," I finally told her. "I wouldn't have made it without you."

"I know." She climbed back up my shirt and hopped into my pocket. "We should get out of here; it will come back to pick through its offal for anything undigested."

"Oh, come on; that just can't be right." I was sure I'd be warped and paralyzed at least. I stood on shaky legs, which I expected, but they held up pretty good.

"The toxin is extremely powerful, but short lasting. Once the stingers are removed it breaks down rapidly in the body."

I was going to do my best to put this entire episode out of my mind. "What now?" I asked as I trod on, in the exact opposite direction of the Polion and the holes.

"We need to get out of the wastelands and into the demon-land proper."

"Sounds charming. And what of you, Linnick? What do you hope to gain by all of this?"

"I do not know, Tallboat. We study the underworld, but we still do not know very much about it. There is a lot of speculating and postulating. Few return from the realm, so obviously it is difficult to gain firsthand information about it. What I do know is that you are somehow unique, possibly immune to some of the hazards of this area, and as such, my best chance of anything beneficial happening. Even my survival, perhaps, resides with you. And for once I have seen something more abhorrent than yourself."

"You saw the Polion?"

"Unfortunately, yes. Breatines have acute night vision."

"I'm not sure why we are together, Linnick, but I think I got the better part of the bargain."

"Undoubtedly." I think she smiled, she said the word with an easy-going lilt. Though, as one more closely related to a bug than a human, it was difficult for me to tell.

I walked for a couple of miles, surprised that nothing or nobody attempted to kill us in all that time. I didn't think letting my guard down was a good idea, though, given our current location. As I've said before, I'm pretty smart like that. And then in an instant, I show just how unsmart I am. Is that even a word?

"So, when we get out of the wastelands is there like, a demon village?" I mean really, how in the fuck would I know? I had originally pictured brimstone, lava, and boiling cauldrons everywhere…maybe evil laughter coming from nowhere.

"*Demon village?* What do you want? Postcards? You knew absolutely nothing about this place and decided a walkabout was a good way to discover the underworld?"

"I'm gonna say there's no town square then?"

There was a cute little slapping sound from, I think, Linnick smacking her forehead, though I did not confirm that visually.

"Think of the underworld as one giant mountain. It has four distinct levels; we are in the bottommost one, the wastelands. This is the lovely place every outcast and malformed misfit calls home—those that have been exiled and have no place among the others."

"Even in Hell there are cliques? That is just the weirdest thing ever."

"Oh, we're not in Hell. Not yet. There's this place, the underworld; the upper world, and then there's Gehenna. Each of those levels has six tiers."

"Of course, it does. Where would 'wandering souls in trouble' be?"

"Every wandering soul in this place is in trouble, Tallboat."

"Fair enough. But how do I go about finding the ones I'm looking for? Is there a directory? For some insane reason, I did not think this place would be quite as vast as it is."

"You use the word 'think' like you actually know what it means. From what I have seen, I do not believe that to be the case."

"You know, usually the people that give me shit are huge, mythical monsters come to life, or, well, even a witch or two, not pocket-sized beetle women. I could pull you out of my shirt at any time and leave you here."

"You would not." She did not say it indignantly, but rather as a statement of fact. "It is true that we are different species from different worlds and that your outward appearance would make a Dredgemire ill, but you have grown fond of me and, although I, for one, still find you completely distasteful to gaze upon, I know your heart is good."

"Insult or compliment?"

"Take from it what you will, Tallboat."

"Fair enough."

"As for your friends…"

"One of them is most definitely not my friend, but go on."

"As for those you seek, it is unlikely they would be in the wastelands or Gehenna, alive, anyway. Both of these areas are significantly more dangerous than the middle worlds."

"And these middle worlds…?"

"Are full of demons and their spawn."

"Sounds absolutely heavenly. And how, pray tell, are those places safer?"

"They are demons."

I might have grunted "Yeah?"

She sighed. "…and as such, are constantly scheming and plotting. Most are focused on finding ways to dethrone the

One that sits in Gehenna. The rest, realizing that goal is futile, are trying to escape their world for any of the alternate realms."

"Alternate?" I asked.

"Worlds such as ours where they can wreak havoc at unimaginable cost to life. They have succeeded from time to time in my world."

"Mine as well," I replied solemnly. "So, the upper worlds, then?"

"It is where your friends most likely are. The wastelands are all about death. In the upper worlds, they might be used for leverage over others or in some devious plot, possibly ensnaring more unsuspecting victims." I felt her hand slapping against my chest. "Like you!" she said, in case I hadn't understood where she was going with that.

"The souls that are sent here, what is their ultimate destination? I mean, what is the end game? I don't know if knowing a little is better or worse than knowing nothing; now I just realize how little I know."

"This is my…our life now. There is no purpose except that which you bring with you. You attempt to do the best you can in the worst situations possible."

"Wait, I'm not getting it. So, the demons, or the One that sits in Gehenna, they don't really give a shit about us?"

"We're not their first priority—that is, not unless you are a *special* one from your world, one who has committed great evils, or has unusual powers… or perhaps was mis-sent, then you might become of great interest. If they feel you can somehow further their cause or be of use they may guide your passage. Almost all that make it through the wasteland become slaves of some sort to a malevolent master."

"What is the purpose of this entire place? Why does it even exist?"

"For the same reason your own world exists. It just does. There does not need to be a reason for this world, for you, for me…for anything."

"I get that argument, I just don't like it. There were a great many philosophers on earth that talked just like that. I didn't do so well in those classes, although it didn't help that I was stoned most of the time...at least I don't think it helped. In retrospect, that might have actually been beneficial. So, no grand design?"

"I never said that. You and I play out parts in these worlds on a much different level than the greater beings. We are more like the Polions who are also trying to survive and escape."

"Speak for yourself."

"I meant only that we live out our lives as best we can; others are living on far grander scales, controlling reality as they move world-sized pieces around on their playing fields."

"Is it always just a game? Because it certainly doesn't feel that way to the rest of us lowly bastards."

"A game of chance, of some skill, and the most powerful factor of all...luck."

I scoffed. "Luck? The one thing we cannot control is the most powerful of them all?"

"I have already witnessed great bouts of luck from you; yet you would discount it so quickly?"

"Luck? Luck has screwed me plenty of times. That was all skill."

"Truly, you believe that?" she asked. "Imagine luck as an entity. It can take the most random of events and either bolster your chances of success or turn a minor situation into an impossible task. How many circumstances in your life, Tallboat, just seemed to fall the right way?"

I couldn't even begin to put my finger on the sheer number of times I had escaped hopeless situations with nothing more than a few bruises and a good story to tell. It had not always been easy, but providence, fate...had seemingly conspired to give me a fighting chance, sometimes in minuscule ways...saved by an inch this way or that. "Like once or twice, maybe," I told her. "Luck favors the prepared."

"I do not need to look into your eyes to know that in this,

you are lying."

"You want me to admit that everything I've done my entire life, the battles I've won, the evils I've outwitted, has been decided purely by luck? Why bother putting forth an effort, then, if I can just sit back and let the pieces move around me?"

"You are misunderstanding. You create your own luck, Tallboat. The actions you perform, the thoughts behind those actions; the approach you take to the situations you find yourself in. These are conscious actions that determine or at least affect your luck."

"Yeah. That's called skill," I said sourly or maybe all surly. We were making good time, I suppose; though since I wasn't entirely sure where I should be going or how far it was, making time was relative. Linnick wasn't attempting to correct my course, so I figured we had to be going the right way, or at least what she thought was the right way.

"Do you know which way you are going?" she asked after a while.

"Yeah. Straight ahead. Is there a problem with that?" It was a sincere question.

"I know a bit about direction down here, not all. I am letting luck dictate our course, since you are such a master of it."

"Yeah, it's going to take me more than an hour to wrap my head around the fact that my entire life has been a fluke."

"Are all humans as dense as you?"

"Either of my wives would most likely tell you that I am my own special kind of dense."

"We seem to communicate clearly enough, but there may be times when certain words don't come across quite right. Luck can also be tied extremely closely to fate, destiny, and providence; are these terms more acceptable to you?"

"Yeah, I don't know how comfortable I am with that either, to think that my pursuits have been planned and decided by others."

"How would you like to think of your life?"

"I prefer to believe that I am the master of my own fortune; that my failures and accomplishments are the product of effort and wit, not the whim of some higher being or an accident of coincidences."

"Accident of coincidences? I do not believe I have ever heard this before, I will keep note of that phase to ponder at a later time."

"Yeah, even a couch with busted springs can seat an ass."

Linnick didn't get the reference and I didn't clarify, if it was even possible.

"So how do we get from this shitfest to the next?"

"Shitfest?"

"How do we go from the wastelands to the upper worlds?"

"There is a gate."

"What is it with gods and demons and their gated communities?"

"They believe themselves to be much greater than we; by instinct this produces suspicion of our kind."

"Yeah, we used to have a lot of people like that back when I was much younger. This gate…they guarding the entry or the exit?"

"Both, I would think, depending on the traveler. There are a great variety of reasons for casting creatures into the wasteland and they are never welcomed back among their kind. Likewise, there are those living inside the upper worlds that would choose to escape their lot."

"Any ideas on how we get in?"

"I would assume you will be allowed. Your soul is intact, and more importantly, unclaimed; that will be of great value to a great many demons."

"And you know this how?"

"Are you familiar with the phrase, 'the eyes are the window to the soul'?"

"I am."

"Then I believe I have explained myself."

CHAPTER SIX
MIKE JOURNAL ENTRY 6

SOMETHING ABOUT MY WALKING, THE swaying action, the heat from my chest, and maybe Breatines just needed a lot of sleep, like cats, but Linnick was out. When I stopped walking I could actually hear her snore, which was kind of funny. It didn't make her even remotely cuter; it was just funny that something that small snored. Off in the distance, I saw what I thought were people. I shielded my eyes from a non-existent sun thinking this would give me binocular vision or some shit and then I peered harder. They were still too far away to tell exactly what they were, but they were the right height and they seemed to move in the same manner as people.

"They could be with them," I said softly, but excitedly, and I started moving at a quicker clip. If I could find Tommy plus one in that mob and get the fuck out of here soon, then all the better.

"Is something chasing us?" Linnick asked as she poked out of my pocket.

"No, there're people up ahead." I was close enough now to be sure of it.

"Tallboat."

I was jogging by this point.

"Tallboat, something is wrong."

I was on the verge of running.

"Tallboat, stop! That is a gathering!"

"I know! It's great, right? They have got to be here!"

"Stop right now!" she screamed with such force I was compelled to do as she said.

"What, Linnick?" We weren't more than a couple of hundred yards away; even as I waited for her to tell me what the hell was wrong I looked for Tommy's profile.

"You should turn around, walk away, and forget you ever saw this place."

"Huh?" But it was already too late, the screams had started. I saw a being easily three times the height of anyone around it. Over its head was a large, black cone-shaped hood. On its body were sharpened metal spikes the size of my forearms. The thing wielded a double-edged axe and was swinging it back and forth as if it were mowing down wheat. But instead of grains, he was lopping off the heads of people. Sometimes he would pick some poor bastard up and pull them slowly into his body, piercing their flesh in dozens of places until they were impaled on his spikes as some sort of twisted meat suit.

"We need to help them!" I said the words but my feet were rooted to their spot.

"There is no help for them," Linnick said sadly.

Had to have been a hundred or more people in that group and the beast was killing them all without impunity. Most he cleaved in two or simply pulled apart with his powerful arms. I watched as he bit the head off one á la Ozzy Osbourne and his infamous bat. I've been on dozens of battlefields and I had never seen any sort of carnage that could begin to match the savagery here. The beast took great delight in stomping the existence completely out from those that lay on the ground, dying. Because of the hood I could not see his features, but his actions led me to believe he wore a large smile as he performed his murderous acts.

"We…I let them die." I took a step forward raising my axe.

"Wait, Tallboat. It is worse; much, much worse."

I watched incredulously as the executioner changed from some sort of deranged medieval hangman into a form that had fueled my nightmares from my earliest memories. The spikes shrank down and melted into colorful dots, the black hood grew scraggly and turned a bright shade of orange. The leather tunic became a large, ruffled shirt.

"A clown," I gulped. "He's turning into a fucking clown." Pretty sure I took a few steps backward before I steeled myself to hold my ground; I did not advance. I wasn't capable. His nose became bulbous and bright red. Opening his mouth to scream, revealed rows of razor sharp teeth. "Is…is this all for me?" I asked no one in particular. He'd already disposed of his previous audience. Or so I thought. The cries for mercy and the screams of pain I'd heard just moments before were completely dwarfed by the tortured shrieks of the damned happening now, as severed limbs and heads, split skulls, broken bones, cleaved midsections, and ribbons of spilled intestines began to repair themselves. People that were beyond human recognition began to heal themselves, it was a slaughter in reverse; every bit as gruesome and obviously just as painful, if not more so.

The newly un-deceased had but a few moments to shake the cobwebs from their reeling heads before the terror started anew and Booze-O the clown began to chop and bite and tear through the throng again. They were as terrified and tortured as they had been by the spiked henchman.

"What am I watching, Linnick?" The depths of pity I felt for those victims was something I was having a difficult time dealing with; and I have seen my share of horrible death.

"The demon you see is a Vlantan. They have the ability to reanimate corpses; very handy for a creature that feeds off the fear they produce from their victims. That gathering is his herd; when the demon is hungry, he will slaughter them a few dozen times before he is sated."

"How long do they get between feedings?"

"It is difficult to say. I have heard it said the Vlantan are insatiable, so it may only be a matter of minutes."

"How long do those…I mean, how long can those people last?" I already knew the answer as I looked out at that group of lost souls. Each of them wore clothes from their prospective eras. I saw a leisure suit from the 1970s, some deerskin clothing that could have been from the 1860s or 2160s. There were mullets, afros, beehives, and mohawks. On closer inspection, I thought a few of the people might not even be considered modern homo sapiens but rather Neanderthal. How bad did a Neanderthal have to be to get to this place? Did he piss upstream of his village? If he indeed was one of my early ancestors, he'd been here for tens of thousands of years, dying multiple times in the most horrific ways, each and every time thinking it was the first. "Surely, they have paid for their sins and then some, right?" The last part I asked to Linnick.

"There is no ledger down here. Once you are bankrupt, you can never repay the debt."

"Fuuuuck." The word dragged out of my mouth.

"We should go, Tallboat. If he spots you he will attempt to draw you in."

"Yeah, we should." My last image before I turned away was of the giant clown sticking a rather large kitchen knife into and through a small woman's midsection. He then pulled the knife up violently, completely cutting her in two. Both halves fell away as if he had just butterflied a shrimp. I'd sort of been stumbling, as I thought more about what I'd seen, then at some point, I just stopped and vomited. There wasn't much there, but the queasiness in my stomach had to be relieved somehow. I didn't feel much better for it, but we soldiered on anyway. After a while, I felt somewhat better, though I couldn't stop thinking about what I'd seen.

"Why only humans?" I asked.

"That is not always the case. But your kind are abundant down here. You have a great proclivity for sin and fear. It is a strange tandem which makes you a sought-after commodity for the Vlantans. My kind are sought after by other demons for their ability to endure pain."

She did not elaborate on the specific reasons, and I didn't want to know anyway.

CHAPTER SEVEN
ELIZA'S REBIRTH

"AH ELIZA! IT IS NOT often we get one of your kind down here, and with your soul intact? This is indeed a boon for me. Although, how I am going to keep news of your arrival truly a secret eludes me. The great one himself, when he finds out, will want you for his own, and that does not suit my plans well."

"Please," Eliza said, "I'm just a girl. I don't understand what is going on."

"That is the beauty of this, my dear! Half of you, the part that was lost so long ago (by your standards) has not even a remote understanding of the events that have transpired around you. But that other half, that piece of you so cunningly hidden behind that countenance of innocence, oh, she knows. She knows perfectly well why you are here and why you must suffer unimaginable and hideous terrors. Your life, or whatever you call this pitiful existence, will be hostile beyond your abilities to comprehend, and you will cry out 'Why me?' They all do. You will endure pain the likes of which you cannot even begin to imagine. So," the demon smiled. "Shall we get started?"

Eliza's first screams ripped through the soft lining of her throat; these were immediately obscured by Jazmixer's laughs.

"It is beyond my scope of comprehension how a being so fragile of mind, body, and most assuredly, soul, is allowed to preside over such an important realm. But, it's of little consequence. All that will change, and soon. While we wait…" Jazmixer first swelled to double his size, then began to fold in on himself. Eliza shrank back as she watched him assume a new shape. His head pulled into a bullet shape then sprouted thick, black hair which parted to reveal very close-set, almost beady eyes. A prominent nose lay nearly flat against the left cheek; as she watched, a heavy, salt and pepper mustache grew below it and covered a mouth that smiled cruelly. The transformation complete, the thin lips pulled back into a malicious leer as he gazed upon his daughter.

"It has been a long time, no?" He stood there with his hands on his hips, he was not a tall man, but he was powerfully built, as if he'd been hewn from a solid piece of oak.

"No papa!" Eliza wailed, she looked for a way out of the enclosure she was in. As she did, even that began to change, to shrink down to a small hut, no more than sticks and mud and a few dirty furs to line the floor. A dying fire barely lit the tiny dwelling. "This isn't real; it can't be." Fat tears fell from her eyes and rolled down her cheeks.

"It's real, Lizzie." Her younger brother, Tomas, had come inside with a meager armful of branches and twigs. "Father hit you hard and you fell over, knocked your head against the fire pit. I did not think you were going to wake up," Tomas sobbed. "I have tended to you for four days and nights; you have lain moaning in your sleep."

"That will teach you to be slow with my dinner," Ellard said as he sat down on the only chair in the room.

"This isn't real. I've…I've been alive for hundreds of years. You're dead. I left this place centuries ago…I'm…I'm a vampire."

Ellard guffawed. "It appears your sister is as weak of mind as you are, boy! How is it my lot in life to support two idiot children? I work until my back aches every day so that you two can stay at home and what, eat bugs together? What exactly is it that you two do while I'm away? Are you two diddling behind my back? Are you cheating on me, my sweet Lizzie?"

"I…we would never!" Tomas shouted. "That's not right!"

"Not right? Not right, the simpleton says. By whose law? I brought the ugly little whelp into the world. I feed her and shelter her; I'll do to her and to you as I please. You should be grateful I don't throw you out or that my appetites don't run towards boys. Huh? What would you think if I pressed my fat snake up your ass? Hmmm?" Ellard grunted and pushed his chair back, thrusting his hips. "I've heard say it's quite the thrill, especially with one so young. Perhaps we will try it sometime; maybe the next time your bitch-sister is lying unconscious. If you don't want that to be tonight, get me my dinner."

Eliza touched the side of her head, it was tender where she prodded around the edges of the makeshift bandage Tomas had wrapped there. "But I'm powerful," she whispered.

"Powerfully stupid." Ellard had said to her. He threw a heavy wooden bowl at her; it hit her in the stomach, knocking the wind out of her. "Fill that." He stood and pointed to the bowl which had rolled close to the fire where an iron pot of gray, bonemeal stew was bubbling over a dirty pit.

She grabbed the ladle and scooped the chunky, boiling liquid into the bowl. She briefly entertained the notion of throwing the hot contents into Ellard's face, but she didn't think this would be enough to kill him and she could not take the chance of merely wounding a dangerous beast. He eyed her warily as she approached, as though he had seen her thoughts. Once she set the bowl down on the table, he gave her a backhand whack with his right that sent her reeling away. Blood leaked from the corner of her lip as she collapsed to the ground.

"I don't like how you look at me, girl. Your mother used to look at me that way sometimes, but I beat that defiance right out of her. Women are things; they are possessions, like dogs. They do as they are told to do, nothing more and certainly nothing less. You mumbled in your sleep about leaving, I heard everything. Who is this *Victor* fellow with the surname of Talbot? Hmmm? Sounds English. Are you tramping around now? I will not allow my daughter to be defiled by others. That is my job!" He grinned as he slurped at the gruel-like substance in his bowl.

He greedily drank to the bottom of his meal, a fair amount getting stuck in his facial hair and falling onto his chest. When he was done he flung the bowl, careening it off Lizzie's head. She yelped in surprise and pain.

"Clean this shit-hole up! I am going to get some ale. When I come home you will service me, as is your duty. I have been saving it up for four long days and this isn't going to take care of itself!" He laughed as he grabbed at the front of his pants, outlining his penis. Lizzie turned away in disgust, Tomas began to wail. They listened to Ellard's laughs trail down the path but did not move until several minutes later.

"Are you alright?" Tomas asked as he helped her up off the ground.

"None of this is real, Tomas. I escaped, long ago. I got away from that pig. I was, I am, a powerful vampire, and I turned you. Oh no! I turned you! What have I done?" She caressed the side of his face. "Your life has been one hell after another. I…I wanted to save you from this place but I should have left you just the way you were. I had no right to do such a thing, my sweet Tomas. This world is much too cruel for someone who is as sweet as you. Perhaps there is something wrong with your mind, or perhaps it is my mind that is warped; perhaps I couldn't hold on to goodness, but you are the way the world is meant to be. How much kinder the world would be if everyone were as tender as you? I have done unspeakably horrible things all these years, Tomas, yet you were always there, always trying to bring me back home. Not this home, but the home of our hearts— one where we could live together, to laugh and be free."

"Eliza, you have gone nowhere, done nothing bad. You have been here with me. I have tended to you, bandaged your head. You were delirious with fever and heat. I thought for sure he had killed you this time."

"You lie sweet, sweet, Tomas, and that is how I know this is not real. My Tomas would have never lied to me; nor would he use a name I adopted long after I left this stupid hovel and that piggish man!"

Tomas laughed as he swelled in size. His chortle growing deeper as he grew. "Oh, my Eliza, I know I put fear into you; I could feel the power of it quake from your skin, if only for a moment. Well done! You have caught me this time, but we have all eternity for me to break you. Eventually, your mind will weaken and I will snap you in two like a dried femur."

"Why? Of what value is my broken spirit to you?"

"Value?" He laughed bitterly. "Why, none at all. It is not the break that fascinates me, it is the journey we will take together, how I bring you there, to that brink; that is what holds the true fascination." The fire, the table and chair, and even the hovel itself all diminished then faded away. Eliza stood in a place of nothingness. "Perhaps that memory is too distant; let us try a different tactic." The shadowy light turned into a uniform gray flatness that stretched to a vast, unseen distance. Lost, lonely, souls glided about, each adrift, contemplating in their madness the endeavors that had placed them in this eternal despondency. Eliza once again found herself floating aimlessly among them.

"I cannot!" she pleaded. "I cannot be here again!"

"I will leave you here to drift awhile. Perhaps it will make you more pliable when next we meet. I will return for you in one day less than eternity." She screamed in anguish as he vanished; though she remembered nothing from before, she sensed the despair that was about to envelop her mind. Even his company was preferred over the crowded lost.

Eliza did not know how much time had elapsed; how could time be measured in a place so devoid of events? Not even the light varied around her. For a while she searched the faces that passed her by, looking for anyone she might recognize, but no one returned her gaze. Finally, they all began to blend into each other, one drab grayness after another. She did not know how much more her mind could withstand. As if he knew this too, she finally saw Jazmixer standing up ahead. She did her best to not react to him.

"It has been many years since we have last seen each other. Do you remember me?" He asked, trying to gain her attention by floating his arm in front of her. She did not blink, she stared through him as if he didn't even exist.

"Excellent. A blank canvas upon which to paint my masterpiece!"

Eliza's heart skipped a beat as she found herself in a darkened alley; a tall man with a hooked nose held her arm fast.

"Are you ready my dear?"

"Ready?" Eliza asked meekly, attempting to wrest her arm away with no luck.

"To fulfill your destiny! To take charge, to right all the wrongs that have been committed against you. Consider this the beginning of your life-long quest for revenge. What will you do with unlimited power over those who once held sway over you? To all who abused that power? How sweet will their blood be upon your hands, in your mouth, down your throat? It will be everything you dreamt it to be and so much more."

"Please, this…this is not the life I want." She pulled more forcibly, yet he did not budge; his grip was unbreakable.

"I do not offer you life, sweet child. I offer you immortality, unyielding death, free from morals, disappointment, and pain. Now you will do as you please, to whom you please, and whenever you wish."

"No. That will make me the same as those who have hurt me."

"The Eliza I know jumped at the chance to avenge her pains, to pay the world back a hundred, a thousand-fold, for what it had done to her. What is this pathetic thing in front of me?" Victor's face wavered between that and the demon he was behind the mask.

"Lizzie?" Tomas shouted from the opening to the

alleyway.

She turned her head to look at the brother she had left behind. In that moment, there was pain and confusion as the vampire bit deeply into her exposed neck. "No!" she cried out as her soul bled out and into the night.

She awoke in Tomas' arms. He stroked the side of her neck, wiping away the twin trails of blood that ran down past her slender shoulders and were striking the dirty cobblestones.

"Get away from me!" she begged. "I am cursed."

"You will always be my Lizzie," he cried.

Her teeth elongated, she rose from his embrace and plunged them deep into the boy's neck.

"Please, please stop!" His eyes grew wide with terror. "You cannot do this—I am your brother!"

Eliza reached out with both arms and held him with an iron vise grip. Tomas' eyes rolled up into the back of his head; his breath grew faint as she pulled more and more of the vital blood from his veins.

"This...is...not...what...happened!" Jazmixer shouted as he pulled away from Eliza's bite and held her at arm's length. "You were, you *are* racked with guilt and doubt for your actions against your mind-hindered brother!"

"But you are not my brother," Eliza said as she stood. She dragged the back of her hand across her lips, smearing the blood rather than wiping it away. She licked around the edges of her mouth to gather more in. "I did not realize that demons possessed blood," she said merrily. "We might have had fun sooner if I'd known. You look absolutely ghastly, by the way."

Jazmixer reeled back and stumbled. Eliza did not hesitate as she sprung from her spot. She dragged her teeth against the creature's neck, opening a large fissure; torrents of dark, thick blood spilled. She lapped at it like a thirsty dog.

"Tell me, demon, can you die?" She moved back, prodding her finger into the large wound. The beast winced in pain yet did not move, too weak from blood loss.

"Others will come once it is discovered I am dead,"

Jazmixer wheezed. "It is not too late, Eliza. I do not have to die. I will be a...a kinder master, we will...be as close to partners as slave and master can be."

"Slave? I am no one's slave, Jazmixer. You have done your best to break me, but all you have succeeded in doing is making me stronger. I am Eliza. I walked my world for five hundred years wielding death and destruction wherever I went. What makes you think I would yield to one as lowly as you? There will be no partnership. I will feed off of you one more time then I will roll your useless carcass into the corner. I will make it my personal mission to find a way out of this accursed hell and back to my rightful place in the world, where those who put me here will pay."

Jazmixer coughed up a ball of blood as he laughed. "No one gets out of here, you stupid twat. If you allow me to live I will show you how to survive. That is the best you can hope for." He screamed as Eliza attacked his neck with such ferocity, half of her face was buried deep within his flesh.

"I have something! I have something—do...do not kill me." His voice was choked, his reserves were flagging.

Eliza pulled back just enough to speak. "Be quick about it, and I may yet let you live."

CHAPTER EIGHT
MIKE JOURNAL ENTRY 7

I HAD A HARD TIME getting the imagery of the gathering out of my mind. It was beyond boggling to think that these people now existed to just die. Sure, a lot of people on earth had that same mentality, but this was different. To be alive at the whim of evil, and not only to die, but to die violently and repeatedly, forever. Maybe I'd feel better if I found out what sin had caused those people to be down here in the first place, but maybe not. I think it would just be a compounding of horrors. That whole "two wrongs don't make a fuck" and all that.

"I'm hungry," Linnick said. "I don't know why. I realize that I'm supposed to be dead; but I have form. I exist in some fashion here, and I thought perhaps it was solely a consciousness thing, like my mind thinks that I *should* be hungry, I get that. But my stomachs are churning up their digestive juices looking for something to work on; that's not my imagination."

"Stomachs? Forget it. What can I find you to eat? Forget it." I now had something new to dwell on; it seems my short attention span had followed me into the underworld. "Great. Now I'm hungry too. How much blood you have in you, by the way?" I made sure I was looking directly at Linnick so she would know I was kidding.

"I do not think it funny to make jokes concerning one's demise."

"What else do we have to laugh about? This whole fucking thing is a joke, don't you think?" I asked as I spread my arms.

"You have a strange sense of humor."

"Yeah, I've been accused of that before. So, what do we eat? I have a hard time believing we're going to come across a cow that was so extremely evil in life it ended up down here. A cheeseburger would be fantastic. I can't imagine seeing anything down here I would want to butcher and eat. I'm thinking there aren't any 7-Elevens…not going to be able to get taquitos. Do you think folks of Hispanic heritage used to walk into one of those stores and just shake their heads when they saw what we try to pass off as Mexican food? Oh, speaking of trying to pass off as Mexican food, well as food at all, I guess…we had a place that supposedly served authentic Mexican food; I used to call it Taco Smell, make a run for the bathroom. Stuff used to tear my innards up like it was alive and wanted to escape out my anus in the fastest manner possible. But—holy fuck was it delicious. I could eat about nine of anything on their menu, minus the bean paste, though. That shit freaks me out. It's brown and mushy and looks like it had already escaped through someone else's digestive tract right before they slapped it on your food."

"There are many nutrients to be found in the offal of other animals," Linnick said with some defiance.

I wisely swallowed hard before I said anything stupid. I know, I know—shocker, right?! Looked like Linnick and I made a pair, not sure what kind of pair, but we made one. I talked shit and she ate it. The hunger I had been feeling so acutely, subsided rapidly. I realized that if I were to find a meal, eight or so hours later so would she, and, umm, that was just not going to work for me. I got quiet, I mean exceptionally so. I started thinking on whether I'd eaten a dish that contained corn at any point recently. For some reason, the thought of Linnick wrestling out a golden nugget was twisting my stomach up.

"You have grown quiet, Tallboat. Do you need to purge your system?" she prodded.

"I think I might just go ahead and reabsorb whatever I need to get rid of."

"You do realize that I am offering humor to you, yes?"

"Wait, what? For the last hour, I've been grossed out near to my limits and you're just having some fun?"

"Humor is not relegated to humans. Are you mad that I was able to fool you?"

"Mad? Hell no. The relief is too great. So, what would you like to eat here?"

"Roots would be preferable; meat if necessary—as long as it is not of demon origin."

"I can't imagine there are many potatoes down here. Kale, maybe. That shit could grow on the side of an active volcano. That is one hardy plant; tastes like leafy dirt, though."

"That does not sound very good."

"It wasn't. My wife, Tracy, was implementing that into my diet right before the zombies came. I was getting a bit of a paunch and I guess she wanted to get me healthy, maybe make sure I didn't check out early from a stroke or heart attack or something like that. That's kind of funny when I think about it all these years later, in a sad sort of way."

"I do not believe crops grow down here. Meat is the preferred sustenance."

"Shit, vegetarians would have gone nuts if they'd known this place was here. Not because they would have wanted to visit but, man, they could so use it as an argument about how evil eating meat is, like, eat a burger, go to hell. Fuck, I mean, this entire place just plays into that perfectly for them."

"Are you considered strange for your kind, Tallboat?" Linnick asked.

I was taken aback. When something that is not familiar with your species and has only known you for a few days questions your mental state you have to take a moment and think about that. "Yeah, I guess that's safe to say," I told her. "Don't tell my wife that though; she doesn't need to have any more reasons to leave me than she already has."

"We will be upon the gates soon. Have you thought about how you will get us in?"

"I guess you really have just met me. You'll understand soon enough that I don't think on any one thing for an extended amount of time; it wrecks my spontaneity. And, in this case, it might actually be a good strategy. I have no idea what we're dealing with or how I could possibly get around or through it; why worry ahead of time about something I don't know?"

"If my teachings are correct, there are seven-hundred and seventy-seven demons that watch that access point."

"That all? Pshh. Piece of cake. Strange number, though…unless there's a casino down here, then it all makes perfect sense. There were churches that preached about the evils of slot machines and gambling; there's got to be at least one card table around. Though…over seven hundred of anything might make getting through difficult. I don't think I could take on that many of you."

"I would think not. I bit your ear and nearly took you down."

"Huh. That's true, isn't it. Son of a bitch."

I had all sorts of incredibly vivid and violent dreams that night. Linnick wisely chose to sleep a good distance from me as I, supposedly, lashed out and rolled around attempting to get away from the monsters that haunted my dreamscapes. I was startled half awake, shaken, on more than one occasion teetering on the brink of demise after demise. I've had my fair share of nightmares in the real world where I was about to die, but they had been spaced out over the years, not binge watched in one frenetic night of horror viewing—Dreamflix and kill.

It got no better; in fact, it was a lot worse that next day. I use day, morning, night, etcetera as a way to express time that will keep me organized in my mind and in my journaling, as a relative landmark. However, in this world, there was no distinction from one moment to the next. No change in light or atmosphere, no sense of moments or hours. I'm convinced that even if I had a working watch, it would not function correctly down here. I believe some demons have the ability to manipulate time for their needs or amusement. It seems for some, tormenting a being for eternity is just not long enough; they like to drag out each second until it not only feels like its own eternity, but it actually is one. The converse is torture as well, to give some poor slob a glimpse at his family and then proceed to increase the speed that time passes. The lost soul must watch in horror as his family ages, withers, and dies right before his very eyes. They probably laughed at Einstein's rudimentary grasp of time travel down in these parts.

Oh yeah, I suppose I should get back to how my day started off pretty shitty, or more aptly, gooey. I was moaning about being chased by a zombie bear that was about to drag me down from behind when I was awakened by a large, green, phlegmy piece of muculent debris that fell, or dripped from the creature standing over me. For a millisecond, I thought it was the zombie bear coming through to finish me off. That thought was quickly pushed aside as I looked up at the green monster. I was back-pedaling on my ass as fast as I could.

"It's a Sludgenous!" Linnick screamed.

The sludge-bag turned to look at her, then back at me. By this time, I'd put ten feet between us—and unfortunately my axe—which it was now standing on.

"That bad?" was all I could think to ask. Superfluous question if there ever was one, like asking if a deep fat fried Twinkie was bad for you. The Sludgenous was every bit the size of a grizzly bear, though it did not have the intimidating shape of one. It was more blobby-looking, like maybe you dropped a green gummy bear onto hot pavement and came back a half hour later to look at it. Its skin, or whatever the outer layer of it was comprised of, looked melted, like it had been in a terrible accident or someone had dripped mountains of candle wax onto it. Lumps morphed and pulsed at various points on its body as if there were burrowing insects trapped inside, desperately seeking a way out.

"Food?" it asked.

Wasn't expecting that question. My first inclination had

been to try for my axe and attempt to cut that thing in half; instead I went all diplomatic on it. "We are not food."

"Tallboat, it took you almost a full minute to tell the creature that we were not something to eat."

"Shut up, Linnick. I don't do well under pressure. I didn't see you volunteering any information."

"It did not ask me."

"You look like food," it stated.

I stood, attempting to look tough and inedible. I don't think that was the appropriate response, as sludge-boy quickly halved the distance between us. Something, I think was a tongue, only it was the size of an Alaskan salmon and as green as an avocado, stuck out from a rough approximation of where one might expect a mouth to be. Although all things being equal, it could have just as easily been a penis judging by how attractive it found me. Yeah, that would have got real weird because that appendage dragged up the front of my shirt and then the side of my face, leaving a gooey slime trail that was nearly a half inch thick. Heavy droplets of the mucusy, drool-like stuff began to fall to the ground. Yeah, drool...I'm definitely sticking with drool. I was already on the verge of going into shock in case it had been some other type of bodily fluid; in that case we were going to have a wee spot of trouble.

"I think it likes you," Linnick said.

"Likes me? Likes me how? "Let's be friends" like, or "squeal like a pig" like?"

"Not food." The thing seemed genuinely saddened that I did not climb into its belly.

"I just got sampled and was found wanting." It's weird how my mind works. As I was frantically wiping away the residue from my new friend's slimy appendage, I kept wondering: *what is it about me that he doesn't find appealing enough to eat?* Not: *Thank God, he doesn't want to eat me!* Who craves validation so extremely that even the rejection of, say, not worthy of being eaten, is enough to trigger feelings of dismay? "I really need a better therapist," I said aloud.

"Not food," I reiterated, in case he had a change of mind. I kept looking to my axe; just because it didn't want to eat me didn't necessarily mean I was out of the woods. "I'm, uh, just going to, umm, get that shiny thingie over there." I started side-stepping, hunched over with my hands up in a universal gesture of harmlessness or "hold on, buddy." Its head moved to watch me, though that isn't an accurate description as there was no true separation between head and body. It wasn't a neck that swiveled, so much as the top third of its body twisted, the gooey folds wringing out some viscous fluid as it did so. Somewhat like an overactive hormonal male teenager's sock might if twisted. Yeah, I'll let that one sit there for a second.

I'd no sooner placed my hand on the axe when the monster floored me.

"You are Michael Talbot?"

I jumped back as if that tongue were coming back out for round two. "How do you know who I am?"

"Michael is not food."

"Right! What the hell?"

"Someone has sent him to look for you," Linnick said as I bent down to pick her up.

"Yeah, but why? What's your name and who sent you?"

The thing made a throat rumbling like it had a lung cookie it wanted to share with the world. I don't know if that was its name or the one who sent it.

"Goober it is," I said, taking the naming rights. I figured I earned it since it tasted me. "Okay, Goober. Who sent you and why?"

"I doubt it is much more intelligent than a Ginses," Linnick said, as if that explained everything.

"Michael Not-Food must pass gate. You are sure you are not food?"

Whatever orders it had, it didn't seem too particularly attached to them. "You can help us?"

I jumped back again when something akin to an arm separated from Goober's side. I had not noticed limbs before;

perhaps it created them when it needs to then just docks them back into its body. It pointed to its back side.

"Tallboat, I do not think hiding behind the Sludgenous will fool all of the demons at the gate."

"How is it that Goober, who is apparently about as smart as a Ginses, can say my name correctly but you cannot?"

"Perhaps it is a show of respect."

"Meaning he has some, or you have none?"

"Yes," she responded.

"Wonderful." Goober kept pointing to his backside and then it got disgusting as he, umm, shoved his arm into his backside. Not, I hoped, its rectum, though I wasn't going to go and see exactly where he was putting his fist. I knew there were some people that walked the earth that thought this was cool, but I wasn't one of them. Plus, can you imagine if it had hemorrhoids? Goober already had pulsing protrusions; that rear canal would be dancing around like those flappy inflated men that car dealerships used to put out front; for some reason thinking that would attract sales. I'm just not stable enough to deal with that kind of thing.

I swallowed hard because otherwise there was a serious threat of bile going the other way. I'm not stupid. I knew what Goober wanted. We were to crawl up inside of him so we could pass through the gate as Goober's cargo; he was a mule. I told Linnick as much.

"Are you insane?"

"Really? That phrase that gets passed back and forth from world to world? I like this one a lot better." I flipped Goober and her off.

"It means the same for Goober as it does for me," she replied.

"I didn't mean it that way!" I was quick to fold my flipped bird over lest Goober got the wrong idea.

Goober pulled his hand free with a wet pop! And, yeah, as one might expect it was dripping all sorts of unsavory fluids.

"Tallboat, he has asked you on more than one occasion if

you are food and now you are seriously thinking about entering his cavity?"

"Well, I mean, it's not his stomach."

"And how do you know where his stomach is or how he digests matter? Perhaps merely getting inside of him starts the process of strong acids melting away our flesh."

"I…I hadn't thought of that."

"Of course you hadn't or you wouldn't think this was a good idea."

"Oh, wait one…I never said I thought it was a good idea. I'm just not sure what else to do."

"Find another way! Does it not strike you as strange that this Sludgenous shows up right now knowing who you are? Every part of this smells of trap."

My first instinct was to say, "Why would he do that?" but there were a dozen reasons I could think of off the top of my head and another dozen that would never occur to me until the trap had been sprung.

"How are you in combat?" I asked Linnick as I studied my axe.

"I prefer to force diplomacy through coercion and blackmail," she replied with not a hint of regret.

"Can you maybe find out Goober's intentions?"

"You want me to see into its mind? I'm not even sure if it has one."

"If we are to have any hope in this quest we need to make it through that gate."

"That is your quest, Tallboat. Not mine."

"You're right, I'm sorry. Could you maybe see what his plans are before we part ways?"

"I owe you that, at least."

I didn't push it, but she owed me a hell of a lot more than that. Maybe a new car with a mounted machine gun, some cold beers in the backseat and Widespread Panic's entire library which I could play on the twelve-speaker set-up. That would be a start.

"Goober." He turned to me. Looking upon that melty shifting face was taking up all of my concentration. "My, err, friend, Linnick, here needs you to, umm, look into her eyes."

"Is she food?" he asked, and I swear his head may have tilted slightly to the side.

"I am not food!" I could feel her tiny vibrations as she shook with rage. "Is this a trap?" Linnick asked after moderately calming herself. There was a long tense silence; I figured Linnick was learning every deep and dark secret that Goober held close, culminating in the fate of all creatures far and wide. This may come as a surprise, but I wasn't even close. I looked down to watch Linnick sag.

"He is either the smartest creature I have ever encountered or the dumbest. I could ascertain nothing, other than he wishes to eat. I think he is a blob of slow-thinking stomach."

"Sounds like my Henry." I thought longingly back to my English Bulldog. "Ask him why he wants to help us."

She did so and seemed even more exasperated.

"And?" I prodded.

"He said 'food.'"

"Is it possible someone offered him food to help?"

"I still suspect it is more likely we are the food. We need to find another way."

"It's 'we' again?"

"My options are limited, so it would seem."

"Well, I'm glad that out of all the possibilities in hell I'm the one you'd most rather give a go."

"We have sarcasm in my world."

"Good," I told her, "then you fully understand what I just said." Goober started vibrating like he was working a jackhammer. I stepped back some more, thinking he was getting ready to explode. Something was pounding on his insides as it worked its way up to his mouth.

"Look, it's his last meal come to say goodbye. That could be us soon," Linnick said.

What fell out of his mouth completely stunned me; Linnick

had to ask what it was.

"It's a fucking Pop-Tart packet." I thought about going to pick it up to see if there was a message hidden inside or something, but it was covered in about an inch of goo. I wisely thought better of it. (The packet itself was the message anyway.)

"Food," Goober said. "More food." His arm formed out from his body and he pointed to the foil, which, when I looked closely, I could see had some small holes in it—not from teeth; Goober's stomach acid was breaking it down.

"You seem pretty excited about a small metallic package; is there a chance you could tell me why?"

"It's a message. Tommy, the person who asked for my help here, loves those and eats them all the time. Though, I'm not sure how he gets a hold of them anymore."

"So that's something this Tommy used to enjoy? Before you decide to jump into the eating machine over there, have you thought that perhaps this is all that remains of your friend?" Linnick's small arm was pointing to the packet that was dissolving even faster now that it was exposed to the atmosphere.

"Not until you just said it, no." I was being truthful.

"It is unlikely to find any type of help nor aid here, Tallboat."

"I found you," I told her.

She didn't have a retort for that one. Not like she could say that she was only with me because it suited her needs; I was sort of using her against herself, if that makes sense. I felt it in my bones that this was Tommy's way of telling me to do this, and I needed to go. But I'd be lying if I didn't want Linnick to go with me. For whatever reasons, we were bonded together. She was right, allies were few and far between and I wanted her to come. Did I like her? I guess I did; she was a companion, and as far as saving each other's lives we were even. Plus, I had to hand it to her, she was a wealth of information. As a team, we had the brains and the brawn. Well, she had the brains anyway. I was bigger than her, at least, so that gave me brawn over her. And, well, I could run way faster. Not a horrible quality when pretty much everything wanted to kill you.

"Goober…so, I just climb inside you and we get through the gate and past the demons?" I asked.

"Food," he said, merrily enough.

"Well, that was a definitive answer," Linnick retorted.

"Alright, let's think this out. Any chance we have of getting out of this world involves going through that gate and the only way through that gate, that we have so far, is in Goober's ass. Is that about right?"

"You are presenting a very limited amount of information and molding it to fit your needs," Linnick said, much too astutely for something that looked like it might be a distant cousin of the cockroach.

"I'm reaching here because I don't have a whole bunch else to go on."

"I am sorry, Tallboat, but this is where we part company. I will not risk all because you are in too much of a rush to seek out better alternatives."

"I'll miss your company, Linnick," I said honestly as I set her on a small outcropping.

"Good luck in your quest. Though, I fear it is about to end violently."

"Yeah, thanks for that. I hope you just plain get out of here," I told her. "You ready, Goober?"

"Foooood." He dragged it out slow and steady. Oh boy, did I get the warm fuzzies about this whole endeavor when he did that. Unfortunately, there is no sarcastic font when one is writing, so read between the words there. Goober turned around, presenting his posterior, and I was inching closer, debating the merits of this, when Linnick spoke up.

"I have had a change of heart," she said.

I turned to look at her and was going to ask why, but that was completely unnecessary. I got my explanation and then some. There was a line of black a mile across and it was heading our way. It looked like the front of some savage storm, and I guess in some respects, it was. "Is that Polions?"

"Many of them." She outstretched her arms, meaning she wanted me to pick her up and put her back in the relative safety of my pocket, although that was about as effective as hiding under the covers when there's a psychotic killer clown in your closet.

"Doesn't seem like something they would do. Gather forces, I mean."

"They don't. Everything I have been taught is that they are fiercely solitary figures; that they will even kill others of their own kind and feed off them."

"Must make mating difficult. Kind of fucks up the mood when your date tries to kill you. Although, I've dated some beautiful women, I'd let a couple of them take a stab at me before we got down to business. If you know what I mean."

"I would imagine even for your world, your problems are significant," she said.

"You have no idea. You ready for this?" I asked as I stepped closer to Goober.

"Food, food!" he yelled. Not sure if it was for urgency because of the imminent arrival of our new guests or he was excited because there were now two things to eat.

Goober's ass or fighting a monster, blind? I'm not ashamed to say it was almost a fucking toss-up. I placed a foot into Goober like one might test the stability of a muddy bank along a river. My foot sank in, surprisingly easy. The tingle I felt crawling up my shin should have been a red flag, but one tends to think of other things when a mile-wide shit-storm is barreling down on you. The tingle got much more pronounced when I was in up to my junk and it wasn't in a good way. Like maybe I was pissing on an electric cattle fence kind of tingle— where my balls were going to ache for an hour or two. I'd once been playing goalie in a street hockey game and I caught one of those orange plastic puck balls in the pelotas, yeah, all you guys that have played before know what I'm talking about; what kind of pussy wears a cup to a street game? Felt like I was going to puke for a couple of hours afterward. This was verging on that. I panicked; how could I not? It got a lot worse when I tried to pull out. Goober's innards had clamped down on my leg and I was held fast, as if he were made from rapidly drying super glue.

"I'm not sure about this, Linnick." Oh, there was a definite hysteria to my voice.

"I am here, Tallboat. Together we will make it through this."

The words held a measure of comfort, it just wasn't enough to stave off the welling terror; besides, she was not experiencing what I was, yet. To make matters worse, Goober had seen the approaching enemy and was having none of it. Three appendages emerged from his sides; they were grabbing at me and pushing me in much quicker than I was prepared for. He was shoving me up…there. Although, who the hell am I kidding? A glacial pace would have been too fast. Linnick screamed when she came into contact with Goober's inner sanctum; I was too far gone for that. I'd stopped fighting it; I had blazed past the first stages of shock and was tearing into the second. I don't remember really having a thought at this point; it's a defensive mechanism. My mind was shutting down to the horror of being eaten alive, because yeah, that was what was happening.

I watched the flesh of my leg melting off. I should have known; I'd seen the holes in the foil packets—had to have some pretty powerful digestive juices to do something like that. I stopped caring the moment I glimpsed the white of my shin bone. The rubber band holding my brain together pretty much snapped at this point. By the time my head was pulled in, I drank greedily from Goober's body slop in the hopes that the suffering would come to a quick and painless end. The end came— that's sure enough—far from painless, though. I'd thought I was well past the ability to feel anything more. That was until I drank of the green acid. My tongue had half dissolved before the liquid could even pour its molten heat down my throat where it spread the fire into my belly and like a bad enchilada, it was ripping through my large intestines, small intestines, and rectum, and then just to ratchet everything up a notch, my anus started to melt. Friends, I've been injured in more ways than should be humanly possible. I have been shot with multiple projectiles; my shattered bones have pierced my skin; I have had flesh rent from my body in wallpaper sized sheets and have bled profusely from every orifice. None of it, combined, matched what was going on in and around my anus. It was like Satan himself was grudge fucking me with a flaming, barbed penis.

"Who's your bitch, who's your bitch!" I added that with my last breath, just for effect.

Then it was over, there was a nothingness. No purgatory, no afterlife, no feelings of regret, of things left unsaid or undone. I was not a ghost, specter, spirit, ravaged soul, just absolute nothing. In my misinformed youth (when I thought I knew everything and was arrogantly certain of my unfounded beliefs), this is what I figured death to be—just…nothing. When you died you simply flat-out ceased to exist. You didn't give a shit about sweet Patty Sue or pretty Johnny. You didn't care, you didn't even remember that you never got that raise, a better job, a nicer car. You never regretted not seeing the Grand Canyon. It was just over; the flame was out. As humans, we are much too egocentric, and too fearful, for most to believe in this, yet I did. Sure, that was before I knew better; I'd not even entertained the idea that there wasn't one world, but multiple ones, all with varying degrees of life after death. How could I have possibly known that more happened *after* you left the *normal* plane of existence? I've met with several versions of afterlife, had my beliefs blown away and rebuilt a hundred times, and finally here it was: Nothing. And I was cool with that.

CHAPTER NINE
THE GATE

"FOOD," GOOBER SAID ALMOST ECSTATICALLY as the human and the Breatine assimilated into his folds. His next thoughts were on the approaching Polions and then, "Need to get far away." He'd never seen so many of them together and had no desire to figure out why that might be. He'd added nearly half again his bulk, yet moved with a fluid grace as if he'd eaten a bowl of helium. He headed to the demon guarded gate without hesitation; he passed through without a second glance. Even the demons that had been assigned to the gate for all eternity and had seen nearly everything that could happen down here were more interested in the approaching horde. Some had even broken ranks to get a better vantage point. Goober shuffled on, pleased that he was able to convince the human to travel inside of him. If he'd had the capability to whistle in happiness he would have done so.

"Stonemar, what are they doing?" Orderg asked. Both were of the lower demon ranks, lacking wings and lacking the favor of the great one. They were forever relegated to the gates, in human terms, they'd pulled fire watch permanently. The ten thousand years would seem an eternity, but even here, demons died. Not generally protecting the gates, as there were very few foolish enough to attempt an assault. Most deaths were from bored higher demons or even occasional fights among the ranks. These, they had to keep themselves amused and sharp, should a true battle ever ensue. Sometimes there were "accidents."

"I have asked you before not to speak to me." Stonemar said, staring at the approaching phenomenon

"Oh, for crying out loud. It has been nearly a thousand years. Can't you just let it go?"

"You want me to just forget that you stabbed me, Orderg?"

"You woke me up in the middle of the night by placing your filthy hand over my mouth and I thought I felt the press of hot steel against my neck."

"Somehow you thought my amulet was a knife?"

"I was asleep, Stonemar."

"I had a way for us to escape this existence. I was hoping you would come with me, that was before I almost bled out on the ground."

"Escape?" Orderg laughed. "I have told you a thousand times. Escape is not possible."

"It was."

"Oh. Now it's not?" Orderg asked.

"It was nearly a thousand years ago, like you said. The opportunity has since passed. It was not that you stabbed me that had me so upset, it was that you did not finish the job."

Orderg sighed hard. "The humans that come down here are always babbling about missing their family and friends, and I never knew what they were talking about until I met you, Stonemar. I consider you my framily. Your petulant silence is making this infernal hellhole even more difficult. As I have said innumerable times, I am sorry."

"It was a passing folly anyway; in my youth, I thought hastily. There is no escape."

"Are we framily again?"

"If it will make the next few thousand years tolerable then we are framily." Stonemar grinned briefly then returned to the event upon the horizon approaching them at speed.

"Do the Polions realize that not one of them has stepped over this line in nearly fifteen thousand years?"

"Yet, they are coming this way."

"Why, what could they possibly want?" Orderg said to himself.

"It is likely they will change course before making

contact."

"And if they don't?"

"I may find my way out of here after all. Legion One! Form ranks!" Stonemar shouted out.

There was an overwhelming silence as the gate demons got back into position. Most did not know what to expect; only a handful of older demons had seen any kind of battle, but the last was one to remember. A large group of dungeon demons were doing their best to throw off the brutal iron yoke of their masters. Hundreds had slithered out from their holes as one; they had fought with the tenacity of the hopeless; nothing left to lose and nothing worth caring about. They were one line away from breaking free before the gate demons rallied. The cost had been savage on both sides, but even more so for the dungeon demons—not one was left alive, nor were the ones that had taken no part in the uprising been given quarter. They were rounded up and executed as if they had been willing collaborators.

The line of darkness moved closer. It was only Stonemar that thought perhaps there was some link between the Sludgenous that had just passed and the Polions that now approached. He could not figure out the significance of the event or the connection there, but regardless, it wasn't his job to figure it out…his job was to *keep* in what was supposed to *stay* in and more importantly, keep out what was banished from his side of the gate. For the first time in a very long time, Stonemar felt fear. It was an unfamiliar emotion and he did his best to suppress it.

"Orderg, go and rouse the reserves," Stonemar said without turning away.

"I will not be back in time for the initial contact." Orderg was angry. The only blood he had ever spilled had been that of his friend some thousand years ago, and he was thirsty for the taste of it.

"Then you had better hurry!"

"It is merely Polions; we will easily defeat them. Do you

send me away because you are still angry?"

"I'm ordering you to get the others because I believe we are about to be tested to our limits and I will not be the second commander to fail these gates." Orderg lumbered off, running with great side to side strides. "Fool," Stonemar said quietly. "I'm sending you off so that you will not die." Something epic and historic was on the horizon; he only wished he had the vantage point to witness it better. Everything in Stonemar demanded that he go out and meet the enemy head on, but his own glory had to come second to holding the line. The gate held its own powers that would aid in its defense and Stonemar could not ignore that; it might be the only thing that tipped the battle in their favor.

As for most creatures that live in the depths, the darkness was not unwelcome. Stonemar's vision adjusted quickly to the pitch black that had descended on the border; he was happy now he could at least see the enemy. That quickly faded when he saw how many of them there were. If he had been asked "how many?" previously, he would have guessed a number a fraction of what he now saw. His seven hundred plus had little chance of holding back the hundred thousand or so that were about to assail his gate, and Polions were not easily killed.

There were no battle cries as the two groups engaged. Long and strong tentacles struck out with withering precision, gripping and crushing every gate demon they came into contact with. Stonemar ducked as one whipped over his head. He spun and sliced through it in one deft movement, the arm shot back like an emptied sling shot. The creature ran forward, almost as if to retrieve its lost arm.

"I had forgotten how ugly you are," Stonemar said as he took two running steps and leaped high, bringing the point of his spear down into the mid-section of it. The six arms shook violently while reaching around its body, slapping at Stonemar's thick legs. The eyes, which were wrapped completely around the squid-shaped head, were open wide in terror, though they could see nothing; it was blind in the darkness its presence created, a part of its proscribed torture. Stonemar had broken the creature's back when he'd landed on it and its back legs no longer worked, though the front two attempted to roll it to the side in an effort to shake the guard off. Stonemar jumped from the dying body to engage the next. He thrust his spear, catching the beast in the chest; a hoof kicked out and snapped the air by the side of his head. He drove deeper, until the point pierced the heart. Its heart burst like an overfilled hot water bottle. Flesh shrapnel tore through its innards, stopping it immediately. Stonemar did not have time to revel in his kills; he had to move on to the next and the next.

At some point, he'd received a deep puncture wound in his side, though he did not remember when or how he'd received it. He knew if he didn't get the blood flow to stop soon he would be in trouble, but right now that wasn't even on his to-do list. His gate demons were fighting with unmatched and unbridled fury, but the enemy's numbers were too great. Every one of his demons were engaged with a dozen or more Polions and the odds got no better though the demons were killing at a ten-to-one ratio. Twenty minutes into the battle and his troops had been halved. They would have been completely slaughtered had not the Polions realized that their ultimate goal, passing through the gate, was at hand. They flooded through rather than to keep engaging, there was no way to stop them.

"Stay with them!" Stonemar shouted as his beleaguered army tried to collect itself. Most that were still alive were wounded in some manner. Stonemar himself collapsed after only two steps. He awoke hours later in a cave. Orderg was looking over him.

"Where am I?" Stonemar asked in a grunting manner as he attempted to move.

"The caves of Debriss."

"We are on the wrong side of the gate Orderg!" Stonemar said in alarm.

"We are. I do not know if this is the escape you sought, but we are out now. Most likely no one will attempt to find us; we will be considered among the many dead. Identification will be impossible; there was so much…detritus…on the ground and all is in such disrepair."

"We do not belong here, Orderg."

"You do not belong back there, Stonemar. What do you think will happen to the commander who allowed a breach of such magnitude?"

"It is my responsibility to accept the punishment I have earned."

"By ancient custom, I have saved your life; therefore, it is now my responsibility to keep you alive. I will not allow you to return. There is nothing anyone could have done to prevent them from getting through. They must have been amassing for a great many years to have had those numbers. How does something so disgusting manage to mate, anyway?"

"You forget they are blind," he laughed and winced at the pain.

"What do we do now, Stonemar?" Orderg had stood and was looking out the opening to the cave.

"I do not know, but I have no doubt we will find out soon enough."

CHAPTER TEN
MIKE JOURNAL ENTRY 8

FROM THE BOTTOMLESS NOTHING, PAIN reasserted itself until it *was* that nothingness. Pain was all— absolute, unyielding, immense, unforgiving, unrelenting, burning, shooting stabs of it. Everything that I was, or would become, was gone. I had no point of reference beyond the indeterminable suffering; there was nothing else to know. Horrible decades sped by in those moments, forever etching the hell into me.

"Mr. T...Mr. T, can you hear me?" A voice passed in and out of my elusive hallucinations as pain endured so deep, every atom of my being screamed in protest. More years, decades, eons dragged on; meanwhile some incessant buzzing in my ear would not go away no matter how much I tried to rest. Imperceptibly, the pain was becoming tamed. It still drew a massive amount of my attention, but at least now I could think; I had "self" again. I was more than the agony.

"Are all humans so weak and spongy?" I recognized the voice even if I didn't have the energy to attempt to put a face on it. I passed out, this time from the exhaustion and exertion of dealing with the pain, not because of the pain itself, that had become a victory of sorts. When I awoke, I had a tingling all over my body as if I'd been scrubbed clean with a Brillo pad. Just as I was scanning myself for the dregs of the agony I'd suffered, I was startled to reality by a pinching pain I knew all too well.

"Fuck, Linnick! That hurts!"

"Tomas! He is awake!" she shouted.

I tried to move but I was stiff, like I'd been wrapped in

Saran Wrap then covered in Elmer's glue and left in the microwave too long, stiff. I mean, not that I'd ever tried anything like that, I'm just trying to draw helpful comparisons. I somehow managed to swivel my entire body; I saw Goober motoring through what looked like his sixth box of Pop-Tarts, if the discarded wrappings were any indication.

"You…" was all I could think to say to the creature that had eaten me and then, what? Decided I didn't taste so good and spit me back up? This coming from a creature that enjoyed eating foil packets.

"He is how we got through the gate," Linnick explained. "We would have been detected if we had not been dissolved."

"Dissolved? What the fuck are you talking about?" I was rapidly moving back to panic mode again.

"Tomas told me that Sludgenous have the ability to liquefy, then re-solidify objects. Mainly they do this with food so that they can enjoy digesting it twice, but they're also handy for transporting large items. Something happens in the liquefying process that renders the parts much less dense than the sum."

"I was a liquid?" This was not going to be easily gotten over.

"An unfortunate part of the reunification process is extreme pain."

"You think?"

"Though some seem to tolerate it better than others," she smiled.

"Well, there's more of me to feel pain. You need to look away for a moment."

"Why?" She seemed suspicious.

I couldn't tell her that I needed to check my junk, but clearly, I had to. What would I do if I looked down my pants and there was a drooped over jello-mold gone wrong in place of my beloved manhood?

"Oh, Tomas said you might want to check on your sexual organs. I looked; everything seems to be in place."

"Well fuck. This day just keeps getting better and better. And how would you know what human reproductive stuff is supposed to look like?"

"One cylindrical component and three spheres, correct?"

"What the fuck?" I scrambled to undo my fly not giving a shit who got to witness me in all my perceived glory.

Linnick, the little shit, was rolling on her back laughing. Like, holding her stomach laughing. "Tomas told me to say that! I did not believe I would get the reaction he promised!"

"Yeah, that's wicked funny." I drove a hand around, did a precursory check…all seemed in order. For some reason, I looked over to Goober; he appeared to be smiling as well. I don't know what it is about end-of-days type scenarios, but I seem to spend an awful lot of time checking to make sure my tackle equipment is in serviceable condition. I'll bring that up with my therapist the next time I schedule an appointment. Gotta be some sort of Freudian issue; lord knows I did enough cocaine in my day to think like him.

"Where is Tommy?" I asked, moving my arms around slowly, stretching the skin ever so slightly.

"He was leaving just as you were waking. He said he would be back soon."

"Is Eliza here?" I asked with caution. Just saying the name seemed to burn as it rolled across my tongue. She had been evil, but I had faced many evils since and she was but one more, and a moderate one at that.

"There were no others."

"Is there any food? I think what little was in my belly our blobby friend over there liberated as cab fare. I don't know that I've ever been so hungry."

Linnick pointed to a rock; I saw another box of the breakfast pastry. I don't know if Goober had other supernatural powers, but he was at my side before I could even rip the top off the box. He was peering over my shoulder.

"What? I wasn't enough?" I asked him.

"Foood."

"You have got to be kidding me." I threw two of the three packets over my shoulder where he scooped them up like an all-star center fielder. I had thought that would give me enough time to at least stuff one of them into my mouth. I don't know who I was kidding. I couldn't even rip the foil before he was once again looking down at me, and what was worse was the green, goopy thing I'm hoping was his tongue that was hanging past my face and not so subtly heading for the packet. As soon as the yellowish saliva made contact with the foil I lost my appetite and just let Goober have it.

Linnick was mowing through what looked like a stack of cricket legs; she was eating them like I would have a bowl of chicken wings slathered in barbecue sauce. I almost envied her meal—almost; it was still bug legs as far as I could tell. Goober looked her way when he finished with the last Pop-Tart.

"No!" Linnick shouted and the brute turned away.

"Really? That's all I needed to say? Dammit." I longed for that stupid pastry. Only for a minute, though. Goober had a horrible habit of playing with his food. He would regurgitate it, reform it, and then eat it again. It was as disgusting as it sounds. It would come out covered in his goo, and most times it would be in different shapes. Once it was just a jumbled ball of material like he'd formed it with his hands then slathered it in a thick saliva frosting.

"Could that have happened to us?" I shuddered as I asked Linnick.

She shrugged her shoulders, a cricket leg sticking out of her mouth.

"That's fucking gross, too," I told her as she chomped it down, she was feeding it in like a thick branch into a wood chipper.

"You don't know what you're missing," she slurped.

"I'll risk it." I sat down, doing my best to forget about the mind blistering pain I'd just experienced and to try and ignore the hunger that was clawing at my belly, even though it felt like a rat boring a hole into my soft internal organs to get a bite. It was maybe an hour later when I heard a noise approaching. I stood and grabbed my hand axe, surprised that through it all, I still had it. Linnick had outstretched her arms. I picked her up and placed her in my pocket. Goober didn't care, he was on his seventh or eighth time through the ball of Pop-Tarts.

"Mr. T," Tommy said as he walked up.

I lost it, emotionally. I'm not ashamed to admit it. I've physically lost more than any man should in his lifetime—and to once, just *one fucking time* get something back, was apparently more than I could deal with. That I was on some level of hell, that I was starving, that I'd just been puked up or shit out by some monster, all of it forgotten. I took two strides and grabbed the boy, hugged him as tight as I could. I realize I was supposed to be the adult in this relationship, but I was sobbing on his collar. It took me a moment to figure out he was doing the same.

"I didn't think you would come," he said after a while.

"How could I not?" I was wiping my eyes and nose.

"It's not like I asked you to visit me in California."

"That, I wouldn't have done. I can't stand earthquakes." We both laughed at that.

"I've met Linnick. Only you, Mr. T, could find a friend down here."

"What are you talking about? You have Goober," I replied.

"Goober?" He cocked his head until I pointed. "Oh, that's Bill."

"Bill? Bill's his name? Get the fuck out of here."

"I'm not kidding."

"Did you know about the pain involved in getting a ride from Bill?"

"Not firsthand, but I've heard about it."

"The next time you have an idea like that, maybe don't."

"It was the only way. The upper demons use creatures like Bill all the time for smuggling things past the gate."

"What? There are rules down here, too?"

"There're rules everywhere. The funny thing is that the gate demons know the Sludgenous are carrying illegal things across, but they've been told that under no circumstances are they to stop them."

"What the hell is the point of the guards then?" I asked.

"Only upper demons are allowed to use Bill's kind."

"Wow. Surprisingly similar to our plane. Only the powerful feel free to break the law and get away with it."

"This place is where we learned those ethics," Tommy said.

"That makes sense. Ok, I'm here. What do we do now?"

"I know where my sister is at."

I couldn't even fake that I was excited. He caught on to that without me having to say a word.

"I'm here for you, Tommy."

"And I'm here for her, Mr. T."

"I get that, and I knew she was somehow part of the bargain. But I'm new to all this. What are we going to do when we get her? I feel like I'm running deeper into a one-way trap."

"That's the problem, you are. We both are. The deeper we go in, the less chance we have of getting out. My sister is still farther in."

"I was hoping you would have a plan and be ready to go once I got here."

"You cannot fault me for taking a page out of your notebook."

"Mmm! I have only known him a short time and I am amazed by his lack of preparation," Linnick chimed in.

"Oh, you guys are hilarious. Is this really the time for jokes?" I asked seriously.

"You, of all people, should not be saying that," Tommy said.

"Okay, okay fair enough. But, Tommy, there's no way you would have sent word out to me if you didn't think there was a way to get Eliza and get out."

"There's a way…I just don't know what it is yet."

"You have got to be kidding me."

"The key is you, Mr. T. Moirai bends to you."

"Sorry?"

"Circumstances, the future; they favor your path."

"Destiny?"

"Sort of, but not that conclusive."

"What are you talking about, Tommy?"

"You are like a miniature gravity well for significant events. You pull those around you into these...happenings. It's not intentional." He must have seen my face. "That demi-god, Poena, when she cursed you, she also blessed you. Maybe it wasn't her intention, but you can't receive one without the other."

"Ooh!! See this face? This is me being ecstatic about this revelation."

"Maybe you haven't admitted it to yourself, but it's the truth. You are a magnetic beacon for things to happen on an epic scale."

"You don't know what you're talking about."

"Should I start naming names?"

I said nothing, maybe even got a little sullen.

"It is not a coincidence, the notable people that are connected to you across your lives. "Tracy, BT, Mad Jack, Drababan, Trip, and Linnick here...Callis, Mrs. Deneaux, Azile, Jandilyn, Winter...." He kept going, some names I knew fondly, some not so fondly. Others were a vague recollection, and still others I'd had no connection that I was aware of, yet. All of those that I recognized were special people, powerful in their own unique ways.

Tommy continued. "In a normal person's lifetime, it is extremely rare to meet even one as special as any of these, yet you surround yourself with them along multiple dimensions. That is not normal. She may lead you to these events, but it is you that draws these beings to your side who gladly aid you in your endeavors."

"Tommy, you're killing me here. You've asked me to help

because you believe that I will somehow alter events in our favor just by being here?"

"Yep. It has already begun."

"What are you talking about?"

"The lower gates have been breached; a massive swarming of Polions is tearing through everything they encounter. It has been thousands upon thousands of years since the gate has fallen and it has never been this bad. This whole level is in an uproar. I do not think it coincidental that you no sooner make your way through and then it is attacked by an unstoppable army."

I had to think on that for a second. That implied that it was known I was down here and that for some reason, I was worthy of all this attention. That was a little too self-centered, even for me.

"No way, Tommy. You can't just mobilize an army on a whim. Whoever did that has been planning it for a very long time."

"I will not debate that; it very well could be true, *but* you do have to admit the timing is spectacularly fortuitous because now we can travel almost without notice."

"Almost?"

"There is no guaranteed safety down here."

"There's another thing, Tommy. If, and I'm saying *if*, that army is looking for me, then someone very high and mighty knows I'm down here and is doing everything in their immense power to find me. I'm really hoping that this is an instance of unintentional cataclysmic chance."

"It is likely that the disturbances you provoke in the fabric of reality can be felt by others and you have been found out."

"I don't know, I mean, I hope not. I don't feel that I have been here long enough for someone to get that many ducks in a row. But if they do know, we need to keep moving because I don't want to be caught again."

We proceeded to leave, Tommy in the lead, well, because I had no fucking clue where we were or where we were going, although it seemed I could just stand still and eventually everything would come to me. Not nearly as comforting as it sounds. I didn't think much of it when Goob…I mean, Bill fell in behind me. It was Tommy that turned around.

"Bill? What are you doing?"

"Food."

"I gave you the agreed upon amount and even more."

"Maybe he has acquired a taste for Tallboat and wishes to stay near him," Linnick laughed.

"You're mighty brave talking that much shit riding in my pocket. Who knows who I meet down here? Could be an old friend and we do a hearty chest bump."

I don't think she completely understood what I was saying but she got the sentiment.

"Food," Bill said again, maybe slightly more urgently. Tough to tell the real meaning of a word that has to swim through the canals of a substantial fluid.

"This is what I'm talking about," Tommy said.

"Huh? Food? What?" I looked to Tommy and back to Bill, whom he was pointing to.

"Bill has been a smuggler for centuries. He does a job, gets paid his price, and moves on to the next with nary a thought to what he just carried or why. Yet here he is, following you through hell like a lost puppy."

"Come on, you got that all from him saying '*food*'?" I did my best to mimic the wet sound of it. Goob's…I mean Bill's head bobbed as I said it. Apparently, we were speaking the same language now.

"I don't need to know what he meant; here he is," Tommy responded.

"You don't really think it's because he wants to eat me again, do you Linnick?" I was looking down at her.

Again, she gave a very human shrug of the shoulders, or at least what I assumed were her shoulders.

"You did feed him once; perhaps he thinks you will do so again," she said.

"Oh, that's true…just like a puppy. I fed him and now he thinks we're besties."

"Sludgenous are highly intelligent, Mr. T. They are mostly brain. As a matter of fact, that is how they reduce an object or a being into its atomic parts and are able to reassemble it. Just because you gave him a cookie does not mean you are friends for life. And before you say anything that he might take offense to, it is not normal for them to speak at all, so the fact that he even says 'food' to you just proves my point."

How does one deal with the knowledge they've been reduced to microscopic particles? "My memories? Are they still mine or have they been altered or possibly erased?" At this point how would I even know what was real?

"Memories are connections made in the synapses of your brain and since he recreates a form precisely back to its original state, nothing will have been changed," Tommy said. I was not feeling reassured.

"Okay, *could* he have changed things?"

"I would imagine, but to what point?"

"To what point? Maybe to just be an asshole. Like maybe he injects in there my hatred for ham, yet it has been something I have loved since I was a little kid. Or possibly, I was a saint growing up, yet now my memories are flooded with remembrances of being inside police stations."

"Please. You have to remember that I was there while you were growing up. You were no saint."

"I'm just saying, I could have been, and Bill over there, in some twisted corner of his brain, decided to fuck with me."

"Well, Bill, did you? Did you screw with Mr. T's head?"

"Food," he nodded vigorously.

"See, I told you," Tommy said as if this explained everything and should have allayed my fears.

I was somewhat certain my memories were intact but truly, how would you know? For all I knew I could have been an accountant my entire life and had ended up down here because I cooked the books. Siphoned off so much from my employers that I retired in Antigua. It could happen. But this was one problem I had to assume was not valid, so I moved on to the next most likely.

"You don't really want to eat me, do you?" I asked. Every time I backed up an inch he came forward two. He was starting to severely invade my personal space.

"Food...no." He had to work hard for that second word. I'd have to take what he said at face value. Honestly, if he wanted to, all he really had to do was walk into me and absorb me into his immensity. Not sure what anyone could do about it, as he apparently contained some neurotoxin that prevented you from moving once he had you ensnared.

We moved out, keeping to the shadows. There really wasn't a choice; the entire place was like a dimly lit basement. Bill was hugging my ass. Usually, I'm okay with someone watching my six, but he was entirely too close. If I stumbled, we were going to become intimate again, just in a different way, and I was not alright with that. There was wailing off in the distance, sounded like your standard damnation remorse or something of the sort...was waiting for the scary music to cue up at any second. The problem with being petrified all the time is that it becomes your new normal. Was I scared? Yeah, sure I was. I was also sick of being scared. But, here's the thing, all the monsters I'd fought in my lifetime were based on humans: zombies—infected humans; vampires—again, infected humans; werewolves—holy shit, I sense a pattern here— again, infected humans. Women...naw... I'm not going there. Plus, they are their own completely separate species. Reel it back in...where was I going? Oh yeah, now it was demons and they were not human; they had not a lick of humanity in them. Did they possess sensibilities and feelings that were not even on our spectrum, or were feelings a universal characteristic of living things and theirs were just at varying degrees from ours? Like maybe the normal mood for them is anger. I sped up a little when some Bill drool, landed on my shoulder.

"Come on, man." I didn't dare to touch it. "Nice friend you

got there," I said to Tommy as I dug through my pockets, looking for anything to wipe away the dripping mass. For me, at least, the next minute or so got worse. I felt Linnick leave my pocket, climb up my shirt and start to work furiously at the glob. And by *work furiously*, I mean *eat*. Thankfully, there was nothing in my stomach to roil over because it was damn near doing back flips on itself.

"You shit on me, Linnick, I'm going to lose it."

She slurped down a particularly long stringy portion before answering. "I'm not a Parnog!" She went back to her delicious meal.

Don't know what a Parnog is, but if she looks down on it, I'm thinking it's fairly nasty.

"A Parnog," Tommy said. He was laughing and shaking his head.

"You know what a Parnog is?" I asked.

"Why wouldn't I?"

"Oh, I don't know…because it's a creature that exists in another dimension would be the easy answer."

"For a being that travels so many realities, I would think you would be more in tune with your varying selves and their surroundings."

"Don't start that shit. I'm barely able to navigate this self through."

"Ain't that the truth, Mr. T." He was still smiling.

"You realize we're in hell, right?"

"Not quite, but I understand what you're saying."

"Yet you're still smiling."

"Would you rather I was angry?"

"Stay out of my head," I told him, figuring he'd been listening in when I'd been meditating on the emotions of the inhabitants down here.

"I shall. It is a lonely place in there anyway."

"I can't tell you how happy I am that jokes can still be made at my expense down here."

"We're not really down…though I suppose that is a

relative term."

"Alright, Mr. Literal. It's just an expression."

His next words floored me. I suppose it'd be better to tell you what he said as opposed to describing my reaction from them.

"I spent a lot of time with your kids."

The excessive slamming of my heart nearly knocked Linnick from her perch as she finished her, ummm., clean-up duty and was heading back to catch a nap after a big meal. I couldn't say anything; I felt like it had been me snacking on Bill's globules and my throat had frozen shut, my mouth open.

"I spent a lot of time up there, in fact, in between bringing cows to you. They missed you terribly."

"After Tracy passed, I didn't have it in me to go on. I wasn't the same person anymore and every time I looked at them I saw her. The pain was more than I could bear. Was I wrong to leave, Tommy?"

"My opinions are not absolution, Mr. T."

"If I'd known then that at some point I could have joined her, that would have at least helped, but to be stuck for an eternity apart? I just…I just couldn't fucking do it. I would not watch helplessly as they all slipped into old age and died in my arms. The temptation would have been too great for me to…to intercede. To curse them, as I had chosen to be cursed."

"I understand. It was not easy for me, either. I was there when each of them died."

"What? I never knew."

"We all meet with circumstances we find difficult to bear. Mine was that I allowed myself to bite you. I hid, watching and waiting. Had you known I was there, you would have turned your angst and sadness into ire and anger at me. Even if you had not meant it you would have blamed me for your lot in life, and I'm not sure I would have been able to deal with it. No, it was better that I stayed away."

I wiped my eyes. "We sure do make a pair. We run into things and run away from them hardly thinking either course of action completely through."

"That's more your specialty, Mr. T, but I have been guilty of it from time to time. Not that I would have, but I asked Nicole, Justin, and Travis each individually if they wanted me to turn them."

"What? And?"

"You raised strong offspring. Each of them in their own manner thanked me for the offer but refused without hesitation. They saw how tortured you were and could not imagine putting themselves, or more importantly, their loved ones through that."

"Well...I did something right, I suppose."

"You did a lot right. Please tell me you are not fishing for pity."

"Maybe a little." I wore a small smile. "How does this work down here—around here— you know what I mean."

"Maybe you should use your words," Linnick added in.

I could barely look at her. Sure, I was getting used to the way she looked, but not what she considered food. Her face was still shiny from the slobber she'd not yet had a chance to clean off.

"The demons, for example. Is there, like, a Devil City where they all live and work? Do they go to torture centers? Like, maybe get assigned a few dozen souls to serve eternal damnation to? Do they clock in and complain about how much they have to pay in health care premiums?"

"In many ways," Tommy said, "this is a world much like our own. For the demons themselves, it is a fairly safe place to exist. From what I understand, there is a lot of scheming going on. Many wish to escape and let loose their evil onto our or another unsuspecting world; a few plot to garner favor with *the one* in a grand attempt to overthrow him. It was close once, but that is a story for another time. It could have gotten quite bad for our world had Sicerone succeeded. He would have opened all of the gates and those here would have flooded to every world. Reigning them back in would have been nearly impossible."

"Wait. So, the one we call Lucifer is actually in charge of all the gates?"

"All save one." Tommy pointed up. "Up is relative in this context." He felt the need to explain.

"What the hell? Who thought that was a good idea?"

Tommy again pointed up. "He thought it was too much power for any one being, even one as mighty as himself to possess."

"This is a little vast for me to grasp."

"Yes, it's not quite as narrow as Earthly religions would have had the populace believe, but like most things, there was a kernel of truth buried in there."

"I'm going to attempt to boil this down to basics. Lead me back if I start to veer off."

"I am not an expert, Mr. T, and I am not entirely confident of my understanding. There are things just not meant for us to comprehend."

"Just going for rudimentary here."

"You should be good at this, then," Linnick said, like she wasn't even paying attention but wanted to make sure she was heard periodically.

"I wish there was a zipper on that pocket. So, there is a main God and a main Devil."

"That is how we labeled them in our realm, though those are not their true titles, if such things even exist. I do not believe they have need of something as mundane as names, but perhaps we do. When you are one of a kind, what is the purpose of a name?"

"True. So, there is a version of our theological good and evil. Fair?"

"Fair."

And it would seem that those of us that attempt a pious life are rewarded and those of us that don't, end up somewhere down, err, around here. Is that true?"

"More or less."

"I'm going with yes because I'm trying to get the worms back into their cans, not open up new ones. So, there are arbitrary judges that decide on a predetermined scale whether our actions were right or wrong, and depending on which way the scale balances out we fall down a chute or ascend up an elevator, to what we thought was Hell or Heaven, but are really just other realities where our soul travels on to and continues its existence. Am I still basically on the railroad tracks?"

"Okay."

"Yeah, that's not much of an answer, but we'll go with it. Now, *this place*, and I would imagine Heaven as well, are way stations for a nearly infinite number of other worlds. True?"

"Sure."

"Are you agreeing to move me along because I am right or because you don't know?"

"It's much more than that, and yet it isn't. We could spend decades discussing this and not get any closer to the truth; there is no absolute Truth."

"I guess I'll just get to the meat of it, then. Why? Why do these realms exist? And who created them? Who felt it was necessary to hold each and every creature accountable for their actions above and beyond what each civilization thought was necessary? I mean, who knows? Maybe eating slime in Linnick's world is completely acceptable, yet to do it in another world and they send you down here to be punished for a thousand years by having a hot poker shoved in your eyeball."

"It was delicious," she said. "Worth it."

"My point is, how could anyone in our world or *any* world know if what they were doing is acceptable or unacceptable to beings we can't comprehend? Seems to me certain rules would apply across the board. Murder, for instance. Universally unacceptable on Earth, but down here maybe they get a hoot out of it. Who the fuck knows?"

Tommy said nothing. It was like asking somebody what was at the edge of space. How could anybody know for sure?

How can anything be infinite? And worse, even if space ends; doesn't something have to be on the other side?

"This is bullshit. Seems like double indemnity as far as I'm concerned." I was mumbling as I headed off. I was pissed off at the thought of "higher beings" and this wasn't softening my mood. "An entire world created just for payback? How fucked up is that. I'm not participating."

"Food," Bill commiserated. He stayed a half-step behind me; my own acid slime stray.

"At least you understand, buddy."

We kept walking on ground that looked like cooled lava fields. And I'm not talking about long ago, either. It was still warm to the touch as if there was an active flow running underneath the thin crust of the material. There were sounds off to our right; I think it was a caterwauling feline in heat simultaneously having its tail stepped on and its claws cut too short

Tommy immediately halted us. Part of me was drawn to see what could make such a racket, a much larger part was repelled. It was a fundamentally alien screeching; whatever was being tortured must be grotesque beyond words and have done unimaginable things in its realm. Again...wrong.

Tommy looked around. "We have to go that way."

"No, we don't," I stressed. The wailing became a prolonged shrieking.

"There is no other way."

"I'm looking at vast fields of other ways," I said spreading my hands out. Though, in reality, I couldn't see much more than a few hundred yards in any direction because of the shitty lighting.

"Well, there may be other ways to go, but that is the way I know. There are traps down here, like mazes, and once you get into them it's over."

"So, I'm thinking you can't just keep your hand on the left side the entire time until you find your way out?"

"Not really. Some are traps of time; you relive the same

moment over and over, or time does not elapse, so you can never move. Some are of space; no matter how far or fast you run, walk, or fly, you will always be in the same place. We need to stay far from them."

"I agree with him," Linnick said.

"Yeah, so do I."

"Food."

"Bill says 'hell yeah,'" I offered.

There are times in my life when I wish I could unsee things, just bleach them from my mind and vision. Like that time I saw a box of condoms in my daughter's laundry. Yeah, she was living in an apartment with her boyfriend and yay, great! (sarcasm font) she was practicing safe sex. However, the beauty of being a man is our incredible ability to make up our own realities in the face of overwhelming facts. Case in point. My daughter was out on her own, but there was no way in hell she was having relations. I mean, how could she? She was my little girl, right? Even if we think it's a possibility we might be making shit up, our next best defense is ignorance. Yup, I said it. We just choose not to believe it, and that's the end of it. That sums up the entire basis of human faith and we need some kind of faith in something to stay sane. My daughter, even after having her own kids, remained pure. She had somehow repeated the Immaculate Conception as far as I was concerned, although then I have to deal with the nightmare of a god having impregnated her, and that really pisses me off…yeah, so some things you can't unthink.

Holy fuck, I was digressing so much because the wriggling mass of demon flesh I was gazing at had me stunned. "Please tell me that's not what I think it is."

"It's a Saturnalia," Tommy said.

"You sure? Because it looks like an orgy."

Tommy didn't say anything.

"Same thing." Linnick had ducked down. Apparently, this was too much even for one who sucked up slobber.

"Oh." It was a chaotic maelstrom of arms, legs, tentacles,

wings....and...other parts. Things of all sizes, colors, textures, and sexes were writhing in...maybe ecstasy? Though, a lot of them looked to be in some serious pain; easy to mistake the two. Fluids sprayed here and there like a very high-priced sprinkler toy. I saw fountains of blood and at least one neck torn wide open in the throes of...passion, I guess. There had to be hundreds of individual beings involved in the collective debauchery.

I squinted hard and furrowed my brow. "I...I don't even know what I'm looking at. Are they randomly procreating? Can interspecies procreate? Because I swear, I see people down in there." There was a large man; I couldn't tell from this far away, but something about the size and set of him was familiar. He was, umm, how do I put this delicately? He was in the middle of a conga line; I wish I didn't know what this was so I couldn't explain it here, let's see...he was getting it as good as he was giving it. Does that help without being overly graphic?

"It's a version of one of the traps I was talking about. Those poor souls are forever locked in the act," Tommy explained.

"Wow, talk about your vicious circles. Fucking bastards even make sex a horrible experience," I said.

"They can never stop. They begin to...wear things raw."

"Stop. Just, stop," I told Tommy.

"Two minutes of elation followed by an eternity of pain and misery."

"Didn't I just ask you to stop? But there are demons in there as well. Wouldn't they know enough to stay away?"

"Punishment for some crime or other," Tommy said.

"How close do we have to get to that thing?"

"Close enough."

"How do we know if we're getting like, you know, too close?" I was nervous. I watched a demon the size of a water buffalo stick a penis the size of an elephant trunk into a small, winged demon not much larger than a deer. The damage was immediate; it was like he was sawing the other thing in half. He was bleeding, the other thing was hemorrhaging, it was..forget it. The deer thing was spun away when the water buffalo finished; there was a moment where everything began to heal up and then they were off, just like that, getting, giving, receiving, accepting…it was all a blur.

"Just don't," Tommy said. "I'll lead the way. Walk exactly where I do, do not stray. Do you understand me?"

"Perfectly."

"I think I want to be in his pocket." Linnick was pointing to Tommy as she watched my head involuntarily spin once again to the scene to our left.

"Traitor," I told her.

"Can you imagine what would happen to me in there?" she asked.

That was all the impetus I needed to not look. I gulped hard and was boring a hole in Tommy's back as my gaze never wavered. Well, not quite. Mostly, sure, but not quite. I needed just one more nightmare to wrap up the event. Tommy had just warned us that we were in a ribbon-sized safe zone not more than eighteen inches across, and that I should pay extra attention to him, when I heard a series of loud, human, guttural grunts.

It was Durgan. The man I had thought looked vaguely familiar, it was Durgan. I was as sure about it as I could be, as he was covered in copious amounts of blood and yeah, other stuff. Sure, he had shot at us at the hardware store, right? I'm not entirely sure; it was nearly two damn centuries ago. I do remember him being a general asshole and even getting into leagues with Eliza. Still, what had he done to earn an eternity of this? Odds were he had been a dickish bully his entire life up until the apocalypse, and that was when his gym muscles really let his inner demons shine. He turned to me; I don't know if there was a spark of recognition on his face, but his eyes did grow wider and I saw a fat line of white all around them. Maybe he was pleading for help, maybe not. I turned away quickly, he looked to be in a misery I thought should only be reserved for those that hurt children. I did take a cursory look for a catsuit; if anyone might enjoy this lube-fest it would have been Fitzy of zombie-fucking fame.

"Mr. T! Mr. T!" I looked up to realize Tommy had got about ten feet ahead of me. "You are right on the edge—do not move. Do you understand me!?"

"Ah, yeah," I told him trying to regain my wits.

"Tallboat!" Linnick bit my nipple so hard I yelped.

"Linnick!" It was all I could do not to slap her away.

"You were moving!" she admonished me.

My foot began to tingle something fierce, I looked down to see that it was embedded in Bill, then Tommy laid a hand roughly on my shoulder.

"What the fuck is going on?" I asked, honestly bewildered.

"We just need to get away from here," Tommy said as he nodded to Bill to let me go. Durgan cried out in orgasmic damnation.

CHAPTER ELEVEN
MIKE JOURNAL ENTRY 9

I WAS STARTING TO FEEL more like myself when we stopped for the day or night; there was no real delineation between the two.

"I think I was in trouble down there," I told Tommy. He had started a small fire, though I have no clue what he was burning; there were no trees to gather wood from. I thought it might be bones, I didn't ask.

"It was a trap and the lure was working."

"What lure? I saw the misery those poor bastards were in. I can't for the life of me think why I would possibly want to join them."

"Pheromones. They take over the more base parts of you, overriding your higher functions. You most likely wouldn't have been able to help yourself. Wouldn't have even realized it until it was too late."

"You, Linnick, Bill, how come you all were able to make it? None of you seemed in trouble."

"Bill would have a natural defense. I think Linnick bit you because she was having her own problems, and me...well, I've been working for hundreds of years on the control of my mind and I'm sorry Mr. T, but I don't think you've ever tried for one hot minute."

"I'd like to tell you to kiss my ass for that comment, but instead, thank you."

He nodded. "I had to. I can't imagine what I'd tell Azile if she asked what happened to you."

"There is that."

Bill was away from the small flame, he had sort of just

flattened himself out, I guess that was his way of laying down. At some point, Linnick had got down off me and formed a small divot in Bill.

"She's got her own gel mattress," I laughed. It certainly wasn't the cutest sight I'd ever laid my eyes on, but there was a measure of comfort that was reminiscent of cuteness. We were four strong down here, and that beat being alone. I thought about using Bill as a pillow, then imagined my head sinking in and starting to tingle, then disintegrate. "Yeah, the ground is plenty comfortable," I tried to convince myself. I slept for what seemed like days. I had, if I remember correctly, a steady stream of dreams. Though the only one I remember with any clarity involved Tracy and Azile. I remember standing off to the side feeling a might awkward about who I should go up to and give a hug and kiss. Occasionally they would laugh and look over at me like they had just discussed one of my idiosyncrasies and thought it was the funniest thing ever.

What I got from it all was that Tracy knew about Azile and was alright with it. Maybe she was now, but what were we going to do when we all got to Heaven? I mean, in the unlikely event that I could still make it, considering my present whereabouts. I believe the current theory is that you are reunited with your loved ones when you go past the Pearly Gates, but how does one define 'loved ones'? There were plenty of girls I told that I loved at some point or another, and in most cases I even meant it. So, are they there, along with those they told they loved? I mean we were going to need a bigger castle in the sky if that was the case. It was going to get mighty crowded mighty quick. Was there a certain threshold of the intensity or the amount of time loved to qualify? Again, lots of questions but few answers when dealing with things outside of normal human influence.

Tommy was standing over me and had gently stirred me awake. Instinct kicked into high gear. It was punctuated when he placed his finger to his lips. I got up quickly, grabbing my axe. I shook off the deep sleep I'd been in as easily as a dog does bath water.

"Demon patrol," he whispered.

I wanted to ask him what that even meant. Why would demons feel the need to patrol? Who fucks with a populace of demons? I went with a more pertinent question.

"How many?"

He held up three fingers. That was four too many. Yeah, I know the math doesn't work but I preferred a negative surplus of demons, *that* makes sense. I heard the smallest of rustling behind me, Bill was forming up. He had an outstretched...something. Whatever the limb was called, Linnick was in it. I grabbed her and placed her in my pocket.

"Be careful," she said softly.

We were all crowded behind some old stone structure. Looked like something left after a significant Nazi bombing run–the ruins of an old church or something. I know that makes no sense, given the locale; just kind of gives you an idea of what we were hiding behind. I heard heavy footfalls approaching. Whatever it was, it was massive. Just once, I'd love to fight something the size of a Chihuahua. Sure, they can be a mean, little, dog, ferocious, even, that can deliver one fuck-nut of a bite, but still, it's the size of a loaf of bread. Odds are if you're not injured and stuck in a house with hundreds of them, you're going to come out on top. But nope, everything I seemed to encounter was somewhere in the quarter to half-ton range. Hardly seemed fair.

There was grunting on the other side of the wall and I heard something thump to the ground with a solid impact. I about lost it when a bright red snake slivered over the lip of the wall. A three-tined forked tongue shot out of it repeatedly, sampling the air, I suppose. I saw no eyes, so we had that going for us. Tommy put his hand out to keep me from doing something. The thing was as thick as my forearm and less than three feet away; why the fuck wouldn't I be doing something? Brown venom leaked from its mouth, sizzling as it made impact with the ground. Then the snake was shooting it right at us as a heavy stream blew out and past that tongue. We all moved away from the impact and splash area.

That's when I realized that it wasn't a snake. Not in the traditional way, anyway. That was a damned trouser snake. There were more footfalls coming and more grunts, but it had a cadence to it. It was their language and they were talking. The other two demons were coming and telling this one to hurry up with his piss. I don't know if this one was ever going to be in a more vulnerable state. I should have felt bad for what I was about to do but, well, I didn't. I moved with a quickness, bringing the axe up and artfully dodging Tommy's hand as he reached out in vain to stop me. The blade of my axe head crushed down on demon dick and went straight through to the stone wall. The shower of sparks my steel made as it impacted the stone ignited the demon's fluids on fire.

He was shrieking and crying out in anger and pain. His damaged dick was afire; he pulled away, waving the stump around in an effort to air out the flame. It wasn't working. The fire quickly crawled up the base and started to burn his delicates. He was howling out what I would imagine was a string of demon swears. The other two demons were looking on with a mixture of shock and awe with a healthy dose of humor. Apparently, one of your mates having his dick hacked off and set on fire was some pretty fucking funny stuff in hell. I mean, I guess where else could you get away with that kind of behavior? Maybe they'd caught sight of his huge package at some point in the community showers and had harbored envy for years and now that he'd been reduced, so to speak, they figured it was all good. Not my job to figure it out.

I jumped up onto the wall and was swinging for the next brute. He was a mottled blue-gray color, nearly nine feet of pure, terrifying muscle. His face resembled something like a bird; a large beak dominated the front, though this beak was lined with razor sharp teeth. Small eyes atop raised piles of flesh and muscle, the face, I suppose, swiveled to take me in.

My axe bit deeply into its chest as I hit him with everything I had, including my momentum. If he moved an inch backward it was due to the shock of my attack rather than the impact. He might not have staggered, but he was fucking hurting. He reached out and grabbed the back of me and flung me away. I had the good fortune to hit Mr. Flombay, and not the burning parts, either.

I righted myself quickly, as did the blue demon. Stumpy wings puffed out from its back. I think he was attempting to make himself look bigger, not sure why, he had me five times over. A luminescent blood flowed heavily from the chest of the demon, his eyes blazed with hatred for me as he dipped a hand down to the wound.

"I got some more for you if you're interested!" I yelled at him. Something about his blood was working on my physiology. Without even asking them to, my fangs elongated and my pupils dilated. The demon paused to recognize one of his own, I guess, or maybe there was a pang of fear. Didn't matter, gave me a second to take the attack to him. If I thought I had some savagery in my attack, it paled in comparison to what Tommy unleashed as he came over the wall. He sprung, he had talons to match the fangs; Wolverine's cousin or something. He stuck his first claw-laden fist deep into the side of the demon's neck, ripping sideways and putting a foot-long gaping hole there. The monster's head lolled to the side as I buried my axe into its beak, shattering it into pieces. It shuddered and cried out as I toppled it over.

"Down!" Linnick cried out as I found my forward momentum going down with the demon, luckily, I might add, as a claw the size of a scimitar whizzed over my head. My head, still attached, landed next to Tommy's. He seemed slightly dazed as he drank deeply and greedily of the demon. He was shaken out of it when he saw me; we both got up and at the ready. The last demon remaining was not the least bit deterred that he was outnumbered. Though he didn't charge, he also didn't flee.

It was this very moment in time that I finally and fully embraced the half of me that was a vampire; for in a way, I had come home. Born in hell to give hell. I grinned as I moved to the left, Tommy to the right. The demon kept its deadly claws up. Not at this exact moment, but I would think on it later; I wondered what the hell he did if he had an itchy nose or just had to, you know, wipe up the old rear-end after taco Tuesday. Those claws must have been murder on his hemorrhoids. Yeah, later I would think on that, but right now, I wanted to open him up like a fish and watch all his priorities spill out onto the ground. Tommy feinted forward and the demon reacted, turning away from me and to the perceived threat. He was in mid-swing when I launched.

I heard bones crack and break as I delivered the axe head into his rib cage. Fetid air from his lungs blew past my face as I dug my fangs deep into his neck. The loss of air, my collision into him, and the blood taking dropped him like a stone. I took my fill and stood, my chest heaving from the exertion and the thrill of the kill. The demon's eyes were wide in fright as he stared up at me, his chest rising and falling quickly as the panic of death set in. I'd seen that look many times in my enemies and unfortunately too often in the faces of those I knew and loved. Everything we do in life mostly boils down to staying alive, so when that very fundamental tenement is threatened, there is a terror that must be met head on. We all pass over; it's just that the transition from one life to another is anything but comforting when you meet it head on.

It wasn't that I gave a shit about the demon's suffering when I shoved the toe of my boot into his exposed rib cage; it was that he was making too much noise and I didn't want him alerting any reinforcements.

Linnick watched as fat blood droplets fell onto my shirt. "Are you alright, Tallboat?" she asked tentatively.

It was a moment before I was able to reign myself in. My teeth slid back to normal and my eyes adjusted. "I am," I said, suddenly feeling exhausted and exhilarated at the same time.

"Mr. T?" Tommy had bent over to get some air.

"I'm good." It was then I looked over to see he was bleeding.

"I'm fine." I had come over to take a look. "Just need a second."

Not sure what he meant by being "fine." You ever see those pictures of that famous Redwood in California where they used to be able to drive cars through it? Yeah, it was like that. I couldn't tell for sure because he wouldn't let me look, but I think I could see through his belly to the other side and out.

I dragged the still warm demon over to him, he fell to his knees and dove in. It was like watching a kid suck on a really good juice box; the sides were collapsing in on each other and all that was left were rattling, sucking sounds as he pulled up airy liquid.

"Just need to rest for few minutes." He was almost completely asleep as I dragged him away from the open area and back to the building. I was looking out at the devastation that was our battle; I needed to hide the dead demons or at least try, but I didn't know how I was going to disguise the fact that gallons of blood had been shed here. It was Bill to the rescue. He came in like an industrial Hoover. He no sooner slid over the bodies than they began to disintegrate. He went through three huge corpses and most of the scattered carnage in under fifteen minutes. Yes, I watched! When the hell else am I going to see somebody eat nearly twenty-five hundred pounds of food in a quarter hour? The weird thing about it was he didn't seem to grow at all from the bulk he was shoveling in. Like, he didn't have an instant one ton pouch hanging from his gut. I eat a piece of birthday pie and I gain three pounds.

"Mmmmm," was all he managed as he passed me by and went to join Tommy for a nap.

"What the fuck did we just watch, Linnick?"

"Not sure I like it down here so much," she said earnestly.

"Yeah, me neither. Do you think he's going to have to shit

soon?" I felt like I needed to know. I mean if a creature near you needs to eliminate that much waste you should be prepared. It could become an evacuation type of scenario in a matter of moments. I didn't want to be one of the next to get a Darwin award. Death by Rolling Waves of Waste; I could see the headline now. Instead of giving me a hard time about my thought process, Linnick urged me to sit farther away just in case there was a releasing of the chocolate hostages; we'd be able to have more of a warning. Those weren't her exact words; I'm embellishing, but the sentiment was clear.

"We shouldn't stay here too long," Linnick said after a while. I was alternating between keeping an eye on the horizon, a resting Tommy, and a belly-gurgling Bill. When I didn't immediately reply, she continued. "If that was indeed a patrol, they will most likely be expected to check in with someone..."

"And when they don't they're going to send more to investigate. You're right. Just a little more time; Tommy still doesn't look all that well."

"He'll look worse dead."

"I mean, I guess there's that. But technically, he already is."

"Is that what you truly believe? Are you not taking in everything around you? We're dead in the worlds we knew, but we are very much alive in this one."

"I'm not dead."

"Oh, but you are, or you could not be here."

I guess I knew that all along, but it didn't stop me from trying to ignore the facts. It's not easy believing yourself deceased. That hardly even makes sense to say, and I'm actually going through it. I didn't argue with her, but I stood, wanting to get away from her. That in itself was futile, considering she was still in my pocket. That's how much she had me befuddled.

"She's right," Tommy said. He was awake, but he had not opened his eyes.

"I know, I know. I guess I've always known, just don't want to admit it. My state of animation is my own business. How are you feeling?"

"Like I've been gutted."

"Well, I mean, technically…you have been."

He laughed. He still had large black circles under his eyes, but at least some color was coming back to his features through that pallid, washed out non-color he had been sporting.

I sat down next to him. "You able to talk?"

"Yeah, I'd prefer it. Helps to keep my mind off the pain."

"When we were fighting the demons, I had a revelation, almost. Well, not almost, it was a total revelation to me anyway. Though, I'm sure not to you."

"Ask the question, Mr. T."

"This was where vampirism was created, wasn't it." I ended that with the upward lilt of a question, but I did not have much doubt in the statement. "Why?"

"The origin is mostly correct; I think possibly a level or two from this one. The 'why' has many possible answers. The most likely is that demons were creating a way to get past the guardians of this place and establish themselves into other worlds."

"Much easier to get a virus past than a whole being," I reasoned out. "Makes sense."

"Fortunately, or possibly unfortunately for us, they were only able to get the virus out and into one world before they were discovered and dealt with."

"Us? Our place was the only one infected? Out of potentially *billions*?"

"It had to start somewhere."

"I suppose, but just….damn."

"Then to top it off, it didn't have the desired results they were looking for. The demons that had created this virus thought the infected humans would succumb to the demon inserted into them. Instead, we assimilated the virus and made it our own, kept most of our humanity intact."

"So…wait one…I had a demon inserted in me?"

"In a manner of speaking. It was mostly inert. The first blood feeding is supposed to jump start it into existence. Instead, as the host, we killed the parasite. A side-effect they could not have known about was the incredible boost to our immune system. We no sooner are turned when our bodies begin to heal themselves of every ailment and foreign body."

I sat back down, this time hard, my hand to my forehead as I wrestled with this new knowledge. "We're basically just a failed experiment to break out of jail, then?"

"If that's the way you want to see it, yes."

"How else can I? We are born from evil with the intention to harbor evil and bring more evil to the world."

"Yet, is that what happened, Mr. T? Are you eviler than you were? Do you wish to harm others merely for the sake of it? Our bodies destroyed the demon. Fundamentally, we are still who we have always been. Of course, our immune response cannot heal the mind; if disease is housed there, it now has a powerful vehicle to further its cause."

"You realize we are attempting to save one that has little regard for any life, don't you?"

"She is my sister. She has been here for nearly two hundred years. Surely she has learned the error of her ways by now."

CHAPTER TWELVE
ELIZA'S RETURN

"YOU FORGET YOURSELF, JAZMIXER," ELIZA said as she sat back on her heels, her face coated in his blood. "There were times, out of necessity, that I dined on lesser animals, cows, horses, even a dog or two. And I can unequivocally say that out of them all, you are the foulest tasting creature I have ever run across."

"Finish me," Jazmixer said softly, his throat burning in pain, his head hot with fever.

"You mean kill you? Heavens no. You're going to help me get out of this place and back to where I rightfully belong."

Jazmixer coughed out some blood as he laughed. "Out? There is no out. We have been trying since time immemorial."

"It says a lot about a place when the inhabitants are doing everything in their power to leave. Does it not? Fear not, I can feel that my idiot brother has come to my rescue and though he is as thick as ogre hide when it comes to me, he has strong connections to other realms. We will escape this place and you will be my pet for a great many years, for I should so like to repay you for the hospitality you have bestowed upon me." Eliza dragged the demon closer to the fire.

"I want you to remember one thing," she said as she moved in close to his massive head and face. "I made you, and as the vampire that made you, I own you. You may believe that you have free will, but alas, that is just an illusion. You are bound to do as I say. Shall we perform a little test of my words? Hmmm?" The corners of her mouth pulled up in a smile.

"Oh, my poor dear! Are you cold? You're shivering. That's just the virus running its course. Here, let us get you even closer to the warming flame."

Eliza placed Jazmixer's foot into the flame. He screamed out in pain but she held fast, her hand and arm burning, as was his foot.

"I'm going to let go now," she said over the searing of flesh. "But you're not going to move."

Jazmixer howled in pain as his foot stayed suspended over the flame, he could smell himself cooking, his skin was blackening and splitting open and there was a sizzle and pop as his grease landed in the fire.

"Your blood may taste horrible but your flesh smells heavenly! Would you mind if I take a bite? It will be small, I assure you. I wouldn't be so famished if you had shared more of your meals. I'm not sure what that slop was you were feeding me, but you will have to give me the recipe because that is what you will be eating for all time. For as long as I decide to keep you, that is." She paused to reflect. "I realize that I was created down here, but I'll admit a lot of ignorance in regard to the rules. When I finally grow tired of you and rip your still beating heart from your chest, who comes to collect you? Not your body…I'll leave that for the carrion birds and worms. And certainly not your soul." She laughed. "That departed the moment I turned you. Oh, talk about your own special hell. Wandering aimlessly, without purpose, forever. Who came up with purgatory? The only reason for nothingness is unbearable torture. I don't know…but if I ever find out whose idea this was I will have them pay as well. Where were we? My head is getting dizzy from the crackling of your skin."

"My…my leg!" he managed to get out between heaving spasms as pain racked his entire body into stiff convulsions.

"Oh, go ahead and move it. I didn't realize you were going to be such a meater."

Jazmixer moved his leg quickly but did not touch it. A large swath of burnt skin hung down. The demon howled as Eliza ripped it free and began to chew on it.

"A little salt and I think we could sell this at County Fairs!" she exclaimed. She gripped part of his calf muscle and tore it free. The pain he'd experienced before had done little to prepare him for what he was experiencing now. Any higher function beyond merely staying conscious was out of the question. Eliza dangled the meat in front of him and leaned in to begin eating it. When she was done she slapped the side of his face, hard. "I think you and I are going to have...well, I don't want to say a wonderful relationship. For me, it might be...not so much for you! For you, it is going to be one of never ending pain and misery punctuated by a brutal death where you find your spirit and your ego will forever be separate. That doesn't sound so bad in the abstract, but trust me, my pet; it's worse than you can imagine. I'll let you rest tonight, then tomorrow we need to figure out how to lead my brother here. Should I act surprised and relieved when he gets here or admonish him for taking so long?" Eliza stood up, placing her hand against Jazmixer's damaged leg. "Sorry." Then she patted the area, he could do nothing but pass out.

CHAPTER THIRTEEN
MIKE JOURNAL ENTRY 10

I WATCHED TOMMY STAND STRAIGHT up; looked like he'd been stabbed in the ass, he shot up so fast. And knowing this place, that very well could have been the case. I prepared to move quickly myself just in case something popped out of the ground.

"You alright?" I asked doing a quick scan of our surroundings.

"Good news, Mr. T." He was wearing a grin that nearly touched his ears.

"Yeah? You found a way out?"

"I found my sister!"

Not really the response I was hoping for, yet I guessed it was the one coming.

"I knew she was on another level, but it was vague, like just wisps of smoke in the distance, but something has changed. She's shining like a beacon now."

"What's changed?" Instead of elation, I felt suspicion. "Why all of a sudden has she gone from dark to bright?"

"Maybe she knows I'm near–maybe she's calling for help. We need to go!"

"Nothing about this seems...odd to you?"

"Should it?" he asked and I kid you not, he was doe-eyed. Looked like he'd just fallen off the apple cart.

"Alright. You already said there is a confluence of events happening possibly because of my presence. Doesn't this fit in neatly with that as well?"

"Does it matter?"

"Well, that's a change of tune."

"It matters little why; she is the reason I am here. Now it will be easier to get to her."

"Or more likely fall into the hands of whoever is setting up the trap."

"I'm leaving. I have a way for us to get through the next gate, but it is not an indefinite window. Are you coming?"

"Tallboat, I need down." Linnick urged.

"Can it wait? I'm right in the middle of something," I told her.

"Oh, it can wait. If you don't mind a messy pocket."

"Fine, fine." I put my hand out so she could climb onto it and began to lean over.

"I would like a little privacy."

"Are you kidding me? Nobody's going to watch."

"I will go in your hand, then."

"Hold on, hold on," I told her as I took a few steps away from the others. I leaned over and was gently allowing her to get onto the ground.

"Tallboat," she whispered, "he is not being truthful." The sentence hit me hard, like I'd been punched with it.

"What do you mean?"

"Were my words not clear enough?"

"Sorry, yes. What is he lying about?"

"I do not know exactly. I only know that he is not being truthful. He is very guarded and adept at hiding his true intentions. You need to be extremely careful."

"Everything alright?" Tommy asked.

"Yeah, yeah, she's just out of toilet paper," I told him.

"Now turn around," Linnick demanded.

"What?"

"Now that I'm down…"

"Oh right." I waited a solid minute then bent back down so she could get back in my pocket. I walked back over to Tommy; I could see him just itching to get going. Bill had yet to form up into an upright position. He seemed about as sure as I did about going. "This next gate, how are we getting through it?"

"I have a way," he said.

"I assumed that. I'm asking you specifically, how?"

He paused then looked at me, his countenance changed from mirth to suspicion to something else altogether. Like, maybe menace. I got a feeling that if I didn't willingly go, he would forcibly persuade me. When he looked downward, to my pocket, specifically, I knew then that he had put it together pretty quickly. That somehow Linnick had given me a peek into his plans. The look he gave her was laced with peril. Like, he wanted to squash her where she was. Would I be able to do anything to stop him? I didn't think so. Bill, who I'd thought had been lounging comfortably, had picked up on the shifting moods within our camp. He was now to the side and slightly forward of me as if he perceived the threat as well. Tommy relaxed and the easy-going kid or, at least his easy-going persona, returned. Bill wasn't buying it; he stayed close, and alert, I think.

"We should get going." Tommy turned.

"Not going anywhere until you tell me how we're getting through the next gate. Otherwise, go. I'll figure out a way to get back. One gate is down already; all I have to do is get by a bunch of cats for the second one, and they fucking owe me. Then I'm home. Can be there for dinner if I'm lucky."

"There's a wizard. He knows a way."

If I thought my danger radar was pegging red previously, well right now, the needle was cracking the glass on the dial.

"Gonna need a name," I managed through gritted teeth.

"He's a wizard; what does that matter?"

"Oh, it matters a great deal. Give me a name, Tommy, or we're through here."

Tommy measured me up, I could tell he was trying to figure out why I wanted to know so bad. I mean, as far as he knew, I'd never had any dealings with wizards. On that account, he was wrong. My experience had been limited to one time, but that time had been unforgettably cruel. Finally, he relented. I guess he was calling my bluff, thinking the name wouldn't mean anything.

"The Green Man. He's called the Green Man, alright?"

I'd known without a shadow of a doubt what he was going to say, but to hear him utter that one word of betrayal was almost too much to bear.

"Ganlin," I said.

"You know of him?" he asked, skepticism clear on his features.

"Oh, we have a passing acquaintance. How much silver did you sell me out for Tomas?" Not sure if I had ever called him that before.

I could see the fake shock and sadness in his eyes, I felt no remorse. When he realized I already knew and that I wasn't buying the puppy dog eyes, he told me *some* of the truth. I wish I could say he "came clean," because that's like making a confession, like he felt bad for it. He did not.

"How do you know the Green Man?" he asked.

"I was a guest of his for a brief period. I'm surprised he didn't tell you all about it when you arranged to have me captured."

"It's not like that."

"No? Well, what's it like, then?" By this time, I had grabbed my axe; if we went to blows I was going to be ready.

"It's my sister," he said, as if that made everything he had done or was going to do all right.

"Yeah. And you're my son, or have you forgotten that whole adoption proceeding."

"Blood is thicker than water."

"Wow, you are laying thick the justifications; did you practice them ahead of time?"

"It's not like that. He just wanted me to bring you to him."

"Not sure how that's different from 'set a trap and capture.'"

He said nothing.

"Did you think he just wanted to say hi? A powerful

wizard in hell wants to see me and, what? Offers your sister, a pretty nice prize down here, I imagine, as payment? Maybe you thought, 'Oh, he wants to catch up on old times...maybe a handshake and a beer.' Was that it? But, no, that can't be it, can it. You didn't think I even knew the bastard. The truth is you just didn't really give a shit what happened. All those years, I thought we were family. I shared a lifetime of family with you; gave you a home, all our trust. Is that how you were able to get the message to me? By using my dearest friends...you know, Mathieu warned me about...forget it, doesn't matter. There's no way you can stand there and believe nothing bad was going to happen to me."

"All those years?" Tommy said angrily. "Most of the time you were a useless lump of flesh, doing nothing, saying nothing. If not for me watching over you, bringing you food, talking to you, you would have withered away long ago. All of your family is dead. I have a chance to save mine."

"I've made a terrible mistake coming here."

"Oh, I'll say," Tommy said as he leaped.

He moved so fast I don't think I could have even gotten my axe up halfway, fucking Bill must have been prescient or at least hyper-sensitive because he was on the move before Tomas. He caught the boy in mid-flight with his body.

"NO!" Tommy screamed in rage as he attempted to twist away from the gluing grip of Bill. It was that mask of rage he wore on his face, though, that will haunt me for a good long time; I'd never seen that boy so much as pissed off. Hurt, maybe. Without saying a word, that face told me that he was going to bring me to Ganlin in one piece or dozens–mattered little.

"You do know, ultimately this isn't about me, right? It's Azile he wants; I'm just the means to that end. Would you so willingly give her up as well?"

"If she's stupid enough to follow you here that's on her, not me."

Yeah, this was stupid of me; they all said as much. But I

went to bat for this traitor. Hindsight is one of those wonderful little Jiminy Crickets of humanity I could do without. Do you think a bear regrets eating an old discarded pic-a-nic basket with spoiled tuna? Nope, not at all. He enjoys it for that moment, he suffers through the torment of a disgruntled belly, and you know what he thinks will make him feel better? A discarded can of tuna. Now I'm just assuming here; I don't know if there was ever a study done, but the bear, in between heaves, doesn't rue his decision to have eaten that food. He does his due diligence and moves on not giving his past actions, a second thought.

Me, though? I had all sorts of regrets and one, well, one of them was not burying my axe into Tomas' head when I had the chance. He was right there, helpless, couldn't do much more than snarl at me. I have to go with the thought that Bill wouldn't have allowed it, that he would have moved to intercept with the same speed he had to thwart Tommy. And that in itself would have sucked, being stuck mere inches away from one I had trusted implicitly, who ultimately didn't give two shits about my welfare or the others that cared for him. I think it was the pain of that realization that made me turn and leave. I was in shock. It's the ones closest to you that can inflict the deepest wounds. Sometimes the cuts they make are through ignorance, or misunderstanding; everybody fucks up at some point. Hell, I know how often I'd hurt my friends by choosing to go forward when I knew we would be at risk. Not so the case with Tomas. He sold me for something he wanted, it was premeditated and intentional and he was going to shove that poisoned blade straight through.

I didn't know how long Bill would hold Tomas; part of me hoped that he would just make the kid "food" and we'd be done with it. But there was another part that still held out hope that maybe I had read the entire thing wrong. Whenever I felt like that, though, I just pulled up my personal video screen inside my mind and paused it a moment to gaze on Tomas's face as he yanked fruitlessly against Bill's clutches. Would be extremely hard to think he wanted to do anything less than major bodily harm with those gritted teeth, furrowed eyebrows, pulled back lips, and the snarl-ridges in his nose. I'd seen Lycan with less hatred. I turned and ran away from them; I couldn't stand to see that face any longer.

"Food," is all I heard behind me.

"We still need to get through that gate, Tallboat," Linnick said after I finally stopped running.

"We can't," I told her. I couldn't bring myself to explain just how easily Ganlin had defeated me and made me his prisoner. There was no way I was going to detail how he had inflicted all manner of torturous behavior on me; the trauma of it was not overly visible upon my body, but it was seared deeply into my mind. "We won't be able to get past the wizard, he's too strong."

Maybe Linnick heard the obviously pained truth in my words or could feel the slamming of my heart as I thought of the man, but she did not question my decision again. Without consciously thinking about it, I found myself heading back the same way we'd come. I didn't know enough about this realm to go blazing new trails. It might have been a full day, I was getting fuzzy on the particulars, but we were once again close to the nightmarish orgy. Whatever power Tommy had to see the borders, I did not possess. I stood on a small rise and looked out over the vast carnal expanse, wondering how I was going to walk the minefield without a map and not cause explosive results, definitely not looking to make a pun; sometimes it just happens.

"How bad is this Green Man fellow?" Linnick asked, worried about the same thing I was.

"Worse than getting your legs pulled off and whipped with them for all eternity," I told her.

"That sounds pretty bad," she answered.

"Yeah, sorry. I don't know why that was the first thing out of my mouth. Linnick, I stand no chance against Ganlin, even with your cleverness and Bill's...obvious strengths. The power he wields dwarfs anything I can manage; and it's not all physical. It would be near to me fighting you."

"And yet I have hurt you," she said, clicking her claws.

"That you have." I smiled, seemed like the first one in a good long while. "Then the battle I would have with him would be worse, a stinging pinch might be the only strike I get in."

"Then?" she asked.

"Back."

"There is no 'back' for me. My only chance lies forward. Even if we could somehow get through the guardians, I do not have a body waiting for me back on my world."

This would have been a perfect opportunity for me to ask what would change going forward. I did not think to do so; damned useless, hindsight. I was wrapped up in my own sour thoughts. This was not how I was expecting the day to go. I had gone from being in a merry band of travelers taking on the entire underworld to being a lonely traveler, scared and lost in uncharted territory.

"I don't know what to do, Linnick."

"I am not asking you, nor do I expect you to accompany me, Tallboat. When we were traveling in the same direction, escaping the same predicament, we were of mutual benefit to each other. Now we must go our separate ways for our ends lie in different places."

"How will you make it?" I looked down at her; she was so damn small.

"I was doing fine before I met you! I will do fine after."

I didn't mention that when I'd come across her she had not been doing too particularly well. We hadn't even parted yet and the regret was overwhelming.

I took a chance. "Azile might be able to do something for you if you come with me."

"Your words have a tremor and your mind is clouded with doubt. You do not know this for sure."

"I can't imagine your kind can stay married for too long

with all that honesty flying around continually. Got to imagine the words, 'Do I look fat in this?' ends most relationships."

"What are you talking about?"

"I'm nervous, Linnick. I'm scared of what could happen to me and to you, mostly to me if you leave. I'm miserable. One of my closest friends tried to sell me to the devil. I feel guilt for not helping you to find your way out and I feel painful remorse for ever leaving my family for what was an elaborate trap all along. The fact they all mentioned that and I fought against them makes it worse."

"Have no guilt or fear for me, Tallboat. I will find my way out or I will not. That I am here, I realize, is of my own doing. I would feel irreparably horrible if something were to happen to you for my sake. As for Tomas, you could not know he would be disloyal to you. He used a familial relationship against you. There is a reason he finds himself here as well. You would be best served by getting back to those who truly love you as quickly as possible."

"You're a true friend, Linnick, and I will miss your company," I told her as I set her down on the ground.

"You are a good being, Tallboat, no matter the doubts that you have. Get out of here while you can, keep that goodness intact."

I wanted to hug her but it didn't seem practical. I waved to her and watched for a few minutes until she was far enough away she was hardly bigger than a speck of dirt.

"Came here alone, Talbot. I guess that's the way you're leaving." I took a deep breath, preparing to pass by The Neverending Porno Story; it got horrible reviews and no awards at the Assies, that's their equivalent to the Emmy's, if you were wondering.

Luckily, Durgan was out of sight; he'd been sucked down into the torrid affair to the point he was out of my range. I was absolutely fine with that. I pulled a Gary–my brother, who fancied himself a rock god–and began singing something that could be traced back to having roots from *Bon Jovi*. It had the desired effect as it kept the siren song from filling my head and apparently it was bad enough that I was no longer attractive to the vast swinger's club.

"Good thing I never sang to any of my dates," I said before moving seamlessly from my half-hummed "Living on a Prayer" lyrics to maybe *Triumph* or *Rush*. Thought about *Widespread Panic* but the temptation to dance would have been too great and this was not the time for a misstep; I was as graceful dancing as I was crooning. So basically, a drunk gorilla in combat boots would look better than me on the dance floor. Of course, I was always allowed plenty of space…but, yeah, there's a visual I don't want to dwell on. I've had enough of gorillas for even my extended lifetime.

It was the closing verses of *REO Speedwagon* when I realized I had tiptoed through the path and was out the other side of the clusterfuck. The sigh of relief I took was palpable. On some level, it did seem weird that basically my entire life I was driven for sex and this time I was doing all in my power to avoid it. I said on *some* level! There were entirely too many atrocities going on inside that pit to be anything resembling enjoyable. With that nightmare behind me, I could begin to focus on the difficulties ahead. I figured for once I might try to wrestle out some sort of plan, typical of hell though, I was not granted the time. The Polion army had advanced pretty far in. I could hear the ringing of metal and the clash of weaponry as the demons must have rallied some sort of defense force and were doing their best to repel the invaders. There were screams and howls as both sides took casualties. In my eyes, this was a win-win.

The best thing that could happen for me was they all killed each other and I could go skipping down Hell's Avenue swinging my arms gleefully back and forth as I whistled a tune. Maybe not the manliest thing to do, but no one was watching. Who was going to be there to revoke my man-card? Second best-case-scenario would be that they were fighting somewhere else because the battle raged directly across my path. I could not go through it, no way. Something was bound to get at me in that all-encompassing darkness. Going around was my only choice, and not only did that make the journey longer; it also exposed me to new and interesting ways to die.

"Fuck," was all I managed to say as I cut a line horizontally against the front. At first, I was doing my best to balance caution and stealth with a decent pace. When I realized I was getting outpaced, I just started hauling ass. In this case, I was more afraid of the devil I knew than the one I didn't. Sure, you'd love to have the ability of foresight, or even a little precognition so you could see what kind of mess you were about to step in. That's just not the way it works; you have to wait for the damned retrospect.

I could not even fathom how many Polions there were as it seemed no matter how far I ran, I could see no sideline. I had even turned away so that I was now heading farther in than I wanted to. What I had not been ready for was the demon militia or whatever the hell they were—wow that expression has way more impact down here—as they ran into the fray. There were dozens of them, just in my general locale, and there I was running out in the open. If it was me they were looking for I might as well have placed a large red bow upon my head. These grotesqueries seemed disinterested in me for the most part. Oh, I got my share of looks, but these demons were defending the homeland or were maybe just looking to get into a fight. Tough to figure out what spurs something that looks like a lizard mated with a pig and maybe has a cross section of Minotaur genes in there for good measure.

That group had no sooner done a run-by when I saw another, even larger group, coming. I figured this one would pass on by as well, that I was merely a curiosity in a full-scale invasion. Like a goat standing on the third floor of a building sheared in half by a bomb blast. Not something you see every day, but when you're being ordered to the front lines by a hard-ass sergeant to go and protect the city you grew up in against the advancing Germans, you're not going to give the goat much notice. Sure, he'll show up in your nightmares for years to come, sometimes it will be eating your face or shitting out hand-grenades, things like that, but right now, it's just a goat.

I wanted to be "just a human" for them. If later on down the road I was stabbing them with a pitchfork in their dreams, that was fine with me. One of the demons, just one, was more curious about me than the battle. Well, maybe not merely curious. It seemed I was its mission.

"You should not be free!" it shouted as it advanced. As far as demons go it was on the runtish side, which meant it was still about four hundred pounds. It looked slender compared to his compatriots, but still dwarfed me. It was a deep golden color with cherry red eyes. Muscles rippled along its arms as it deftly wielded a spear that was fifteen feet, maybe longer. It had spikes on its head in an oval pattern; I thought maybe it was some sort of helmet or even a crown. Come to find out it was bone structure.

"I know! I've been telling my wife for years I should charge her for the right to be near me." I turned my back to the advancing battle. I had my axe and little else, by that I meant a chance. I had a *slim* chance. And then it got worse.

"The Green Man is looking for you." So, it knew who I was and not just some random human that had possibly, temporarily, loosed his bonds or climbed out of his sink hole, but someone he was actively seeking.

I wanted to have a witty comeback, but just the sound of that name started to close my throat up in a big clotting of fear. He'd bested me without breaking a sweat; I'd been his bitch for weeks as he'd tortured and beat me, without a hint at a bargain. I didn't have any reason to believe it would be better down here. In fact, pretty sure it would be worse; I'd be paying now for my rude escape.

"You will come with me," it said as if I would just fall in behind him.

"I'd like to, I really would, but you see, I have this appointment. Massage therapist, actually. Big Swedish dude.

And if I show up late, he takes it out with some terribly painful deep-tissue moves using his elbows. And I'll tell you, it just fucking hurts. I mean, you're lying there thinking you're going to get this nice relaxing stress-relieving massage and then all of a sudden, you're being told to breathe through the pain like you're giving birth to a child. If you ever get a coupon to visit one of those licensed torturers, my advice is to re-gift. So, you see, it's very important that I show up on time." I was backing up slowly.

"He told me you would not agree to come. I did not believe him. Nobody ignores a summons from Apollyon's creation."

So Ganlin wasn't the boss. Made sense, explained some of the crappy attitude. Not sure if that information helped me at all, but I'd store it away for later. The demon had not moved, yet his spear did; not in the traditional "he tossed it" way, but rather like it was Pinocchio's nose and it had just lied. The shaft was elongating with alarming speed; I watched as the jagged-edged tip came at me like a dart. I ducked and rolled to the side as the blade narrowly missed my shoulder. It retracted enough to be back in front of me as the demon readjusted his aim like one of those lizards with the sticky tongue; they just sit still and fling it out there and grab a moth. I swung my axe out and shattered the shaft. I'd not been expecting it to be that easy. Most likely that's the reason I ended up with the broken, splintered end getting embedded in my left shoulder.

With some difficulty, I smashed that shaft as well. This time I was smart enough to move before it could thrust into me again. I could only play "dodge the spear" for so long before he got me in a vital spot. Maybe I wouldn't die but I'd be immobilized while I got carted off to see my old pal. The shaft nicked the edge of my arm, scraped the living shit out of it. I was on the move, this time not away but rather toward the weapon wielder. I'd like to think I saw a brief second of surprise or fear. Didn't matter, though, he was already reacting and pulling the shaft in by whatever magic or technology it used. It streaked past me, had a brief second as he switched the transmission from reverse to forward and once again tried to make me his own personal olive.

I cried out. He nailed the same spot he'd hit previously with pinpoint accuracy. Pushing the splinters in even further. This time I had the presence of mind to grab the shaft. I'd like to say, "the smarts" but I wouldn't go that far. At first, he tried to pull it free but I had a tight grip on it and I was rapidly heading back to him like I was the new spearhead. He struggled as he wielded my weight around. That he was doing it was a feat all on its own. Wrestling two hundred pounds on a stick nearly fifty feet long is impressive, plus he was winning. Have to take this guy spear fishing sometime. Soon enough though he'd had enough of that. When he realized I wasn't going to let go he decided to make it go forward. That, I had not been expecting. With all of my weight going forward it was not much of a surprise when we reversed direction that the shaft went right through me.

I could hear tendons and muscles tear as the wood sought an exit, and that was nothing compared to the shattering of my shoulder blade. That was a unique sound followed by an even uniquer pain, and I don't give a shit that "uniquer" isn't a word. You weren't there, it needed a new word to describe it. Still, I held on. If nothing else, I'm stubborn—I mean to a fault. Like, even when I know it's to my detriment, and I have plenty of folks that will back me up there. The Horney-crown demon seemed to be getting pissed off. It's nice to know I can bring anger and frustration to others everywhere I go. He started jack hammering that spear, he was sending it back and forth at a porn star fucking pace. Maybe I should have said humping rabbit pace; it sounds less violent and is actually much quicker.

I didn't know what else to do except hold on. There really weren't many choices available for me. My vision was blurred as my head snapped back and forth rapidly. All I could tell was that as I was being shaken like a paint can impaled on a mixer, we were getting closer to each other. He was reeling me in like a hooked swordfish, which basically I was. I was in trouble, especially if there were more coming. My left hand, which had been the primary gripper of the wooden pole, was beginning to lose feeling and more importantly, power, as he just tore shit up with that damn stick. I was fearful to grip it completely with my right as I was still holding the axe and I could not afford to drop that.

"Now or never," I said through teeth that were clenched tightly together. With my flagging left hand and arm strength, I pushed myself off that stupid spear shaft. With a loud, squelching popping sound I found myself dislodged from the pole. I was twenty feet away from Thorn Boy when I got my feet under me, ran for a few steps and leaped. For most of that fraction of a second or two, he had been getting his spear under control and had not realized the threat for what it was. That changed quick enough, he caught me on the side of my arm mid-flight. Bad arm I might add. It was enough to send my trajectory off course but I still got a swipe in.

The blade rang out as it struck one of the boney protrusions atop his head. I figured his crown was going to go spinning off onto the ground. Instead, I got a hollow ringing as the bone snapped and then the howl of one in pain or rage. Maybe he was pissed because it took decades to grow those. Like maybe he was a reggae lover that had passed out early at a party and some of his douche-bag friends had thought shaving a patch in his dread-locked covered head would be hilarious. But the screech kept going, I was thinking rage was not it, especially when I saw the eruption of a thick, deep yellow fluid gushing from the broken head spike. Looked like molten gold as it poured down the side of his face.

I was tallying up the score, I had just awarded myself round two when that stupid fucking spear thwacked me in my side. He had enough force behind the stroke, my body wrapped itself around it, just about cracked me in half. Pretty sure I could add lacerated liver and split spleen to my list of injuries. I might be tough to kill but it wasn't impossible and I was starting to come down the other side of that bell curve. From a damned pointed stick! Now that I knew just how painful and tender those thorns were, they were a flashing bonus target. It was time to go for another. And that was exactly what he was expecting. The spear whizzed over my head like a helicopter blade in full rotation.

I didn't give him a chance to readjust, the spear fell to the ground with half of his right hand. I split it between the third and fourth hooves. Yeah, they were more hoof looking than phalange type digits and there were only four of them and that included some weird opposable thumb-ish thing that was high up the arm thus making it six or so times longer than any of his other finger-things. Thorny was pissed off, that much was obvious, but he wasn't exactly about to lay down and call it a day. That's the thing about fighting for your life. If you're in a fist-fight, maybe you're drunk, you say something stupid about someone's date or football team, and someone gets in a few good pops and dazes the living shit out of you, you tend to tell them you've had enough. Most times you splayed out on the ground looking up at the stars is enough for them to realize they've won and everyone goes back to drinking. In a life or death struggle, something else clicks in the brain, you do until you can do no more. You fight with everything at your disposal, wits, hands, teeth, bricks, doesn't matter. To retain life is the primary focus, there is no timeout or halftime or uncle.

What I'm getting around to saying is that I should have expected the strike to my face. It was something like a punch, only his hoof fingers were not curled nor fleshy, so he carved my face up like a Thanksgiving turkey, or like being stomped repeatedly on the face by a bull. I didn't dare reach up to feel the damage, first because it would hurt like hell, second, it would give him an opening, and thirdly I didn't want to be touching my facial muscles, which I was sure were completely exposed. I was in instinctual mode now as I lifted my blade to deflect his next blows. My axe cut lengthwise down his arm slicing his right thumb completely off. He was bleeding at a good pace in three areas and I still think he was getting the better of me. His hoof hand knifed into my shirt, piercing my side–though not far.

I was covered in a fair amount of my own blood and also his. This triggered my primal side again, the need to feed that dark side. I wasn't sure what golden demon blood was going to do to me, but it was my only chance. I latched onto his damaged arm like a cat might a person that was harmlessly, tenderly scratching its belly. Oh, you know what I'm talking about. You can still be a cat lover to realize that for some reason that crazy animal both loves and loathes that particular form of attention from its human caretaker.

At first, he shook me around to the point I thought my eyes were going to roll out of my head and still, I held on and more importantly, I drank. Even as he was dying I felt better, strange, but better. He fell to his knobby knees, yet, bless him, he kept punching my head and shoulders doing his best to dislodge the fat tick attached to him. I was getting loopy, like his blood was laced with hallucinogens or I'd just shot-gunned a twelve pack of beer and chased it down with a couple of bong hits. Not that I'd done that recently, but some things never fade. Bringing a bottle of this shit back to Trip crossed my mind, as did other bizarre notions. I was getting restored and fucked up, I just hoped not beyond repair. Hey, getting buzzed from time to time is fine, but if that becomes your new normal it's not such a good thing. I was losing contact with his arm; I don't know if it was because I couldn't control what I was doing or I just didn't care…hell, maybe he was empty. I fell away from him like Alice did down her famous hole.

It seemed to take an hour before I felt my head impact the ground and then another hour when I heard the thud of him land next to me. Maybe my body realized I hadn't completed the healing process or I just wanted to get a wee bit higher, but I managed to shift my body weight enough that I lined back up to that arm and again planted my fangs in. He was still alive, or at least his heart was still pumping as the blood gushed into and around my mouth. It spilled down my throat, some of it inside, some out. I passed out when I saw four of him.

CHAPTER FOURTEEN
MIKE JOURNAL ENTRY 11

"TALLBOAT...TALLBOAT." IN MY DREAMS, I kept looking for these tall ships the mystery voice spoke of. "You must awaken."

"Fuck off," I croaked. My throat was raw, and my head was splitting. Whatever rager I had attended last night, I had over-indulged. I could not remember a time when I had been more hung-over. I could not even open my eyes, they were crusted over in thick sticky breadcrumbs. I dug it away from the corners of my eyes and the ends of my eyelashes as best I could, attempting to break that seal. When I felt as if I succeeded I opened my eyes only to realize that I couldn't see. My brain was as foggy as a fall night in San Francisco as it struggled to figure out what was going on.

"I'm blind," I choked out.

"Shut up, Tallboat," the voice hissed.

"Linnick?" I asked.

"I will bite you and not let go if you do not cease to make noise."

That threat cut through all the other bullshit. We were either back to the first time we'd encountered the Polions and I had been killed and hallucinated all that had happened afterward or this was the next time and she had found me. The first explanation seemed much more likely.

"You're so little; how could you have found me?" I asked, and true to her word she bit my earlobe with enough force that I think her mandibles were touching. I shut up, and I shut up quickly. Yeah, I was overjoyed my friend was back but if she didn't stop chewing through me I was going to be forced to do something about it. Finally, she released her grip and sat back.

I should have been more petrified, I knew this on a bunch of different levels, I just couldn't muster enough feelings inside of me to give a shit. Thorny had nearly taken me out, I should be celebrating the fact that I was alive and petrified that I was about to hand that hard-fought victory into the jaws of defeat. There was a very good chance it was Thorny's blood that was funking me up. I still had a residual buzz and the true beginnings of a bitch-slapping hangover was on the horizon.

Have you ever partied your ass off on a Tuesday night hoping that Wednesday was still days away? No? Come on I'm not the only one. Your alarm goes off crisply at six fifty-five in the a.m., you are approximately a sheet and a half to the wind and you know your ass, which you figured looked pretty good in your jeans last night, is going to be flailing and dragging on the ground the entire day. Sometime right before Carl from accounting asks you what you're doing for lunch, your head is going to start drilling spikes through its own skull, your eyes are going to begin to smolder from the burning sensation, and your poor abused stomach is going to grumble and bumble its distaste at your choices in life. And that's not even getting into your sphincter which will be flapping in the breeze because your broke ass was drinking something swill-like that came in a bargain breaking twenty-five pack. Yeah, because it's that very last beer that cements the fuck-fest you're going to be for the next twenty-four hours.

Right this very second, I could see Carl coming over, his early receding hairline the only thing visible above the cube walls. "Geez Talbot, you look like shit, want to get some sushi?"

I didn't lose my lunch that time, but I made up for it this time. Steaming wet, semi-chunky jets of something gold-colored was tossed forcibly from my stomach and onto the ground. Linnick was losing her shit and I hoped not literally. Because the last thing I needed right now was warm runny whatever she crapped running down into my ear canal and leaking into my brain. I'd no sooner got done unfurling my body from the severe cramps when I heard a shifting. That's the best way I can describe it. Like whatever the monster was that had the good and common decency to just pass us by unbothered, had now had a change of heart. Or more accurately, figured that he'd walked right past something to kill and eat.

I wasn't in any condition to fight. I didn't need Linnick to whisper in my ear to stay down, I tried to lift my arm that was holding the axe but either my bones had turned to rubber or Thor himself had taken over my weapon, and since I wasn't a Nordic God…well you know the rest and if you don't it just means only Thor can lift it. The thing was coming. I could hear the squishy noises it made as it moved and there was a thumping as it must have been sending an arm out, pounding on the ground to either locate its prey or maybe scare it off so it would start running. If it was coming to eat us, I just wanted it to be over with. I'd deal with whatever was on the other side of this encounter when I got there. Anything would be better than to keep feeling like I'd downed a case of Maddog 20/20. If you're reading this, there really isn't any chance you've stumbled upon some in your scavenging hunts and you should consider yourself lucky. That shit would have definitely eaten through its bottle by now. I think they made it from those fake plastic grapes that everyone's grandmother had from my original time. You have no idea how many times as a kid I tried to eat those. No one ever said I should have been in Mensa.

Where was I? Oh yeah, the part about not giving a shit. Yeah, that ended the moment one of the tips on one of those arms brushed across my face. Everything got real, real damn fast. Still wasn't a whole bunch I could do except get petrified, but at least it became my primary emotion. The rest of the monster was coming, having discovered something of interest. I put an image of Azile, the babies, and Oggie into my mind; that was what I was going to hold on to in the after after-life.

This suddenly seemed like something a cat would get through, and just like that, I let Sebastian into my final mind-photo.

I heard what sounded like wet rope constricting, then there was the shattering thud as a heavy object was pummeled into the ground, then again. I felt the cool spray of blood rain down over me, then there was the meatier (poor choice of adjectives) internal parts as Thorny was hitting the ground like he was a brush beater and the ground was a rug. Or the ground was a fly and he was a fly swatter, or the ground was a cockroach and he was a boot heel. I mean, you get it now, right? He was getting destroyed. Seemed good-old Thorny was taking one for the team, I always knew he was a team player. "Cheers to Thorny! I'll drink to that." Were pretty much my last words before I decided unconsciousness was a better state.

"Tallboat, you must awaken now. We have been too long in this place. I will bite you if you do not listen to me."

"My mom never bit me when I was running late for school," I mumbled. I was face down in the dirt, felt like I'd been eating some of it. I sat up, drooly mud caked the side of my mouth. My head so light I thought it was going to lift me all the way up and we'd go floating around like a hydrogen-filled balloon, ready to explode. That did wonders for a belly standing on the edge.

"Perhaps if she bit you, you would not have been late."

I couldn't argue with that.

"That demon," Linnick asked, pointing over to something that once was a being, which had now been reduced to almost a paste. The Polion had smashed it into oblivion, maybe concerned that if enough was left it could regenerate itself. I could happily report that was not going to be the case, though I did shudder thinking I was about six inches away from that having been me.

"What about it?"

"Did you feed on it?"

She asked it in a way that did not sound good–like possibly I'd eaten an ill-prepared puffer-fish and was about to die a horrible death.

"Why?" I stalled as if this were somehow going to halt whatever inevitability she was about to tell me about. If I didn't know, how could it affect me, right? I'd lived most of my life that way. I wasn't seeing any good reasons to go and shift away from it now. Especially *now* in fact.

"That was a Luvier demon."

"And?" I prodded gently, not really *wanting* to know more, but needing to.

"They are among the third hierarchy of demons."

"Out of?"

"Three."

"So, they're the fat cats? Linnick, I don't know what you're driving at. Thorny kicked my ass and I drank of him to keep me in the fight and alive. What happens now?"

"I do not know," she replied. "Lift me to your face." She studied me like she was getting ready to paint me. "Have you always had gold flecks in your eyes?" she finally asked.

"No. I don't think so...." A pit was beginning to deepen in me. This was merely a cosmetic change but I'd never seen one that didn't imply other, more fundamental, changes as well.

"Hmm," she said to my answer.

"What's going to happen to me, Linnick?"

"I don't know, Tallboat. I have never heard of a Luvier demon dying by anything less than the hand of an archangel, and surely none of those types ever consumed their defeated opponent. You should not have been able to kill him." If I thought she was laboriously studying me before she had upped her game.

"You're freaking me out a little, Linnick. Can I just put you back in my pocket so we can get out of here?"

"That might be for the best. This body is sure to garner attention."

I got my feet up under me, swayed like a tall tree in a wind storm, righted myself and started to walk. I felt decent, but I kept having a nagging thought of something horrific happening. Like maybe my eyeballs would melt and run down my face or my feet would catch on fire and I would be doomed to run for all eternity to make sure the fire did not continue past my ankles. You know, normal type fears and concerns; I mean at least for hell.

"Are you real? Is this real? I mean we parted ways. How could you have possibly found me and so quickly?" I asked after my head cleared enough that I could even form a question somewhat intelligently.

"I turned around almost immediately."

"Sure, Linnick, but I'm huge compared to you. How could you possibly keep up?"

"At a full sprint, I can run four miles an hour."

"That was about the pace I was walking," I said in astonishment. "Damn, Linnick! Those four miles would have been like me running for fifty."

"More," she said, but did not elaborate.

"But why? And aren't you exhausted?"

"You ask a lot of questions. Yes, I am exhausted, and I don't quite know why. Instinct, I suppose. I have begun to accept your hideousness and even worse, your company, and thought we would be better off keeping our forces united for the time being. It is a very good thing, too, or else the Polion would have gotten you."

I had to halt her there. "How do you figure that? If you hadn't awakened me I would neither have moved nor thrown up."

"You were snoring loud enough that you would not have gone unnoticed."

"Oh. Well, thank you for that." And I meant it. "But even if we are a good team, which I agree with, by the way, you yourself said your only way out was forward, not back."

"There is more to your value than my eyes can see Tallboat, you are not just an ugly biped with little wit. You destroying the Luvier is proof of that. I suspect my best chance of salvation lies with you."

"Sure do wish I had a tape recorder, ain't nobody anywhere that's ever known me going to believe someone just uttered those words to me."

"You mean about your unsightliness?"

"We need to get a few things straight, I might not be Brad Pitt handsome but I'm not Quasimodo, either." Right after I said that I was thinking on the bone scraping wounds Thorny had given me on my face. "Linnick if you can get past your prejudice of my apparent repulsiveness to you, could you please let me know what the damage that Thorny did to me looks like? He hooved me in the face a couple of times and opened me up like a can of tomato sauce on Prince spaghetti day.

"You have four immensely large scars, nearly as long as I am and are very thick–almost the width of my arm."

I breathed a sigh of relief. In terms of damage it wasn't all that bad; basically, I had some scars about the size of an Amazonian beetle. I had bigger scars from workshop mishaps. Size is as relevant in every world.

"They also have a golden tinge. But only sometimes, when the light hits them a certain way."

"Great, it's going to look like I've gone to a strip club and Goldie the big bosomed blonde shook her sparkles all over me. I'm sure Azile will be okay with that and not put a witchy spell on me."

"Wait Tallboat, Are you talking about Azile, the Red Witch, Azile? How am I just putting this together?"

That kind of took me aback. I mean Azile was a unique name; how many of them could there be running around? "The better question is how do you know her? I'm married to her."

"Oh…now I don't know if it is wise for me to be with you or if I should get as far away as possible." She seemed panicked. "Married, as in a union? Were you coerced, possibly held hostage? Enchanted to do her bidding?"

"Really? Is she that bad?"

"She is not called the Red Witch because of the color of

her cloak. Are you sure you did not come here to get away from her?"

"No, I did not come to hell to get away from my wife. I'm definitely enchanted by her, but not in the bad way."

"How would you know? Wouldn't that be how it worked? I doth think the enchanted doth protest too much."

"You have got to be kidding me. Are you paraphrasing Shakespeare?"

"Never heard of her. You might be safer staying here."

"I'll take my chances going back. The question, my little friend, is why did you come back? And don't try any of that old pal, old buddy crap."

Her whole body sagged, maybe in relief or maybe in defeat, I didn't know which until she started to speak. "There is no way back for me. My path has already been forged. What would I go back to? I have no vessel there to call my own. This is my home now, though I wish it were not so."

I felt defeated for her. My chances of actually getting back were pretty slim but there it was, I still had one. A chance, I mean. Nothing she did would allow her to escape.

"I'm sorry, Linnick," I told her.

"How I chose to live my life is nothing for you to apologize for."

"I'm not apologizing for that; I'm being sympathetic to your plight. If I could, I would help you."

"Who knows, maybe you can. Only archangels can defeat Luvier demons."

"Yes, that's me. Tallboat the Archangel. We've got to get out of here. I've got at least two, maybe three pretty powerful beings actively looking for me, several doing their hunting for them, and everything else that dwells down here is just trying to kill me for fun."

"Not everything, but I see your point. Does this happen a lot?"

"To most people? No. To me, it tends to be the standard operating procedure."

"Tell me more of your version of the Red Witch," she requested after we were back on the road, such as it was.

"I am not enchanted," I stressed.

"We'll see...but I am curious about her through your eyes. She is a mighty and powerful warrior in my world, the shaper of histories."

"Well, she's that where I'm from, too. I met her long ago...damn, she was just a kid then, barely older than my daughter. She had some power back then, though I don't think any of us knew about it except her. She stayed and fought alongside us for a while before leaving on a quest to discover what she was truly capable of. It was about a hundred and fifty years later and we were once again in the midst of a war–she saved *me* this time, sent Tommy to get me out of my, umm, current situation, even if I didn't want to be saved. I'm not sure when it happened. When it went from resentment, to fear, then to love. It was a relatively smooth transition."

"Enchantments are smooth."

"Will you stop it with that?"

"I am looking out for your and my best interests, Tallboat. It could have been her plan all along to get you down here."

"You don't know what you're talking about."

"Perhaps I do. You said she first sent Tommy to save you, is that correct?"

"It is, they stayed in contact the entire time. I decided to wait out the world in my brother's basement. So, what's that mean?" I knew she was firing blanks; I'd be damned if I was going to give her any live ammunition to fire. It had been Azile that said she was in contact with Tommy and again it was Azile who knew a way for me to come down here. But that made no sense; I watched her kill the Green Man. Didn't I? Or had it all been an elaborate ruse? Was this somehow her payment come due for all the magic she used? Was I the silver coins? Kind of fucked up that I'd be the one paying for my own betrayal.

"Anyone who has ever known the Red Witch has paid a

price of some sort for that contact."

"First, I pay plenty and get my share in return. You don't know her like I do." Though I felt my words were feeling a little hollowed out in the middle.

"Is there a chance you do not know her at all?"

I wanted to tell Linnick to shut the fuck up, she was raising wild doubts in me about the woman I loved. Wouldn't be the first woman that screwed me over, but this would be on a whole other set of levels. I honestly wouldn't have anything to compare it to. I've had plenty of women tell me to go to hell, and with good reason, but to actually send me to hell? Holy fuck that's some messed up shit right there. Did I deserve to be here? I sure had my moments of reflection where I accepted this to be my final destination. But a woman I loved, married, had babies with? Could she be capable of this? Save Eliza, Azile had known Tommy the longest and that boy was about to throw me to the wolves. And I had adopted that kid, called him my son, brought him into the family; if he could fool me…

"This can't be happening." I shook my head.

"I do not need to see your eyes to realize that you are doubting your words."

"It's just this place; it's screwing with my perception."

"I have seen males around her just as confounded as you, though by the time they realized their mistakes they'd had their throats cut or intestines spilt to the ground. Where she travels, death follows. And he brings his friends: travesty and destruction."

"Enough Linnick. I cannot take any more. I have to believe in the woman I know, not this creature that you speak of. I can't, I won't believe it until I see it on my own."

"You should open your eyes then and look around."

"I will put you down and walk away if you say one more fucking thing. Do you hear me? I came here. Me. My choice, not hers."

She said nothing, though she nodded. My head was spinning with the potential implications. What kind of web had they spun for me? Was the entire thing from the first cow delivery all a set-up? Had I been the patsy even back then? If so, Tommy and Azile were in it for the long game, knowing full well I never think much beyond what is immediately in front of me. They most certainly could have used that against me. Could Tommy's death have been staged? Like maybe he wanted to die? Now that I look back on it, he didn't give much of a struggle for one so powerful. And then what are the odds that we would find each other in purgatory? There would have to be some heavy magic involved to make that happen. But the Green Man...he had that kind of magic, didn't he?

What about the body preservation thing? How much energy did she expend to do something like that? And for what nefarious reason? I was very much feeling like a puppet that was having every string yanked violently. How did Gabriel work into all of this? It was Tommy that pointed out that baby was special, and sure as shit if that prophecy didn't come to fruition. Now, come to think of it, pretty fucking coincidental that someone with that much power lived down the road from me. Had been placed there, actually. Linnick said I drew the special ones to me. I was no more than a fishing bobber in a turbulent sea, bobbing around like an idiot wherever the storm took me, tantalizing bait for the really big fish.

"No," I said aloud. "I'm twisting facts to make your devil's advocacy sound plausible for whatever self-abusive reason. The Green Man had me; in fact, he has always known pretty much where I am, if that's what he wanted." I'd no sooner said the words when I remembered it was never me he wanted, it was Azile. I was a means to an end. Therein lay the real truth; it all made sense. He was the debt collector and her bill was well past due. She said there was a price to be paid for what she did; did she know I was her comeuppance? Or was she trying to use me as her chip, maybe as a way to get rid of those involved; why wouldn't she just tell me that? I knew who would know. I turned around.

"What are you doing?" Linnick asked.

"I'm going to see the Green Man."

"I thought the idea was to stay as far away from him as possible."

"Yeah, I thought that too, but now that the can of worms has been opened I'm having a hard time shoving them back in. They keep getting cut up on the sharp rim and worm guts are leaking down the outsides and all over my hands. I can hear their little worm-screams as I sever heads and split bodies."

Linnick was looking at me with her mouth open.

"I'm sorry…do you, do you have worm friends? Did I just insult you?"

"I do not have worm friends; I am merely concerned for your state of mind. If you believe that the Red Witch is trying to entrap you, why would you possibly go toward that which she is using as the snare?"

"Because I know nothing, and I can't live with this kind of doubt. That's not the way I work."

"Yes, once you are captured, tortured, and killed you will have proven your case."

"I'm doing what I have to."

"Or what you've been told to do."

"I swear Linnick–you need to give it a rest."

"I am looking out for your well-being; you still have an opportunity to leave this place."

"If what you're saying is true, I have a lesser chance than you. The Red Witch…I mean Azile, my wife, mother of my children, is watching over my body. If she doesn't want me coming back there's no chance I could do so."

"That is a logical statement."

"Yeah, and now that I've said it aloud I feel sick for it. Do you want me to leave you here?"

"Why would I do that?"

"Because even if this is not something my wife has laid out for me I am going to meet the Green Man, and he's a dick."

"Life or death, Tallboat, I stand with you. You may be my redemption, though that is not why I have chosen to stay with you."

"I know, I know, you've fallen in love with me. Not hard to do, I've seen it happen a hundred times before."

"I would rather mate with a Gordand."

"I'm taking it that isn't some sort of god on your world?"

"Worms look down on them."

"Fine, I'm glad you're coming as well," I told her and I meant it. I'd made up my mind to confront Ganlin. If I had any semblance of smarts I would have re-made it and turned the fuck back around. Hopefully, Linnick would survive the encounter and carve out a decent existence in this world.

My mind was running around in circles, simultaneously disproving and validating every argument I had for and against Azile and Tommy. At one point, I was even convinced that my initial rescue of Azile in the semi had all been part of the plan. If that were the case I was so far out of the game I wasn't even sure what we were playing anymore.

As if Linnick had read my earlier thoughts in regard to her, she spoke. "If we can somehow get past the Guardians to the underworld, there are places in that realm that we could live. It would be bleak and we would not have much, but we would exist."

"When you say it like that, maybe I should just turn around. Not sure what our kids would look like or how we'd even...you know, do the deed, but I'm always up for a challenge."

"Please do not be as ugly on the inside as you are on the outside," she said in all seriousness.

"You know, my wee friend, you're starting to give me a complex. Verbal abuse can be more painful than physical."

"Is it wrong to say, if it is the truth?"

"I wonder how much protein your body holds."

"Rude," was her reply, but at least she shut up for a while. She was starting to make me feel like Quasimodo's bastard brother who'd been forced to wear an iron mask because he was deemed "the ugly one."

CHAPTER FIFTEEN
MIKE JOURNAL ENTRY 12

WE STOPPED AT SOME POINT, just because that seemed the normal thing to do. I suppose I could have walked indefinitely, but I still had reservations about my present course of action. I was about to go get my ass beaten to hopefully prove Linnick wrong, although I was still going to get my ass beaten if she was right. There wasn't much of an upside, as far as I could tell. If I thought stopping to think on it would help, I was wrong. With all that walking around a desolate landscape, I had dwelt on it even more, twisting scenarios and reassuring myself with fond memories. My rationale began to solidify to continue onward with my destructive course of action.

"Are you fucking me over, Azile?" It hurt to even say the words. I looked down into my pocket, Linnick was curled up sleeping or at least pretending to. She did not respond to my question. In my heart, I knew Linnick was wrong; if she wasn't, then several of my past lives had been for nothing.

"Hey, fuckface!" I spun my head to the sound of the voice. A monstrous clown was bearing down on me.

"Whoa!" I got up quickly, pretty much in panic mode, putting my hands out in front of me. I'd rather take on a pack of rabid werewolves than have one clown do me a magic trick. And from the looks of this beast, the only thing he wanted to pull out of his hat was my head.

"I know you!" it said, raising an oversized gloved hand and pointing a finger.

"Yeah, I doubt it. I typically avoid your kind."

"What kind is that?" He was still coming quick and I was

backing up.

"Well, I'd like to say assholes, but I tend to attract them more than anything. Clowns, I avoid clowns. You guys are fucked up. That giant red nose and curly red hair coupled with the white face paint and huge red lips and that seizure inducing clothing you tend to wear—just all of it, man. Skeeves me the fuck out wondering what kind of crazy thing is hiding under all that pretend fun. Stephen King wrecked your kind a long time ago; why you didn't have the good graces to just curl up and fucking die I don't know. The world would have been a better place for it, that's for sure."

"You shot me!"

"I don't remember ever seeing you in my life, and, uh, trust me, man, you are one thing that would have been burned indelibly into my mushy mind."

"You were with a big man, colored, I think and no...no it wasn't you, you were a pussy back then, too. It was your wife that shot me."

"Listen, friend. I don't know what you're talking about. Why don't you go find a little car to pile into then drive it off a cliff into a pool of lava or something...please? Honestly, I'd pay to see that."

"Friend? Tim doesn't have any friends!" he roared.

This thing was dangerous. Couldn't tell if it was a demon or a deranged human under all that freaky make-up. Though they were kind of the same thing, weren't they? And those teeth, not many people walking around with pointed ones. Though they looked rough enough they could have been filed. I automatically rubbed my tongue against my own pearly whites thinking about the pain and discomfort that would cause.

"Listen...Tim? Tim, you said?"

"Don't you ever fucking call me Tim-Tim!" I could feel the gale force wind from the yelling of those words.

"I didn't really call you Tim-Tim. I only called you Tim, Tim." Yeah, that wasn't the right thing to say. He started running at me.

"It's always the bitches that kill me!" he was screaming savagely. "Your little bitch redhead first. Then that bitch blonde, and then that bitch brunette!"

"Got a feeling they were justified," I said pulling my axe and getting into a fighting stance. He was just blind rage and muscle, I settled that blade deep into his thigh as I spun and moved to the side. Not far enough, as he bowled me over before he fell.

"You cut my leg!" He rolled over to look at the damage. He seemed completely offended that I would defend myself as he tried to avenge some apparent slight it seemed my wife may have committed. He'd somewhat described BT and Tracy and he said he knew me, but if so, it wasn't from any timeline I was aware of. "You can't cut my leg!" Even injured he was able to get up as fast as I did, which led me to believe he was more than he seemed. I had him pegged as a clown demon. Who knows what powers they possess?

"Let's talk about this." I was stalling. He didn't seem the type that would hug it out. "I don't know you and I'm about ninety-five percent sure my wife didn't shoot you."

He got low, leading with his head, his eyes upturned now, somehow giving him an even more savage look. "It was in the first few days of the zombie attack. Little pecker kid bit me, turned me into one of those things."

"That explains your wonderful disposition." I was circling, not giving him a stationary target, he was turning to match my pace.

"There I was, eating my own business, found an old girlfriend and BLAM! Your asshole wife put a round right in my forehead."

"When you say it like that I can't imagine why she would have done that. Right in that giant melon you call a head? Speaking of which, where do you get a wig big enough to cover that dome? And does that make you feel slightly effeminate wearing one?"

"I ain't no fag!"

"Never said you were and don't give a shit, you freak. Was just wondering what you thought when you wore things that are more traditionally used by the fairer sex."

"You sound like her." He put a hand up to his head as if he were remembering a particularly hurtful memory.

"Who, my wife?"

"Yorley, you fucking twat!" He said it with enough force I thought he was going to renew his attack.

"Listen, Tim, I don't know Yorley, I don't know you. I don't remember ever meeting you. I suggest maybe you go and play out your little psychosis somewhere else."

"Oh, it was you alright. I think you were trying to talk your way out of it last time too. You see, I remember pussies, every one of them, the ones I fuck and the ones I fuck over."

"Your social graces are without equal. So where did all of this go down then?"

"San Francisco. And you know that."

"I've been there once in my life and it was long before I met my wife and I can guarantee you the girl I was with back then didn't shoot you. She was a card-carrying bleeding-heart vegan liberal that hated all things gun. If you were a zombie she would have advocated for your rights and allowed you to eat her before she would have ever harmed you. She was weird like that."

Rather than seem confused I was making him angrier by doubting his version of events.

"First I'm going to snap your back in two, making you paralyzed. Then I'm going to bend you over my knee."

I thought he was going to say something about a spanking now, and that in itself would have been strange, but it was much worse than that.

"Then I'm going to force my arm up to my elbow into your asshole."

"What? What the fuck are you saying right now?"

"He's telling the truth." Linnick was watching the entire

event.

"I figured that, but who does that?"

"Who are you talking to? Doesn't matter. Then when my arm is halfway up your body I'm going to grab a fistful of your intestines and drag them out. If you could feel anything, you'd be screaming for your momma." He got a smile on his face thinking about this sequence of events. "This is where it gets fun."

"Here? Glad you told me, might have missed something." He completely ignored me and continued with his, well, what I hoped was a fantasy. He might have been dancing in a daydream, but he was still aware and wary of me. I did not have an opening from which to strike or I would have–just to chop that fucking nose off his face.

"I'm going to roll you over so you can watch me eat your insides."

"Just so I'm sure we're on the same page, you're going to shove a fist up my asshole, with the express intent of grabbing my shit filled intestines so you can snatch a snack? Is that about right?"

"I'm going to eat all of you, motherfucker!"

"Starting with my shit-filled intestines. Roger that. Wow, man, just wow. What in the fuck happened in that childhood of yours that made you such a twisted individual? Is it the clown outfit? Does that give you the anonymity you need to act out these deviant desires? Got to tell you, buddy, it's usually a little less over the top, though. Most folks that dress up, for like Halloween and shit, just want to have a night off from normal mundane routine constraints. Maybe that one night, they're a sexy nurse or a bad ass wolverine. But, uh, yeah, you've ratcheted that up a few notches, haven't you? I knew a wonderful dog once; her name was Riley. Just a big bundle of love she was. She had this habit; if you got into her face she would lick you. You just had to time it right and pull away or she'd catch your cheek, couple of times she got my lips. Even one bad day I got to taste some tongue, yeah that was a rough week."

"I don't care," he hissed. "Why are you telling me this?"

"Hey! I had to listen to your gross-ass intestine thing, you can hear me out!" Surprisingly this worked. "Anyway, this one morning, I don't know, I was tired as shit, BT and I had found a bottle of vodka and had proceeded to polish the thing off the night before. I was at half speed that next morning, when I went to say hi to the dogs, got my typical sneeze from Henry and…and…"

"Go on, just tell me. You'll feel better for it," Tim urged, almost like he was sympathetic to my plight, but I think it was more so I would hurry this along so he could slurp my innards up. I mean is that possible? Could he create enough vacuum on my…forget it. Not sure why I even wanted to go there.

"I told you I had been drinking, right?"

"Yeah, yeah, man, keep going." He wanted to kill me in the worst way but he also wanted to hear the story. I think if I kept it up I could have made him even crazier if such a thing were possible.

"So, there I am, in her face, just smooshing it up and it happens, lightning quick. That tongue darts out of her mouth so fast, like one of them crazy rainforest frogs snagging an insect, although instead of a bug it's my eyeball. That tongue dragged across the surface of my eyeball before I could so much as blink or pull away, that's how fast it happened. I know you don't know much about me other than mistaken identity and all, but, I have this thing about germs. Can't stand the little fuckers, something I developed when I had kids. I had no idea of the sheer amount of the nasties they could track through the door with them from school."

"Where are you going with this?"

"Shut the fuck up, Tim!" I yelled. "How long you been down here? Couple of hundred years, right? What's your rush? I'm finishing this story. I've never told anyone and now that I've started I feel the need to finish, like a sort of catharsis. Do you know what the word means? I'm not asking like you're stupid, I just want to make sure I'm using it in the right context. I'm going to say by your silence I did alright." Actually, at this point, I think he was kind of stunned into submission. Had a feeling the crazy clown didn't have many people spilling their life story to him. "You're lucky; I mostly remember where I was or I'd have to start over again and you seem mighty impatient like you have a pineapple enema waiting, and not pineapple juice, but like a whole pineapple. Saw it on South Park once; kind of funny that the animated show was the first hint that made me start thinking Lucifer and Jehovah were in cahoots."

"I don't even know why I'm asking; it doesn't seem like you're capable of finishing a thought but wait for it…I'll bite." Then he laughed like he'd said the funniest thing in the world. The truth of it was, that even considering the circumstances, it sort of was. Sure, it was me he wanted to bite, but still.

"You should kill him now," Linnick mumbled softly.

"What's that?" Tim leaned in. "I heard something!" He was looking around.

"So, as I was saying." I looked down sternly at Linnick, though she was having none of it. Tough to be afraid of me when a walking talking nightmare was directly in front of you, and I had to agree with her completely. "It was when Satan was shoving a pineapple up…whose ass was it? Hitler maybe? Saddam Hussein? Can't rightly remember, some dictator's ass. Anyway, I guess it doesn't matter; whoever it was, a pineapple was being shoved up his ass."

"Why do you keep talking about things being shoved up asses? You some sort of queer?"

"Me? I mean I don't really think so…there was that one time at band camp but I think it was more of a misunderstanding."

"I knew it! That's why you're down here!"

"I was kidding, Tim, relax. Pretty sure you have to do something more than love someone of the same sex to be down here. You're proof of that."

He seemed to ponder this.

"I did what I did to survive. I have no regrets," he finally replied.

"I get survival as a top priority but it can't be at the price of everything and anyone around you."

"What the fuck do you know?" I'm the most important person to me!"

"Shit, man! Is there any chance your mother's name was Vivian?"

"Finish up, little man. I'm getting hungry."

"You seriously enjoy eating people?"

"It's an acquired taste, but I think I'd enjoy you even if I didn't like it so much. You talk more than anybody should."

"Been accused of that before. Which one do you want me to finish? The tongue story or my theory on hell?"

Tim motioned with his hand for me to continue; I was going with the assumption he meant both. Normally I'd wrap this up with an axe strike to the head, but just because Tim seemed to be listening to my story didn't mean he wasn't cautious. Dangerous fucks rarely let their guards down, and now that he knew I could hurt him, it was doubly unlikely I'd get a clear shot. And like I said earlier, this guy could give BT a run for his money in the size department. Not to mention that clown suit was really throwing me for a loop. Anyone that deliberately drew attention to themselves in this pit of despair obviously had little to be concerned about. Which, rightfully so, had me extremely concerned. He'd made a mistake, but I had the feeling he wouldn't do so again. And that gouge I had forged into his thigh had completely stopped bleeding; every once in a while, when he moved his leg, I could tell that the wound was somehow stitching itself up. Wasn't entirely sure what he was, but dangerous was part of the equation and I'd feared clowns for too damn long to be done in by one now.

"So, anyway, I think Heaven and Hell are working together as opposed to against each other, as my Catholic teachings would have you believe. I know–it sounds weird, right? But you're sent here if you're not a good person, right? I mean look at you. Heaven throws the gate shut and says fuck off, then you end up here, and I presume get huge barbed objects shoved up your rectum."

"I got nothing shoved up my ass!" Tim was shaking with rage.

"I think someone doth protest too much," I said through the side of my mouth.

"What? What the fuck does that mean!?"

"Nothing, nothing. Just something Shakespeare was quoted as saying. So, if hell was the place you had to go because of your actions and it was in direct contrast to Heaven, shouldn't it be a big party down here? I mean a lot of hooting and hollering, drinking, drugs, heavy metal music...and really good sex–not that super-chaffing circle jerk I passed a few miles back because there is no part of fucking to bleeding raw that appeals to me, am I right, Tim? But no! It's one gigantic torture chamber down here. This is consequence for all the shit you wrought above. It's payback. So, personally, I don't think Lucifer had a real falling out; I think it was a set-up. They have this big fake blow out and God is like, "and don't come back!" and all the time they're winking at each other because they're in the know. Satan comes down here and sets up shop, giving people the punishments they so rightfully deserve, but that a fair and loving God cannot. Make sense? Hmm...not sure I ever thought this out further than that, but that makes God a little duplicitous, doesn't it? Forget it, I'm stopping there. Me and him go way back and I'm hoping he's not done with me. We meet again, I don't want to have to try and explain where I was going with my story."

"I like it just fine down here," Tim said evenly. "I can do whatever I want when I want and there is no society to piss on me when I do."

"I think you're missing the point of this place."

"No, you are. With the right attitude, this place *is* a party. Full of tasty treats and delightful deceits."

"You're a fun one, Tim."

"Don't give me shit, you holier-than-thou fuck. You're down here too so it's not like you were walking on water your damned self–you were wading through the shit just like the rest of us."

"Technically, I chose to come here before my time."

"Uh huh, just like no convict is guilty, right?"

"I mean it, I know it looks bad, but I'm really on a mission from God."

"So now you're Elwood Blues? I was going to have you finish up, kind of a last hurrah thing. I'm not totally unsympathetic to the plight of those here, but man I really just can't stand you. Got to think you were a loner topside, nobody wants to deal with a mouth flapping like yours on a constant basis."

"Got me there."

Tim took a step in. "You're a little too fast. So why is that?" He circled. "I didn't catch your name."

"I wouldn't think you'd want to know the name of someone you wanted to eat."

"Makes it more personal that way. Know what I'm saying?"

"No, I really don't."

"I think you do, Michael." He sneered when he said my name. "That's who you are, isn't it? Michael the douche-bag Talbot. Can't believe a chick that was stupid enough to let you fuck her would be able to shoot me."

"Great, so you know my name. I still don't know what you're talking about. I'm not privy to whatever alternate reality we met on; like I said, I would definitely remember you."

"Have I ever told you that I don't believe in coincidences?"

"We've known each other for ten minutes. I don't think it has had the opportunity to come up."

"Fuck the Green Man and his little hunting party. I've never eaten a vampire before. Do you think your meat ages like wine, or are you going to be all tough and sinewy? I don't really give a shit, it's all delicious to me, just wondering. Come on, we need to get this party started. As much as I'd like to take my time savoring every morsel of you, I can't afford for his minions to stumble across our little dining experience."

He was even more off his rocker than I thought if he assumed I was going to up and quit and let him start gnawing on my forehead.

"Let's do this…Tim-Tim." I said with more than a hint of sinister malice. Might as well have thrown a match on gas-soaked tinder. He pounced, and I mean fast, like there were springs in those big, floppy shoes. A meaty, closed hand struck me flush on my cheek. I felt my jaw and neck jerk violently, one down and the other to the side. I'd been hit by nearly every conceivable weapon, by every conceivable monster, and Tim could have taught them all a thing or two. My jaw felt broken, though with difficulty I could still move it around. I had at least three teeth rolling around inside my mouth like cast dice. I was surprised he'd not added my neck to that list of busted things. A cloud of static had rolled into my skull; it was Linnick that removed it. Surprising what a bite on the nipple can overcome, or start, for that matter.

He'd been in the midst of tossing another haymaker, this one I just about dodged. He caught the tip of my nose with enough force to almost push the thing into my face. I fell back hard enough that I did a complete reverse somersault. Blood was pooling in my mouth and falling out the corners of my lips which I could not shut properly. Tim wasn't the kind to gaze upon his impending victory; he was diving back in even as I fell, and leading with his razor-sharp teeth. I rolled shoulder to the side; he ripped into the material of my jacket not more than a couple of inches from my neck. I could feel his teeth trying to seek purchase in my trapezius muscle, no idea why I know what it's called, it's the one that Spock used for his Vulcan nerve pinch, if that helps, and one I used to practice on my kids when we were playing. Ended up being more ticklish than deadly, at least, in that context. Right now, it hurt more than I could express. Especially since my jaw wouldn't allow me to scream.

I threw left after left into the side of his head and face. My right hand was pinned and I couldn't get the weapon into him. The first half dozen didn't even faze him, like I was hitting him with a puffy pillow, but I kept at it and it's not like I'm not without my own power. He started to rock, blood was free flowing from my knuckles but more importantly, from his head as well. He seemed confused that I still had fight in me and even more so that I was inflicting damage. With my last punch, he rolled away before it had a chance to land, unwilling to take another strike. He stood quickly, wobbled, then righted himself.

"I'm gonna pop your head like a fucking pimple!"

"Like I haven't heard that before," I mumbled. I was also standing; my shoulder was on fire from the pain. I couldn't check to see if he'd broken skin–even if he hadn't, he'd compressed the muscle down to a quarter of its width and it was protesting that fact right at this very moment.

"I'm going to lift you by that dome of yours and just squeeze it until my hands touch!" He mimicked the movement; it looked impressive. His muscles rippled, I could see them even through the loose-fitting material of his outfit.

"You and Durgan get your 'roids at the same discount store? Hemmie's Roid Emporium." It hurt to talk, but it didn't stop me. I'm smart like that; still have to get my digs in. Yeah, I was stalling. My right arm wasn't working up to its normal capacity, and I was going to need it at some point. Tim-Tim moved in quick; I swung with my right–looked like I'd gone up to bat and tried to switch hit, having never done so before. If you are not practiced at "switch-hitting," as it is called, you can look fairly spastic going through the mechanics. You can go through roughly the same motions, but the odds you're going to hit something with any degree of effectiveness are pretty slim. It was enough to make him jump back, I got a fraction of a second where he was afraid, then he must have seen just how wildly I missed.

"Shoulder a little fucked up?" he grinned.

"Come on over and check it out." I must have said it with enough malevolence that he was rethinking his charge ahead strategy. Even if it sounded like I had marbles in my mouth.

"I think you're bluffing." He never gave me a chance to respond as he came in again. With his left, he was able to deflect the majority of my hit; the blade turned sideways and I broadsided him in the head with the flat of the blade. Rung his bell pretty good. Not a death-dealing hit, by any stretch of the imagination, though. His huge hands wrapped around my head and I suddenly found myself levitating six inches off the ground, suspended only by my neck. I immediately wrapped my left hand around his forearm in an effort to relieve some of the upward pressure he was exerting on my spinal column. Wasn't making the damage in my shoulder any better. The pain so excruciating my first inclination was to let go of the axe and use my right arm to keep my weight out of his hands. I had enough foresight to realize how short-sighted that was. How long could I keep that up? Eventually he would just shake me around like a rag doll until he snapped my neck, and if I didn't die right away, I would have the distinct pleasure of hearing him dine on me. Something I didn't think I could stomach.

With all I had left of my flagging reserves I brought the axe high over my head and brought it in close, hitting his left forearm in the middle. I hit him hard and true; his howl of pain was immediate as I snapped both bones and almost cut completely through. He dropped me like a hot potato and I fell away. He was screaming bloody murder as he danced around, reminded me of when you smash your thumb with a hammer on a particularly cold day.

"You can't hurt me!" Seemed to be the gist of it. Blood was spraying all around as he shook it back and forth. If I wasn't so frightened for my life, I would have been completely grossed out by his nearly disconnected hand flapping around like an elephant ear, as it tried to cool its host on a hot summer day on the savannah. "I'm going to fuck you up, asshole."

You've got to be kidding me? I thought as he came at me again. I was scrabbling on the ground, trying to get my feet under me to get back up. Just as I did, he struck out with the said damaged hand. Those two severed bones hit me in the cheek, ripping through the meat on my face and once again spinning me to the ground. The victory I'd achieved was rather short-lived. What normal fuck still tries to attack when they get their hand chopped off? I kept wondering why everyone was trying to bust up my face–I could not help but wonder if they had talked to Linnick. Maybe it was blood loss or the realization that he was forever going to be called Rightie the Clown, but after he punched me he took a second to look at his severe wound. He even propped it up, like he'd poured a healthy dose of super glue and was now waiting for it to set the arm back in place. This, at least, gave me enough time to stand.

"You're dead, Talbot!"

I had all sorts of witty comebacks. My personal favorite was "if I had a nickel for every time someone said that to me I could put a down payment on a house, or retire in the Bahamas, maybe build my own amusement park, fuck maybe even pay the bondsman to get your mama out of prison." I didn't have it in me to say it aloud, though. This thing before me was pure savagery. If he'd ever been a man, as he claimed; he no longer could be, could he? This was something possessed. I wanted to bury that axe into his head, repeatedly, I just didn't want to get close enough to do it. His look alone could have murdered everyone that I'd ever known, if looks could...do that. Still, he held that hand up and it finally dawned on me what he was doing. Much like with the thigh injury, he did have some kind of super glue. He was somehow healing himself. I was fighting a hydra monster with a big rubber nose.

"Just a second longer." Either he mumbled it or I was thinking it–I was out on an island with this one. I've fought more vile creatures than I can imagine but this one might have them all topped. He wasn't the biggest or strongest, but there was something so disconcerting about fighting what should have been more human than monster, not to mention validating every childhood fear, and it was fucking me up in the head. I could not let him have that hand back to start the fight anew. I went after it with a single-minded determinedness; probably why I never saw him let go with his right and drive a fist into the side of my skull. I toppled stiffly to the ground like a hewn oak tree. My eyes closed before my head touched down, my mind screamed "tiiimmmber!." Surprisingly enough, it was the sudden pain from making contact with the ground that woke my ass back up. My motto is to fight concussions with concussions; it's always better to pile them on. Just ask any neurologist.

"Get up, Tallboat! It's coming!"

I've seen professional fighters pretty much get their bell not only rung but cracked through like the Liberty Bell and somehow muscle memory kicks in and gets them up off the mat, even though they are pretty much dead on their feet. Yeah, that was me right then. Turns out my stumbling around may have saved my life. Tim had sent another fist-sized locomotive to travel down the tunnel of my throat–as luck would have it my left leg buckled and I dipped to that side. His fist mostly grazed the side of my cheek, but since the nerve endings were exposed, the brilliant electric shock of the pain was enough to burn the low-lying fog out of my head before he could follow up. How the hell I was still holding onto my axe is a mystery; there were probably so many things wrong with me I no longer had the ability to tell my hand to unclench– that seemed the most logical explanation.

I swung out to my side and kept turning with the momentum until I lodged that blade into the small of Tim's back. There was a satisfying crunch and a sickening snap as I did some major spinal damage. He yelled out something about making my mother his bitch as his legs caved in. One moment they were supporting the monster and the next they just no longer worked. Much like the Silver Bridge of Mothman fame, I had severed the connection. I wrenched the blade free and walked a few steps away. I was winded and wounded and a little bit terrified. He was face down in the dirt but that stupid polka dot material was still rising and falling with his breaths.

"Just fucking die," I said with my hands on my knees. I was hunched over but keeping a constant vigil on Tim. I wasn't going to be like those horror movies in the seventies where the hero/heroine always turns away from the psycho killer after they confidently delivered the killing blow only to discover the twisted maniac was playing possum. I mean really, how many times has that been done? I was going to guarantee it didn't happen here. And damned if his legs didn't start to twitch like something inside of him was rebuilding the connections. I could picture little workers throwing repair cables across the span of the downed bridge.

"What kind of demon are you, Tim?" I asked softly as I crept up closer.

He turned his head, a wicked smile was the first thing I noticed. "I'm not one of those scum. I came down here with nothing! Nothing! They thought they were going to make me pay for my sins! Isn't that rich?" He laughed until he coughed, very unsettling. "For fifty years they did things to me that only I should be allowed to do to others! Then I got a chance, my chance. I tore Kalder's wings off–well chewed through one, ripped the other clean off. A funny thing happens when you take a demon's wings; they don't lose all their power, but they lose enough–yeah, just enough. I put him in the same restraints he'd kept me in all that time. Then I carved him up...piece by piece. I can't say I'm overly fond of demon meat, but each bite of him was a savory-sweet victory. It took me a year to eat him. Want to know what the beauty of it was?"

"No. No, I really don't."

"Gonna tell you anyway. He was alive for most of it. Of course, those last three months he was in and out, might even say clinically insane, but yeah, he was alive. Those demons are some mighty tough fucks. I choked him down and made him watch. One of the most satisfying things I've ever done. But even that is going to pale in comparison to what I have planned for you."

This, boys and girls, should have been the time for me to go screaming into the night like a wild banshee. Not figuratively, but quite literally. I did a quick ball check, guys know what I mean, and I moved in. I brought that axe down into him so many times that if someone stumbled onto the scene they would have a difficult time telling where I stopped and Tim began. Dog food companies would have rejected the substance I made of that fucking clown.

"Fix that, Blowzo," I said. As I stood up, heavy chunks of viscera fell from my lap and chest. Blood sluiced off of me in great runny runnels, pooling in puddles that even the ground would not accept. "You alright, Linnick?"

"What was that?" she asked. Not sure if she meant Tim himself or the frenetic beat down I'd just pulled on him.

I shrugged my shoulders; more slop fell from me. "I sure would like to get cleaned up." I was just about carrying an extra person's body weight on me. I wiped my face, but when your sleeve is just as gross as the rest of you, it's difficult to make any headway. I waited for my heart to slow to a more normal pace; the cranked-up adrenaline finally sputtered and quit and my arms were leaden when I started to walk away.

Linnick had crawled from my pocket and up my shirt to sit perched on my shoulder like a pirate parrot. "Tallboat…" she said softly. "Tallboat, you should turn around."

"I'd rather not."

"I think you should."

I had a good idea what I was going to see. I'd already foreshadowed it by talking about all those campy horror movies. I'd turn and Tim, in all his comic ugliness, would be standing there, polkadot pajamas, red wig, red nose, and white makeup–good as new. The oversized red lips would be pulled back in a huge, frenzied sneer when he came at me with a chainsaw. I mean, that's how these things go, right?

I turned. Sure as shit, Tim was lunging towards me. He had a scimitar the size of the Reaper's. The edge looked sharp enough, so odds were I wouldn't feel too much; naturally I'd have a couple of uncomfortable seconds where I looked up at my body as my head rolled around on the ground. Eventually, my body would fall alongside my head and my brain would stop functioning. Those last few seconds, though, they were going to be a drag. Do you think all those things we heard about the guillotine were true? Is that why they held the head up? Icing on the execution cake? Would you have enough faculties to actually realize you were looking at your own body? You would. Terror is all in your head, along with your eyeball function. What a fucked-up thing. Pretty sure they already made their point by separating your most vital piece of equipment from the machinery, but then to go and rub habanero-infused salt into the wound? Well, that's just taking being a dick to a whole new level.

But it wasn't Tim getting ready to off my head, not saying that would have been a more welcome sight, but it sure would have been a lot less weird. His parts were starting to meld together, not like the liquid metal Terminator, where it pooled together and reformed–nope nothing that normal-ish. All his scattered pieces had sprouted insectoid legs and were scurrying to get to where the other pieces were, and it was in a completely hectic fashion. There was no order to it. The best way I can explain it is they seemed to just run around crazily until by sheer chance they hit another part, and then when that happened they fused with a hollow, drawn out popping sound and as the parts got bigger those damn legs got bigger. Inch worms were becoming caterpillars then becoming millipedes, and then there was a damned weasel-sized centipede. I was beginning to look for an exit sign from this fucking circus side show when Linnick spoke.

"You can't leave him like this."

For a mistaken second, I thought she wanted me to help him. Then she got specific, and it was worse.

"The head. You have to take the head."

As of yet, the caved-in skull had not sprouted any legs. It was still canted on its side, one eye closed, the other lying about a foot away, still attached by a thick, wet rope of optic nerve. It was right this very second, I thought maybe I was back in my own world and I had finally slipped over into the uncharted waters of true insanity as that loose eyeball began to track me. It was watching me. I'm as sure of that as I was of Azile's undying love. Wait…scratch that one for now; I'll revisit it later.

"No fucking way, Linnick. First off, the thing must weight thirty pounds and secondly…just fucking ewww." I'm glad none of my manly friends could see me saying "ewww" to a tiny female buglet giving advice from my front pocket.

"He'll be back together in an hour; less if you don't grab that thing."

"We can get a good jump on him in that time." I could hear the little legs clacking along as they did their hideously disgusting job.

"He'll come for you; he'll never stop."

"Have you seen *The Terminator*, too?"

"Tallboat! You cannot let him re-form."

"Sure I could." But of course, I wasn't going to let him, I was moving forward, just at my own pace. I halted my progress almost immediately when I saw something move down my leg, Then off my boot and down my jacket. The pieces of him that were stuck to me were moving to join the fray, either by their new locomotion system or just by liquefying and rolling off me like I was made of Teflon. On one side of the spectrum, it was pretty cool that I was getting cleaned up, but the other side…well it was kind of freaking me out a bit, like a meth head who believes there are bugs crawling all over and under their skin, freaking out. Only this was true and I didn't even have the benefit of being high out of my mind. I was not opposed to stripping naked, pouring gasoline on myself, and doing a little spring cleaning.

"What is going on here!?" I pleaded, though no one was listening.

"The head. Take. The. Head," she repeated through tight lips, like a broken record stuck skipping on a song I can't stand. Something was poking inside Tim's cheek and finally broke through–it was a leg, nearly the width of a finger; another sprouted from his mouth, then the vacated eye socket. Like his damn noggin knew what I was going to do to it and was going to make a run for it. Five more legs popped out, some at impossible angles to be able to do anything but flail. When it started dragging that trailing eyeball around I was sick–yeah, I've seen a lot, but a spider clown head was more than I could stomach. Once I finished getting rid of the little bile rising in my throat, I was going for Tim's head. I used to think I had a cast-iron stomach back in my Corps days, with the amount of alcohol I could drink and not get sick. Some things do change. Unlike all the other little pieces of him, his head had the power of sight and was actively, err, headed, for its stumbling parts so I couldn't mess with it. On one side, it wasn't all that fast or agile, like all the legs really weren't on the same page kind of thing; on the other it was a damn shame because I caught it relatively quickly. And by "caught" I mean I squashed the optic nerve under my heel to halt its regrouping effort.

The legs started stabbing at my boot, thankfully ineffectually; finally, something funny about a clown. There was no way I was taking this horrendous thing with me. I couldn't do it. I could, however, make it extremely difficult for it to find me when it became whole again. I reached down and in one deft movement, freed the eyeball from its constraint. The other one swiveled up at me in panic. The legs started scurrying when they realized exactly what I was doing, though they could not free themselves.

"This just sucks," was all I could manage to say as I brought the flat of my blade down on the top of Tim's skull. The crunching of skull plate is a uniquely disgusting sound and unfortunately, I'd heard it more than anyone should have to. It took five good whacks until his right eye finally popped free, though I could not stop myself until the tenth or eleventh. If Tim was to recover from this, I wanted to make sure it took as long as possible. I cut that eye free, grabbed the spongy red nose and scooped both orbs up into it. Almost stuck it all in my pocket when I realized that there was no reason to think that these things wouldn't grow their own legs and then they'd be scuttling around in my pants. Yeah, that wasn't going to happen. While I had been busy working up the nerve to hinder Tim, his body had been gaining steam in the regeneration department. He had a couple of pieces that were as large as rabbits stumping around now. It wouldn't be long until he was performing his routine again.

I stomped on one of the larger pieces, a forearm or maybe a calf, I don't know, I just wanted the material covering it. I cut the pajama-like silk free as the body part struggled against me. I made a hobo bindle and stuck my prizes inside it. I was wishing I had a long stick so I could carry it over my shoulder. I cinched it tight and then tied it to a belt loop. It was now going to be important for me to forget what was in there so I could focus on getting out of here.

"We should go," I told Linnick as I surveyed the general area, recovering my wits. A horror writer with a sick, twisted imagination who had been off his meds far too long could not have come up with a more disturbing scene. I mean, I suppose he or she could, *but why?* I don't know how I was ever going to forget watching all those Tim parts running around. Booze—and lots of it.

"We should go," Linnick echoed from the bottom of my pocket. She'd also seen enough, so it would seem.

I was sort of in a fugue state, so I'm not sure how far I'd

walked or how much time had transpired, but when Tim let go a full-throated scream that he would find me, that shook the cobwebs free and I picked up the pace. The clown bag was thumping against my leg, I did my best to pretend it was the movement of my walking that caused it to do that; the illusion quickly dissipated, though, when I stopped to get my bearings and it still kept struggling. The next best thing I could come up with was Mexican jumping beans; that was the band-aid I chose to slap over the gash in my mind. Worked pretty good, too.

CHAPTER SIXTEEN
MIKE JOURNAL ENTRY 13

"DO YOU THINK IT WISE to stop?" Linnick asked. Just as I was sliding down what could be considered a tree, though I doubt anything this warped and stunted would ever have a chance to live in my world.

"I'm just kind of at a loss. I'm a little worn out, both mentally and spiritually. Physically, I'm pretty good, but I'm in the midst of a serious head-fuck and I need to sweep around the edges in there."

"Not only are we in hostile territory, but we are being actively pursued on many fronts."

"Linnick–yeah, I know, but my son tried to double cross me and my wife might be in on it. I don't know much about your world but that shit is most definitely not normal where I'm from. It happens, but it's more likely one of those things you see in a movie and you're like "how fucked up is that?" Then drink your coke and eat some popcorn, not dwelling on it too much because it doesn't apply to real life. But when it happens to you, when those closest to you–the ones you'd trust with your life–are the ones trying to stab you in the back? It kind of makes everything else look trivial. Oh, Oggie, I miss you. He'd never try to screw me over."

"Did your father ever bring you to an auction site and sell you off to the highest bidder?"

I halted my personal pity party to look at Linnick. "I am so sorry…I had no idea. No wonder you turned out the way you did."

"What does that mean?" she asked, definitely taking offense.

"I…I'm just saying that might be why you're here, though that doesn't seem fair…how could one that had evil perpetrated against them be held accountable when they, in turn, did evil acts? One of them perpetual motion machines type of thing, I guess."

"You should stop talking."

"Hurts too much to think about?" I asked. I was concerned for her.

"No, because it didn't happen to me."

I got a stunned expression. "Then why would you say something like that?"

"I've…seen it done, and I did nothing."

"Are you feeling guilty? You can't be responsible for fixing every travesty. Especially given your size."

"I now see why those that love you might be tempted to travel down darker paths."

"Ouch, Linnick. Little low with that punch."

"I was attempting to distract your mind by telling you there are worse fates."

"Yeah, the old 'stab me so I'll forget the bullet wound' routine. That doesn't usually work so good; you just end up with two holes. I honestly don't know what to think. I mean, she begged me not to come, but she absolutely knew I would, so that doesn't hold much weight."

"What does your heart tell you?"

"That there is no way this could be happening. That I'm either missing huge pieces of this butt-fucked picture or I'm making too much out of it. But since I am now trapped in an underworld I don't belong to, I think I'm allowed a little over-reaction."

"You will want to get over it soon."

"Are you channeling my first wife now?"

"Maybe if you didn't have more than one mate you wouldn't be in trouble."

"No wiser words ever spoken."

"When will you be ready to continue?"

"If I get up and start walking, will you shut up?"

"That's a distinct possibility if we are moving, yes."

Little shit was sleeping less than ten minutes after I started walking; I think she just wanted the rocking motion I produced. "Glad to see one of us is enjoying themselves. Sweet dreams." I told her. "You wouldn't fuck me over, right?" I was looking down at her. The part of me, the trusting part, thought *no fucking way. We were in this together, through thick and thin,* but when I peeled down a little deeper than the superficial emotional layer that I had fabricated to protect myself with, I was left with a completely alien being whom I'd only known for a few short days, and she says she can't get out; is that because she belongs here? If a boy I'd known for two hundred years could try to shove a knife in my back, why couldn't she? What's in this horror trek for her? I didn't want to be a Deneaux and distrust everyone, equally; what kind of life had that been for her?

Speaking of the old bag, I was wondering when I'd run into her. Has to happen eventually, doesn't it? I guess I should count my blessing that she wasn't with Durgan's little party. Wouldn't that have been fun? Probably would have liquefied my eyes right there and then and my damned glass belly would have just shattered. The only good thing about her was you always knew where you stood; there was no two-faced treachery. She was always going to do what was best for her, screw whoever stood in the way. You can always count on a liar to lie, so you can trust them, in a twisted, but dependable, way. What happened to her was necessary, though I find myself thinking about her more than I should. She was a necessary adversary, if that makes sense. As long as your goals aligned with hers, there was no one better to help you achieve that end. "I wonder if she's a bounty hunter down here?" That was enough for me to do a quick scan of the area. No Deneaux, no Tim-Tim, and near as I could tell, no nothing. I looked down; Linnick was still out. Now was as good a time as any to sit. I found myself exceedingly tired and a little depressed, truth be told.

"Tallboat! It is time to arise!"

"Why?" I half opened one eye.

"To keep moving."

"There's no purpose to it, no reason to continue on."

She said nothing as she climbed out of my pocket and onto my shoulder so she could get a higher vantage point; I hoped she wouldn't bite my ear. "How could you?" she asked, turning.

"I don't know what you're talking about and could you get out of my face?"

"You wandered into the pit of despair."

"Seems like I've been circling the rim since the moment I adopted Tommy."

"We have got to get out of here before it gets worse!"

"Before what gets worse? My life? Huh! How could that get any worse? My family wants me dead! I'm surrounded by creatures that want to torture me or use me for some other nefarious purposes. I miss my dog. I'm, I'm tired, Linnick. I'm just going to stay here. I'm better off."

"You don't know what you're saying. It's this place! It drains serotonin from the body; if it pulls it all from you, you will never recover!"

"Leave me alone, Linnick. I don't care. I'm done. I've been done for decades; I was just too stupid to realize it. I should have thrown myself into a volcano the moment my wife died instead of holding on...holding on for what? Was I that thick to think that others wouldn't try to use me?"

"I am not a fan of this version of Tallboat! Where is the one that is all mouth and bravado?"

"That dipshit? He just had a rude awakening and realized he knew absolutely nothing, was absolutely nothing." I rolled over so that Linnick had to jump off or get trapped under me. Sleep...that was all that mattered. It was the only thing that would offer any type of escape from the feelings of hopelessness and desolation coursing through my body. At

---

least one would have hoped so. My dream started off good enough. There, in a fancy gold frame was a wide, beautiful portrait of everyone I had ever loved…a big, loving bunch of family members and good friends I considered family. I felt a surge in my heart at the sight of them, smiling, standing shoulder to shoulder…and *somehow*, I knew what was going to happen next. I felt choked up, something wasn't right; one by one they were overlaid with a black cross, signifying their deaths. I knew the cause with each new cross. Most met with violent ends; others simply wasted away against the worst enemy of all…time. In the end, they were all claimed. I was looking at a field of black crosses; my perspective drew back. In my nightmare, I was on my knees, sobbing into my hands. The burden was too much for anyone to carry.

At some point, I was awake–I guess nothing mattered to me, not my head scraping across the strange surface, not the tingle in my feet, not the constant chattering of Linnick in my ear. I wanted nothing to do with any of it. If I'd had a knife I would have jabbed it through my temple repeatedly until the signal was lost and I could no longer move my arm. What was left of me would leak out onto the ground. I should have dragged my axe blade across my neck but I couldn't even be bothered to move. I was no stranger to depression–I'd suffered through a few bouts during my time walking the planet, but this was orders of magnitude above and beyond anything I'd ever experienced. I was so utterly devoid of life, I could not even contemplate that a different state of mind actually existed. Who I was, who I'd ever been, who I could ever be was shrouded over by a curtain made from cold, indifferent steel.

I knew just how fucked I was when even sex held no appeal. Not that there was anything here enticing me, just that I wasn't even thinking about it. Thoughts of love making ceased to cross my mind and, as a mostly normal male, that's just never the case. Sure, usually I could chew gum and read a book and maybe not think about it for a while, but well, it sure wasn't ever too far from the forefront of my mind. Right now, though? It was absent to the point that it never existed. This was the point I should have thought, "Hey. Maybe I should give a shit." I didn't. I think my face was hurting; still didn't make me turn it or try to lift it up. There was no will, no desire. I had never been so empty, even when I was dead. How can you have less than nothing?

I fell asleep again, not that I cared. The blackness behind my eyes was not disturbed with any imagery from my mind, and that was what it was. I did not care one way or the other. When I awoke I was looking at Linnick standing up on Bill's head; their backs were to me. Bill did not rotate his body; his facial features sort of swam through the goop he was made up of so that without ever turning around, he was now looking at me. I realized this held some interest to me and it prickled–the way your skin feels after brushing through nettles. Linnick turned when she realized I had moved.

"Bill?" I sat up and immediately pitched over as if my head was a bowling ball. "What the fuck?" I asked, propping my hands in an effort to get into a perpendicular position.

"You should stay down," Linnick said, "at least for another day."

"How long?"

Linnick said nothing.

"How long, Linnick?"

"You were in the pit for nearly two months."

"What?" I sat up and was met with the exact same results, like my head was tied to an anvil with a bungee. I love when I validate the insanity argument. You know the one, doing the same thing over and over and expecting different results; I was constantly testing that hypothesis.

Bill's eyes shifted up so Linnick was almost standing on them. They knew something I didn't.

"Spill it." I wisely stayed down this time.

"You were asleep for nearly another one."

"Another what? Day?"

"Month," Linnick managed to say.

I shut my eyes. For three months, I'd been trapped in a hell of my own making; no one can punish you more effectively than you can.

"It will be months, possibly, before you have restored the chemicals in your brain to their appropriate levels."

"How did I get out?"

"When I realized that I could not do it alone, I sought out Bill."

"You never cease to amaze me, Linnick. In the most dangerous of worlds you let nothing hold you back." I told her. The insides of my head were such a mess I actually cried. Couldn't help myself. Linnick might have thought it a normal human response. Bill somehow knew better and rotated his eyes away, though, disconcertingly, left his mouth where it had been. Just to complete the damn Picasso, he'd spun his nose half way.

"You could just say thank you." She was looking at me, trying to peer through my haze of tears.

"I am." I blubbered. Great, here I was, big bad Marine vamp, slayer of all things supernatural, and I could not shut off the water works. I don't know if it was better or worse that those that were witnessing my meltdown were not human. I've had moments throughout my history where I felt on the verge of losing control, where I was barely holding on. But right this very second, I was certain I was in the midst of a breakdown. I could no sooner tell myself what to do than I could teach a pack of rabid hyenas to fetch.

"Is the salty water leaking from your eyes normal?" Linnick asked. "It somehow makes you even uglier, if such a thing were possible."

She'd not intended it, but that cheered me up some. "Humans crying is normal enough. Most times men, for some reason I've yet to figure out, don't cry in public and definitely not me, but…" I started choking up again. "Oh, this is going to get old soon," I said when I could.

"Food," Bill got out. He formed that appendage thing and pointed. I couldn't really see through the curtain of tears I had going on. I wiped furiously at my eyes willing them to dry the fuck up. When I got it down to a pinhole leak I still couldn't see anything.

Didn't really need to see it, though, I had some Spidey sense tingling in me. Tommy was on the hunt and actively pinging for signals. In the best of times, I would be hard pressed to block him out and yeah, I was not at the best of times.

"We have to move." I could sit up, I wobbled like my head was still too heavy for my puny neck, but at least it wasn't anchored to the ground.

CHAPTER SEVENTEEN
AZILE

"MATHIEU, IT HAS BEEN OVER a month. We cannot stay here indefinitely."

Mathieu looked upon Lana, he knew they could not linger forever. Denarth was in one of its happiest times, but it was not without problems; their leader could not be absent for long stretches. He was torn. His best friend lay inside, cold and lifeless. He would die many times over to help him, yet it was not within his power to do so. He could be no more than an observer in this conflict. It was difficult. He and Lana both helped with the twins while Azile performed rituals over Michael almost constantly.

"He would not want us to sit here on our hands while he was gone," Lana said.

"In this you are right, woman. Michael was never…is not one for inaction. I will talk to Azile."

"About what?" Azile had come out onto the porch.

Mathieu stammered.

"We cannot stay much longer," Lana spoke up. "I have Denarth to look after."

Azile was close to letting, "You would not have Denarth to look after if not for that man lying in there" slip out, but she bit it back. Instead she said, "I understand." She knew it was selfish to ask them to stay longer. Their help with the children had been invaluable. She was not sure if she could watch them and watch over her husband at the same time.

"We could take Gabriel and the babies," Mathieu spoke up and then looked at his wife to see if he'd said something out of place.

Lana's face lit up. "That would be perfect! We could get back home and you would have the time you need!" She lightly clapped her hands.

"I cannot ask that of you."

"You didn't ask it of us; we offered. We love Michael; you know that we would do anything for him. Let us watch your children, Azile, that is the help we can offer," Mathieu said.

"You are indeed good friends. Michael certainly has the fortune to surround himself with those that remain true and loyal to him."

"The actions of his heart demand it. I would like to say that he befriended me because of those same qualities, but I think it was mainly the beer," he smiled.

"How will you watch over Michael and yourself if we are no longer here?" Lana asked.

"I will send Sebastian back to tend to us."

Mathieu seemed dubious but said nothing.

"And you do not need Gabriel?" Lana prodded.

"There are other ways. Obviously, it is easier with one that can naturally open a doorway, but yes it can be done."

Within the hour, Azile had bundled the children up with their belongings and was kissing them goodbye. "I will miss you both so much." She hugged them tightly and placed them gently in the small wagon.

"Send word when he comes back," Mathieu said.

Concern grew in Azile's belly as she watched Gabriel depart. The boy was the key and that she could no longer draw on his power to pull them back sat uneasily with her. Still, she waved.

IT HAD BEEN OVER TWO months since they'd left, and

more importantly, since she'd last seen her children. She was rapidly losing hope that Michael would travel this realm with her again. He'd been gone three months on a fool's errand; she hadn't heard from him since those first few days, when he had gone in axe swinging. She had no idea where he was or what type of situation he was in. She received a partial answer not more than two days later.

"Azile! Remember me!?" The house shook on its very foundation.

Azile stood and looked around. The voice was coming from no single place, but seemingly from everywhere. "Ganlin?" she said softly.

"We have some issues to settle, you and I! I don't take kindly to my neck being singed. I have been biding my time, wandering through other realms, gathering strength and waiting for my opportunity."

She figured this would be the part where he wanted to barter Michael's very life and soul for her own.

"You should come out from behind your barricades. I know you are close!" Azile waited a few more seconds before she started to laugh. "You don't have him," she said merrily. "You can't get him and you're getting frustrated, isn't that it? That's why you're here trying to get me to show myself. You are attempting to rattle me. It won't work."

"I will rip him to shreds! There will be nothing left of him once I am through! Mark my words I will–"

"Please. If you could have, you would have. You're as pathetic down there as you are up here. Go run back to your little demon handlers and ask them to kiss your boo-boos. Perhaps if you are lucky, Michael will not seek you out to repay you for the kindnesses you bestowed upon him while he was your guest." The Green Man's presence had faded back into another realm.

"He is fine," she said to herself, holding on to the first glimmer of real hope she'd had in quite a long time. "Come back to me soon." She picked up his hands and pressed them against her face. She'd fallen asleep with her head on his chest like she had on so many previous nights. She started awake when she heard another voice. This one much closer.

"Tommy? Is that you?" He sounded faint, urgent.

"Not much time," he said. "Do you know where Mike is?"

"Don't you?" Anxiousness rushed up inside of her. "And why are you calling him Mike and not Mr. T?"

"We were separated." Tommy did not answer her question; in fact, avoided it.

"Is he alright?"

"It would be better if we were together," Tommy said.

A fat finger of doubt was riding alongside her anxiety. She found it strange that she had heard nothing from anybody in months; now, on the same day, she heard from Ganlin then Tommy. Could they somehow share an agenda? That was preposterous, wasn't it?

"I know that you have given him aid, Azile. It is imperative that you lead him back to me."

"That sounds more like a demand than a request, Tommy."

"I need him!" Tommy yelled.

"For what reason? Are you working in concert with Ganlin?"

There was a pause.

"No…that's not it," Azile said slowly. "But you promised him Michael, didn't you, Tomas? Give him my husband and you get your precious, twisted little sister? Was that the deal? He is…we are your family, you ungrateful little bastard! I wish your father would have smashed your head against that hearthstone hard enough to spill your diseased mind all over that dirt floor. Go fuck yourself, Tomas. You will burn for all eternity down there before I would ever give him up!" She severed the link and spent a few moments clearing her throat of the sobs that caught there and clearing her mind of the encounter she just had.

"I'm coming Michael, and hell hath no fury like…well like me, I suppose."

CHAPTER EIGHTEEN
MIKE JOURNAL ENTRY 14

EACH STEP I TOOK HELPED to dissolve whatever was going on in my fried head. I could almost have a complete thought without careening off into a variety of directions or crying. You cannot sympathize with one with mental illness until you think a thought in their mind. It's like, if someone tells you they have sciatica, you look at them with concern and you sympathize and then you tell them to hurry up because they're lagging behind on your walk. Then the day comes where you get the mind blistering pain that starts in your lower back and travels down one or both legs only it's impossible to touch or pinpoint. It's like someone shoved a screwdriver, hilt deep into the small of your back and slowly twists it back and forth, all day, every day, even more so at night so that you can do nothing except think about the intense discomfort you are in. We can empathize to a point, we can have true concern and care deeply for something afflicting another, but until we experience it firsthand, we cannot *feel* it.

For all those that had mental issues and my rote answer was "buck up," I am truly sorry. There is no manner of physical pain that I would not endure repeatedly, rather than suffer through the quagmire that is an ill-firing set of synapses. That thought no sooner pervaded my mind and I started to cry again. Funny enough, the Marine part of me told me to "buck the fuck up." Fuck, I'm an asshole–even to myself. We're hardest on those we love. I got a grim smile of satisfaction for that thought. I'd mostly been walking with my head down, following Bill, so when he said "Food" from behind me, it was a little bit of a surprise.

"He says Tomas is gaining ground on us," Linnick interpreted.

"You got all of that from 'food'?" I asked. When I turned to look I still couldn't see a thing on the horizon. "Is it worth picking up the pace or do we stand and fight? It seems that Bill can have his way with him."

"Fooood." Bill drew out his answer.

Linnick took a second, I guess tabulating her answer before she replied. "Bill says he surprised the boy the first time and it would be unlikely that he would be able to do so again. They had a deal already worked out between them. Tomas would not have expected Bill to react like that."

"So, you were working with Tomas? What changed your mind?" I asked. Bill's features rotated away from me, apparently, he was not in the mood for answering questions. "I guess in the end it doesn't matter; that we are together now is what counts. I mean unless, of course, you struck up a different deal with someone else."

"Food." Bill was allaying my fears, I hoped.

"He says you have the mark upon you; it is subtle and could be easily overlooked, but it is indeed there."

"What mark? Like a scarlet letter? Am I considered a harlot?"

"Of the being, you call God."

"Is that good or bad?"

"It got Bill to be your friend."

"That's true. Why subtle, though? Was God not sure he wanted to be my friend? Did he figure if he placed it on lightly nobody would know? Am I like a fucking scooter?"

"Scooter?" Linnick asked.

"Yeah, everyone thought they were fun to ride until a friend saw you on one."

"You believe your god only wanted to be your friend as long as no one became aware of it?"

"Well, I mean it sounds a little stretched thin when you say it like that, but yeah, that's what I was thinking."

"Perhaps it is meant to protect you. If those around you are unaware, they may not attempt to use it against you."

"Great. I'm getting logic lessons from an insect."

"Stop being so ugly on the inside!" she berated me.

"Damn, Linnick. You are one tough cookie. I'm honestly pretty happy I have this size advantage on you."

"You should be. You look strikingly like something I have dined on from time to time, though you do not have arms that end in sharp points."

That rustled the leaves of a memory way down the tree of my thoughts before the wind stilled and I thought no more about it.

"Alright, let's figure this out. I am apparently blessed by the hand of…"

"Not blessed, touched," Linnick explained.

"There's a difference?"

"According to Bill."

"I'm really going to need the Food-to-English translation handbook sometime soon. Fine, touched, for whatever that affords me; there are still three of us against one." I had a hard time adding Linnick into a conflict situation but she would have been offended if I had not and would have let me know. Besides, Bill pretty much counted as two anyway, so my original number still held up.

"Tomas has help; we would be overtaken."

"Oh, come on, Bill didn't even say anything this time. I think you're making shit up now."

Bill shuffled past and definitely picked up the pace. Linnick looked at me as if Bill's moving was all the evidence she needed to prove she was right. Which she was, of course, she always was; she was female. When has a female ever been wrong? It's like they feel the need to always be right since the whole apple from the tree of knowledge fiasco. Which I'm sure was Adam's doing. Like he begged her to make him an apple pie for his birthday or some shit. So, we've been giving Eve crap since the dawn of time for fucking up the Garden when it was Adam's cavernous stomach that was really the undoing. Yup, pretty much a normal string of thoughts for me, but then I wept for the loss of the Garden. Jacked up hormones were going to be my personal undoing.

"Bill, how did Tommy get away?" I asked. He never slowed as his features twisted around to look at me, then they just kept going until they were front and center again like he needed an exorcism. He did not deign to answer.

"It is still too painful for him to answer that."

"How do you know that, Linnick?"

"Did you not see it on his face?"

I wanted to tell her that all I saw was melting green wax. Instead, I nodded like I knew what the hell I was saying.

"Ow! Dammit Linnick, stop biting me! I'm moving just as fast as Bill."

"I didn't touch you." She was standing on my shoulder; the bite had come under my arm.

"Fuck!" Bill turned at my shout. "Something bit me again!" I was still looking accusingly at Linnick like she had somehow done it.

I had to sidestep Bill, who had stopped. I felt a flash of heat travel up my neck and cover the top of my scalp like I'd put on a heavy knit cap.

"Bill, wants you to show him where you got bit."

"It's…nothing." A wave of euphoria flooded over me.

I attempted to bat Bill's hands away. But have you ever fought jello? It can absorb a hell of a punch.

"Oh, oh." This from Linnick, once my shirt was off.

That doused the feelings of wellness I was experiencing.

"Oh, oh?"

"You have Thrimes."

"That doesn't sound so bad. Shit, I had chicken pox once, that sounds way worse."

"It's a parasite that can kill you."

"Like a tick that steals your blood and infects you with a horrible bacterium or a gold-digger who latches on and leeches everything financially from you?" I asked.

"I do not know what either of those is, but a Thrime feeds off your memories. It consumes them to the point that you will no longer know how to make your heart continue to beat."

The weepy side of me wanted to say "Yay. I can forget all the crap that's been going on." The side getting pumped with endorphins didn't give two shits. The Thrimes were welcome to my memories. Hell, most of them sucked ass anyway. Yeah, that was until I first felt them being leeched away. I don't even know how I can explain the unraveling of a memory. It was a moment I'd nearly forgotten in the annals of time. Something small, but poignant; one of the baby building blocks that led to the love of Tracy. It was one of our first dates; I was pretty nervous, which in itself was weird. Now I'm not saying I was Mister Smooth Moves, but I'd dated enough to have the basics down, so the fact that I was nervous meant that my higher self, sort of already knew this was the real deal. Weird, but what clued me in was that she didn't automatically laugh at my shitty jokes.

I had some pretty good witticisms, and she got a kick out of that, but when I missed, she wasn't too shy to let me know. And fuck, if I didn't find that endearing. There was no fakeness to her; she showed you who she was up front, and that's a rare quality. I could feel the hammer of enamor being dropped. That was the memory the Thrime was first showing me and then devouring.

"Get them out, Bill!" I started clutching my head and running in circles. I couldn't imagine all the things housed in my head that were there for the taking. My wedding days, the birth of all my children, our first night with George the adopted wonder bully, the meeting of wonderful friends. Sure, there were thousands upon thousands of shitty memories they could take, the death of so many of those I loved being at the top of the list, but I don't think I had the option or ability to pick and choose what they took; and I certainly couldn't risk the sweet to purge the nasty ones. I reached to scratch at one and was met with something like I'd touched an electrified thorn, and that wasn't anything compared to the pain that rocketed from the bite. Bill immediately grabbed my hand in his, but it wasn't like I was in a rush to try that again.

"Food." Bill shook his head solemnly.

"I've got something to tell you, Tallboat, and I don't think you're going to like it."

"You mean it's worse than bugs that eat your memories?"

"It's a matter of perspective." I noticed she was in hurry to get off of me. She was speaking as she headed south.

"What the hell, Linnick?" I should have known she was distracting me, I never even got all the information or the option to disagree with this plan of action. My entire right side went numb as Bill moved in. "Wait a min–!" Was all I managed to get out before I was once again completely engulfed inside of him. Somehow, knowing about the pain makes it worse; you tense up. Or maybe the second time around just is worse, like your body absolutely doesn't want to handle the stress of being reduced to the atomic level and then put back together again and again, like Humpty-fucking-Dumpty. I didn't even have the advantage to visit a happy place as I recovered because I couldn't even imagine such a place existed. I won't go into the pain again, why would I? It was worse than the first time and altogether an experience I wish the Thrimes had taken with them.

At some point, I realized we were mobile again, though I was certainly not under my own locomotion. Bill was carrying me half inside of him like I was luggage tucked under a fat man's arm and his body had wrapped around the bag. Linnick would occasionally lift an eyelid to see how I was doing, or ask, but I could do little more than grunt that I yet lived.

"How long this time?" I asked. My throat was rough and raw like I'd chugged scalding grapefruit juice, heavy with pulp and seeds and those little bits had burned into the soft flesh of my esophagus.

"It has been five days since you were bitten."

"The Thrimes?"

"They are next to you." I tried to move away but I was wedged tight and now that I thought about it, I was claustrophobically wedged tight. Tight as in: Let Me the Fuck Go. Now. tight. You ever have an older sibling hold you down and torture you? Yeah, that kind of squeezed tight.

"Let me out, Bill." At first, it was a statement, then it moved quickly to a demand, then right off into pathetic begging. Bill released his grip. It was sort of like being released from a giant jello mold replete with squishy and glopping noises. I fell to the ground. For some reason, I felt like a recently birthed hippo calf. I don't know why; perhaps because I'd just dropped unceremoniously to the ground and I was covered in what could be considered afterbirth. Bill's features circled his head like a damned lighthouse in a particularly foggy night, warning mariners of the dangerous shoals, although I knew he didn't want to warn anybody but us of impending danger.

"What have I missed?" I asked Linnick when I felt I had the ability to stand again. My eyes went immediately to the two Thrimes still encased in Bill. They were the size and shape of a birthday candle, except for the mouth and head part that looked very much like a tick from my world. The head was small and dominated by mouth parts that burrowed and locked into its host with evolutionary amazement. Little fuckers.

"Tomas is much nearer; we must not stop moving."

"I am really sick of this movie. I think I might ask for my money back at the concession stand."

"Bill, says that you have to eat the Thrimes."

"Um, fuck no."

"They have eaten memories important to you and the only way to gain them back is by eating the Thrimes."

"No, Linnick. Have you seen those things? They make you look like a Disney Princess. And who gives a shit about a few memories? If I can't remember them what do I need them for? Kind of like a junk drawer–you stick everything in there that you're too afraid to throw away because you figure someday you'll need it. But you know what happens? Ok, I'll tell you. First you forget it's in there, so you go get a replacement which might also be swallowed up by the drawer. Another likely outcome is you never ever need it again and all you do is completely fill the damn drawer up. I had a house once where we had three...*three* active junk drawers. Who does that shit?"

"Tallboat, what is your daughter's name?"

"Huh! That's easy enough, Nicole. My daughter's name is Nicole."

"Your other daughter."

"What?" I was completely perplexed. I had absolutely no idea about what or whom she was talking about.

"You had twins with Azile."

"I know Azile!" I said triumphantly. "And MJ, yeah I know him. Even Oggie and the damn cat!" But there it was, a hole where I knew something should be. Like when something small has been removed from a not often dusted dresser top. I could see a bunch of pictures on there...but, yeah...why is that one spot free from dust? I knew there should be a frame housing a picture, but of what?

"He says you do not have much time, that he has slowed their systems, but once they eliminate, their gleanings will be lost forever."

"So, you're saying that once my memories become shit, they aren't retrievable? I mean that's what he's saying, isn't it? Oh, just fantastic." I swallowed hard, looking at the worm-like parasites. Maybe shouldn't have done that. I saw hairs, thick hairs that covered a fair amount of their bodies and the parts that didn't have fur were scaly. I psyched myself up as best I could to do what needed to be done. "I'm ready, Bill." He pushed them closer to the surface where I was able to grab one. I tilted my head back and dangled that wiggling mass above my head; I was going to do the goldfish swallow. Not that I'd ever done it, but I'd seen it done before.

"You have to chew them up good, Tallboat or they can

attach inside your body."

"Oh, for fuck's…you suck, Linnick." I stuck the first one in my mouth and chewed like I needed to break rocks, trying to avoid my tongue, which is impossible, by the way. The entire thing tasted like a blister pill of bile and had the consistency of a raw oyster. There was not one redeeming quality about the entire experience…until some lost memories rushed back into their respective holding spots inside my head; suddenly, there was Mathieu, holding a mug of deep brown ale up to the light. I'm not going to say, I couldn't wait to devour the last two of those juicy little suckers, but I wanted what was mine. The second one, after watching what had happened to his friend, was wriggling with extreme prejudice making sure those barbed hairs were touching me continuously. He was hoping I'd drop him and he could go about his way. Not a chance. I ripped his head off like a geek on a chicken. I chewed, choked, and chugged that thing down, saddened that I had nothing to wash the bitter taste away with.

"Alianna!" I raised my head triumphantly. "Her name is Alianna!" It didn't completely make me forget about the taste in my mouth, but it helped. "How could I ever forget that?"

"It is good to have you back, Tallboat. You umm…have a little bit of gore in your facial hair."

I wiped it away quickly with my sleeve, definitely not my tongue. I could only hope that what I wiped away was something like the discomfort from a diaper rash I suffered when I was a year and a half old, I'd be alright not recalling that one.

It took me longer than it should have, I was still trying to get over the lingering ache from the transfer and the bitter bugs I'd had to swallow but I finally got around to thanking Bill.

"Hmmm," he grunted.

"Well, that's different."

"He's worried."

"Do tell."

I couldn't help but think Linnick was making this up as she

went along. Sort of like my Nicole used to do with her baby brother Justin. We'd be in the car on a hot summer day and Justin, at eighteen months or so, would utter something that sounded like Klingon, but not quite, and his "big sissy" would decipher it for us and it would usually sound something like "Justin says he wants ice cream" or "Justin said he wants to go to the water park" when I'm pretty sure all he was saying was "red truck!" or "my farts smell."

"We had to stop frequently while you were recovering, and in that time, Tommy did not move much closer, though he should have been able to. Also, the demons are beginning to push the Polions back–straight toward us."

"So, Tommy is merely keeping an eye on us, which means he has a healthy fear of us and/or he is waiting for backup. Doesn't make much sense. He would not keep tailing us for all this distance without coming in for the kill."

"Hmmm," Bill said.

"Not kill, so much as confront," I told Bill, "caught between a vampire and a war. What if we brought the fight back to him?"

"You mean turn around?" Linnick asked. "Bill says that's a bad idea."

"Linnick, if you're going to make shit up for Bill, you should at least wait until he says something."

"Bill?" she questioned.

"Hmmm, food."

"See!"

"*What?*" I asked.

"It amazes me that something as appalling as you can also be that dense. Do they not have natural selection on your home world?"

"Should have left you in your friggin' hole. Just tell me what you think he said."

"He asked if you have already forgotten about the Thrime field."

"Oh shit. Um, maybe I did. Maybe that was one of the

memories they took from me." After that, though, I did shut up about going back. I don't think I was mentally equipped to deal with another unraveling. "What's the plan then? Surely he has one."

"He doesn't."

"How far until Gate del Gato?"

"Too far," she said vaguely. I prodded for more info, but it was not forthcoming.

"I don't understand, then. What are we supposed to do, just sit here and wait?"

"Bill shrugged."

I was going to tell her he hadn't moved, but what was the point?

"Maybe the sneaky fuck is waiting for help but not in the way we're thinking."

It was now Linnick's turn to ask what I meant.

"Maybe he is waiting for the Green Man, or the Green Goddess, or even the Jolly Green Giant."

"Oh, I've heard stories about that one. We'd better hope he doesn't show."

"He's real?"

"You just mentioned him."

"Yeah, he was an ad mascot for frozen vegetables."

"Not here. He smashes everything he encounters with a large mace until it is mainly soup and then he slurps it up with a large hollowed out log."

"I hate this place."

"Tell me about it. So?"

"Sorry, I was thinking about a giant slurping up body parts through a tree straw." I shivered. "Okay, so the demons are pushing the Polions right to us, that means the light."

"Unlight."

"Sure, unlight goes more unny."

"Dark."

"No shit, Linnick. You going to let me finish?"

"Maybe if you used the correct words, you could do so

faster."

"I use words that make sense to me. Plus, you know damn well what I'm talking about–you're just being difficult."

She didn't reply to that which led me to believe I was on the right track with her, but if she were like any other female I knew, this would be when she would dig in for the extended version of the confrontation. She caught me again off guard; it's not really all that difficult to verbally or mentally trip me up. I'm a Marine, absolute hell in a firefight. After that…well there's no guarantee I won't say or do something stupid.

"Hell's not getting any cooler."

"Salty little thing, aren't you? Probably go good on a pizza." I muttered that under my breath. I don't think she heard it, but Bill "hurrumed," which might be construed as a laugh. "Okay. So, when the unlight dies and it goes all-dark and we are surrounded by all manner of horrific demon and monster alike, we will be at our most vulnerable. It would be at that moment that Tommy would strike."

"Will he not be at the same disadvantage as us? Maybe worse?"

"Not at all my little friend. He's been slinking in the shadows for ages; he knows exactly how to hide from things. Nope. That's it. He's waiting for his opportunity to strike. Now the question is, how do we stop him. Sucks that I know his plan but there isn't much I can do about it."

Like a violent storm off in the distance, we watched as the battle lines were continually redrawn, it was not difficult to see that even though there was some ebb and flow to it, that storm was definitely heading our way, and with a quickness. The Polions seemed to be in full retreat, at times stopping to protect their rear echelon, while forward creatures escaped. Could all this be laid on the Green Man's shoulders? He'd spurred them on and when it suited him he forsook them. If that was the case, his timing was impeccable. Tommy must have a way of communicating with him. In Western movies, cowboys could use a stampede to flush out their enemies. But weren't we the ones that were supposed to be wearing the white hats? Right now, Tommy had us fucking corralled and on the ropes. I sort of wish I had a Claymore mine to blow him into Kingdom come, and then again, I didn't. He'd betrayed me and I wanted to make his death an up close and personal statement. And yet again, he was family. Well, as much as he could be. The boy he'd shown me, the slow, big-boned kid that I'd fallen in love with was a far cry from the man he ended up being–a cold, calculating and quick, vampire. But I had adapted that love to encompass this new permutation; maybe I shouldn't have. Because I'll tell you, being betrayed by an enemy or a stranger, while it definitely does suck, the pain is tempered by the fact that you knew double dealing was always a distinct possibility; you'd invested nothing of yourself in that enemy. But a family member, someone you love, shoving a pitchfork in your back and tossing you into the baler? That's a whole other level of fuckery. So, yeah–I wanted him dead, but after I'd had a satisfactory explanation of why he was doing what he was doing. And still, I'm lying to myself. I was holding out hope that there was an explanation that was going to make me say, "Oh! That's why you did that! I understand, son," and all would be right with us. It was going to be that naive attitude that was going to get me killed unless this was just some cruel plot twist.

You know the kind. Someone is set-up to be the bad guy the entire film, but at the end, you realize they were undercover or were doing bad things for all the right reasons. It was the handsome, well-spoken gentleman that was the villain the whole time. That kind of thing. If I hesitated for just one moment when, and if, I had the opportunity to kill him, then he would kill me. Obviously, the worse problem was what if I was wrong and I killed him and he was indeed not scheming to get me tortured and killed or using me as bait to get my wife tortured and killed? And, as for Azile, I was just going to let her kill me because if she could pull the wool over my eyes that far, then I damn well deserved it. To think she was so willing to commit to her course of action that she would bear my children just seemed too far-fetched, even for someone who fully believed in some of the more "out there" conspiracy theories. Plus, if she wasn't out to get me and I told her that I suspected she had been, she'd kill me anyway. Very few trust-issue scenarios with a woman don't end in a lose-lose scenario.

"Tallboat, you should come back and join us." It was a very small and scared looking Linnick. At some point, I had wandered away from our strange group and was watching as the war encroached. Hadn't really been thinking about the death, destruction, and devastation that was swirling around in that horde…in fact, hadn't really been thinking about much of anything. A feat almost any man can do with hardly any prodding but which a woman cannot for the life of her fathom can truly be accomplished.

"Okay," I said as I shook away the cobwebs from the underused corners.

"Bill has an idea–says he can protect us from the Polions, but not so much Tommy if he does indeed show up, as you believe."

Bill's idea was ingenious. He was basically going to be a…I wanted to say human shield, but well, he's not really human. He was going to drape himself over us like an umbrella. Sort of. We weren't going to have much room, kind of like hiding under a canoe. All great and fine until something finds you, then you're kind of screwed because you can't really escape with any speed. Used to play this awesome game as a kid, Night Jail. Kind of reverse tag. A team of three or four loaded up with flashlights and walkie-talkies would attempt to find the "escapee." We had set boundaries and a time limit, so if you evaded capture for say, a half hour, you won. Wow, you know, now that I'm talking about it, it's no wonder I have trouble with authority, I was learning how to get away from authority figures pre-pubescent, and it was a blast. Holy shit, the revelations that can come when you start to write things down. So not the point. Anyway, in one of the yards within bounds, barely, was a huge weeping willow tree, the branches hung so low they swept the ground. It was dense, too, like a hedgerow, an area that just seemed entirely too difficult to even bother with. Well, this particular night, Paul and Dennis were closing in; I was the escapee. I don't think they'd seen me yet, but they would soon enough.

I chanced it and wormed my way in and through that impossibly thick forest of branches and leaves. Was like I found a damn Hobbit hole in there. Had my own burrow, could barely even hear Paul and Dennis yelling back and forth at each other if they'd found anything. I'd won that particular round. Then I'd started dipping a little too often into the well. After I'd won a few rounds, the searches got more intense, and once my hiding spot was discovered, it was always checked first from there on out. I hoped as Linnick and I wriggled under Bill this would be one of those times we weren't found; he was a pretty obvious spot, after all.

"Bill, you going to be alright?" I asked. Thinking that maybe it was a bit late to ask that; what could he do about it now?

"He's neutral in all of this No one will touch him."

"Bill is the Switzerland of the underworld? Weird, man. Shit just keeps getting weirder and weirder."

The cacophony of those being eviscerated was upon us, Bill's bulk muffled some of the screams but not enough. I had some serious misgivings about our present predicament and maybe more than a little bit of panic worming its way into my head. Always fun to desperately want to run out into the open when you know doing so would result in conceivably one of the most violent deaths ever possible. The hurt zone and all its fallout was swirling around Bill. He seemed immune to all of it, an impartial island in a sea of war. It sounded like the worst of it was passing us on by when the really bad part started. Bill, who wasn't overly fond of words, expressions, gestures, or anything else that resembled communication began to shriek. It was a halting, loud, blaring sound, like an asthmatic at a kazoo testing facility. Bill was most definitely under attack, someone had decided that Switzerland was theirs for the taking. At first, I thought riding it out underneath was the best bet, but he was getting brutalized out there and I couldn't just lay here and let it happen. Unfortunately, come to find out I also couldn't move; Bill had clamped down on our impromptu fortress. I'd gone from the relative comfort of being under a fifteen-foot tiny home to a seven foot kayak. His flesh was pressed up against my nose and descending.

"Tallboat!" Linnick also wasn't liking our present situation.

There was a wet tearing sound; I wanted to pretend it was anything but what it really was, the sound of Bill's flesh being cleaved. But the shrill sound that came from him and the shuddering of his body was the only proof I needed that Bill was losing the fight.

"Let us out Bill! We can help!" I shouted.

At first, there was nothing. Possibly the pain was too much that he couldn't even process the information or maybe he was going to see to our safety right up until the end. Maybe it was a reflexive thing or he'd finally taken all he could, but when we heard another large rip, an opening revealed itself to my left. I didn't hesitate as I rolled out from under. Seriously though, what was my alternative? Get crushed under his bulk or slowly vaporized? Neither was all that appealing. The unlight was back, the demons and the Polions had pushed past. I was dealing with a whole different monster now. Tommy was in attack mode, his teeth were elongated and the muscles rippled down the lengths of his arms, as he tore into the much larger Bill. Bill, for all his size and strengths was no match for Tommy, who somehow seemed unaffected by Bill's attacks. Bill was inflicting pain on the boy but was not dissolving him and was not able to keep him held in his clutches.

Hunks the size of briskets were being torn off Bill and wetly discarded to the side. Tommy had been so focused on Bill he had not realized I'd come out from under him. My guess was it was taking everything he had to stay one up on him. This had gone on for long enough. Never one to ponder, I grabbed my axe and attacked. It was possible he had most of his attention on Bill, but he had more than enough to thwart my attempt at cutting his fucking head off. He arm barred my attack hand with enough force to throw me off course. I had some satisfaction when my killing blow missed his head but bit into his shoulder. Not deeply, mind you, but when a razor-sharp blade slices a deli meat sized sample off of you, you're going to feel it and react.

I'd given Bill the reprieve he'd earned, though now I had the full attention and ire of a large, pissed off vampire. Good times, good times. I'd been bounced away after my hit but had recovered before Tommy could. We were now squaring off; I gave the briefest of glimpses to Bill–there would be no help from that quarter. He was listing heavily to the side and a gel substance was pouring out of him in quantity. There was no question he was dying and by the look on Tommy's face, I'd be joining him soon.

"You're no match for me, Mr. T."

"Fuck you, Tommy, and to you, it's Mister Talbot. I renounce any familial ties we ever had." Don't know if that struck a chord or the slight slippage on his face was due to something else. Whatever my words had affected, anger was part of it. He launched his attack. He moved so fast I never even saw the fist that pounded into my jaw. Felt it though, oh yeah, that wasn't a problem. I skidded away like a leaf in a gale. He attacked before I could even begin to think about countering. Fists were reigning down upon my face and head. It felt like I was fighting five ninjas because I'd screwed all of their girlfriends. If I was supposed to be delivered dead, he could have made good on that at any time. My brain was swimming in its own concussive juices, my vision was blurred, and I'd been less drunk the time I asked the statue of Paul Revere out on a date. Yeah, I'd even got pissed that it had not responded to my advances–like drunk-idiot me was the catch of the damn day.

Don't know when I'd dropped the axe, or even when I fell to my knees and onto my back. I do remember the waking up part, the boot to the side forcing the air from my lungs. My face was in the dirt and my hands were tied tightly behind my back. Nope, not tied, manacled; I'd heard the clanging of the metal. I rolled over, the cuffs biting into my back.

"You traitorous, treacherous, fuck. I should have cut your throat when I had the chance."

"You never did. Have the chance, I mean." He was staring down at me. "It's time to go, you've already made me late."

"Yeah, I wouldn't want you to miss your turncoats anonymous meeting. I heard they were having apple turnovers."

He roughly grabbed my shoulder and wrenched me up and onto my feet.

"What makes you think I'm going to walk to my own funeral?" I sat back down hard, the jarring impact traveling up my spine. I was going to have to rethink my acts of protest, especially when I couldn't use my hands.

"You walk or I'll squish her." He held up a small bag, there was something in there, could have been a stone for all I knew.

"I see her first."

"Get up, Mr. T."

"I'm going to put this as eloquently as the Marine in me can. You should take your own male sexual organ and push it past your anal sphincter with enough thrust that you can taste it in your throat. If that was too haughty for you, I'm basically telling you to go fuck yourself." The kick to the side of my head was enough to send me spinning and cause me to black out again. Brown out, really. I still sort of had some cognitive functions, enough to see Bill, who had turned a sickly gray color in his death, as I was being dragged past.

"You fuck." I was finally able to mumble when we were a few yards past the grisly scene.

"You getting up now?"

"I see that she's alright or you can keep kicking away. I'm getting used to having my face scraped off."

"You have no idea how many years I tried to figure out if this idiot persona you portray was a cleverly crafted façade. When I found it was truly who you were, I have to admit I was surprised."

"Yeah, that's me," I grunted as he pulled me up into a sitting position.

He reached into the bag, I was hoping Linnick would bite his finger off. My heart nearly stilled when he pulled out a non-moving form.

"Stop the possum playing. If you don't move, I'll rip an arm off," Tommy told her.

She quickly reacted; there are chances you'll take and there are ones you won't. This was definitely a won't time.

"Hello, Tallboat." She was scared. So was I.

"Satisfied?"

"I'll be satisfied with your head on a pike and I'm parading it around Mardi Gras with topless women showering me with beads."

"The women got beads for showing their breasts, not heads on pikes."

"My fantasy, I'll have beads thrown any way I want."

"Get up and walk or I crush her, kick in your skull, and drag your ass."

I got up. There was no reason to think this an empty threat. He'd killed Bill, knowing there were repercussions to that act. Who was going to give a shit, other than me, if Linnick got killed? And at this moment there wasn't much I could do about it to make him pay. I stood up. It was then I noticed I had manacles around my ankles and a chain a couple of feet long, giving me the ability to take a decent stride, but nothing with any speed.

"Where are my eyeballs?" I asked looking for the small bag I'd had tied to my waist.

Tommy didn't even acknowledge that question, like when

a person asks where their hat is while they are wearing it. I didn't push it, right now. Tim coming back and finding me was low in the queue.

"Are you that afraid?" I asked, looking at all the hardware I was wearing.

"Not at all. You're a lot less powerful than you think. I could kill you easily enough; the chains are for me not you. You're just stupid enough to keep trying to escape and I'm afraid that one of those times I'll just kill you instead of delivering you safe and sound. Here's your stupid bag; not sure why you're carrying around eyeballs and I don't want to know." He shoved them in my pocket.

"How long?" I asked after a while. "How long have you cared so little for me? Is it this place that turned you or was it ever since the Walmart roof?"

"I hated you the moment you exited your mother's womb. Your lineage destroyed my sister."

"Oh, the fucking saintly Eliza. Listen, I'm sorry she had such a shitty childhood, actually breaks my heart, but I think it's your dear old da' you should be harboring feelings of hatred for. It was that twisted fuck that started her off on her course. And oh yeah, your saintly sister is anything but. She's destroyed hundreds, if not thousands of lives in her unnaturally long and cancerous existence."

"Careful where your words tread, I care more for a fallen hair of hers than I do your survival."

"So, you've made a deal with Ganlin. And what makes you think he's going to honor it once he has me?"

"Oh, Mr. T, look at you and your rudimentary attempt to enshroud in doubt my contract with the mage. I can assure you, our agreement is based on something stronger than mere word."

"You're just going to hand me over and walk away? Then what?"

"I would think your life will have become unimaginably horrible by that point. There are things that can be done down here that cannot happen to beings in our natural realm due to physical limitations. I will get my sister, we will have a pathway forged for us past the Guardians, and from there we can escape back to your world. By then Azile will have attempted her own rescue of you, at which she will have failed miserably."

"She killed him once. What makes you think she can't do it again?"

Tommy outright laughed. "It was all a set-up! Every facet of it. The idea was to get her down here, where her rather significant powers of light could be drained and used against her, taken, and then unleashed in your world. Speaking of which, when my sister and I are once again free, our first plan of action will be to rid the world of all those who knew and loved Michael Talbot. I would not think there would be very many; might only take us a few days, but it will be so fulfilling."

This just wasn't making any sense. This wasn't even a one-eighty from the boy I knew; it was someone entirely different. Was it possible that this wasn't him? How could this thing have lived and fought right alongside me for so long without the barest hint of its true nature? No fucking way. There is *no fucking way*, something like this can hide for so long right in front of you and not give any indication of what truly lies beneath. There would have been a slip of the tongue, a sneer when he didn't expect somebody was looking, whispers of hatred in his sleep. Something. Nobody can wear such a complete mask, it isn't possible. Humans aren't capable of it. And that was the rub; he wasn't human, not anymore. I almost severely screwed up and told Tommy that if he laid a finger on my children I would kill him, but he didn't know about them, and right now their best defense was to stay hidden. Though if Azile did come down here, the only people she would entrust with them would be Lana and Mathieu and Tommy sure did know about them.

"Getting your head ripped off by a couple of werewolves–

that part of the plan, too?"

He didn't answer that one. It did seem at the end that he had given up, but really? Allowing your head to be ripped off? That's a pretty extreme way of calling it a day. There were too many variables. It's possible he could figure out a way to make us meet up in the way station we had found ourselves in; but then the doorway? Was it all a giant conspiracy and even now I had no idea the breadth and scope? And why move my piece around so fucking much if it was Azile they truly wanted? Was I really her only weakness?

"Can almost hear the creaky wheels spinning in your head trying to figure out what's going on."

"You could just tell me."

"I could, but I'm not going to. In the off chance you pull a rabbit out of your ass like you're wont to do, I don't want you having any more information than you should."

"Aw, that's just the pussy in you talking, boy," I said it as derogatorily as I could. His next step hesitated before he started back up. A loud scream, at a key I didn't even think possible issued forth from Tommy's chest. I ran a couple of steps before he turned with an evil smile on his face.

"Don't even think about it, Mr. T. She's a fucking bug to me. I care for her even less than I care for you. The only reason you're alive is because you're my bargaining chip. Her?" He held up a visibly distressed Linnick. "Dead or alive makes no never mind to me. How about you?"

"Fine, fine. Have it your way. Just leave her be; put her back in your pocket."

"I love it when I see the dawning of realization in someone's eyes as they figure out that I am truly and wholly in charge."

I said nothing. I'll take a punch or two for a snarky comment, somehow makes me feel good inside that I pissed off someone enough to earn a hit from them, but he'd just crush Linnick. This wasn't just a threat; it was the truth–I could see it on his face. Time was just becoming a blur. My body and my soul was one giant ache, my shoulders from having my hands clasped behind my back, the constant rubbing of the metal on my ankles, the worry for my friends, this trek wasn't doing me any wonders. That and the fucking halting shuffle steps I had to take was wreaking havoc on my thighs.

"I'd like to take a break."

"Keep moving."

That was it. I could grumble about it all I wanted; he seemed pretty set in his ways. So, walk we did. Blood began to run from my wounds and onto the ground; it had been doing so for a while. Tommy turned to look at me when he got a whiff.

"How long…how long have you been bleeding?" He was looking down at my ankles and the trail I was leaving. Like Hansel and Gretel only grosser.

"I don't know. Been in and out of dazing for a while. Couple of miles, maybe."

"Fuck," he said, very uncharacteristically.

"You worried about my well-being?" I asked and gave a dry laugh at the end.

"I'm worried what your blood might attract. Leaving a blood trail is like chumming for sharks down here. Anything could stumble upon that."

"You mean I could get eaten before you have a chance to hand me over? Well, that sure would be shitty for all parties involved."

He pushed me down, I fell like a plastic army man, had not been expecting it at all. Landed hard on my ass, nearly bit through my tongue–I had been in mid-word. "I fucking cried when you died."

He'd pulled up the cuff of my pants. I tried not to look but I did anyway, wish I hadn't. I was looking right at my shin bone and some of the muscles attached to it. The manacle had worked straight through the flesh. On a side note, in twenty or thirty more miles I might have sawed through my entire leg and would have been halfway free from my constraints. Probably wouldn't have put up much of a fight by then, but it would have been the principle, that I was halfway free. And completely free to bleed out. Tommy roughly ripped off my shirt and then made strips to wrap around my legs. He tied the left tight enough my foot began to tingle from the loss of circulation. I said nothing, I did nothing, as he worked on me. That was until I saw Linnick poke her head out of his pocket. She was going to make a run for it.

"Your sister," I started. "That whole, 'she hates you and you love her' thing you have going on." Linnick had swung out and was reaching for the heavier jacket where it was less likely he would feel her.

"What about it?" He was making another strip for my right.

"That real or fake?"

He thought on it. "No harm in telling you that. It's true enough."

"As much as I would like to be mean about this I am not. I am merely curious. What makes you think that springing her from this place is going to change that? You think that all of that time she's been leading you around the world by your short hairs will go by the wayside? That she's just going to be so appreciative that you rescued her, that she's going to fall into your arms and profess her undying love?" He started to notice something on his leg and was about to check. "A little unnatural!" I said louder than I needed to. "That love thing you have going for your sister; you sure you don't have a little more of your father in you than you care to believe?" Yeah, that got me a nose flattening strike to the face. Blood had burst away from me in a radial pattern. He'd fuckin' hammered that thing in like a stubborn nail. *So worth it*, I thought as my head bounced back onto the ground. I'd watched as Linnick had bounded off his leg and run to parts unknown. When I awoke, we were once again on the move. Tommy was dragging me by my foot.

"Time to walk." He dropped my leg to the ground.

"How long have I been out?"

"Too long. Been dragging you for almost an hour."

"Then you can go fuck yourself. I'm not walking."

"You are just the stupidest man I have ever had the displeasure of meeting."

He reached into his pocket, then felt around frantically.

"Missing something?"

"*You knew?*" He looked at me savagely.

I was smiling. "How could I? Been having my head dragged."

There was a quick moment of panic, maybe indecision, as he looked around, desperately trying to find a sign of Linnick. Maybe he was worried she would get help, I don't know where the hell she was going to get it from, not like she could call 911 down here. I just hoped she ran and kept running.

"Get up!"

"Come on ma, can't I just sleep five more minutes? I'm so tired! School won't miss me."

"I will beat you senseless."

"Some would say that's already happened. Naw. I ain't moving without some rest and maybe some water. A little food would be decent as well. A deep tissue massage, but not that Swedish stuff, too rough."

"This look like a hotel?"

"Was it hard?"

He looked at me quizzically.

"The act, I mean. You played it for so fucking long. Was it hard?"

"Humans see what they want to. When I needed some down time from dealing with all of you that was when I would check out."

"The silent times. Man, I knew you were deep in thought, I just never figured it to be because of your hatred for us."

"Now you know. Does the new knowledge make you feel empowered?"

"No, just sad. Sad that I wasted my breath on you. Sad that any moment with you was one I could have had with one I loved and loved me back."

"Boo fucking hoo. Who's the pussy now?"

"That came full circle pretty quick. Karma usually gives you a little break before it comes back around."

He weighed carrying me; he could have done it easily enough–I'd seen him heft twice my weight without breaking a sweat, but this wasn't the world to be caught with your hands full of chained human. He went a few feet from me and began to do some rhythmic chanting. It was spells; I'd seen Azile do enough of them to realize what he was doing.

"You're a fucking witch?"

"Warlock, idiot. And shut-up."

"That's how you got all those gross ass Pop-Tart flavors. And the foreshadowing…that had nothing to do with your vampirism, it was magic. How in the fuck did I miss all this?"

"We've already discussed your intelligence level."

I don't know what cosmic grocery store Tommy was shopping at but he pulled out a couple of large bottles of water and of all things, an MRE, mac and cheese, to be specific.

"I take it you can pretty much get whatever you want and it's an MRE?"

"Plenty of calories and protein. I don't give a shit what you do, but this is the last time we're stopping. Your little fucking bug friend could screw this up for me."

I asked how, he responded by telling me if I didn't eat now, I wasn't going to be able to.

"I don't have my hands," I said as I looked down at the nuclear-proof packaged meal sitting on my lap.

"I'm not your mother."

"You sure? We had a complicated relationship, too."

"I'm not feeding you."

"I'm not asking you to. Undo my hands so I can do it myself."

"This some sort of trick?"

"My legs are shackled, you've beaten the shit out of me for countless miles, you have been stronger than me since the day I was born. What trick do I have that you could possibly not know? You are handing me off to an asshole who is going to use me for all manner of abuse and torture. Is it too much to ask that I can enjoy one last fucking meal, such as it is, before that happens?"

He eyed me looking for some different truth. "You try anything and I will chop an arm off." He was behind me, undoing the cuffs.

My shoulders, thankfully, slid back into place as I moved my sore arms. It was a few moments before I even had use of my hands to open up the package. I'm not going to say I took my sweet time, because Tommy would not have allowed it, but I sure did savor that food knowing that is was very likely possible that I would never dine again. I had a feeling that prisoners eating their last meal went through this. At some point, we all eat our last meal, but most of the time we don't know that it is, and that's a key difference. I think maybe cosmically, the universe owes us the ability to choose what we want for that last meal. I mean, come on, convicted assholes that do the most heinous of crimes used to be able to order whatever the hell they wanted. Probably didn't taste so good knowing you were about to be electrocuted or hanged, but still...naw. Forget I asked, better keeping it as a mystery.

I was squeezing the remnants of a tube of peanut butter into my mouth when Tommy told me to stand.

"I see it in your eyes, Mr. T, you're thinking about taking a shot. I'm advising against it, you just got the feeling back in your hands and your shoulders are burning. You can't get into a decent fighting stance because of the leg irons. All that's really going to happen is you're going to suffer more damage."

"Yeah, it would appear you're damaged enough for the both of us." I turned to give him my hands, this wasn't the opportunity I was looking for. Who knew if I was ever going to get one...but this wasn't it.

CHAPTER NINETEEN
ELIZA

JAZMIXER HAD BARGAINED ONE FINAL nugget of information before Eliza had killed him.

"Ganlin, the Green Man...he was born of your world, remolded down here and sent back."

"Tell me more." Eliza said with her mouth full of demon. She had stopped pulling the blood from him in great floods yet kept her canines in position. The desire to feed was too strong to stop. She was not sure she could have stopped even if he was capable and willing to open a door out himself.

"That's all I know. The demon that created him was betrayed and another was attempting to control Ganlin's actions for his own goals," Jazmixer said breathlessly.

"And what were those goals?" Jazmixer winced as Eliza gently tugged at the main artery with her front teeth like she was pulling tenderly on a lover's neck.

"To escape this world."

"And that demon's name?"

"Trinitor..." He could barely get the word across his lips.

"I have two names and forever to find them. It has been a long time since I have been on a quest. I will not leave any loose ends like I did the last time. A Talbot killed me, though she was not of the blood; it seems something like that was always pre-ordained. I do not know whether I should laugh or cry. Oh, but the thrill of it all. The Michael Talbot clan was so special, he fought me at every turn. I am glad I did not kill him those first few times we met, it would have been easy enough. I've never told anyone this, but I visited him once when he was five. Tomas knew I had been close and he kept a vigilant watch over the Talbot's. For all the power my brother has, I am his one true weakness. Getting past him was remarkably easy."

Jazmixer began to shudder.

"Hold on a little longer, darling, this isn't a lengthy story. It was past the hour of the witch when I crept up to that boy's window, and you know what? He was standing by that screen watching me the entire time. Yes, there was fear fluttering in his small chest but still, he stood there, not frozen from his fear but rather in spite of it. That was partly why I did not kill him then. It was not his age nor his frailty that kept me from that most wonderful of feelings. It was that I saw a worthy adversary in him if I but let him mature. Was that folly on my part? Hubris perhaps. But when one slaughters sheep for hundreds of years, just the sight of a ram can be invigorating. We stood looking at each other for close to five minutes. Because even though intrigue was prevalent, the thought of dining on his blood kept invading and I am smart enough to know that I would have eventually caved in to my vices. But that boy grew into a magnificent man, everything I thought he would be. It might have been much wiser of me to turn him in his younger adult years when he would have been more malleable. But by then Tomas had grown in his powers and proved very adept at keeping Michael safe. He'd somehow figured out that this man was a key of some sorts. I do not know if he was the key to killing me, because he did succeed in that, or perhaps there was some other great feat he accomplished. By this time, I was distracted." Eliza smiled, remembering her time in purgatory.

Jazmixer coughed up a ball of bubbly blood which Eliza grabbed out of the air with her hand, brought to her face, and licked off her palm.

"Is there a deeper underworld for those that are considered bad down here? Truly what is the penalty? Or are you without consequence? Perhaps you are forced to go to heaven; I would imagine that would be its own hell for someone like you. I am glad we had this talk, you and I." Eliza reached into his throat and with one savage motion tore it out. She threw it onto the ground and stood.

"Off to Trinitor's house, I go. I have not felt this alive since Victor's bite. Once I am free to roam the world, I believe I will continue to destroy the Talbot line. I wonder sometimes how much time has elapsed since I last walked the earth. It may be that there no longer are any Talbots; it's difficult to decide whether that would be a good or bad thing."

CHAPTER TWENTY
MIKE JOURNAL ENTRY 15

"WE ARE HERE," TOMMY ANNOUNCED.

I think I immediately started sweating. I'd already gone a few rounds at the hands of Ganlin, there was nothing about that experience I wanted to relive. "Where?" I asked, hoping he was wrong. This place looked as featureless and empty as any other.

"It is protected like Azile's."

If he knocked, it was a psychic thing, for I did not hear anything and he did not move, yet a moment later, something of a doorway shimmered into existence. I don't know which of the three of us were more surprised when Eliza came to the opening.

Tommy looked like he was going to fall to his knees. Eliza's gaze swept over him and to me.

"A housewarming gift? How thoughtful." It was tough to call the thing that pulled up the corner of her mouth a smile. "It's customary to bring wine, Tomas, but we will drink from him nonetheless."

"Lizzie...how? Has Ganlin already freed you?"

"That useless disfigurement? He tasted nearly as vile as he looked."

"What?" Tommy shouldered past his sister as she stepped aside. I saw what looked like a crime scene from a b-list movie made by an overzealous prop designer who'd had the good fortune to come upon a dumpster of fake gore and blood behind a Halloween superstore and wanted to use them all before they dried up in their containers.

Can't say I was overly distraught with the Green Man's

passing, though staring down the double barrel of Eliza and Tommy wasn't as appealing as it sounds.

"Oh, my. Are you soul rich again? What a truly karmic event." Eliza had come over to me and was pulling in long drags of scent. "It is ambrosia! I've just finished dining, but there is always room for dessert."

"Eliza, what have you done!" Tommy shouted from inside whatever I was looking at. "The mage was our way out of here! I was to offer Michael up in exchange for you!"

"Michael and I are now of equal value? My, my, my, Michael! What have you been up to in that life of yours?"

I said nothing.

"How long has it been since that bitch wife of yours and that witch sent me away? Speak!" she demanded when I still said nothing. "I know how fond of their genitalia men are; I could rip yours off and shove it down your throat before the crippling pain could make it to your brain."

"Two hundred years or so." That seemed to take her aback.

"Two hundred years? She cost me two hundred years? She must be brought to pay for that. But alas, humans are frail. Time wears them away faster than a raging stream does a muddy bank. Tell me, Michael, as the years passed, did you grow weak and turn her so that she would forever be by your side? Please tell me that this is truth. Because if it is, I will find her, and the joys we shall share together. My joys, her torment, really. But you understood that."

She had gripped my chin and forced me to look into her eyes. "Tell me what I want to know!" she demanded.

When tears came freely from me she knew the truth.

"You let her die? You surprise me at every turn. There are few that would have allowed that. What did Ganlin want with you? There is nothing especially interesting about your soul, other than it is stained with your humanity."

"It wasn't him he wanted." Tommy sat down hard, his head in his hands. "It was his wife."

Eliza looked confused. "This Ganlin was powerful enough

to reach up and snatch her from the heavens?"

"Not that wife. He is married to Azile now."

"Azile? How is that possible? She had power! I felt it even as she wed my soul to me, but not that kind nor that much."

"She grew more powerful."

"I understand that, Tomas. She lives after two hundred years. Perhaps you should start at the beginning and fill me in on the parts that I am missing, so we can figure out what our course of action is."

"There is no course of action now, Eliza, don't you see that? You destroyed our way out of here."

"Oh, Tomas. Always the doomsayer. If nothing else, we have a wonderful meal."

"No!" Tommy looked up. "No. He could be our way out of here. "You're right, Azile is powerful and she has the child, Gabriel. He is a Veil Piercer. They could possibly be made to comply."

"Pity," Eliza said as she dragged a long fingernail down the side of my face and neck. "I think at some point we will be able to revisit this," she whispered in my ear.

Tommy spent a few hours recalling in detail all that had transpired; the rest of the zombie apocalypse, a lot of the things he had done during my downtime–some of which he never shared or alluded to during our time together. For that, I'm glad. The talk of the farm he cared for, and the human livestock he tended was a little more than I could stomach. Eliza grew much more interested in the Lycan wars, especially at the part I played and the time I'd spent with Ganlin.

"You are something of a legend now? There always was a purpose in you, Michael. I'd not seen it in those early years, though I could sense it was there, like a sparrow singing in the dark of night."

She'd said it almost tenderly, like a mother would coo to her newborn. It was unsettling because I knew she was just wondering if this would somehow reveal more of my weaknesses or make me sweeter to eat.

"I am sort of surprised that with all your abilities, you had never once seen my brother for who he is. He never really had a chance, well neither of us, really. Physical, verbal, sexual abuse at such an early age tends to fundamentally change who you are, and then when the soul is removed, well, there goes any semblance of a governor to those tormented thoughts and the need to act out on those dark desires. Although, I must admit, Tomas has always been able to hide his true self. I have never seen a need to be anything other than myself, yet he would use subterfuge to his advantage. In the end, it brought you to me, so perhaps, there is some value in it."

"We should get away from here. The scent of blood will bring company we do not wish to entertain," Tommy said as I sat down.

"I'm done," I told him.

Tommy looked like he was about to blow a faulty gasket in his neck. He stormed toward me; Eliza looked bemused. Tommy hit me hard enough to the side of the head I made an indentation in the ground. I sat back up.

"All that time and still you have grown no wiser. How is that even possible?" Eliza asked.

"It's a talent, really," I told her. "As for you, dickhead, I ain't moving, not with these chains on. They fucking hurt. My ankles are killing, my shoulders are killing, and if I could feel my hands, I'm sure they'd be killing. Either finish me off, carry my ass, or take these things off. I can't imagine between the two of you I'd be much of a threat; or are you still afraid of me?"

"Afraid of you?" Tommy scoffed.

"Then take the chains off, dear brother," Eliza said.

"You do not understand, sister. He is slippery; a pig covered in lard."

"Yes, but think of the bacon once caught."

"Oh, all right. I get it. You want to eat me. At this point, I don't even give a shit, either do it or shut up about it."

"Have you grown so full of yourself, that you no longer

fear me?" Eliza asked.

"You know what? I've faced more enemies than I care to think about. As far as I'm concerned, you're just one more. What's the worst that can happen? Either I kill you or you kill me. Though if you think about it, I've buried hundreds, nope, I take that back, *thousands* of potential killers."

"Ah, but Michael, you forget that so have I. But, that's not really it, is it?" She was peering intently at me. "There's a part of you that is ready to die. You are far too young for that to be from your vampirism. Many simply cannot live past five to six hundred years; they lose purpose and become so despairing of how the world has changed that they lose their minds and themselves. No... you want to be reunited! How sweet! That is most likely not going to happen for you, but how sweet."

"We'll see."

"You were a worthy adversary back then, but I do believe I am liking this older version even better. Free him, Tomas, so that we may depart."

"This is not wise."

"Do it, or I will stay beside him until whatever comes, comes."

Tommy hefted me up, undid all the chains, and pushed me roughly forward.

"It is always so shocking to those involved when he shows his true demeanor." Eliza laughed as she said the words. "I'm not always there to witness the revelation, but when I am it is an exquisite delight."

"I am so sick of vampires; you're all lying sacks of shit. I met a few friends of yours, Payne, Charity, and Sophia. Ring any bells?"

"What about them?" She eyed me.

"I…" I was going to put the fear of some deity into her but just then the earth began to move and not in a love song type of way. Like California was about to drop into the ocean and make Arizona ocean-front property type of way.

"Run!" This from Tommy. I saw it on Eliza's lips, she was

about to protest that running was undignified or how it was beneath her or some such shit. When I saw the roiling, rolling wall of what I could only think was lava heading our way, I didn't really give a fuck what she thought. I was on the move, amazing how boiling rock and earth can make all your aches and pains mysteriously disappear. For all her potential griping, she caught up to us fairly quickly. We could hear explosions behind us as the wall consumed everything in its path. The heat it was throwing off was beginning to become a factor. At first, it was just a warm summer breeze, then it was that gust of heat you feel when you open an oven, and it was rapidly moving to singe inducing steam, the kind that comes from a screaming tea kettle. It would not be long before our clothes caught fire and our skin began to slough off in crispy sheets, like packaged seaweed. I spared a glance at Tommy; he was off to my left and slightly ahead. "Fuck it," I mumbled, my plan as half-baked as I was about to be.

I moved over and kick-tapped his right leg so that it crashed into his left, tripping him up. Under normal circumstances this is hilarious to a pack of drunk buddies. I knew there was more than a fair chance that I would become entangled with him. Was pretty fucking happy when I landed it perfectly and barely lost stride. I managed to reach down and grab my axe he had tucked into his belt before Tommy, went down into a rolling heap.

"Fuck you," I mumbled as I continued, didn't even chance a look back. Neither did Eliza, when she heard him scream out; so much for big sisterliness. I looked over to her and was pondering the same maneuver. She gave me a look that dared me to try; an Eliza on the prowl was far too dangerous. We'd been running for at least three miles when the land had an upturn; it wasn't much of an incline, not at first anyway, but it did begin to give some much-needed breathing space between us and the fiery wall of death.

Then it started to rise in earnest and the lava was not flowing fast enough to fill the basin below us. Still, we ran–in case it got a second wind. When we got to the top I'd like to say we had an expansive view of the beautiful vista, but it was basically a brown turd of tundra, featureless and boring.

"You killed Tomas?" Eliza asked when we stopped. I was winded, had my hands on my knees; she looked like she was getting ready to go out to spin class or something.

"I hope so." I did not look away from her, odds were we were about to go at it. For all my strengths, I did not think I had much of a chance against this waif of a girl.

"I do not believe the Michael I knew would have had the stomach to do that."

"Probably not. And how do you feel about it?" I stood tall, in a vain attempt to look more imposing, though I'm thinking my heaving chest gave my pose away.

"Family must be avenged."

"I can stand behind that comment. That's why I did it. He threatened those I love, I won't suffer the chance he makes good on it."

"You realized that killing him would force me to kill you, correct?"

"Didn't give it much thought; just seized the opportunity, like he did when he sliced Bill into chunks. Tell me what's different Eliza? You were going to kill me anyway. But before you go and do something rash, I know something else."

"Do tell."

"You are a self-serving vampire. And yes, I took out Tommy, but I am still your best chance of getting out of here. I propose an alliance until such time as we can conclude this war of ours in a more traditional setting."

"Why should I believe you? Perhaps I somehow come into some compromising situation, why would you not take advantage of that?"

"We're not friends, never could be. Too much loss. But you were always who you said you were. I always knew where I stood with you. We are combatants; you've wrongly hated me for something a very distant ancestor did to you. Which by the way, if we're being honest, I think you actually liked. Had Victor not come around, you would have died long ago, in the dirt of some shitty city. Instead, he changed you, allowed you to enact every sick and wrong thing that flutters about inside that head of yours. He made you, Eliza, and you love who you are. Your brother, on the other hand, pretended to be something he was not. And he was so good at it I adopted him, made him part of the family, when all the while he loathed me, I'm thinking more than you do. And I've got to tell you, that pisses me off to no end that he did that; I can never forgive nor forget it. He was a friend–no, a brother to my boys, my daughter. Another son, who was secretly plotting the downfall of everything I cared for. Fuck him. And oh yeah, fuck you. But I'll honor my end of the agreement because I don't want to stay here, either."

"Kiss me."

"Not a fucking chance." I was thinking back to our first encounter when she was more zombie than vampire and licked my eyeball as I was frozen, rooted to the ground, good times.

"Pontius Pilate sealed his fate with a kiss."

"I don't see any silver coins." I extended my hand. She looked at it like I'd uncoiled a fistful of snakes. "A normal human gesture a little too much for you?"

"I am not human!" she said with vehemence.

"It's more for me than you."

"If you but let go of that part of you, that weakness, I could show you your real potential."

"Your apprentices don't have much of a shelf life."

She laughed, she genuinely laughed at that. I had just murdered her brother by lava flow and she was laughing.

"I will take your hand Michael Talbot; we will escape this place, and then you will give me what I am due."

"First," I said, pulling my hand back before she could make contact. "This ends with us. Should you kill me, your war with the Talbot lineage dies with me."

"Why would I agree to such a thing?"

"Because I won't fucking move otherwise."

"Oh Michael, I could make you punch yourself until your hand split open and you were cutting deeply into your face with the shards from your broken knuckles. I've done it more than once; it is fairly entertaining."

"What good is that going to do you?"

"If I can make you maim yourself, what makes you believe I couldn't make you travel alongside me?"

"I'd say nine times out of ten, Eliza, you could kill me easily enough. Won't even argue the point. But I will resist you with everything afforded me and just like I told your brother, at a time when you may need to be at your best, you will be strained. If that's the route you want to go, let's do it."

"I am a vampire through and through. Lying is no more consequential to me than telling the truth. Why would you believe anything I may or may not agree to? In the end, words are merely words. How many times have false ones been spoken?"

I didn't even know what to say. If someone tells you that they are just as likely to be telling the truth as not, how can you trust anything they say?

"How many of the Talbot lineage still wander the earth?"

It was not an answer I was prepared to give. First, because I really didn't know. The Northern Maine compound Talbots had flourished; though I'd stopped checking in on them after the last of my children passed. There was no way of knowing how many of them there still were, or where they were.

"Two...there are two."

"That is truth, though you hold something veiled which I cannot see."

"Great. You can peer into minds as well?"

"It is a talent I kept hidden from Tomas. It was unclear to me if at some point he meant me harm and I wanted the weapon kept secret."

"Well, now you know. They, along with Azile, are to be forever free from your wrath. In fact, you will not even seek them out, even just to get a peek. You will go back to England or whatever it is called now and set up your new life."

"She played a part in my undoing. What kind of vampire would I be if I let that go without reprisal?"

"Azile is not one to be taken lightly; it would be better she did not know how I met my end, for she might take vengeance upon you."

"That almost sounds like a challenge."

"Eliza! We make this deal and you honor all facets of it or good fucking luck–and that's sarcasm by the way–I don't mean any of the luck parts. If we go our separate ways now, I hope you find your way into a dendrun hole filled with scorpions."

"I could just follow you."

"What? Like a lost puppy? I would think Eliza would be above that."

Her eyebrows furrowed as her eyes took on a distant stare. I prepared for a fight that she did not launch.

"Tommy yet lives," she said evenly. For all the inflection, she could have been talking to a fellow commuter about the weather.

That wasn't good at all. Tommy would try to snap me in two the second he saw me.

"He is asking for help."

"And?" I asked.

She began to walk perpendicular to the line of lava below, which may have been receding, sucking back down into the bowels of the earth, where it belonged. This is what happens when Earth eats a giant hot sauce slathered burrito, upset stomach causes massive heartburn reflux and explosive fiery diarrhea. Oh, come on, you know what I'm talking about, remember that first time you had something really spicy? Your stomach was gurgling in protest, then a few hours later you were wondering why your asshole was on fire. Doesn't seem right that something should be hot on the way in and out.

"Shit." This was one of those times when my fight-or-flight reflex was totally out of whack, had one of those "Out of Order" signs hanging on the side of my head. Running could give me some much-needed distance from this damaged duo, but dammit if I didn't need Eliza. She'd killed Ganlin, just because, and had not suffered one bit. She was powerful, no doubt about it. Odds were she could take care of just about anything we'd encounter, which somehow worked back to the fact that I should put as much distance between me and her as I could. Let's restart the vicious circle; it seems to be working so good for me. The thing that could kill me the most, and wanted to, I need to add, was also the same thing that could also kill just about everything else that wanted to kill me. I always kind of thought the saying "pick your own poison" was a throwaway idiom; really didn't like the fact that right now it carried the utmost importance. I trudged in tow.

The ground looked scorched, I seemed to remember seeing something like this at some point in my life, but just couldn't find the right time, or more likely, the right me. I was smart enough to realize there were or are or had been multiple timelines of mine that had played out and sometimes those memories bled. They'd gotten less intense as the years progressed. I think because, yes, I was getting screwed on a cosmic level but the demi-god was still bound by the natural length of my life, and it was against great odds that I was infected with a vampiric virus in too many of them. I sincerely hoped that I was the one taking one for the Talbot team and no other "Me" had to go through this.

I bumped into Eliza, it was getting a lot like the Three Stooges with all the slap stick. She'd stopped in front of me and I'd been absorbed in other thoughts. Her head was turned to her left; a burnt, disfigured tree branch sticking up from the ground had her fascinated. When it spoke, I knew why.

"Help me," Tommy begged, barely above a whisper. If the rest of his body looked half as bad as that arm, his lungs would have been lumps of coal. That he was still somehow alive was a testament to his strength.

"He is not yet beyond hope." Eliza was looking to me.

"Me? You want me to help him? I'm the one that put him in that position. What makes you think he would want my help?"

"Have I not put you in your present position? Yet, still, you seek my assistance."

"Don't start." I walked over to that outstretched arm. When I got closer I saw that half of his body was encased in cooled or cooling lava; he had become a less noble version of Han Solo encased in carbonite, though where Hans was perfectly preserved in gun metal silver, Tommy was twisted and blackened. Their faces, full of pain and a beseech to stop were similar, though.

"Possessed."

That was all he said; I understood the implications clearly. He was saying that everything that he'd done was because he'd been taken over by a vengeful demon and now he was fine. That was pretty convenient, as far as I was concerned. He'd been feeding me heaping helpings of shit for hundreds of years; what was a few teaspoons more? Eliza had confirmed his false nature just hours before, but if what he spoke was true, then it was quite possible I could be saving–or not–the Tommy I thought I'd known all along. I could also be doing him a huge favor if I ended his suffering. I'd have to live with the guilt of killing him.

"Was he lying to me the entire time?" I asked Eliza.

"It is not for me to say." She had a sly smile.

"This fucking funny to you?"

"Watching the tortured thoughts race around your head? Yes, I find it very amusing."

"He's your brother, for fuck's sake!"

"Truth?"

"What? What are you talking about?"

"We are not related by blood."

Well if that didn't just send my reality spinning off into space.

"My mother was caring for Tomas for another woman in the village who was foraging for food. She fell off a small cliff and snapped her neck. From that day forward, he was ours, though it meant less food for us all."

"Your father–he said that your mother died giving birth to Tommy."

"Oh, she did. My father killed her for bringing the boy into our hovel. Even then he was a coward. He didn't kill Tomas because he knew my mother would seek retribution. He waited until she was asleep and he crashed a rock down on her face, twenty times by my count, and then he made me clean up the mess while he dropped her body off the same cliff Tomas' mother had fallen from. I was five years old, scraping my mother's bones, blood, and brains from the floor and bedding. I've hated Tomas ever since that day."

"You lie. I don't know which part of it, but at least some of that story is lies. I saw you with Tommy on a couple of occasions. You cared for him; you protected him. I saw when you were bitten–you tried to keep yourself from hurting him. You are considering saving him right now."

"NO! Now it is you that lies. You cannot know these things!"

"Yet I do."

Eliza changed her stance a few degrees but kept her eyes on the fried arm of her brother. "I once held care for him; that is true. When it was us against my father we were allies, much like you now propose for us."

"So, it makes no difference to you what happens to him now?"

"Only in so much as I am curious as to what you are going to do."

"Was he possessed?"

"How is one to know?"

Oh, she fucking knew. She just wasn't going to tell me.

"Mr. T please…please help. It's me, T…Tommy."

He almost had to add in that extra part. If I'd stumbled

upon him I would not have recognized him.

"Blood, I need blood," he begged.

"You'll get none from me."

There was nothing for what seemed like ages; I thought perhaps he had died. Had given up hope when he realized help was not coming.

"I will not interfere if you want to help him," I told Eliza.

"As if you could. No, I will not help. I am enjoying the torment this is causing within you."

"My mental anguish is more important to you than Tommy's suffering?"

She said nothing.

"I…I love you," Tommy cried.

My heart was attempting to wrench itself from my chest. To shed its bodily moorings and enfold the boy in its loving, life giving beats. I stepped closer. I could be cold-hearted when circumstances dictated, this wasn't one of those times. It was an improperly cooled piece of rock that changed everything. The brittle piece under my foot gave way and I fell through past my ankle. I expected pain from a sprain or maybe a piece of molten rock that had not yet cooled. I got neither. What I did get was some verbal wrath from Tommy.

"Hurry, the fuck up,'" he hissed.

I pulled my foot free and shook away the sharp rocks that wanted to slip inside my boot and tear up the soles of my feet at the most inopportune of times.

"You know what? I'm going to pass," I told him.

That seemed to be the last hurdle for him to overcome in regard to his filter.

"Come closer, Talbot. Once I begin to feed, I will not stop until you are a dried husk that will wither and blow away in the breeze."

"You deserve this, to be roasted in the fires of hell, I mean, in case I wasn't clear. I'd no sooner allow you a drop of my own blood than I will shed another tear for your death." I knew that was a lie, I wonder if he did. I would cry a great many times for the death of the person I thought I knew.

He started to laugh, it was a dry thing absent of all humor. "All those around you eventually die–most because of you. You must be used to it by now."

"Goodbye, Tommy. For a while, I will remember you for the person I thought you were, then I will think no more of you. I will never talk about you again; you will be completely forgotten as if you never existed. A legacy of none." I fished into my pocket and tossed Tim's eyes, striking Tommy on the head. "Little parting gift."

Nothing but one final cough and the dim light that still shone was flaming out quickly.

"He will not have far to travel," Eliza said as she began walking again.

"Hard fucking core," I mumbled as I followed. Surreal did not even scrape the surface of what was happening here. I'd come to hell to get Tommy back, to dissuade him from the craziness that it was to rescue his sister, the woman that epitomized all that was evil. Yet here I was, traveling with that woman as my temporary ally as we sought a way to free ourselves from the grip of this world, both of us having let Tommy die when we might have saved him. This was a twist I could have never seen coming, not if I'd thought out every possible outcome for the next hundred years. None would have ever involved Tommy betraying me. I would need to maybe seek out the reality that he had truly been possessed, had stayed true deep inside. Although in retrospect, what kind of mind fuck would that be? I'd choose to remember how I saw fit, and I'd drink the rest away. I'm not sure why I was worried, odds were heavily favored that Eliza would be dining on me some time later this evening after having watched a fine show.

CHAPTER TWENTY-ONE
MIKE JOURNAL ENTRY 16

ELIZA WAS ABOUT AS CHATTY as a pair of socks. Which for the most part was fine, wasn't like we had a whole bunch of common ground to bond over and her voice gave me the creeps. She was relentless in her pursuit of escape; she was a wild animal caged in an eight by eight enclosure, a t-bone steak just out of her reach. So far, she'd torn into three demons; only one had been smaller than her, but none had stood a chance. A lioness destroying a squirrel would have been less lopsided. She only fed off the first one; the other two had the unfortunate luck to merely cross her path. Well, I guess it wasn't that lucky for the first one, either. He'd at least died a fairly quick death as she pushed his misshapen head to the side and pulled his blood free. She'd dropped him to the floor when she was done, just another concert-goer dumping an empty beer can. The other two had been torn apart like a poor Princess Penelope doll in the hands of a spoiled five-year-old who really wanted a Princess Peach doll. Sure, it was demons, but watching a head get popped off is not something one considers entertaining after the first couple of times.

"You have any ideas on how to get out of here?" I asked after maybe a solid day of traveling.

"That's the reason *you* are here. Is it not? Because otherwise, I may as well dispatch of you and your incessant jabbering."

"Incessant? That's the first thing I've said all day."

She didn't reply. I guess we were back to the silence. Which would normally be fine, but in this location, it was unsettling. The non-talking was opening my ears to all sorts of disturbing noises; rumblings, distant maniacal laughter, and there was this constant hot wind that sounded very much like the moans of the damned as it passed by your ears. And the damned don't sound overly optimistic about their lot.

"There's the gate. Now what?" Eliza had an expectant countenance like I had a bag of catnip and that was going to make all the Guardians abandon their posts as they frolicked about, stoned out of their kitty gourds. Now that I'm thinking about it, I wonder why there was never some PETA protest about getting cats high. Wasn't a pet shop you could go into that didn't sell bags of cat weed and nobody seemed to give a shit that we were getting felines fucked up. Because, make no mistake, that was definitely what we were doing. Come on, tell me you never smoked a fatty with some of your friends and then gave your household cat a toy absolutely laced with catnip? Just me? Whatever. Talk about cheap entertainment. We would laugh our friggin' asses off as the cat would dance and roll around, never letting go of that toy–the stuffed mouse with a bell on its neck that contained all the answers to life, and he wanted to be the only one to possess that knowledge. And, like too much knowledge, that weed cooked his little cat brain, so much that he would mewl, pounce, and prance, the happiest creature on earth. Then, of course, he would bite you as you bent to share the merriment, because that was what he did. Might have been because I took his stash back. I would have done the same thing.

Telling Eliza that I had "no clue" what to do was akin to me putting a gun to my head. But I had no clue. "You watching me isn't going to magically make an answer appear. Shouldn't a being with unlimited time be a tad more patient?"

"I have been lost for two hundred years. I do not wish to waste more."

I sat back against a rock, a prominent feature of this landscape.

"I will not suffer this for long." She said, almost as a threat, before she also sat.

I looked over to the girl, and that's what she was, really. I don't think she was a day over eighteen or nineteen when she'd been turned. But that didn't make a whole lot of sense if what she'd told me was true, because that made Tommy around thirteen or fourteen, and I'd peg him somewhere closer to twenty-one. I was going to keep him at that age. Thinking I'd offed one that had just reached the age of puberty was not another strike I needed for my wounded psyche. To just look upon the girl, not knowing who she was or having seen her at her ferocious worst, she was stunning. I mean she was the kind of beauty that huge companies would have clamored for to push their jeans and makeup, as if their products had some magical way of transforming women into beautiful swans, from the ugly ducklings they would lead women to believe they had been beforehand. When she turned to look at me, that illusion was gone, those cold, indifferent, black eyes were filled with death and hate. It oozed from her in a toxic stew.

"Besides Victor, you were my favorite Talbot."

I didn't think I liked her using the past tense when she referred to me. Most likely in her mind, she had already disposed of me. I didn't think it wise to bring it up.

"Victor was a favorite of yours?" I asked, tough to think that, since she'd killed him.

"I was thinking about your words; you were right."

This is where I would normally go off on a tangent about actually having a woman admit I was right for once but this was not the person nor the place for that. A new leaf was turned over as I wisely remained silent.

"Without Victor turning me into a vampire, I would have died long ago. My pathetic excuse for a father would not have missed me, Tomas, perhaps, for a little while, but once he died I would have been forgotten. Returned back to the earth in a shallow, unmarked grave dug by an apathetic, grave man. An unremarkable life filled with nothing but pain and ending in misery."

I could not argue her that; I had stolen a glimpse into her

life. Death would have been a service to her.

"You lived a life of misery, I agree with that, I do. And even at that young age, you realized it for what it was. But then you went and gave it all back tenfold."

"Should I have perhaps been a saint?" she asked, and she was serious.

"Wouldn't have been the worst thing you could have done."

"Oh, those pious puissants always spewing forth the good word, most of them had been more perverted than the general population, they just hid behind their own illusions of grandeur."

"We're talking saints, didn't they have to go through a pretty serious vetting process by the Vatican?"

She let out something that could be considered a derisive snort.

"We are vampires, you and me. We do not possess many choices in the things we must do to survive."

"I think I'd like to disagree with you on that point."

"Do not cheapen your existence by hiding behind what you believe yourself and your qualities to be. Have you killed?"

"I have but…"

"It matters not at all if you believe that your killings were merited or even in self-defense. A life was taken. The only difference is that I enjoyed my kills, whereas you seem to live under a mountain of guilt. If you but shed that one trait, you could do great and mighty things."

"Apparently my guilt is the only thing keeping me from becoming you; I think I'll keep it where it is."

"Whatever allows you to continue on. Eventually it will consume you."

"Why did you come to the States? You can't tell me you had eradicated all of the Talbots from Europe."

"Lisdon Tunning."

"What about him?"

"Her, actually. She was one of the greatest warriors I had

ever known. I am not merely speaking of the Talbot line, but of all time. I stayed very close to the Crusades; the Knights Templar were their own brand of vicious, though they fought in God's name." Her eyes let me know that she got a kick out of that. "I could slaughter and eat to my heart's content and not draw any attention to my doings. It was a wonderful time. It was not unheard of for me to kill and consume ten to twelve people in a single day. European and British knights, Muslim freedom fighters, the innocents, I took them all. There was so much death there I could not be noticed. Not until Lisdon anyway."

"Wait, I know that name…that's your surname! Had you been following her?"

"I did not even know she existed, it was just happenstance that we met. Although, perhaps I am so closely tied to that great bloodline that there is no corner of the world I can travel without confronting one. Or maybe it is just that they breed like rats and inhabit all four corners."

"Tunnings are sluts?"

"She was a sight to behold; statuesque, tall for that day and age. She had gleaming silver armor and a heavy long sword that men larger than her would have had a difficult time wielding, yet she did so effortlessly."

There was rapture in Eliza's eyes as she spoke of her ancestress.

"I did not think women could be knights."

"There were none that would tell her otherwise."

"I like her already."

"I watched her for three days as she led almost every charge into a Muslim stronghold. She would not be deterred; she fought with such abandon I thought that she might be one of my kind, hiding in plain sight. More than once, I saw her pull the still beating heart from one of her conquests; she would inhale of its essence, savor a small bite, then consume the heart entirely. A wonderfully ingenious performance if one wanted to conceal their true nature; she could feed while proving her ferocity and worth to the other knights."

I had been digging this Lisdon, right up to that point, where we come to find out she was pretty much insane. That trait flowed like gravy at a meatloaf festival in Eliza's relatives. I could empathize to a point. I'd danced along that edge a great many times and for fairly long distances. Something or someone always shoved me to the more or less sane side, eventually.

"It was on the evening of the third night. She had finished rutting with two of the men and had walked over to the fire. She was naked, and the blaze glowed upon her, turning her skin into a polished golden color."

So, she had once admired this woman; possibly loved her. Well, I could see why.

"That was the first time I'd heard her accursed name. One of the men had called out from the tent for this 'Tunning' to get him some water. I spun around, looking for who the man was calling to, when the golden warrior herself swore at him. She told him to get his useless ass up and get it himself."

"Then you turned her?"

"I did. Something inside of me snapped, anger blistered; I wanted to tear her limbs from her torso. That name, that she could possibly have anything to do with my father, was more than I could handle. She fought savagely, valiantly, to hold onto her soul. Even without her sword, she was powerful. She had broken two bones in my hand, my nose was split open and bleeding and I had damage to one of my eyes where she had tried to pull it from my head. Her blood was of the sweetest nectar I had thus far tasted. It made me giddy with the power of it. She had been blessed with some force I was not aware of. It was almost my downfall. The two she had lain with heard our commotion and rushed to the sound with their swords drawn. If I had risked staying there to finish her, I would have found myself dying next to her. I was certain there was no chance she could survive, losing the amount of blood I had withdrawn."

"She lived, though?" I asked.

"She did. Her company laid vigil over her for a full five days, expecting that she would not recover. When she did, they wanted to kill her, fearful that the devil had taken over inside her. They almost had it right; they would have been correct to kill her. Instead, they stripped her of her armor and clothing and shunned her away. Without clothes, money or protection on hostile, foreign territory, she still managed to find her way back to England. Though she had never been an ordinary woman, now she was extraordinary."

I was starting to see glimmers of where this story was going, but I'd been wrong once or twice so I let her continue.

"She fought every impulse she had to satisfy her blood craving. She arrived back at her home, pale and withdrawn. Her betrothed, who had been injured in the crusades some two years previous, recognized her sickness for what it was. He supplied her with blood from his farm animals, nursing her back to strength. By now, the news was beginning to spread throughout the small town. Fearful that the villagers would rise up and kill the woman he loved, he booked passage on a ship for the New World. He'd read about the savages and their ways, and reasoned that if anyone could help it would be their shaman."

"You were on the same ship?"

"I was."

"How did you avoid her seeing you? Pretty sure she would recognize the one that tried to kill her."

"She stayed in her cabin throughout the voyage. I thought about killing the entire crew, even the man she loved. It sounded like something that might entertain me."

"I'm not sure if I like the way that you kept allowing her to live. I suspect that somehow this story is going to come full circle."

"The ship made port in Boston. The couple left during the cover of darkness. Lisdon was having greater and greater difficulty hiding who she was. I followed as they slowly traveled west. It was in Wyoming, Yellowstone, that they came upon a shaman who would be willing to cure her *sickness*."

"This guy she's with has some stones, doesn't he? I mean, traveling with a known vampire and into the wilds of America where any great number of things could kill him, including the natives. I guess it makes sense that Lisdon would be attracted to someone as strong as herself. Mercy is not your strong suit, Eliza. It can't just be curiosity that is keeping you at bay."

"There were other forces here, playing a much larger game than I had ever imagined could exist, but finally I had to admit I was taking part. Lisdon, her mate Brentford, myself–we were but pieces being manipulated into various positions; you know how I hate being told what to do. The only way to combat this was to figure out who was rolling the dice."

"Yeah, sucks being a Monopoly piece on a chessboard." I was thinking about my own sets of circumstances. "Don't really have a valid move." I didn't think Eliza would understand the reference, but she agreed with a slight head nod.

"The shaman could sense my presence in Lisdon's life and he shielded her from me. She became invisible to my senses. I lost track of her for years, until I started to realize that it was not her I needed to look for but rather the lack of her."

"The hole where she should have been. Yeah, I get that."

"By then they had moved to Colorado. Far into the wilderness and high in the mountains, they had carved out an existence. The Tynes had two children and a small farm...."

I slipped off my perch. "What? The Tynes? Oh man, those pieces have been shuffling around far longer than I realized. Again, you let them live?"

"I tore Brentford's throat open as she watched. She was paralyzed with indecision, whether to fight me or to drink from her husband. I would have kept her around for a while, had she eaten. The guilt and torture that would have emanated from her would have been cause for a great many of my smiles."

"I don't understand, you killed them?"

"The parents, yes. I was so wrapped up in their deaths I forgot about the children who had already run from the scene."

"They survived...so somewhere down the long and twisted line, it was inevitable that I would run into a descendant of Lisdon. I guess it shouldn't be that big a surprise that your finger was swirling around inside the fish bowl. Well, I guess I can see why you would hate the Tynes' as well. Did Tommy know all this?"

"He pieced it together over the years. I never related it to him like I just did you." She looked off to the side like she was wondering why she had.

I was stretching the thought out. "Odds are if you had never been introduced into Lisdon's life she would have either died somewhere in the Middle East or back in England of old age. Coming to the New World would most likely be out of the equation. So many outcomes; who can be the captain of all these ships? And what's the eventual outcome? Did it already happen, or is it ongoing? I hate this kind of thinking. Plenty of questions and zero answers. I don't want to be some god's plaything!" I was standing and now I was pissed. I loved BT like a brother, no I take "like" back, he was my brother. But the fact that our meeting was pre-ordained by some uppity higher power irked the living shit out of me. It was trying to cheapen what we had for its own amusement or interests. It was apparently a foregone conclusion we were going to meet, but there was no guarantee of how we would interact; I guess that's where our own will takes over.

"No more stories, I have no desire to know how you influenced my first wife's relatives. I was just lucky enough she wanted to date me." Those words had no sooner come out of my mouth when I thought on the influence Eliza had wielded and was currently having on my present wife. It seemed this vampire was a catalyst for a great many aspects of my life. It was like Victor was reaching out from his grave and influencing all things Talbot; and what about before Victor?

There was a time in my life when I more than half believed in a great many government-led conspiracy theories. Maybe there had been something to them, if only I had set my sights a little higher or lower.

Out of the blue, I blurted it out like an awkward teen might ask a girl to the prom, not the same words, obviously, but the same manner and screeching tone. "Do you like having your soul back?"

She regarded me for a few moments; I thought I saw the flicker of a smile. She thought about it before answering. "It is a part of me, but it is a burdensome one. It has a weight to it that I do not care for."

"Does it affect who you are?"

"Michael, I believe your conception of a 'soul' is flawed. It does not *contain* morals, it does not *dictate* how you act; we are neither 'good' because of it nor 'bad' for its lack. It is a manner of connection to other worlds, a leash, might be a good description. It is a conduit of control. And I will not allow that; not from anyone ever again. I will shed this choker when I am able."

"A harness? You're saying we're harnessed?"

"Man is a horrible creature. Surely you have been around long enough to realize that."

"There is a lot of good as well."

"Oh, that old argument. When I left the earth, the civilizations of man were on the verge of collapse. Did Michelangelo's paintings or Widespread Panic's music save it?"

My head shot up at the reference.

"Sometimes there are creatures so misaligned that the gods feel taking control is the only way. Souls were created for this."

"That doesn't make any sense. If we were so controlled, why did things still go bad?"

"You can spray perfume over a pile of cow dung; in the end, it is still sweet-smelling cow dung."

"Yeah. Talk about shit, I think you're full of it."

She laughed. "You can feel any however you want, the truth affects people in different ways. Now, I have given you enough time to ponder our escape from this realm; have you done so?"

"Yep. Got it all figured out, as a matter of fact." I was fine with not exploring that line of thought anymore. "Going to go down there and demand our release. Tell them that they have the wrong people–that we don't belong here."

To her credit, or more likely naiveté, Eliza took my often-used prison words at face value. It had never worked in any of the shows I'd watched, there was no reason to think it would work now. What the fuck else was I going to do, though? I don't know if you've ever had that feeling that something was wrong only because it was too easy. I know that makes about as much sense as saying something tastes so delicious because it's bad for you. Wait…that one is wrong, because that's usually the case…it's either fried or loaded with sugar. Forget it, the analogy isn't important. But most times when you think something is too easy something is wrong. It's not because when you're stealing the crown jewels from a museum you were really being set up by MI-6 so they can catch the infamous thief. No, it's usually where you walk into Starbucks at peak time and no one is there, or you go to a McDonalds drive thru and they understood you the first time around and by some weird twist of fate got your order right. So…that means invariably a cop is going to pull you over for going through a stop light on your way home. It's a way of balancing out the little highs with little lows. Can't have one without the other. Nope can't just let a good thing slide for a while, got to throw a hatchet straight at the heart of it. But I'm not fucking bitter.

There we were, just walking to this shimmering gate like we own the place, gigantic cat guards are leisurely padding back and forth on their side, I could see their tails swishing, looking again like they are on the other side of that bubbly shower door glass. The cats had Eliza's attention; I don't think she'd seen them before as she'd taken the express train down here. It was the glimmer of movement that caught my eye, like something was there but hiding effectively, some active camouflage or damn invisibility cloak. I only caught a fleeting glimpse when whatever it was, was on the move–like its camouflage needed a millisecond to react completely to its new surroundings, thus giving a brief window for me to "see" it. I really wasn't sure I wasn't just seeing things. I could almost hold on to that thought, right up until Eliza was picked up a good ten feet off the ground and hurled at least double that.

A normal human would have broken in half, like a worm-eaten stick. She was a little out of sorts, but she recovered quickly and looked to me angrily as if I'd had something to do with it, tricked her to stand in the ejector spot or something.

"Trust me. If I had that kind of power, things would have been a lot different. You can only see it out of the corner of your eyes; it's an intermediate shimmering." I could mostly keep an eye on the thing and it knew it as well. I had my axe up and I was going to do my best to bury it deeply into its flesh.

"I have it." The cords on Eliza's neck were pronounced as she strained to hold it. "Kill it," she muttered.

The first thing I wanted to utter was "You caught it, you kill it." But playing games with Eliza was like playing hide and seek with Charles Manson, the ramifications are too frightful to explore. "It's still moving," I told her, though it only seemed to be repeating a five-foot loop.

"So strong…can't hold long. More…com…coming." Each word was halting and took longer to come out than the previous.

"I hope this sucks more for you than me," I said as I ran to it. My axe resounded like I'd struck iron. The vibration threatened to pulse the handle free from my grip. I thought I'd hit some sort of armor, but the piercing screams the creature issued told me I'd done something to incur some pain. It had no plans to suffer much at my hands. A vise-like grip wrapped around my neck. Now when I say vise-like, I'm not even using a turn of phrase. It was cold, and when my hand went up to yank on it, I would have sworn it was iron or some other indifferent metal. Pulling on it was not going to produce anything soon. I would be blacking out from lack of oxygen as my windpipe was shredded against my spine. I did the only thing afforded to me; I started swinging my axe. The vibrations made my shoulder feel like the socket was going to be rattled out of its own pocket. The squeezing on my neck intensified for a few moments and then began to subside as I relentlessly hacked away. The screams, along with the grip, finally faded and I was dropped unceremoniously back to the ground.

"Keep going," Eliza said hoarsely, she was partially bent over like she'd done a couple wind sprints and was trying to catch her breath around the burgeoning gorge that wanted to force its way up.

It is difficult to have an intense fury for something you cannot see, but I gave it my best shot, repeatedly. I was confused at first by what I was seeing; pieces of things, like misshapen burnt crayons were all around me. Then I realized I was hacking pieces of the monster off and they were landing all around me. Not that this whole thing wasn't weird but this was slightly stranger than the rest; each piece was a unique and different color. There were the major three, red, green, and blue, then some pastels, of all things, even a terrible teal, some gold and silver, some that glittered, some that shimmered. It was like once each piece had been removed from the part of the brain that controlled the camouflage aspect; it just went haywire.

One would think that it couldn't get much weirder, well that asshole would be wrong. Some of the pieces portrayed imagery of landscape, like an oil painting of its surroundings, and some looked eerily like the Grand Tetons. Then faces formed– people, animals, monsters, demons, life forms I couldn't even describe or had any basis of familiarity with. There was a being with the top of its head white and eyeless and the bottom half was jet black with a toothy, worm-like pucker for a mouth. That one struck a chord deep inside; I did not want to play. I kept going even when I recognized Eliza's words that it had been stilled.

"Michael, we must go. There are more coming and I will not be able to control them."

I was covered in multi-colored gore, looked sort of like I'd walked through one of those car washes that shoots that tri-colored foam all over the place only this was from a psychedelic murder fest. It had been kind of trippy to watch after smoking a fatty back in the day. Right now, I just wanted it off me.

"I don't really have any idea of how to get through this," I said as I reached out and touched the unyielding wall.

"I do. We will need to bite each other."

"What? No! No fucking way. You think whatever you want about souls but mine is my ticket to the promised land and I'll not yield it again."

"Oh, that drab area. You will have a place in my castle…that place? Like a dog being kenneled. You are far better without your constraints than with them."

"You've already admitted being the queen of deceit. Hell is not where I start believing you."

"Fine, Michael. I don't really care what happens to you. Bite me so that I may pass."

"That won't work, will it? I can't make you more of a vampire, can't take what you don't have. And now that I'm on that train of thought, why the hell does it take your soul away?"

"There were mages and witches that discovered our tether and ways to shed it."

"Wow, talk about the cure being worse than the disease."

"You are free from those who would control you. Out from under your masters."

There was no way I could hide my feelings from myself.

The way she presented it, sure, it definitely held some appeal. I'd always had issues with authority, at least with earthly authority. For example, a boss or a commander, but you had a good idea why they were doing what they were doing, even if they were fucking with you. This cosmic shit, on the other hand, well it's no fun being played in a game where you don't know the rules and you can't possibly win.

"Then if they are using souls as leashes or collars or whatever the fuck they're using them for, where would they go if not up or down. Huh, tell me that?" I'm not even sure why I was arguing the point.

"You have a thickness to you that is not easily penetrated. There should not be souls. Crocodiles, giraffes, ants, most of the animals and insects do not possess them. It is only the higher creatures, and for the reasons I have already told you."

This was something I'd often wondered about, animals having souls, I mean.

"This is all a bit much for me–I'm going to need some time to sort it out."

"I've had all the time I need. You will bite me, I will travel through the gate and kill anything that attempts to stop me. You may come with me or not. I suggest you decide quickly, as more of those creatures are coming and one was nearly our undoing."

That spot between the rock and the hard place is so fucking uncomfortable, and I was wedged in tight. "If you bite me can I get mine back?"

"Why do you care so much?"

"I have a family. I want to see them again."

"You're a fool. They are gone, you are here. That is all that matters." She looked over my shoulder, I spun. There was that strange shimmering effect and this time there was a line of it, indicating an army of the beasts were coming. I was scanning through my options for one that had even a pinch of decent in it. One: I stayed and fought the invisi-monsters and Eliza took off. Two: Eliza and I ran away and then she killed me for not un-attaching her soul. Three: I bit Eliza, she went through the gate, I got skewered by the monsters. Or: we bit each other and made good our escape and I leave my soul behind. Nope, I wasn't going to do it again. "Maybe everything you said was true; more likely it was merely your skewed version of the facts as you believe them. Whatever it is, I have some knowledge of the after-life and I'm not going to pass up on it again. I'll bite you." I told Eliza.

She stood right in front of me, tilted my head down so she could look into my eyes. "When I tell you to stop, you will do so. Yes?"

"Trust me, yes."

"Do it. Time grows short, we will both be weakened. We will need as much time as we can to recover."

My eyes narrowed as my teeth elongated, I placed my hand on the small of Eliza's back. She was so small, delicate, even. It was unimaginable that her frame could house so much pain and misery. I leaned her back. Her mouth opened in a slight sigh, her eyes half closed. Her breathing became heavy, goose pimples raised up along her arms, heat flushed her neck as I plunged in. She let out a gasp. I pulled at the sweetest blood I had ever tasted. It splashed across my tongue and down my throat. She leaned into me, letting more of her weight fall onto my hand. Her long, jet black hair nearly swept the ground. She seemed to grow lighter as I drank more of her. Her hand came up to my face. At first, it was a slow caress as I felt the fluttering of something slowly fly past. And still, I drank.

"Stop, Michael," she said breathlessly. I knew to stop, I wanted to stop, and yet I didn't. I could not. I was not thinking of ending Eliza so that she could not be let go on an unsuspecting world. I was not thinking of any ramifications. It was only her blood, just the blood; it was all I cared about. She began to struggle against me, her caress turning into a push. I gripped her tighter. "You will stop!" she said this both internally and externally and still, it was not enough to override the drive that had been triggered within me. Her hand became a fist, and blows were ineffectually striking my face, each had less power than the one before it.

"You are killing me!" she begged and when I opened my eyes it was Tracy I saw. She was the one I held in my arms, she was the one whose life I was draining. I don't know if I was more mortified, wondering what she would think of what I had been doing or concerned for her well-being as I pulled free from her neck. She cried out as I caught her, she was as weak as I'd ever seen her.

"I'm so sorry!" I told her as I knelt to the ground with her in my hands. Tears fell from my eyes as I gazed upon her face. "I have missed you, each day, every day since you have gone. I have missed you." I hugged her tight like a lost child might his favorite stuffed teddy bear. I eased up so that I could kiss her, as my lips pressed against hers the façade began to lift. It was Eliza in my arms, it always had been. She reached an arm around my neck and pulled me close. I will be ashamed until the day I die that I did not immediately pull back from that small bit of intimacy. But I already had a plan in place that made me think it would not be a guilt I carried for long. I pulled back and pulled her up onto her feet. She braced against me for a moment as she got her equilibrium.

"Now you," she said, breathlessly.

"Where I go, I travel alone." I dropped to my knees facing the enemy. I wanted my demise to be swift and hopefully as painless as possible, but in reality, once again I didn't really give a shit.

"Our time together is not quite complete," Eliza said. I screamed out as she plunged her teeth into my neck.

CHAPTER TWENTY-TWO
AZILE

"SEBASTIAN!" AZILE SAID AS SHE saw her old friend. "It has been too long." She placed her forehead against the large cat's.

"I have stayed here, waiting for his return. Even you must know, it is not likely he will do so."

"I know you think little of him, my friend, but there is more than you and I are aware of."

"I believe that you believe those words, Azile."

"Sometimes, Sebastian, I would not mind you keeping your opinions to yourself."

"As your familiar, it is my job to look out for your well-being. I would not be doing it correctly if I didn't say what needs to be said."

"You have delivered your message…repeatedly."

"Yet, still you have not heeded it."

"He is the father of my children, whom you love, by the way."

"Completely."

"And I love him. I am not asking you to, but I would appreciate if you two found some common ground to share, or at the very least pretended the other did not exist."

"The latter…I can work toward that."

Azile scratched behind his ear. He wanted to purr but thought better of it in front of the Gate Guardians.

"I need to go past that gate," Azile said.

"No."

"Excuse me?"

"The purpose of familiars is to keep their charges from doing something too dangerous or from drawing too much power. To watch over them. I have given you nearly free reign in all that you do because of the extenuating circumstances your world endures. But this is too much; it simply cannot be. And you looking sternly at me only works on Michael. You and I are equals, it is Michael you hold sway over."

"Is it a condition of being male that you are all built to infuriate me as much as possible?"

"If preventing you from your own death is cause for infuriation, perhaps you should turn that ire inside. My feelings for Michael aside, he is but one man. You have two children at home, you have good friends, and perhaps more than all of that combined, a world that needs your guidance as it once again rebuilds."

"You have been of great counsel through the years; an invaluable ally, and above it all, a true and beloved friend, Sebastian."

"I know this speech Azile. You are going regardless of what I say."

"I have to, Sebastian. Even though his soul may be tied to another, mine is hopelessly entangled within his. I must go to him; he is in trouble."

"When has he not been?"

"Tommy has betrayed him." This information perked the cat's ears up.

"Did he have reason to? I have known him nearly as long as you, I cannot believe he would have done so without cause."

"He has reasons; his own selfish ones. He was going to turn Michael over to Ganlin in exchange for his sister."

"He was to barter with that abomination so that he could bring his sister back into the world?"

"Yes."

"You will need this." Sebastian reached into his fur and pulled out a small bag made from burlap. "Do not open it here," he told her when she began to unravel the knotted drawstring. "You will know what to do with it when the time arrives."

"The children are with Lana and Mathieu. If I should…"

"I will watch over them until your return."

"Thank you." She petted him again, this time he allowed himself a small purr of contentment. The Guardians moved aside as she strode among them and through the gate. She took a moment to look back at the impenetrable barrier between herself and her world before opening the bag Sebastian had given her. "Two blood crystals?" she asked as she held them up to the unlight. "Oh!" She exclaimed before placing them back in the bag and securing it tightly.

"Now, if I were a crazy vampire with a penchant for not planning anything, where would I go?" She looked out over the expanse. "I will not dwell on it, as one choice is as good as another. Too bad there is not a fire raging or a tornado twisting, for then I would know immediately where you went, my love. You are very predictable in your unpredictability."

The first twelve hours of traveling, Azile encountered no living being. There were plenty of dead ones. A battlefield's worth.

"This is a new war, she said as she walked around the multitudes of the dead. "Did you directly or indirectly cause this Michael?" She did not much believe in coincidences, those were for the uninformed. She knew too much about the workings of the world and the other realms to ever think that much happened by chance. There was too much at stake to "let" things happen of their own accord. "I will follow the mayhem, that usually leads to your doorstep. I sometimes wonder what my life would have been like had you not saved me from that truck. A lot less interesting, that is for sure, and certainly much shorter." She smiled at her thought, doing her best to shield herself from the carnage all around.

"I'm not sure what to do now," Azile said as she looked around the desolation. She was certain she would have seen a sign of some sort by now. She could perform a locating spell, but it could be her undoing. It would be like putting a spotlight into the sky. Many more beings here were in tune with the forces of nature and magic and would notice her draw from the source. She did not think it would go unchecked. She sat down, wondering if perhaps there was some obtuse way she could find him that would be less obvious. It was in this quiet that she heard a small scrabbling, and then a soft, choked coughing sound. She said nothing, though it was clear whatever was making that noise was in distress. The scrabbling was coming closer.

"He…was…so ugly! But…but he was my friend. I…I should not…have left…" The spasmodic coughing continued. Azile spotted the tiny creature as it came up over a small knoll. The creature, as of yet had not looked up. Azile quietly stood.

"Hideous…really," the creature sniffled. "Something that…ugly should have been locked up…but he was not…not ugly on the inside." Linnick froze when she finally looked up.

"The…Red Witch?" Linnick asked.

"You know of me?" Azile asked, confused.

"It would be more strange, had I not."

"Who are you, and what are you doing here?"

"My name is…Linnick. I have…"

"You are Linnick!? Where is Michael?"

"Tallboat?"

"Yes." Azile stepped closer, Linnick scurried back.

"If you wish to kill him…it…it may be too late."

"I am his wife. And while I often wish to kill him, it is more allegorical than actual. Now tell me what has happened, little creature."

Linnick filled Azile in, from Mike saving her from the dendrun hole, their meeting with Bill and all about Tommy, his betrayal, the killing of Bill, the imprisoning of Michael, and her escape. "By now they will have reached Ganlin and Tallboat will be his prisoner."

"There are a great many problems presented here. Ensuring Michael's freedom is my top priority, but Eliza on the war path will have to be dealt with soon. She can wreak whole new levels of destruction. Finding Ganlin should not be extremely difficult." Azile was disappointed in herself that she had not thought to do this beforehand. Ganlin would never be bashful in his draw of power; she would simply follow his beacon. She chalked her misstep up to Michael dominating her thoughts. "If we are to survive I must not have my thoughts clouded again. Thank you for your help, Linnick. Michael spoke kindly of you when we communicated."

"I would like to stay until the conclusion." She reached her arms up. "Michael let me ride in his chest pocket."

"I welcome and like your company; I do not, however, possess a chest pocket. Will you be alright on my hip?" Azile pulled out the material to show her the opening.

"I will not have the same vantage point, but it does look comfortable."

They had been traveling for a while; Azile was concentrating on picking up some magic trails. "It is not polite to stare, Linnick." Azile could not help but notice the small Breatine had not yet taken her eyes off of her.

"It is the grotesqueness of your species; it fascinates me."

"What?" Azile stopped.

"Are all humans as disfigured as you two? Is that why you are mated? Perhaps you met at a healing, as you attempted to cure the calamities that had befallen you."

Azile laughed.

"It is good that someone as crippled with ugliness such as yourself can still find humor in the world."

"Were you this same way with Michael?"

"He is somehow even more disgusting to look at than you, of course, I told him as much. Kind, he is, though. He has a determined benevolence that shines through all that he does. Unfortunately, all of it is shrouded by a great deal of pain which he does his best to hide from the rest of the world. You love him?"

"I do, from the first moment I saw him. Even then, when

he was more than happily married and nearly twice my age."

"You mean him no harm, then?"

"I…wait, Linnick. What are you doing? I can feel your presence. It is not polite to invade the thoughts of another."

Linnick groaned as Azile entered into her head. "That is NOT the same!" Linnick shouted, forcing Azile from her. "I am seeking the truth, not sorting through your memories. One is a violation of privacy; the other is diplomacy."

"Both are invasions as far as I am concerned. You ever do that again and I will drop you right off."

"It is alright. I have already discovered all I needed to know. Had you not cared for him I would not have helped lead you to him. Even though he is ugly, he deserves no more pain– in this world or any other."

"What is it about my husband that makes people instantly love him or hate him for life? There are no in-betweens when it comes to Michael."

"It is that he presents the truth. There is no deception. He is what he shows himself to be. There will always be those that despise unabashed honesty. I knew immediately that he would not harm me, if I did not harm him. That is not typically the case, in fact, with almost everyone it is the opposite."

"True, his idiotic charm has a way of making you feel safe, and at ease to be yourself, as well," Azile smiled.

"Not the words I would have used, but we have come to the same conclusion."

"I have detected something; it is more of an echo, though. The ripples of something major that happened here."

"Is it this Ganlin?"

"I cannot tell, but it is the only lead I have to go on. And wherever great events occur, it does not take a leap of faith to believe that Michael has had something to do with it."

"You do not want to go the way you are heading; those are the Dendrun holes."

"It is the quickest way."

"And the last way."

"Fear not, little one," Azile smiled.

Within an hour they were standing on the western most side of the Dendrun fields.

"Michael, with all his tendency for folly, would not have come back here. I beg of you go around."

"The ground is only dangerous when you touch it; I do not plan to do so." Azile spoke a short incantation; her feet rose six inches from the ground.

"Oh!" Linnick said, surprised. "And how long can you hold this?"

"Indefinitely. I have tied the spell off. It is as if I have sent a round stone down a never-ending mountain side."

"Yes," Linnick started as Azile hovered over the new ground. "But what other manner of debris will that tumbling stone push down the mountain as it falls?"

"Did you say something?" Azile asked.

"I am implying that your actions could cause an avalanche."

"We will be fine. Now let me concentrate on these echoes, for they are growing fainter."

Linnick had desired a good long nap; she had not had one since she left Michael. Azile was not talking and the gliding force that propelled them had its own soothing effects, not like Michael's rhythmic footfalls, but it was quiet. Still, there was that constant fear of where she was. Here, she had, by some strange twist of fate, been spared a miserable death being buried alive. That she had willingly gone back, was keeping her awake. She'd diligently been watching the horizon, waiting impatiently to spot the white cliffs that marked the far edge. She rarely looked down because she held no desire to see this ground. She froze briefly as she peered above the hem of Azile's pocket. She then gently and carefully climbed farther out, clinging tightly to the soft fabric so that she could get a better look at Azile's feet. She could not help but notice the witch's toes were nearly dragging.

"Azile…" she said after she climbed back into the relative

safety of the pocket.

"Yes, little one?" Azile asked without looking her way.

"Something is wrong. You are not nearly as high up as you were."

Azile had to refocus after she pulled back from her tracking spell. She nearly stumbled as the toe of her boot kicked up dirt.

"I thought you could do this indefinitely?" Linnick was beginning to panic. "I cannot be in a hole again, Azile. It is a terrifying way to await your death."

"We are not going to die here," Azile said, though the words seemed forced. "Some…something is wrong." Azile's left foot touched down briefly before regaining flight.

"You did not need to orate for me to figure that out."

"The spell is somehow unravelling."

"Retie it! Retie it, quickly!"

"I cannot; the edges of the spell are being broken up. I cannot explain it; I have never encountered anything like this. My magic is not only being undone, it is as if it never existed."

"I should have stayed with, Tallboat," Linnick lamented.

"All is not lost. How far is it until we are out of here?"

"Twenty, maybe as many as thirty pedronts."

"I don't know what a pedront is."

"Much too far! If you go to the ground now, the hole will be above your head in less than five."

"Where are you going?"

"I have an idea," Linnick said as she climbed down Azile's leg and onto her boot. With one leg on the lip of the boot sole and her arms clutching the lace, she dragged a foot onto the ground.

"I don't see how this will help."

"You don't worry about this, you worry about whatever magic is working to counter your own."

Every so often Azile's foot came down, this was happening with more and more frequency until finally, she was standing on the shifting ground. Linnick bounded down and stood a few feet away.

"We need to go," Azile said as she worriedly looked at the ground moving away from her feet. She thought it was very much like what happened when she was a child and her mother brought her to the beach. She stood right at the shoreline as the waves rolled in, and as they pulled away they took the sand out from under her. It always gave her the feeling she was moving and she liked the tickling sensation it caused. The only tickling this ground caused was the tug of worry in her belly.

"You will not make it."

"We have to try."

"We are trying."

"You're just standing there! That's not helping."

"This is how Michael and I escaped. He traveled in my hole."

Azile got down to get a closer look at the ground under Linnick. "It is not moving."

"Not yet. I already have a hole assigned to me, and I cannot believe I am saying this, but I am hopeful it is even now racing to capture me again."

"How can that help us?"

"The holes are lazy; they only do as much as is necessary to trap the host within."

"Linnick, I will need more than that if I am going to trust you enough to stay here."

"You will have to do as Tallboat did and travel within my hole."

"That worked?"

"It did; though he complained the entire time. That made his features even more difficult to look upon."

Azile did not like this plan, not in the least, and she was having great difficulty finding out how to weave her magic back so that they could once again hover over this accursed ground.

"It's coming!" Linnick shouted excitedly. "Wait, something is not quite right." She was squinting, doing her best to see far off into the distance. "You should perhaps begin running."

"What?"

"Run!" she shouted.

Azile needed no further warning as she bent over, grabbed Linnick, and took off. Linnick climbed up Azile's arm so she could look over her shoulder.

"There is a massive hole coming for us."

"Massive to you or to me?" Azile asked through breathes.

"To a gargantoid it would be massive."

Azile didn't need to ask. With a name like that, she correctly assumed it was enormous. She dared a look over her shoulder; her fears were confirmed when she saw great plumes of dirt as the hole roared forward.

"I will not be able to outrun it." She slowed and then stopped. "Our only chance is levitation."

Linnick began her death chant as Azile began her incantation. Linnick had climbed back down into Azile's pocket just as the bits of dirt being forced up from the leading edge began to strike them. At first, Linnick was elated when she felt them rise up, thinking that Azile must have been successful in her spell. A short moment later her stomachs rose up into her throat as they found themselves in a sort of flight, though not the way they desired. They were falling deep into the depths. Linnick looked up to watch as the sky diminished. She possessed some happiness that the suffering would be brief as they struck the bottom at deadly speeds. She wasn't sure if she wanted Azile's body to cushion the fall for her or to be completely compressed under the human.

"You are not screaming," Linnick said, more as an observation.

"I need to concentrate, but we're going to be alright. This isn't a trap, it's a doorway."

"Yes, but are we welcome?"

It was some minutes later when Azile's feet gently touched down, as easily as if she had jumped off a small chair. She looked up; she could no longer see the sky. The chamber they found themselves in was easily over sixty feet in diameter.

"I do not wish to sound ignorant, Azile, but I do not see a doorway."

"Nor I." Azile had done a small spin to see if anything looked different in the mountainous walls that encircled them.

"Are you sure?"

"As sure as I can be." Azile took a step; the wall moved with her. She stopped, so did the wall. Whichever direction she walked in, the wall moved away from her. "Perhaps we are not there yet."

"And which direction do you believe that we need to go? There are no signs."

Azile walked a few more steps; the small smile she was wearing grew as she knelt down. "Here are our signs," she said as she brushed lightly at markings on the ground.

"Runes," Linnick said with amazement.

"Gaelic runes, as a matter of fact."

"Do you know what they mean?"

"I would be asked to turn in my witch-card if I didn't."

Linnick said nothing.

"Really? That wasn't funny to you? Michael is constantly talking about losing his man-card, yet I say something about a witch-card and I get nothing but crickets chirping.

"Ah, crickets chirping! Now that's funny!"

Azile looked at her. You don't even know what crickets are, do you?"

"It is just good that you know the way out," Linnick frowned at Azile.

"It is rather a way in."

"To?"

"The upper-world."

Linnick swallowed hard. "Out of the wastelands, past the underworld, and into the upper-world? A passageway we just happened to stumble upon? I would like to say this is fortuitous, but right now I feel this is an invitation we should refuse."

"What about this invitation infers we have the ability to refuse it?"

"Just a suggestion."

"It will be alright. I have my magic back. The one wielding his spell is powerful, but not without flaws. They tried to conceal the source, make it appear as though it no longer existed. And, in truth, they have blinded me to it. But I do not need to see it to know it is there and to use it."

"Use it now. Fly us out of this."

"That would not be wise; the element of surprisc falls to us if they believe we are helpless."

"You are playing a dangerous game in which you could easily be outmatched."

"Perhaps that is the case, Linnick, but the answers we need lie there. Any chance you have of redeeming your life lies there as well."

"There are worse fates than the one we exist in now."

"There are also much, much better. Are you so willing to throw that chance away?"

Linnick bowed her head and then lifted it as she spoke. "Breatines understand the consequences of their actions in life will send them to this place, yet we do some of these things for the greater good of our primary existence. I think that finally, I would like to do something that was good for all my existences."

"Does that mean you wish to continue?"

"I am not seeing the alternative just yet."

"But if one appears, you may wish to use it?"

"If something better comes along, I would not be opposed to considering it."

"Smart girl."

Azile continued on, occasionally stopping to read the runes they encountered and alternating course when necessary.

"I am going to need to rest at some point, Linnick. I grow weary."

"I sure do wish we could make it out of here first." Linnick looked up nervously.

"I have a feeling, my little friend, that this may be the safest place in this entire realm."

"If that was supposed to make me feel better, it did not."

"I understand. If you wish to stand guard, please wake me up in a couple of hours." Azile got as comfortable as she could, and within minutes was breathing softly.

"I am having great difficulty believing I am traveling with the powerful and terrible Red Witch," Linnick whispered. "She doesn't seem particularly wicked." Linnick ducked back into her pocket, curled up and was immediately snoring.

Azile's dreams were plagued with images of Mike in all manner of life-threatening situations, the least of which had him running from a pride of lions into an ocean full of sharks. She awoke with a start right before her husband could be bitten.

"You can't even stay out of trouble in dream realms, Michael." Azile sat up. "Linnick, you should wake up." She gently shook her pocket.

Linnick poked her head out. "Is it brighter?" She had placed an arm up to shield the light.

"I guess that answers that question. The runes are different as well."

"What does that mean?"

"We are still traveling in the right direction, but someone thought we were moving too slowly and has ushered us along."

"I don't like that."

"Nor do I, and without us knowing…that is cause for alarm."

Azile pondered on how their escort could be anywhere, with any possible agenda. Other than this constant caution, Michael and her children dominated her thoughts. That was of course, until they came to a door.

"Azile?"

"I see it." She had stopped. The great wall of material in front of them had stopped moving forward. A large, arched, unadorned oak door was now neatly outlined.

"What if we were to go back?" Linnick asked.

"I do not believe that would be advisable. Someone has invited us here and they might construe our turning around now as a rude gesture. And considering exactly where we are," Azile looked and pointed up, "with a mile or more of ground above us, I think that might be our only choice."

"Not much of an invitation if you have no choice but to accept it."

Azile walked over to the door. "There is no handle."

"Is it not customary to knock?"

"I swear, I had manners once upon a time." Azile made a fist and knocked lightly on the door. She'd hardly made a sound, between the stoutness of the door and the sound dampening effects of the wall she'd doubted anyone could have heard her rapping. Even so, the door began to swing slowly inward.

"You ready for this?"

"If I said no?"

Azile stepped through. Blinding white light replaced the drab of the Dendrun hole. She stepped upon a white marble floor. Marble columns marched off into the distance of an unimaginably long corridor. "I'm guessing we're not quite there yet."

"This does not sadden me," Linnick replied.

They walked in an uneasy silence, Azile's footfalls echoing in the mighty chamber. It was not overly long before she could just make out something in the distance. "Is that a dais?"

"Someone or something is upon it," Linnick added.

They'd gone another hundred yards when Linnick spoke. "We should turn around if it is at all possible."

"What do you know that I don't?"

"That is Lamashtu."

"Are you sure?"

"Head of a lion, ears of a donkey, hairy body…suckling a pig and a snake. There is little doubt in my mind. She is evil."

"I know this, little one. She may be the well-spring from which evil manifests. She answers to no one–Man, God or Demon. You are right in your desire to leave, though I fear that is not an option we have."

Linnick ducked back into the pocket.

"Azile, the Red Witch," boomed from the entity on her throne. She stood as Azile approached. "It is good of you to come."

"Had I a choice?"

"No. It was determined the moment Gabriel was discovered."

"And the reason for this determination?"

"Your husband, Michael Talbot."

Azile could honestly say that wasn't a surprise to her.

"Have I been summoned here to pay for his transgressions?"

"Quite the opposite. You have been sent here to stop him."

"Stop him from what?"

"There is a delicate balance between life and death, good, and evil, yin and yang; you know this. Those are the terms your kind are most familiar and comfortable with. Though it is a much more ancient and powerful force, it is something akin to that which you call magic. Even with all your talent and might, you have no idea of the source power you tap into. It is responsible for the heavens, the hells, the stars, the planets…for every bit of life on all of it. The creators of this are beyond even my understanding, and I have been in existence for time untold."

"How do my husband and I affect this mighty balance? We are aware of our place in the worlds."

"SILENCE!" Lamashtu yelled. The walls shook, Azile took an involuntary step back. "You are as aware of this balance as a stone is to love. Your mate, perhaps ignorantly, perhaps knowingly, is on a very dangerous path, one that could upset this balance forever. The consequences he tempts would be most grave."

"You wish me to stop him? I know of Michael's conversations with Jehovah. Why would I go into league with you, while he has been empowered to battle evil in the worlds?"

"You are a fool. I thought perhaps bringing you here would bring you more understanding. It is not for the side of good which your husband fights."

Internally, Azile was rocked, though she stood her ground and concealed her thoughts.

"You cannot hide your shock from me. Michael is with Eliza and they are close to tearing down everything that has stood since the creators. Eliza has killed the one assigned to keep her, and Michael has destroyed Tomas."

"Lies! All of it lies! You brought me here to deceive me in person! I will not submit so meekly!" Azile pulled hard of her magic, creating a vortex of purple arcs of lightning.

Lamashtu stood and waved her hand; a shimmering image of Michael walking side by side with Eliza was displayed in front of her.

"That is indeed him," Linnick was looking as well. "She speaks the truth."

"This…this cannot be." The lightning slowed and began to dissipate.

"You will need to stop them both."

"They are but two beings in a universe of trillions. How is it that they would be able to accomplish a deed of such magnitude?"

"They have help."

"Your kind! It's always 'help.' You puppet us lesser beings here and there to do your bidding, to kill, to spare…maybe if you just left us the fuck alone, the universe wouldn't always be on the brink. How's that for an idea? You want him stopped? I suggest you personally do something about it. Just know I will be doing all I can to protect him."

"As easily as you can crush that Breatine in your pocket, I can do to you. You exist still because I allow it. You will do this, Red Witch. The alternative for you, at least, is unimaginable." Lamashtu once again waved her hand; the image changed to Lana and Mathieu riding through the woods, the children in the back of a small cart. Mathieu was looking around as if he sensed something was not quite right.

"You will not harm them!" Azile shook with rage.

"Harm them? Oh no, I wouldn't dream of that. They are unique and powerful. A vampire demon that has bred successfully is relatively unheard of. A demon that has bred with a witch? Something like that has *never* happened. I will bring them to me, suckle and raise them as my own. They will be powerful agents, eternally fighting to accomplish my goals."

"You cannot!"

"Because you say so?" She laughed. "To your primitive mind, there is very little I cannot do."

"Except stop Michael," Azile said through tears.

Lamashtu thought on this for a few seconds, then smiled. "This is correct. Let us try a different tactic. If your husband is to succeed on his quest, it would be preferable for your children to be here with me. Realities will begin to unravel, worlds that should not meet will collide and forever be united. The end of humanity will be long and violent. Finally, there will be nothing left, anywhere."

"I just have to stop him?"

"Ah, even you cannot be that naïve. Michael is too large a threat to continue. He is unique in that both sides have touched and have laid valid claims to him. He walks that line dangerously; no matter which side he chooses, he is ultimately an influence for revolutionary change. He must die while he is separated from his soul."

"I know no magic to do this."

"The hard part is done." Lamashtu pulled up the images of

a crying hunched Michael being bitten by Eliza.

"No!" Azile put her hand out. "My poor, Michael."

"The destroyer of worlds deserves no pity."

"He has done nothing yet; no one, not even you, Lamashtu, can foretell the fate of all worlds. I will stop him, but in my own way. I will not kill him for you, for anyone, not even for everyone."

"This is not a negotiation."

"Perhaps you are as mighty as you say, but I will not die without a fight."

"Die if you must, then. I will find another way to deal with him." A pin of light as bright as the sun formed above Lamashtu's head.

"Wait!" Linnick cried out. "There is another way!"

EPILOGUE
MIKE'S EARLY YEARS

IT WAS IN THE MOUNTAINS of Afghanistan that I found out there is more to the world than I had previously known. Although how much could a young man with a rifle really know to begin with? My unit had been sent on a search and rescue mission, seems a patrol had gone missing. Not an unusual occurrence, given the circumstances. The mountains there could be just as savage as the animals and the people that inhabited them. Now I mean "savage" as in fierce, not making any moral judgments here. I can't imagine how "savage" I would have been if another country had invaded my home and I was fighting for everything I knew, high up in the Rocky Mountains. Anyway, we were looking for a SEAL team, one of the best, so I was told. They had been on a special mission to capture a leader of one of the kabals; that all of the team members would vanish without a trace was highly unlikely.

I got that they were highly trained, smart, motivated individuals, but that wouldn't stop a bullet or more likely a mortar from killing them. I'd seen enough death already to realize wasn't much that would stop a rocket. I had mixed feelings about these missions. If the shoe was on the other foot, of course, I'd want an entire battalion and maybe a few boy scout troops looking for my ass, but when I was doing it I always questioned the sanity of endangering more lives. I didn't say I was without selfishness. Watching limbs blown off, losing lives or seeing a friend grieve when those things happen tends to enforce feelings of self-preservation. But the stronger bonds of the brotherhood and sisterhood of those in arms always won out. Plus, my lieutenant would have had me court-martialed and sent to Leavenworth to make little rocks out of big rocks. And let's face it, no matter what Linnick keeps saying, I'm too pretty for jail.

We had a helo insertion, got us to the tree line somewhere around ten thousand feet, which sounds pretty high, but when you're talking the Himalayas we were barely making base camp. They were talking about a raging storm barreling down on us and the chopper couldn't risk the brutal cross winds, the mountains were famous for. Glad to see that command wasn't too concerned with our welfare, though. And people are always asking me why I have issues with authority, well here's example two thousand three hundred and twelve: ordering us peons into hostile territory during hostile weather. We ran from the helicopter, which was hovering a few inches off the ground; the pilot was in such a rush to get the fuck out of there he wouldn't even land. We set up a defensive perimeter until our only ride was back high in the sky, just a rapidly vanishing dot.

Been on more than a few missions since being dropped off into the world's armpit. Now that's not to say Afghanistan didn't have some incredibly beautiful parts, because it did. It was the people, and I'm including us, that made it a cesspool. War. Just doing our part for population control. Not trying to devolve into a political rant because my true ignorance would shine through and it has absolutely nothing to do with the story. So, another mission, get through it, get back, get shit-faced off of Charlie's home-brewed hooch. I've had cherry-flavored cough syrup that went down easier, but it did what it set out to do, burn away the memories of the day, and I mean with a prejudice. Like it targeted those thoughts and just boiled them out, bleach on grass stains.

Where the fuck am I? Oh yeah, the helo is gone and I get this fluttering in my stomach. At first, I'm thinking it's the shitty MRE I'd eaten an hour ago. You haven't lived until you've eaten beef goulash from a bag; pretty sure it was just every ingredient left over from all the other meals. But instead of sitting like a stone like they usually do, this one kept rising, trying to force itself from my throat. It was nerves. Sure, nerves were a normal part of the equation, but this was different. This was one of those precognizant things, a "sinking feeling" of all not being right. I might have paid it more attention if I actually believed in clairvoyance or if the L.T. wasn't force marching us up the side of a mountain at double time. Nothing quite like jogging up a mountain wearing combat boots, carrying seventy pounds of gear to take your mind off your nerves.

"Talbot, you're point!" Lieutenant Denkins shouted.

"Of course I am," I mumbled as I took the lead. I'd been on his shit-list for the last week. The army had sent us over some ten-day old cupcakes, things could be used as hockey pucks. Didn't stop us from eating them, though. I was serving dinner that day and by the time he got to my station, all of them were gone. Like somehow that was my fault? I mean, sure it was because I had lifted a whole tray for my friends, but I'm pretty sure he didn't know that. Or shit, maybe he did and that's why he was pissed…doesn't matter. Hadn't gone more than a couple of clicks when the wind picked up. Went from a sunny, decent day to gale force winds and storm clouds that would make folks in Kansas concerned. L.T. was a hard ass, but he was smart and he wouldn't unnecessarily risk the safety of his men.

"Talbot, find some cover!" He had to shout because even though we were only twenty feet apart I could barely hear him over the ripping of the wind.

I did a quick scan, there wasn't much of anything except loose rocks and a few stunted, twisted trees, nothing a whole squad could find sanctuary behind or under. I kept going up, not entirely sure why; I guess because that was the direction I was pointed in. The wind was screaming down the side of the mountain. I couldn't even look up anymore to see where I was going because of the rain pelting into my face. I was soaked– everyone was soaked. I'd easily added another twenty pounds onto my load. We were going to be in serious danger of exposure if we didn't find a place to call home for the night.

SEE! This is the shit I'm talking about. Command absolutely knew this storm was coming and still they green lit the operation. I felt bad for the poor bastards they were going to send in to retrieve what was left of our asses after the mountain goats were finished dining on us. Yeah, you keep telling yourself goats are herbivores; that's until most of their natural food source is blown away by ordinance and they're starving. Goats eat just about anything. Until you say you've seen a pack of goats ripping the flesh off a dead person, you really can't say you've seen it all.

"No fucking way," I said aloud. "I am not going to go out by goat." I raised my head. By now the rain was beginning to freeze and tiny ice shards were trying to pierce my eyeballs. I raised my hand up to shield them as best I could. I couldn't be sure, but I was fairly positive I saw something a little further up and off to our left, a darker blackness where everything else was a drab brown. It seemed as good a place to head as any.

"L.T!" I had to shout it three times before he heard me and raised his head to look. I pointed to where I was going. He looked, nodded, and off we went. My teeth were chattering and my muscles were firing off almost to the point of uncontrollable shivering by the time I got to the mouth of the cave. In terms of a mouth, it was more of the closed lip variety. The opening wasn't much bigger than your standard dog house door. I'd be able to fit but only after I'd taken my backpack off. I waited for the rest of the squad to show up.

"Let's go, Talbot." The L.T. thrust his head to the hole.

"Fuck off," was at the edge of my lips. But I was freezing, my friends were freezing. This was our only chance, but man, that was not a place I wanted to wriggle my ass into. It looked tight and I didn't want to get stuck or even consider the alternative, that the enemy was already camped out in there and as soon as I showed my face I'd get a knife to the side of the neck. Then they'd pull my profusely bleeding and dying body out of the way, waiting for the next guinea pig to check it out. Instead, I said "Fuck," as I shucked off my equipment.

"Be careful," Charlie said as he grabbed my gear.

"Let's go Marine," L.T.'s version of a pep talk.

I put my rifle in first, hard. If anything was up front I was at least going to get a shot off. There was a moment of panic as I initially got in to the entrance and realized I didn't have much room for maneuverability. I turned my vest flashlight on and wriggled forward, looking for any signs that I might not be alone. The entrance tunnel was maybe fifteen feet long and steadily got bigger, which was fine by me. By the time I got to the chamber proper I was walking, albeit hunched over. I was happy; I was in somewhat of a fighting stance, anyway. I pulled my flashlight out to get a better look at what I was dealing with, would have been better off with a lighter for the amount of area it shone. All I could tell was the place was big enough for the squad to fit, it wasn't raining ice in here, and as of yet no one or nothing had tried to kill me. Those were all plusses.

"It's clear!" I shouted through the opening. I dropped off a small edge and into what we would soon find out was a vast chamber, measuring almost a hundred feet across and fifty feet wide.

Charlie was the first to come through. "You good?" he asked.

"Right as rain."

Within fifteen minutes the entire squad and our gear was in and we had a burgeoning fire going. Someone had been in here before us, many some ones, as a matter of fact, and there were plenty of wood stores.

"Good job, Talbot," the lieutenant said, smacking my shoulder.

With the fire going as high as we could get it, we could see the opening in its entirety. Besides the wood, there was a fair amount of animal offal, discarded empty food cans and even a box of interestingly old MRE packets. If it was from our

SEALS it was very uncharacteristic; they usually traveled ultra-light, and if they did have food on them, they would have most certainly cleaned up after themselves, so as to not leave a trace of their existence. So, either it wasn't from them or they'd left in a hurry, unless they'd been taken. When Denkins saw those, we became all business-like again.

"Talbot, perimeter check."

"I'm not off point yet?" It came out before I could even begin to rein it in.

He pulled me in close. "Next time there are fucking cupcakes and your sticky fingers steal a tray, I get mine. Now hurry up. I want to sit by this fire and dry off."

"I'll go with him, sir," Charlie volunteered.

"He the one that got my cupcake?" Denkins asked. I said nothing. "Yeah, go, Blaylock. Have fun."

Everything was damn near fine; we were coming up on the very last part of the chamber when Charlie noticed a mostly hidden passage that went farther back.

"Do we tell him?" I asked.

"If a bear comes out of here later tonight and we knew about it, we'll both be cleaning latrines for the rest of our enlistment, and Denkins will make sure that the men have burritos on a consistent basis."

"What the fuck is wrong with you?" I asked him.

"Come on, let's go," he said as he brought his rifle up. I followed. I figured for sure it wasn't going to go much more than the fifteen feet it had taken to get inside in the first place. I was wrong. We traveled a hundred yards or more through a twisting passage. Thankfully, it never got much tighter than an ordinary hallway; at times, it was twenty feet across.

"Chuck, man. I'm thinking we should tell someone where we're going. We are way too far away."

"There's light up ahead," he whispered. "Go back."

"Where the fuck have you Mary Janes been?" Denkins asked when we got back.

"There's a passage, sir," Charlie said. "And I saw a light

at the end of it."

"Shit. Hobbs, Wilson, watch the entrance. Stiller, Cowlings, you'll watch this new passageway. The rest of us, gear up. Let's go."

When we got back to the new passage, the L.T. nodded to me. This shit was getting old. It wasn't too long until I saw the light Charlie had seen. It was white, not the flickering of a flame or the yellow of a flashlight, it looked like a natural source. Wasn't sure how that could be; the sun had been setting and we were in the midst of a typhoon when we came in. I edged forward, heart pounding. I was fully expecting to come across the whole of the Afghani rebel army. That may have been preferable. A leg; I saw a camouflage covered leg. Not too particularly weird, except this leg was embedded in the side of the cave. At first, I figured it had been blown off with enough force to stick it there, but when I got closer I saw that there was no blood or damage to it at all and it seamlessly went from material to stone, more like they'd been fused. I backed up. Nothing in my training had said anything about this.

"Uh, L., there's something up ahead you might want to see."

I think my face was sufficiently ashen that he didn't question me.

"What in the fuck is this?" he asked when we got back to the leg. He looked closely at the boot, his flashlight causing a glint off of the dog tags tied in the laces. "Hold this." He handed me his light. He grabbed his knife and cut the laces free. "Collins, Trent," he said, reading the tag. "This is one of our guys."

"What happened to him, sir?" I asked.

The lieutenant turned to the rest of the squad closing in. The rest of you, go back, get warm, get some chow, but stay vigilant. Me and Talbot will be back soon."

Charlie looked over to me, I shrugged. We'd gone another ten feet when my light caught the shine of one eye, only one because the other half of its head was encased in solid stone. However this man had died had not been pleasant; his mouth was forever frozen in a scream.

"That another one?" I asked.

Denkins grunted a "yes."

The light was getting stronger the farther we went. We'd come across five of the six men we'd been seeking. None of them alive. The only one missing was John Stephenson. My guess was he was fully immersed somewhere and until the tectonic plates shifted, wasn't anybody going to find him. Still, we pressed on until we came to another opening, this one made what we'd just seen seem almost normal. We were gazing out over a vast, lush valley that belonged more in a rainforest than halfway up a barren mountainside. Wherever or whatever this place was, it didn't belong here. In the back of my head, I knew I was staring at something that was not supposed to exist. Denkins was staring at the vista before him slack-jawed. Just because he was an officer didn't mean he knew everything, just meant he was good at ordering people around.

"We need to check this place out, Talbot."

That sounded about as good as eating pigeon wings. "Sir." I pointed to something almost as far out as we could see. It was a shimmering ripple that was expanding outward. My gut said that wasn't good and I let him know.

He stared for a second longer before he came to the same realization. "Run." Like a good officer, he let me take point again, this time I was fine with it. I don't know how or why those men had melded into the side of the mountain but I was pretty fucking sure of what had caused it and it was a golden shimmering ripple currently barreling down on us. The L.T. and I were hauling ass as fast as you can in a winding corridor. We'd maybe gone half way when we heard a deafening sound. Ever put earbuds in tight, load your mouth up with pop-rocks and toss some soda in there just for fun? It was like that, only to the point where we could hear nothing else. I was sure that the entire cave was coming down on itself, and still, we ran.

I could see Stiller up ahead, his flashlight illuminating his face. "You guys hear that!" he shouted.

"Run!" I told him. No explanation needed when someone yells that. He turned and tailed it. I was five feet from the exit when I heard a thud. I skidded to a halt to see that the L.T. had gone down.

"Fuck." I went back reached down and yanked him up and out for all we were worth. The crackling sound was upon us as we fell through. I thought we had died–it had gotten so quiet, so quickly. The sound had stopped; we'd not been bombarded by rocks the size of trucks and not even a wisp of dust shot out of the opening.

"Shit, Talbot. Thank you," Denkins said.

"You're welcome, sir." I went to roll over when I realized my leg was held fast. I panicked, thinking my leg was now enmeshed with the stone. "Sir, I'm stuck," I pleaded.

"It's alright. We're going to get you out of here."

"Yeah, I want all my parts to come with me."

He just reiterated that he was going to get me out. "Relax, kid. Let me look." There was a small laugh of relief soon after. "Just your heel Talbot; just your heel. You're going to be fine," he said as he undid my laces. The bottom of my boot was held fast in that rock, most likely still there today.

The Corps didn't believe us, the DOD didn't believe us, neither did the FBI, the CIA, nor any of the other alphabet organizations, though they kept interviewing us about it. We were debriefed over and over again that what we hadn't seen was classified as top-secret and that if we said anything about what we did not see, it would be grounds for lengthy prison terms. Sometimes I think the CIA did something to us to repress that memory because I can't ever remember discussing it with anyone, ever again. I mean, not until now. Especially after what I'd seen with Jack and Trip. This had to tie all in together right? Fucking Thrimes. I know it was them that shined this penny up for me to see.

About The Author

Visit Mark at www.marktufo.com

Zombie Fallout trailer

https://youtu.be/FUQEUWy-v5o

For the most current updates join Mark Tufo's newsletter

http://www.marktufo.com/contact.html

Also By Mark Tufo

Zombie Fallout Series book 1 currently free

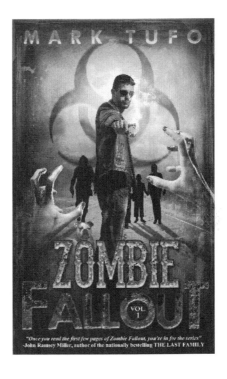

Lycan Fallout Series

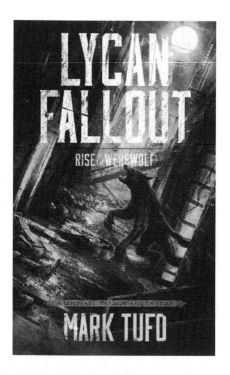

Indian Hill Series

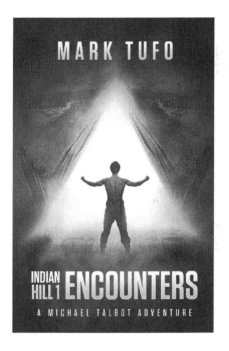

The Book Of Riley Series

Also By Devil Dog Press

www.devildogpress.com

Burkheart Witch Saga By Christine Sutton

The Hollowing By Travis Tufo

Humanity's Hope By Greg P. Ferrell

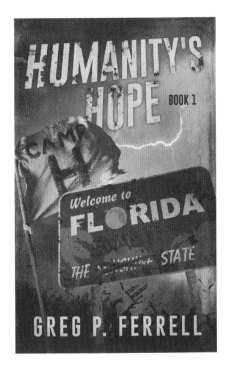

Revelations: Cast In Blood by Christine Sutton, Jaime Johnesee & Lisa Lane

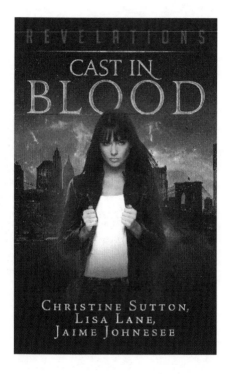